# SUMMER OF
## SEVEN

D1367053

# SUMMER OF
## SEVEN

BY
**CANDACE CHRISTINA**

MONARCH AVENUE
A PUBLISHING COMPANY

*For Colleen and Summer, my first and second princesses*
*And Andrew, my prince*

Published in Atlanta, Georgia by Monarch Avenue, Inc.

Monarch Avenue, Inc., books may be purchased in bulk for educational, business, fund-raising, or sales promotional use. For more information please contact the Sales Department: sales@monarchavenue.com

Publisher's Note: This novel is a work of fiction. Names, characters, places, and incidents are either products of the author's imagination or used fictitiously. All characters are fictional, and any similarity to people living or dead is purely coincidental.

Library of Congress Control Number: 2010906983
ISBN 978-0-61534-179-8
Printed in the United States of America
7   6   5   4   3   2   1

# Contents

iv

V

"I tell you the truth, anyone who believes in me will do the same works I have done, and even greater works, because I am going to be with the Father."

-Jesus

*Chapter One*

# ⊗ LAST DAY FIRST VISION ⊗

Bump-bump, bump-bump, bump-bump, rattled Chris' head against the dingy window of the big yellow school bus, that roared down Ellington Road, delivering Chris and his little sister home after a long day of school. Although the blaring noise of the engine shuddered him sore, he became one with it and followed his heavy eyelids into a peaceful sleep, that is, until he was awakened by a poke in his side.

"Chris, wake up!" Casey whispered pulling her short brown hair back into a ponytail. "Cleofus is coming!"

Chris' eyes popped open and he sat up as if an alarm had gone off in his ear. It was the last day of school and he didn't want any trouble, however, everyone knew the name Cleofus was synonymous with trouble and Chris knew that's exactly what he was bringing. His little sister Casey sat with her arms folded and watched his every move.

Cleofus made his way down the aisle with his two loyal followers Pete and Everett in tow. This small, but villainous crew brought fear and intimidation to most of the kids on the bus and picked on those who let them.

Actually, Cleofus was the one to be feared. The victims often looked into the bus driver's big rearview mirror hoping to make eye contact with her image - a trite cry for help. But instead, she would ignore the pitiful blushed faces, focusing her eyes back on the road, pretending she didn't see a thing because, she too, was intimidated by the bully and did not want to get involved. Instead, she often rushed Cleofus home first to put the children out of their misery and her out of her irritation.

Cleofus stopped at the seat in front of Chris and Casey, and grinned down at the helpless passenger who sat there. It was a boy named Emanuel Amin, small for his age, and frightened speechless at the sight of the bully. Not knowing what to expect he tightly clenched his empty book bag with a gaze of terror fixed on Cleofus' face.

"Hey Pete," Cleofus called turning around, "how much have we collected so far?"

The crony pulled a crumpled wad of money from his pocket and began to count.

"Thirty-two dollars and seventeen cents," he said giving Emanuel an unfriendly smile.

Cleofus turned back to Emanuel.

"Pay up little punk!" he spat. "It's the last day of school, and I need enough dough to get me through the summer!"

"I…I gave you five dollars this morning! That's all the money I had," he rebutted trying to control his breathing.

"Well," Cleofus said balling up his chubby fist, slowly hitting it inside of his other hand, "Looks like you're gonna have to pay … for not paying up!"

"But I did, you took all I had!" Emanuel cried.

Chris had seen and heard enough. All eyes were glued and ears were peeled waiting to see what Cleofus might do to Emanuel if he could not produce anything. Even though the others truly felt sorry for him, they were too afraid to intervene and cast down the biggest bully in the entire school.

However, Chris looked at Cleofus and tried to figure out what was it about him that had everyone so afraid.

*Is it the big mole on his chin that looks as if it possesses some type of super power?* He thought. *Or, maybe it's his huge belly that peeks through the bottom of his shrunken shirt.* He couldn't exactly figure out what it was, but he pondered crazy possibilities.

Chris looked at Pete now, who was tall and thin. Chris wondered,

*Now why does this guy obey this guy's every command?... I know, I know, Cleofus probably told him he would feed him if he would listen to him.* Chris laughed to himself.

Cleofus had Emanuel by the collar and was about to strike him when Chris jumped up from his seat.

"HEY!" he shouted, startling Cleofus.

He froze in mid-swing, fist in the air, and look at Chris as if he'd lost his mind. Emanuel's small body was rigid with fear and his eyes were shut tight anticipating a plunging blow when Cleofus answered, annoyed.

"How can I help you?"

"I just have a question for you," Chris stated sarcastically. "What makes *you* think *you* can just go around beating people up if they don't give you what doesn't belong to you?"

Embarrassed Cleofus looked around and saw that everyone on the bus was snickering.

"I'm about to shut that smart little mouth of yours," Cleofus said to Chris, releasing Emanuel's collar.

"Whoa, whoa wait a minute," Chris chuckled, "I don't do well with threats. It's three of you and one of me, and I'll still take you down!"

"We'll, see about that," he said with a grin.

"Casey, move to the back," Chris demanded.

"No! I'm not moving anywhere. It looks like it'll be two on three," she said standing up looking Cleofus straight in the face.

"I don't have a problem hitting a girl – especially one that's out of line," Cleofus said.

"Three on three!" A voice yelled from the back.

A guy Chris recognized but didn't know stood up.

"Four on three!" another voice yelled.

"Five on three!" someone else chimed in.

Chris smiled as he watched the bus gain confidence; he looked up at the bus driver and saw her smiling too. She was so excited she decided to make Cleofus her last stop to make sure he got what he deserved. The children continued to count off, six… seven… eight… nine! Chris placed his hand in his brown hair, raised his thick eyebrows, and gave Cleofus a victory smile.

Emanuel stood up and said, "Fifteen on three!"

Cleofus jumped at him as if he was about to attack and Emanuel jumped back and hit his head on the window.

Cleofus laughed and said, "Looks like it's still fourteen on three."

"No matter what it is, you're out numbered," Chris said. "So if you're smart, you'll take your seat in the back."

"Not before giving me my money back!" a voice screamed from the front.

"Yeah! He took my money too!" another person shouted.

People started to complain about the money Cleofus had taken from them and how they weren't able to eat lunch. The bus became filled with loud, chattering complaints and kids clamoring to get their money back as Cleofus' face turned tomato red.

"Well, Cleofus, looks like your gonna have a broke summer after all," Chris said.

Those who had been bullied all year by Cleofus approached Pete with their hands out. Pete looked at Cleofus, and when he didn't say anything, he started returning the money back to them. Cleofus stomped to the back and took a seat, looking at Chris with rage in his eyes.

Chris held out his hand to Pete, "Five dollars please."

"We didn't take any money from you!" Pete complained.

# Last Day First Vision

"Emanuel's money," Chris insisted and waved his head towards Emanuel.

Emanuel held his hand out; Pete rolled his eyes and shoved the money in his hand. Emanuel smiled as he looked up at Chris with a sigh of relief because Pete had given the whole thirty-two dollars and seventeen cents away; and there were still kids in line waiting for their money.

"I don't have anymore!" Pete shouted with his hands up.

"You should've thought about that before you started taking our money!" One little girl yelled.

"Yeah!" More kids retorted, as the angry mob ganged up on Pete and Everett forcing them to the back.

The bus pulled up to the middle class neighborhood where Chris and Casey finally got off. The bus came to a slow screeching halt as Chris left his seat and headed for the door. He looked back and saw one of the kids in a nose-to-nose combat with Cleofus and shook his head with a smirk.

"I don't care if you're outta money. Give me your watch!"

"But my dad gave me this watch," Cleofus argued.

"And my mom gave me the money you took!!"

"Yeah!!" The kids began chanting.

Chris and Casey made their way to the front of the bus.

"See ya later," Chris said to the bus driver.

"Have a nice summer," she said smiling at them.

They waved good-bye and got off the bus.

"Wait!" They heard a mealy voice call out. "I'm getting off here, too!"

Chris turned and saw Emanuel hurrying down the stairs of the bus just as it was preparing to leave. Just then, Cleofus let down his window and yelled out, "You're a dead man Chris!"

"Aw!" Chris hollered back, "why'd you wait until I got off the bus?" He flicked his hands in the air as the bus tore off down the street.

"Can't stand him, Chris," Casey said.

5

# Summer of Seven

"Ah, don't worry about him, he's no threat," he said to his little sister. He then turned to eye Emanuel and said. "So, I haven't seen you get off here before."

"I just want to thank you for what you did for me," Emanuel said timidly.

"Not a problem." Chris responded, "but you gotta learn to stand up for yourself or this will happen again."

Dropping his head Emanuel acknowledged that Chris was right.

"That's why he never messes with you, huh?" he asked Chris.

Chris felt really sorry for him. Throughout the school year he had witnessed Emanuel being bullied at least a dozen times, not just by Cleofus, but by others too. They preyed on his size and his weakness.

"How old are you?" Chris asked him.

"Thirteen," he responded looking up at Chris.

"Thirteen?" Casey yelped. "I would've guessed ten!"

"I know, I'm small for my age," he said scratching his messy head.

"Why don't you tell your parents that he bullies you?" Casey asked,

"So they can contact the school - ya know – fix the problem!"

"My parents are in Israel, I live here with my aunt, who doesn't speak much English," he explained. "Plus…it's embarrassing. If she knew this was going on it would only upset her."

"You just need to gain a little confidence and stand your ground even if it's a little scary," Chris told him.

"You should hang out with us for the summer," Casey offered.

"I would really like that," Emanuel said nodding gratefully.

"Well alright! We look forward to it, but, for now we better head on home," Chris said.

"What's your name again?"

"Emanuel."

"E-man," Chris said matter-of-factly

"No, it's E-man-u-el," he said slowly.

Chris smiled and patted him on the shoulder, "I know, but we will call you E-man from now on…it's more fitting."

E-man smiled back, as he accepted his new name. "Ok," he said, happy to have made some new friends, too.

"It's burning hot out here. You live far from here?" Chris asked.

"Oh, no I just live two blocks down," he said, turning to head on home.

"We'll see ya soon," Casey said waving good-bye.

When E-man was well on his way Chris turned to his sister, cracked a little smile and said, "Race ya home!" and took off running before she had the chance to agree.

Casey darted off swiftly to try and catch him, but she was too far behind.

"That's no fair! You got a head start!" she yelled as she watched his back getting farther into the distance ahead of her.

Moments later, Chris arrived at their house while Casey lagged behind. He was out of breath, crouched over, leaning on his knees trying to catch his breath when Casey arrived. But when he looked up and saw her coming, he threw his arms up and did a victory dance.

"Yeah, yeah!"

"Whatever, Chris," she said as she walked over and socked him in the stomach.

"Ugh!" he moaned, doubling over in more shock than pain. "What you do that for?" he asked, faking a cry.

"Because…you…you cheated!" she said out of breath.

He chuckled and yanked at her ponytail.

"No, you just lost," he declared.

"Come on, let's get inside. It's too hot out here."

Chris took the chain from around his neck with the key on it and unlocked the door. The house was still clean from the night before because mom had made them stay up half the night spring-cleaning, or in this case, summer-cleaning.

Relieved to be home, they dropped their bags down in the foyer, as was their norm, and then Chris went straight into the game room to play his favorite video game—as was his norm. Casey trailed behind him for a minute until she turned off and found her spot on the big plush sofa in the living room. She snatched up the universal remote and began flipping through the channels and blurting out commands.

"Chris, call mom and let her know we're home."

"You do it, I'm busy!" Chris shouted as he was rumbling through his box of games.

"I always call. It's your turn. Plus, you know if mom doesn't get a call she's gonna hold you responsible because you're the oldest!" she smirked at her brilliant comeback.

Chris let out a hard sigh and stopped what he was doing. Dropping his games back into the box, he reluctantly meandered over to the phone in the kitchen to call his mother mainly because he knew Casey was right.

"Oh, she gets on my nerves!" he mumbled to himself then thought. Well, I have been fussed at a thousand times before for not calling…no point in taking another bullet.

On the way to the kitchen he turned and looked at her only to find a smart-aleckie smile splashed across her face and one little leg swinging from the edge of the huge sofa. Chris cut his eyes at her and said not a word as he went on to the kitchen.

"I thought you'd see it my way big brother," she said rubbing it in.

He picked up the beige wall phone and dialed his mother's work number. While he waited for an answer he scanned through the refrigerator looking for a snack.

"Hello?"

"Hey, Mom."

"Hey, baby."

"This is Chris, Mom," he said grabbing a lime Gatorade and a hand full of white grapes out of the bunch.

"I know that, and you are my baby!" she said obviously smiling.

"Mom, I told you already, I am not a baby," he complained, annoyed by her endearment. "I mean what if you slip up and say that in front of my friends?"

"That's right. Sorry. I forgot you're my little man. Is it okay to slip up and call you my 'little man?'"

Chris rolled his eyes and sighed.

"Anyway, you guys ok?"

"Yeah," he said throwing a grape into his mouth. "Casey is watching TV and I'm on an important mission to save the world!" he answered hoping to rush her off the phone.

"Oh, you're playing that video game, uh?"

"Yeah, so I'll see ya when you get home ok? Love you. Bye!" He clunked down the phone and popped another grape in his mouth. He flicked off the kitchen light and headed off to the game room. He was walking up the hallway with his mind on his game when he was suddenly stopped in his tracks.

All of a sudden, he was paralyzed, not able to move anything except his eyes. He could not call out to Casey for help either. He was like an upright mummy desperate to be unraveled.

*Why can't I move?* Chris panicked.

His eyes were wide and searching when suddenly a small screen resembling that of a transparent television appeared on his sight.

*Oh! What is going on? What is this?!*

Fear was beginning to grip him. He could not move or open his mouth; screaming was out of the question.

*What in the world! Why can't I move...HELP!* Chris thought to himself as he was being taken over by terror.

He kept telling himself to scream but his mouth just would not open and no sound would come out. He stared at the screen in front of him and noticed that he could actually see through it. He saw the back of Casey sitting on the sofa.

*Casey turn around! Casey! Casey! Turn around so you can see this!* He called from within himself, but she didn't turn from the entertainment on the real TV screen because she couldn't hear him, of course.

Right there before Chris' eyes the screen began to have moving figures and color changes. Chris felt like he would faint, but his neck stiffened tighter as he had no choice but to watch as a vision began to play out no differently than an action packed movie with all the cinematic effects. He watched the screen as it revealed his next door neighbor's mother rushing off to work. He saw her zipping out of her driveway and up the street to the interstate. He watched as she was singing to herself in the car. But, as she merged onto the highway he watched in horror as her little white car was slammed in the rear by a big dump truck thrusting her into the 18-wheeler truck driving directly in front of her. Her car slid underneath the 18-wheeler, where she became helplessly trapped, until a Life Flight helicopter arrived on the scene of the accident.

Chris could hardly believe the scene as his neighbor was rushed to the hospital hanging between life and death. He watched in horror as she was flown away by helicopter. The scene continued to play on and progressed into the night allowing him to see her in a hospital bed. Initially her eyes were at half-mast, but then they fell shut followed by the piercing sound of the life monitor. Chris watched in dismay as he then observed the green flat line rip across the face of the monitor.

Doctors and nurses did their level best to revive her, but to no avail. Mrs. Harris passed away right before Chris' eyes and he could do nothing about it but stand frozen and take it all in.

In a snap, as suddenly as the screen appeared, it disappeared and he was able to move again. As he turned around he found himself facing the kitchen window just in time to look out and see Mrs. Harris next door, alive and well, and fumbling with her keys in an apparent rush. She darted to her car and got in.

*Oh, no!* Chris thought and raced to the front door to try and stop her.

When he ripped past Casey, he grabbed her attention away from her TV show. She jumped off the sofa and followed behind him. Not knowing what was going on she looked back over her shoulder as perhaps an intruder had invaded the house or something.

"What's wrong Chris?" she asked fearfully running close behind, but Chris did not answer.

Chris dashed through the door and hit the ground running. He tore across the lawn in an all out effort to get to Mrs. Harris before she pulled off, but to his chagrin, her car was already backing out of her driveway. By the time he could get close enough she was already rolling down the street.

"Wait!" Chris cried out as he tried to catch her.

When Casey realized that he was running after Mrs. Harris, she stopped cold in the middle of the front yard and threw up her hands. She was not sure what was going on or what she should do, so she put her hands on her hips and watched and wondered.

Chris kept running with all his might. He waved and hollered out,

"MRS. HARRIS! STOP...STOP! PLEASE! MRS. HARRIS STOP!!"

After running halfway down the street, Chris accepted that it was not humanly possible to catch up to a speeding car. His sprint turned into a jog, and his jog into a walk. Panting, Chris put his hands on the top of his head and closed his eyes tight. He was devastated by what he had seen and upset because he was unable to stop her. A single tear streamed down the side of his face. Batting his eyes he slowly walked back to the house. He passed by Casey as though he didn't even see her.

She threw her hands up and asked, "What's wrong with you? What exactly did Mom say to you on the phone?"

Chris kept walking but shook his head with frustration in response to her and remained wordless. Casey stayed on his heels relentlessly determined to get to the bottom of his strange behavior.

"Chris, what is wrong?" she practically begged him.

But he kept silent. He sat down on the couch and recalled the intrusive vision trying to make sense of it.

Casey began to panic, "Chris you are scaring me! Please...talk to me!"

"I saw Mrs. Harris, she...she was crushed by the truck," he stammered.

"WHAT? There was no truck out there?" she said pointing outside.

Chris sighed and dropped his face into his hands.

"No, not out there. It was in front of my face," he said massaging his temples.

"In front of your face?" she responded. "Well...where was your face when you saw this?"

"In the hallway."

"The hallway?" she repeated sarcastically.

He turned and glared at her, again wordless.

"I just want to understand you Chris. You saw Ms. Harris get crushed - by a truck - in this hallway," she said pointing behind her.

"Yes," Chris said knowing just how crazy it sounded.

"Ok. Mom is right about those video games rotting your brain out."

"For the first time you might be right," he said reclining on the couch.

"Glad I never got into those video games," she mumbled under her breath as she took a seat next to Chris on the sofa.

"Well, how about we just watch some TV, now. I think that's safe," Casey suggested hoping Chris would feel better.

At 5:14 p.m. Ms. Prentice pulled into the cluttered garage. Casey heard all the commotion and ran out to meet her to tell her what had happened earlier, but Chris remained sunken in the sofa. He flipped through the news channels to see if there were any accidents reported. Ms. Prentice came through the kitchen door and dropped her briefcase on the kitchen table and went into the living room to check on Chris.

"How ya doing?" she lovingly inquired.

Chris said nothing and sprawled himself out on the sofa. Concerned, his mother found a spot, sat down next to him, and put her arm around him.

"You ok, sweetie?"

"Casey told you what happened, didn't she?" he finally responded.

Casey gave a guilty shrug upon hearing her name as she had been standing in the doorway eavesdropping.

"Yes, she did, but I am asking you how you are doing," his mother insisted.

"It was clear as day Mom! I saw Mrs. Harris get crushed by a truck! I tried to run and warn her, but I wasn't fast enough…I couldn't catch her!" he lamented. "I feel like it's all my fault."

"Listen Chris, Ms. Harris is going to be fine. People sometimes imagine that bad things might happen to people, but they usually don't. When your father was still with us and we'd fight, I use to wish that bad things would happen to him but they never came true. That was wrong of me, of course. My point is: just because a little thought runs through your head, doesn't mean that it will happen, ok?" she said rubbing Chris' back.

"Mom, it wasn't a thought that ran though my mind! It was a…," Chris hesitated. "Something popped up in front of my face!"

"Chris, you have always had a vivid imagination," she said getting up. "You should be grateful that you are not like a lot of people who can't see past what's in front of them. Look, I will even call the Harris' to prove it to you."

"Yeah, okay! That will make me feel a whole lot better," Chris quipped.

Ms. Prentice walked over and picked up the phone and dialed Mrs. Harris while Chris and Casey watched from the doorway of the kitchen, but there was no answer. She hung up the phone and turned to assure Chris, "Honey, everything will be fine," she assured him.

"No one picked up because she left an hour ago. I thought you were calling her cell phone, mom!"

"Why don't you go on up and get some rest," his mother suggested as kindly as she could, considering that Chris was becoming frantic and even a little rude.

Chris schlepped on to his room feeling somewhat defeated and plopped across his bed until dinner.

⊗ ⊗ ⊗

Later on that night the house was dimly lit as Ms. Prentice enjoyed the peaceful hush that had fallen over her home, especially now that Chris and Casey were fast asleep after a hearty spaghetti dinner. Ms. Prentice decided to take a seat on the sofa and brush her hair in front of the Eleven o'clock news before retiring for the night.

*My sweet Chris*, she thought. *I pray he has peaceful sleep and will be done with all that nonsense by morning.*

She raked her brush through her long thick hair and heard the ending of a T.V. commercial that she hardly paid attention to. She threw her head, tossing her hair over her lap and began sectioning her hair when she heard the music typical of a nightly news breaking story.

"BREAKING NEWS…a fatal traffic accident earlier today has claimed the life of one of Atlanta's own citizens…"

Ms. Prentice lifted her sights toward the television and was perplexed as she saw swarms of police and story hungry reporters on the scene.

"Two Eighty Five's northbound traffic was brought to a standstill earlier today. Traffic was backed up for hours," the news anchor reported.

As the reporter explained the accident the view was panned over to the wreckage still on the scene. Ms. Prentice was aghast when she saw the mangled car.

"Oh, my God!" she lamented covering her mouth.

*It looks exactly like Ms. Harris's car! But, I'm not sure. It's demolished almost!* Ms. Prentice stood to her feet oblivious of her falling hairbrush and rollers. "IT'S HER! NO!" she whaled.

She stood in the middle of the floor, screaming with her watery eyes glued to the television. Chris jumped out of bed and ran over to the staircase and hooded over the banister to see what was wrong. It took no time for Casey to follow suit. With her face crumpled with concern she shot out of her room and darted around the corner to where Chris was still looking over the banister. He held on to Casey as they both took in an aerial view of the T.V. and saw what their mom was watching.

"Oh, my God! I don't believe this," Ms. Prentice screamed.

She fell back into her seated position on the sofa. The kids watched as their mother sat on the edge of the sofa with both hands over her mouth sobbing.

"No, no, this can't be!" she lamented.

Recognizing the scene on T.V. to be the same as the one he saw during that frozen moment in the hallway, Chris dashed down the stairs leaving Casey behind. Ms. Prentice turned and stared at him speechless through red weakened eyes, speechless.

As a mother, she felt helpless; she had no answers. Her mind quickly scanned the day that her husband abandoned her and their children. That was the last time she remembered feeling so helpless and void of answers. Chris drew closer to the television peering at the familiar scene while Casey looked on from the top of the stairs, afraid.

Ms. Prentice took off to the kitchen and dialed next door to the Harris' residence all the while looking out the window into their yard, into the windows hoping for some activity, any activity. The phone rang and rang, but there was still no answer.

"Sean might be home," Chris said.

"They wouldn't leave him home alone, you think?"

"Mom, he's almost eleven."

"Well, let's go see," she said wiping her eyes with the back of her hand.

They left Casey and ran over to the house and knocked on the door. After a moment Sean peeked through the window and opened up the door.

"Hi Sean, are your parents home?" Ms. Prentice asked.

"No, my dad got a phone call and said he had to go to the hospital and he would be back. I asked him could I go but he said that I had to stay here."

He turned his gaze to Chris, then back at Ms. Prentice.

"Why are you looking for my parents, and why are you crying?" he asked suspiciously.

Completely ignoring his questions Ms. Prentice asked, "Have you heard from your mother?" She was still hoping that she had mistakenly identified the car on the news.

"She doesn't get home from work until later on tonight. What's going on? Why are you asking me these questions?"

"Oh, just need a dessert recipe," she lied. "Well, I'll just stop by tomorrow."

"Yeah, sure," he responded dryly. Ms. Prentice and Chris turned and walked briskly back to their house. As soon as they entered the house, Ms. Prentice ran into her room and retrieved her purse and cell phone.

"Where are you going?" Chris asked.

"To the hospital, I have to know if it is Mrs. Harris."

"I'm going too," Chris said.

"No! You stay here and watch Casey," she said snatching the couple of rollers out of her hair that she'd put in earlier.

"She can stay here and go back to sleep. She won't get into anything. She knows better," he argued.

"No, Chris" she said grabbing her keys off the table.

"Well, let her come too!"

"No, Chris," his mother insisted. Chris stood looking into his mother's face obviously hurt and quite irritated.

Ms. Prentice took in a deep breath and blew it out hard, not sure how to make her son understand.

"Chris," she said breathy, "please, don't be mad, sweetheart. This is the type of stuff you just don't need to see."

"I already did!" he snapped, and stormed off.

When Ms. Prentice arrived at the hospital it was not long before she knew for sure that Mrs. Harris was indeed the subject of that ghastly news story on T.V. as she heard the wails and sobs of someone who had obviously been given woeful news. When she turned the corner of the long corridor she spotted Mr. Harris bowled over as if he was sick. Nurses and orderlies surrounded him, some holding him, others scrapping with him just to ensure that he'd stay put and not return to the room where Mrs. Harris's battered body lay still beneath a winding sheet.

Mr. Harris wailed and cried uncontrollably. He weaved and bobbed like a man lost and without hope now. All Ms. Prentice could do was watch writhing at the sight of a good friend in the throes of pain. She too cried continuously because she could do nothing to help. "My God!" she cried clasping her hands, bringing them to her chin. The more she listened to Mr. Harris's sobs the weaker she became.

"Oh, Mr. Harris," she whispered walking over toward the crowd in which he was the center. Mr. Harris was bent across the shoulder of an orderly, weak with sorrow, when he lifted his eyes enough to see Ms. Prentice. She stood and stared, her eyes equally teary. She reached her hand out and placed it gently on his head, the other over her mouth. At the feel of her touch, he went into rolls of sobbing.

The small crowd of helpers walked Mr. Harris over to a lounge chair and folded him into it then gave him a sedative. Ms. Prentice could not take another moment of grief especially since she could not do anything to change it, and made a bee line to the exit.

Heavy hearted, she drove at a snail's pace all the way back home. When she arrived Chris was still up and met her at the door.

"Is it true? Was it her? Did you see her?" Chris asked beginning to cry.

"Yes," she whispered, nodding. The two of them fell into each other's arms and wept until they were drained.

For the next couple of days Chris was numb to everyday life, he didn't eat, he didn't sleep. He lounged in front of the television in an almost unconscious gaze and took in nothing. Walking by and seeing her son in the same posture she'd seen now for the past couple of days caused Ms. Prentice to grow more and more concerned.

"Baby, you want to talk about it?"

"Nope," Chris responded. "there's nothing to talk about. She's gone and I didn't stop it."

Upon hearing this, Ms. Prentice was not only painfully surprised, but she decided that now was the time to let Chris in on a little secret of her own.

"Chris, sweetheart. I've been talking to someone who I believe can help you and all you have to do is talk," she explained.

"Help me with what?"

"This obvious trauma you have experienced through first seeing all that happened, before it actually happened, and then it coming to pass. Honey, that's a bit much for anyone especially a young guy like you," she explained rustling the top of his head. "I'm worried about you, so, I've gotten some help…"

"… in the form of…" Chris pressed.

"Well, a therapist. A nice lady who specializes in traumatized children, Honey."

"What's her name?"

"Dr. Gabriella Host. She is one of the best therapists in the town and came highly recommended."

"What if I don't want to go, Mom?"

"Well, son, that is when I would say, 'I am the mother and you are the child who I care the world for.' Just trust me on this one, okay? I've heard that her clients always get results."

Sighing, Chris agreed. Just then his mother put him in a playful headlock and began covering his forehead with kisses.

*Chapter Two*

# ⊗ THE DOCTOR'S OFFICE ⊗

It was 3:07pm when Ms. Prentice finally found a parking space in the congested parking lot of the doctor's office. As soon as she was nestled into a parking spot she yanked her keys from the ignition, grabbed her purse, and looked over at Chris who was staring up at the tall shinny building, to beckon him on.

"Come on, Chris," she said eying her watch.

Chris was lost in a mental replay of the recent events surrounding Mrs. Harris.

"Sweetie, did you hear me? We are seven minutes late. Let's go."

He snapped back to the present long enough to open the car door and spill out of the car and onto his feet. He and his mother hurried across the parking lot and into the building. In no time, they were in the midst of a plush lobby that had what looked like a huge rock garden, appeared to have a tall marble wall growing up from it, set right in the middle of the lobby. It was captivating as the soothing sounds of the water cascaded down the back wall. Ms. Prentice quickly eyed a security guard.

"Dr. Host's office?" she asked walking toward the elevator.

"Seventeenth floor," he responded with his face never leaving his newspaper.

She flung him a 'thanks 'and clicked in march-time along the green marble floor. She hurried to their destination, but Chris crept along not excited at all. He did, however, muster enough interest to press the up button then leaned on the wall to wait for the elevator.

"This is a waste of time and money, Mom," he complained.

"No, I don't think so. I have never heard of anybody having such a vivid vision and it coming true!" She stammered for lack of clearer words.

"I just hate seeing you like this, baby."

*Ding!* The elevator door opened and they stepped in.

"Chris, try to be open to what Dr. Host says. Don't just write her off because you've made up in your mind that this is a waste of time."

Chris remained numb and stared at the wall. His mind began to drift off again putting his mother's words in a winnowing distance.

Chris thought to himself, *I'm the fastest runner in my class! But why wasn't I able to stop her? Maybe if I shouted a little louder she would've heard me – then she would still be alive to thank me for the warning.*

Ms. Prentice sadly looked on at her son's nonchalant demeanor. "I don't understand why you won't let me in; I thought we were closer than this," Ms. Prentice said.

*How random was that?* Chris thought still refusing to utter a word.

Ms. Prentice was growing increasingly frustrated and began to fear that she would lose Chris if something didn't happen quick.

*Oh, I hope Dr. Host can do something miraculous and fast!* she thought doubting that she could.

*Ding!* The elevator doors opened offering them their destination at last— the seventeenth floor with the one who would finally clear this peculiar mess. Ms. Prentice walked up to the very attractive receptionist to get further direction.

"Good afternoon, how may I help you?" the receptionist asked pleasantly.

"Yes, we're a little late. Prentice is the name, and our appointment was at three o'clock," she said, her brows high and tight.

"Oh, yes, Dr. Host is still expecting you. Follow me."

Ms. Prentice had to practically drag Chris along now. When they arrived at the door, the receptionist knocked twice and opened it. Dr. Host was sitting at her desk reading over some material.

"Dr. Host, your three o'clock is here," she announced ushering them into the office.

She slid her reading glasses off the bridge of her nose and stood to her feet to greet the mother and son.

"Thanks dear," she told the receptionist. Ms. Prentice couldn't help but notice the paintings of beautiful landscaping that garnished her office walls.

"You must be Chris," she said walking over to him with her hand extended. She was noticeably endearing. Her long blond hair and radiant skin contributed to her striking beauty which Chris was struck by immediately. "And Ms. Prentice, how are you today?"

"I'm fine, thank you. Sorry we're late," she interjected backing up slowly to take the seat that seemed to press flush to the back of her knees.

"It's not a problem," Ms. Host said taking her seat, too, behind her cherry desk.

The office was large and impressive. Behind her were two tall windows that stretched from the ceiling to the floor and framed out the skyline overlooking the city. Two colossal bookshelves stood tall in the corners filled with books and figurines.

"Ms. Prentice, I know we talked briefly over the phone, but if you don't mind, I would like to hear Chris tell me exactly what happened," Ms. Host began.

She crossed her hands and turned toward Chris.

Chris slowly and deliberately told his story to Ms. Host and left out not one hair-raising detail. Upon finishing his story, the room fell silent for an awkwardly long time. Chris sat in hope that, alas, when the silence was done, it would be replaced with answers coming from Dr. Host. Answers that would not only make him feel better, but answers that would give full explanation to his new found, albeit uncomfortable, gift. He stared at her curiously without batting an eye. If only he could pull something out of her to put him out of his misery.

Ms. Prentice broke the silence, "How could this be? Could it be a coincidence? What is going on with my son, Doctor?" she begged.

Ms. Host had no response for her but instead kept her gaze fixed on Chris as his was certainly fixed on her.

She asked Chris, "Has anything like this ever happen before?"

They both answered in unison, Ms. Prentice saying, "No!" and Chris saying, "Yes!"

Ms. Prentice turned to Chris overwhelmed by surprise.

"What? When Chris? Why didn't you ever tell me?" Chris shrugged his shoulders. .

She frowned and stared bewildered at the doctor.

"Sometimes I have these dreams, and a day or so later it happens just like I saw…sometimes good…sometimes bad," he confessed.

"Ms. Prentice, I need to ask you a question," Dr. Host asked still looking at Chris.

"Yeah, go ahead."

"What is your religion?"

"We're Christians, but… we haven't been to church lately," she said a little embarrassed. "What does that have to do with anything?"

"Well, it sounds like God is trying to use your son."

"What? Like the prophets in the Bible or something?" she asked.

"Well, yes, you can look at it that way."

"Chris, do you remember when these visions and dreams began?"

"I was about ten," he spoke reminiscently.

Ms. Prentice interjected again, "That's when we first joined the church - when we gave our lives to Christ!"

"You may already know," the doctor began, "but I feel the need to say it anyway. When you accept Jesus into your heart, at that point, you are born again."

Ms. Prentice nodded in agreement.

"Often times, when you are born again, God chooses and gives you what are called spiritual gifts."

Her nodding slowed to a halt as her mouth fell open in surprise and question.

"And it sounds like Chris has been given the gift of prophecy. Many are given this gift, but it comes in different ways. For some, God simply whispers a message in their ear or gives a message for someone else. For others, when they dream, an angel comes and gives them instructions on what to do with the situations around them. There are many different ways the gift of prophecy is given. But sometimes when people receive the message and they are not in tune to God's voice, they miss out on their assignment. In extreme cases, like in Chris' case, God is calling you for something. He is saying it loud and clear because He can't afford for you to miss it," Ms. Host informed Chris hoping Ms. Prentice caught it all.

"Miss what?" he asked anxiously.

"Whatever He's calling you for…whatever He needs you to do," she answered.

"Well, what is it that he wants me to do?" Chris asked.

"I don't know. He will let you know when the time is right."

"Well, if he was using me, when he showed me the vision of Ms. Harris, why couldn't I save her?" he asked frustrated.

"It was not for you to save her. It was her time. There is no way you *could have* saved her, Chris. God revealed that to you, to get your attention."

Chris looked troubled and confused.

"In many cases you see things ahead of time so you can warn the person right?" Ms. Host asked.

"Yeah."

"This time was different. There was nothing you could do to change the outcome. Even if you caught her before she left, she would've died another way that same day, same hour, same minute," she said.

Ms. Prentice raised her hand as if she were an eager student in class. "I have a question doctor," she said.

"Yes?"

"How can Chris have this gift when there are perhaps hundreds of people at our church who are more mature in Christ, and none of them have any spiritual gifts?" Ms. Prentice asked.

"They do," she smiled.

"Ms. Prentice let me ask you, what natural talent do you have, something you were born with?"

"Well…I can draw well," she answered.

"Let's say when you were a child, you drew all of the time, and at the age of eight you stopped and never drew anything again. If you picked up a pencil now, do you think you would be able to draw well?"

"No."

"Why?"

"Because I haven't been practicing," she said.

"Exactly! When you have a talent, you practice, you spend time getting to know your craft, and you get better and better, right?"

"Yes."

"It's the same thing with a spiritual gift. When you spend time with the Lord, getting to know him by reading the Bible, and through prayer, that is when your gifts begin to develop and you can begin to work miracles in His name. Many are still infants when it comes to doing the will of the Lord. They are still eating baby food when God is ready to serve steak," she closed her eyes and frowned.

"It's really sad when a saint who is being obedient begins to do what God has called him to do, whether it is healing the sick or raising the dead. People get shocked and amazed when they shouldn't be because they should be doing similar things to bless the Kingdom of God."

As she finished she looked up at the brass wall clock hanging behind Chris and his mother.

"Well, it's almost four o'clock," she announced.

Ms. Prentice asked, "Well, what do you suggest that we do?"

"I suggest that you send Chris away for the summer to take in a different atmosphere and relax. He needs some time off from the usual… may I suggest a place?"

"Sure," she answered unsure.

"There is a camp called Camp Come Along, and it's in the mountains, far away from everything, and I hear that the camp is serene. Ms. Lambert has been running the camp for years now, and this will give Chris the chance to get away and get his mind off things. They're enrolling now."

"Do you have their information?"

"Sure do," Dr. Host said ripping a piece of paper from a pad on her desk. As she was writing down the information, Chris noticed the beautiful gold ring that she wore on her thumb. It had a blue stone with a golden hollow circle in the middle of the stone. She handed the information to Ms. Prentice and stood up.

"Why don't you give them a call when you leave here today, they will give you further instructions."

"Should I send my daughter, Casey?" she asked getting up as well

"Why not? It will be nice for you to have some time to yourself."

After thanking Ms. Host, they left in better spirits. Once they got out, Ms. Prentice asked Chris, "How do you feel about what Dr. Host said?"

"I'm fine, just trying to understand all of this…take it all in, you know, Mom?"

"You and me, both," she said raising her eyebrows. "How do you feel about going to camp for the summer? You guys haven't spent more than two nights away from home in your life."

"Actually, summer camp sounds kinda fun. The kids at school that go are always talking about how they can't wait to go back. They brag about all the fun stuff they get to do."

"Well, that's good. I'll call when we get in and get you guys out there tomorrow," she said starting up the car.

"Oh, and Mom, get Emanuel's number from Casey and ask if he can go with us!"

"Who's Emanuel?" she asked.

"A friend from school. Don't worry. He's a good kid. you'll like him."

## Chapter Three

## ⊗ CAMP COME ALONG ⊗

The sun was beginning to set when the Prentice family mini-van turned into the parking lot of Camp Come Along. Emanuel beamed with excitement and could not stop thanking everyone in the car.

"I want to thank you again for bringing me along. I was so bored just sitting at home! Thanks guys! Really, thanks!"

"I'm glad your aunt let you go," Casey responded.

Ms. Prentice pulled into a vacant space and turned the car off.

"Ok everyone, I expect that you will be on your best behavior, right?" she insisted turning to eye each one.

"Yes, Mom," Casey and Chris sang for appeasement.

E-man on the other hand, said it and meant it, "Yes Ma'am!"

"Very good, E-man. You are so welcome." She turned back around and looked at Chris who was sitting behind her.

"You alright?" she asked.

"Yeah," he said feeling better than he had in a while.

"I want you to relax and try to have some fun, ok?" she encouraged him.

"Alright. I think I can do that, Mom."

"Ok let's go! It's getting hot in here," Casey said opening the front door.

"Pop the trunk."

Chris and E-man got out of the back and helped Casey get the bags.

The air was clean up in the mountains at Camp Come Along, not a cloud in the sky. Already, the kids could feel the air moving gently taking the countless trees along in a slow sway. It was evident that a body of water in the form of a pond or lake surrounded the camp too. Ms. Prentice got out of the car and took off her shades.

"Come gimme a hug, Baby," She stretched her arms toward Casey, and gave her a tight hug.

"I miss you already, Mom," she said with her eyes shut tight.

"I miss you too, Sweetie."

"Chris," she said motioning for him to come over so that she could enwrap him too. For him, her hug would be two-fold. "Remember what Dr. Host said…seek God," she whispered in his ear.

"I know. I will," he assured her though exasperated. She released her hold and locked a gaze onto him.

"There's one thing I need you to promise me," she said.

"What's that?"

"That you will look after your sister. Make sure that nothing happens to her."

Chris looked at his little sister and made a face.

"I'm not sure I wanna keep that promise," he said smiling at her.

Casey cut her eyes at him and quipped, "Don't worry, Mom, I'm eleven-years-old. I can take care of myself."

Ms. Prentice laughed, "I know, Sweetie."

"Well, Mom, I guess we'll see you in five weeks," Chris confirmed tossing his overly packed backpack over his shoulders.

"Oh, wait. Come here Chris," Ms. Prentice said licking her thumb.

"There's something by your eye."

"No, Mom! You know I hate it when you do that!" he protested wiping his eye before his mother got the chance.

"Sorry, Honey" she smiled.

"We better get going for sure now," Casey said.

"Ok, let me get my hug from E-man."

E-man kept his eye on the thumb in question hoping it wouldn't touch him.

"Come on, let's go," Chris politely insisted. "See you later, Mom."

"When you go in ask for Ms. Lambert. I've taken care of everything so all you have to do is check in. I love you guys. Call me if you need me," she said watching them march away.

The camp was approximately one mile long and one mile wide— a fully developed peninsula. Seventy-five percent of it was surrounded by water and the remaining twenty-five percent of it was covered by posh greenery because of its connection to a forest. Two large bridges sloped up and reached outward like a gigantic two prong fork. One side led to the parking lot and the other side led into the forest.

The bridges were arched by thick wood planks and had thick wooden rails going down the sides. The excited campers crossed the south bridge that led to the camp.

"Wow! Look at this place!" E-man exclaimed.

"This might not be so bad after all," Chris added looking around.

The crew trekked along until they were half way through the entire camp observing everything. They especially appreciated the discovery of really nice, large cabins along the campground. Kids were engaged in different sports and activities everywhere; some were swimming, others were playing softball. There was even a group engaged in a rigorous game of dodge ball. Chris, Casey and E-man were aglow with anticipation.

"Wow!" E-man huffed.

Over to the right of the west bridge sat the main office. As the kids approached the door to go in, they noticed at the top of the doorpost was nailed a wooden sign with the words 'THE COME ALONG OFFICE' carved in it. When they entered, they came face-to-face with a petite woman with thick, blond, wavy hair tamed back into a ponytail. Her skin was noticeably red and peeling. Casey noticed an obvious difference in the skin color around her eyes. Apparently, she'd been wearing sunglasses while sunbathing or something.

"Hello, we're Chris and Casey Prentice and this is E-man," Chris announced introducing him with a quick glance.

"Amin, Emanuel Amin," he corrected.

"Oh, yes," she said in an almost piercingly high-pitched voice.

"I spoke with your mother yesterday, and she took care of everything over the phone. Hold on," she said grabbing her clipboard.

"Christopherrrrrr," she sang while trying to locate his name on the sheet with her index finger, "....Casey, and Emanuel here you are," she said. "You can go and place your bags up against that wall, and they will be placed in your cabin by our staff."

A boy walked in, sweaty and out of breath, holding a flat volleyball.

"Ms. Lambert," he said tossing the flat ball up into the air, "we need another ball! See, what happened was: the other team thought they were winning, and I spiked the ball so hard-"

"One minute, Bo. Let me finish with these three," she said warding him off for a moment.

Bo took the towel he had and wiped over his amber colored face. His wiry hair was low-cut with streams of sweat running noticeably throughout his scalp. He leaned on the counter to catch his breath.

"Ok, you three are in cabin number thirty-seven," she said.

"Hey, we're roommates. I'm in that cabin too," Bo said looking a bit confused that Casey was also a roommate. "Wait, all three of you are in 37?"

"Yes," Ms. Lambert clarified.

"But, she's a girl," he contested.

"I noticed that," Casey said.

# Camp Come Along

Bo snickered at her sarcasm.

"Normally, boys and girls don't share cabins," he said.

"I...I know that...this year will be a little different. We have some new rules," she said with a worried look on her face.

"Co-ed cabins? I'm not complaining," Bo said.

She quickly pulled out another volleyball from behind the counter and tossed it to him.

"Thanks," Bo said.

"You play ball?" he asked Chris tossing the ball in air.

"Never lose," Chris quipped.

"Oh, really? We'll see about that," Bo responded dashing off toward the field.

Chris wasted no time and was right behind him.

"Come on guys!"

Casey cut her eyes at him at the sound of the command before following along with E-man in tow.

By the time they got outside, the sun was beginning to set casting a grey hue over the area. Remembering that his mom commissioned him to take care of Casey, he glanced behind him to see if she was still coming up the rear.

"Case, E-man, you two coming?" Chris called.

Casey waved them on letting him know to go ahead without them.

"So, what do you think about the camp?" E-man asked.

"I think it's beautiful. All the trees and the water makes it so peaceful," she explained.

"Yeah, and there's so much to do," E-man exclaimed.

Some of the kids were row boating while others were racing and playing tag. As the two of them trekked along, a giant flat rock appeared in the near distance with a fellow camper perched at the top of it. He was reading a book. As the crew got closer, they w;;;';ere able to shout out,

"Why aren't you out playing with everyone else? You're not getting any exercise sitting up there all alone," Casey shouted.

"Well, I would rather relax and read," the boy spoke back in a thick British accent. "Besides, I am getting plenty of exercise."

"You're not even moving. How are you getting exercise?" E-man asked.

"I'm exercising my brain - the muscle few enjoy working out," the boy called back.

Casey sucked her teeth. "You know what we mean," she said now close enough to climb the rock for a face-to-face conversation. E-man was right behind her. "I'm Casey and this is E-man."

"Nice to meet you both. I'm Alex."

"You're not from around here, are you?" she asked with her brows furled.

He was watching the kids play volleyball.

"No, not actually. I was born and raised in London, England," he said squinting his eyes towards the field. E-man turned to see what Alex was looking at, and that's when he got an eye full.

"Hey, isn't that the guy you two came with," Alex asked jumping to his feet and pointing to the raucous activity he spotted.

"Fight! Fight! Fight!" on lookers shouted.

Casey stood up on the rock and saw Chris throwing punches and kicking an opponent. He lunged on the guy sending the two of them falling hard onto the ground.

"Oh no!" she said, "That's—"

"Cleofus Sline!" E-man hollered.

"What's he doing here?" Casey asked.

"Cleo-who?" Alex asked.

"I'll explain later," she said rushing down off the rock to the fight.

All she could think of was helping her brother. E-man stayed and observed from the sidelines of the great rock with Alex. Two other campers jumped in the fight and plunged their fists into Chris' body.

Left...POW! Right...THWACK!

This provoked even Bo. He, too, jumped into the fight, snatching one of the guys by the neck, hemming him up into a stable headlock, while kicking the other guy off of Chris. In the heat of the brawl, two camp counselors got wind of the news and went running to break up the fight.

"Move - MOVE!" Jill, one of the senior counselors, shouted shoving her way through the excited crowd.

"Break it up! NOW!" she yelled.

There was no doubt that she had some authority around Camp Come Along. Small in stature, but tall on rules, she began the process of tearing the boys apart. The other counselor barreled her way in too.

"Alright!" she bellowed. Break it up! Go back to your activities... this show is over!"

Looking over the rustled boys, Jill asked, "What's the problem?"

The heaving boys said nothing. Chris had set an unmovable menacing stare on Cleofus. His face was contorted from the anger that brewed within like that of a bull right before he charges his subject.

"Jill," Bo interjected, "it's not Chris' fault!"

"Yes it is!" Cleofus fumed.

"That's enough! You boys come with me!" she commanded.

They followed her into the camp office. Ms. Lambert was standing at the front desk when they arrived; however, one look at the tattered boys took away all pleasantries.

"Good heavens! What has happened here?" she inquired as she came from behind the desk with her arms folded.

"They were fighting," Jill informed her.

"But Chris has only been here two minutes," Ms. Lambert said.

Chris finally spoke. "He pushed me," he nodded towards Cleofus.

The office door burst open. It was Casey out of breath.

"Chris didn't do anything wrong! He was only defending himself! I heard Cleofus say on the bus that he would kill Chris when he got the chance!" she tattled.

"What?" Ms. Lambert said.

"You better shut your little brat-sister up before I do!" Cleofus said low enough for Ms. Lambert not to hear.

Chris charged at him, catching Jill and Ms. Lambert off guard.

"Hey, you! Stop right now!" the two counselors shouted as they pulled Chris off of Cleofus.

"You boys are out of control," Ms. Lambert scolded them.

"I will not tolerate –"

The front door opened cutting into Ms. Lambert's speech to the boys.

"Could I have a word with you Sarah?"

"Floo-Ellen, right now I'm in the middle of –"

"It's urgent," she said calmly looking her in the eyes.

Floo-Ellen was a matriarch at Camp Come Along. She had crow's feet about her eyes and mouth - a mouth that barely smiled, if ever. Her thin white, sun-spotted skin was an immediate source of conversation among those meeting her for the first time. Her hair was dark with a streak of grey cutting through the center of her coif, which was always pulled back off her face, pinned up into a bun in the back of her head.

Placing her hands on Chris and Bo's back, gently inching them along, she commanded, "Jill, take these two in the office with you."

Turning to Cleofus and his two companions, "You three sit down here," she instructed pointing to the bench. "I will be back to deal with you in a minute," she quipped as she exited the office with Floo-Ellen.

The dubious trio dragged over to the wooden bench that sat up against the wall while Jill escorted Bo and Chris into the office, closing the door behind them.

"Have a seat," she offered.

The office was a relic of the 1970s, which the teen boys knew nothing about and had no flare for the green and orange plaid woven sofa they now sat upon.

"Who is that lady Floo-Ellen?" Bo asked.

Jill was pulling the foldout chair from behind the antique desk as she answered the fair question.

"Floo-Ellen is Ms. Lambert's new assistant."

"Oh."

"Chris," she said turning her attention to him, "you have got to control this little temper of yours!"

Chris was flustered by Jill's indication. "Obviously, you did not hear what he said to me," he argued.

"It doesn't matter what he said to you. He is just trying to provoke you so you will get into more trouble! Aren't you a Christian? Aren't you supposed to love everyone?"

"Wow, Jill!" Bo exclaimed turning to Chris. "How do you just assume he's a Christian?"

"Well you are a Christian, right?" Jill insisted.

Chris gave a confirming nod.

"Well this sounds so convincing coming from an atheist!"

Chris looked at her to see if it was true.

"My beliefs have nothing to do with this Bo."

"Well it's funny how you don't believe in God but you believe in his word - when it is convenient for you."

She was sitting with her elbows resting on her knees as her fists were a ledge beneath her chin.

"Man, you should have heard her last summer quoting different scriptures for different situations – I just knew she was saved and sanctified!"

No one spoke for a moment.

"Why don't you believe in God?" Chris asked.

"Why do you?" she snapped.

"Because I have seen his miraculous miracles first hand!" Chris said.

"Well maybe my views will change when I experience '*miraculous miracles*' first hand…. Now, tell me what happened out there, Bo."

"Me and Chris were playing volleyball when dude came up like a mad man and pushed Chris down on the ground yelling, 'I keep my promises'. I got involved only to help Chris up off the ground, and they started fighting. Chris was beating him down and that's when his friends jumped in; and when they did, I did!"

She turned back to Chris, "Fighting is not the answer."

"It is when someone is throwing punches at you," he responded.

"Like my sister said, I was only defending myself."

Jill sat wordless observing Chris closely; his dark brown hair sticking to his sweaty face which matched his crinkled eyebrows.

"You're right," she finally said, "but you should try to avoid trouble at all cost. Tonight you could have walked away," she said.

"Jill, the guy pushed him on the ground!" Bo interjected.

"It's all about making the right judgment call, and Bo you know the rules here!"

Chris glanced over at Bo.

"What are the rules?"

Bo took a deep breath. "Chores," he said, flatly rolling his eyes.

"Yes. For the next week you guys will be responsible for helping the cleaning crew clean up after breakfast, lunch, and dinner. We also have a new landscaper this year to help us keep the grounds looking decent. You will assist him with anything he needs. If you are not able to stay out of trouble, then harsher punishments will be enforced," she emphasized sternly.

"Like what?" Chris inquired.

"Like spending the rest of the summer not participating in any camp activities, becoming a maid to your fellow campers, and if you are not asleep - then you're cleaning!"

She looked at her watch.

"It's after eight, we need to head out. Dinner has already started. Let's go boys. " she said and they went over to the Mess Hall.

*Chapter Four*

## ⊗ EAT AND MEET ⊗

The sound of rushing voices filled the Mess Hall and thickened its air monotonously for the duration of the hour-long meal the noisy partakers enjoyed. Continuous chatter bounced from one table to the next as everyone seemed to have the uncanny ability to chat while chewing. People were everywhere - kids mostly, grown-ups too - in line awaiting their food, while others were seated or finding one around the circular tables stationed throughout. In the middle of each table stood a cardholder with large laminated index card that displayed the cabin number.

"You guys know your cabin number?" Jill asked.

"Yeah," Bo said pointing to the table, "number thirty-seven is over to the far right by the window."

"Good. So go and fix your plates and take your seats over there," Jill instructed.

"Not hungry," Chris announced still recovering from his earlier tussle in the dirt.

"Me neither," Bo said.

At this, Jill was not in the mood for kids who wanted to go against the grain. "Oh," she said nodding her head as her hands were perched on her slack hips, "you guys too pumped up to eat, uh?"

Chris gave a chuckle and threw her a comment as he walked off to his appointed table.

"Yeah, something like that," he said and Bo agreed.

Hyperactive adolescents were talking and bragging 100 miles a minute about who won the games that were played, while others made excuse for why they lost. As they made their way to their table it was hard to ignore some of the people whispering when they went by about the fight earlier. One guy pointed at Chris and punched the air as he described to his friends his version of what happened. Chris pretended not to see and focused on Bo's direction to their table even harder. This was definitely not the attention he wanted – being new to the camp and all.

When Casey saw them she stood up and said, "There he is – this is the one I was telling you about."

She hugged his arm and gave him a warm smile. Chris had a troubled look on his face and wondered what all she could've possibly told them in this short period of time. The last thing he wanted was people judging him before he had the chance to introduce himself.

"Here, Chris," she said pulling out the chair, "sit by me."
"Uh, thanks," he said hesitantly.

He gave her one of those looks that spoke loudly without him parting his lips. Telepathy was in order for sure as he was trying to get her to tell him what in the world she'd told them. Bo took the seat on the other side of Chris.

Chris leaned over to his sister and whispered, "You didn't tell them about what happened at home, did you?"

"No, of course not!" she said above a whisper.

He gave her an 'I'm not convinced' look and turned away.

As the partakers around the table became full and satisfied, empty plates were pushed toward the middle of the table and everyone was beginning to mingle, shuffling about the cafeteria. The sound of clanging dishes, silverware, and clinging glasses was like music against the endless voices that were even more voluminous than before.

From around the table, a young lady introduced herself.

"Well, I'm Leena, and I'm from Alabama," she said flashing a smile then taking a bite of her roll.

Casey observed her fairly thoroughly and asked, "Are you Chinese?" Leena swallowed the last bit of her bread and prepared an answer.

"No, I'm a lovely mixture," she said as a matter of factly.

She wiped the edge of her mouth with her napkin. "My mother is Japanese and my father is black."

Her short hair spiked out through the rubber band that was in the center of her head.

"Oh," Casey said understanding where she got her signature Asian eyes from.

"Hey, I'm Jacqueline," a newbie called, "but you can call me Jacks. I'm from Jersey and live in a Puerto Rican household by virtue of my Puerto Rican parents," she said with a smile.

"Which makes you Puerto Rican," Casey imputed.

Chris gave her a curt look and Casey instantly wished she could take her comment back.

Jacks was tall, slender, and wore a thick headband to keep her lengthy, sometimes overbearing, brown hair out of her face.

"I'm Alex. I saw you two earlier running over to play volleyball – I was sitting on the big rock sitting in the middle of the field," he said looking at Bo and Chris.

Bo squinted his eyes tapping his index finger on his cheek.

"Oh yeah," Chris sang out.

He and Bo were nodding their heads pretending they remembered seeing him as well.

"Well," Alex continued, "I'm from London England, and I've been in the States now for three years," he said in his thick British accent.

"How do you like it here?" Jacks asked.

"I like it. It's a little different than what I'm use to, but I like it."

"I bet it's nice there," Jacks commented.

Alex shook his head and took another bite of his food.

"What about you?" she asked addressing Bo. "I was born and raised in North Carolina," he said crossing his hands behind his head leaning his chair back on two legs.

"And you are?" Leena asked.

"Bo, of course!"

"Well, how are we supposed to know who you are?"

"Because I'm a man that needs no introduction," he said lightly popping his shirt.

"Oh, whatever!" Leena said waving him off like she would a mosquito.

"What?"

"Anyway, let's move on," she insisted turning her attention towards Chris now.

"Me and Chris are from Atlanta," Casey squeezed in.

"What about you E-man? Where are you from?" Jacks asked.

He pushed his plate away from him.

"I'm from Israel, but I live in Atlanta not too far from Chris and Casey," he said in his signature small voice. "Most of my family still lives there. My parents sent me away to live with my aunt because of all the fighting."

"I like E-man! He's so soft spoken and sweet," Casey said smiling at him.

"Thank you, Casey. You're a real nice person too."

"Wow," Leena said sniffing the air, "is that… love I smell?"

Casey sucked her teeth and gave her a disapproving look.

"Girls and boys can be just friends!" Casey quipped.

"If you say so," Leena responded looking off catching the table sign in her view.

"There must be some mistake. We can't all be in the same cabin," Jacks said changing the subject.

"That's what I was thinking," Bo added. "For the last five summers I've been here, boys were never allowed to visit girl cabins - let alone share one."

"Well, maybe the numbers mean something else," Jacks said.

"Yeah," Leena said turning to Alex, "remember last summer we all stayed in the same group during the day? Well, maybe this is the activity group."

"Possibly," Alex said, "or, we could be roommates."

"We are roommates," Bo said. "Lambert told us in the office the cabins are co-ed this summer."

"But what about –"

A makeshift intercom became live in an instant. The irritating sound of tapping fingers on the head of the microphone and electric squealing pierced everyone's ears as the microphone screeched sending the cutting sound permeating though the room. Everyone turned their attention towards the back where they saw Ms. Lambert standing in front of a long rectangular table where all of the camp councilors were seated.

"Hello everyone, as most of you know, I am Ms. Lambert…"

She took a hard swallow and wiped the little beads of sweat that started to form on her forehead.

"…I've been the camp director since the camp opened fifteen years ago, but this summer will be a little different."

Mumblings just above a whisper began to fill the room. It was obvious everyone wondered what the change would be.

"Please everyone," Ms. Lambert said raising her hand for them to quiet down.

She moved the microphone cord away from her feet and stepped aside.

"Most of you guys know the Come Along counselors," she said and introduced the councilors from the past. "But there are a few new faces," she said moving to the end of the table. "This here is Floo-Ellen."

She stood up with a pleasant smile and waved to the crowd.

"Floo-Ellen will be taking over my job this summer as camp director. So from this point forward, all orders will be given by her, and they are to be followed."

The whispers of speculation grew louder. Jill caught Ms. Lambert's eye and frowned with shock - as did most of the faculty, and all of the children.

"Why does Ms. Lambert look so nervous?" Jacks whispered.

"I noticed that too," Chris added.

"Jill told us Floo-Ellen was just hired as her assistant. Why would she make a crazy change like that?" Bo asked.

"Looks like the camp counselors are just as shocked as we are," Alex said reading the looks on their faces.

"What's so wrong with Floo-Ellen?" Casey asked.

"I don't know," Leena frowned, "but I don't like this."

The crowd grew louder. "Please everyone listen up," Ms. Lambert pleaded.

Floo-Ellen came from behind the table.

"Camp activities will still go on the same way, and nothing will be differ – "

"Actually," Floo-Ellen interrupted taking the microphone from Ms. Lambert, "there will be some changes made that I believe you will absolutely love and will be in your best interest. Like Ms. Lambert said, there are a few new faces that are on the staff, myself included. In fact, would the new crew please stand up?" The four counselors stood up all decked in blue polo shirts and blue jeans.

"This is Bella at my right hand," Floo-Ellen began.

Not only was Bella young and clever, she was strikingly beautiful.

"This is Herman and Scott," she continued. Herman and Scott were complete opposites because Herman was an easy 6'5" and 300 pounds, while Scott was a mere 5'6" and a featherweight.

# Eat and Meet

"And finally I introduce to you, Zanku!"

There was no mistaking that this one was her favorites for some unknown reason. It was like he was a trophy or something.

His skin was thick and dark as night. His eyes were as blue as the bluest sea. He had a deep scar that started at his temple curving all the way underneath his left eye. Floo-Ellen walked back toward the center where she began.

"As you can see, each table has a number. That number represents what cabin you will be in. So, that means your roommates are sitting next to you at your table," she said.

"But there're girls sitting at my table!" Cleofus shouted out loud.

"Yes, I noticed. The cabins are co-ed this year. We're trying something new this summer."

"Is that legal?" someone whispered.

"Now that that's understood," Floo-Ellen said under her breath,

"like Ms. Lambert informed you, I will be taking over this camp this summer and things will be better than they ever were before! So, you are all lucky to be here this summer," she said.

"I feel truly honored to be in this position, and I can assure you that this will be the best summer ever!" she said to Ms. Lambert.

Ms. Lambert pressed her lips together and nodded her head to acknowledge Floo-Ellen.

"Children, this will be a summer that you will never forget because for the first time in history, this camp is throwing The Come Along Competitions! Each cabin will compete to win, and the cabin that has the most wins by the end of the summer will win $20,000 to split amongst your cabin mates!"

There was a collective gasp throughout the entire room.

"She just tryna give me some money – just forcing me to take it!" Bo said.

"She can't be serious," Jacks said.

"Is this a joke?" someone yelled out.

"I assure you, this is not a joke," she spoke slowly into the microphone.

Casey asked, "Is that possible?"

"All things are possible," Alex said.

"You know what I mean!"

"I don't like this…something's not right," Leena said dubiously.

"What's not to like? You got competition and lots of money," Bo said not understanding where she was coming from. "With Chris and me on the team we will surely win!"

"I don't know," Leena said.

"Stop being so negative," Bo snapped.

"It is a good opportunity," Alex added.

"$20,000 for us to split? I agree with Alex – it's a good opportunity!" Jacks added.

Floo-Ellen tapped the microphone cutting right into the chatter to get everyone's attention.

"These are the rules. Each day three cabins will compete in a contest. The three cabins that will compete will be announced at breakfast every morning. The winning cabin for that day will collect their medallion, and at the end of the eighth week medallions will be turned in and tallied up for the grand prize."

Bella whispered something in her ear.

"Alright everyone, talk it over with your teammates and decide on a name for your cabin. Bella here," Floo-Ellen said placing her hand on Bella's shoulder, "will come and verify that you are in the right cabin and at that time, she will collect your team name. Be sure of your team name because that's how you will be identified for the rest of the summer. We have a busy day ahead of us tomorrow. You are dismissed. I will see you all for breakfast tomorrow morning at eight o'clock sharp," she said putting the microphone back in its stand.

Everyone sat for a moment still stunned talking about the new and sudden changes. Ms. Lambert was in the front explaining something to Jill.

44

Bella handed Floo-Ellen the clipboard and as she looked over it they left the room.

"MS. LAMBERT!" Leena stood up and shouted in front of everyone loudly enough to grab the attention of everyone present, including Floo-Ellen and Bella.

"What would possess you to make such a foolish decision?" Leena belted.

Ms. Lambert was stunned by her boldness. Floo-Ellen peered at Leena as she spoke not saying a word.

"Why are you acting so afraid of her?" she asked pointing to Floo-Ellen. "What did she do to—?"

"Please, Leena! Please!" Ms. Lambert whispered rather loudly.

Placing a defiant hand on her hip Leena snapped, "What?"

"Don't say another word!" she asked as if her life depended on it.

Meanwhile, Ms. Lambert smiled and gave Floo-Ellen a light wave to show that things were under control as people returned to their conversations increasing the hum in the room. Floo-Ellen and Bella proceeded to the kitchen area as kids were making their way out of the Mess Hall. Everyone at the table was in a quandary as to why Leena would display such behavior.

"Leena, rude outbursts will not be tolerated!" Ms. Lambert scolded.

"But Ms. Lambert you looked like you were being drafted against your will or something!"

"And if that were true – and it's not - that still doesn't give you the right to yell out like that in public!"

"Well, I'm sorry. I just don't feel right about her," Leena argued.

"Well, I assure you, Leena, Floo-Ellen is an upstanding lady and an asset to this camp, young lady! There will be no further discussion on this matter either!"

With that, Ms. Lambert stormed off.

"See, I told you to calm all that down," Bo said.

"You're lucky you didn't get chores like us," Chris said.

Leena stood with her arms crossed and said nothing. The others got up from the table and pushed in their chairs.

"I think she will be fine," Casey said to Leena. "Nothing to worry about."

"Except Cleofus!" E-man added.

"And he's definitely nothing to worry about!" Chris rebutted.

Bo held the door while everyone went through. Leena was the last to come out and Bo released the door and hung his arm around her neck.

"Stop looking like that, Leena. I don't think she's that bad."

"I don't know for a fact that she's bad; I just feel that she is. My feelings have never steered me wrong before! I can see it in her eyes," she explained.

"Just relax anyway, please." Bo was trying to be as comforting as possible.

People slowly made their way to their assigned cabins to discuss their strengths and weaknesses in trying to come up with strategies to win in the competitions.

When the crew made it to their cabins, Alex opened the unlocked door displaying three sets of bunk beds up against the walls in the huge room in the back. In the front room, however, was a small red sofa - apparently a convertible bed. Excited, the kids ran in and claimed their bed territories by putting their stuff on it. Some pounced on a bed or laid out on it marking their space. Chris put his bag on one of the bottom bunks as Casey grabbed the top bunk above his. E-man also got a top bunk.

"This is a pretty big cabin," Alex declared peering into the bathroom.

"Supplies!" Leena said. She was looking in a chest that sat in the front. "We got flashlights, batteries, and tools and some other stuff!"

While Leena was scouring through supplies E-man had gotten busy trying to destroy a spider web on a vent that was too close for his comfort. So he tried with all his might to tear it away by reaching as far as he could to get it with a tissue. But instead, he ended up falling headlong off the top bunk, flipping over and onto the floor, and twisted his ankle as well as busted his knee. E-man let out a bellowing cry.

"Oh no!" Casey screeched jumping down off her bunk.

Everyone ran over to the weeping small fry to examine his injuries. E-man cried and cried.

"Besides the skinned up, bloody knee it looks like he has a really badly twisted ankle," Alex said examining his leg as he if were a doctor.

Everyone crowded around him focused on the limp leg. Alex even tried to turn it.

"Ooouch!" E-man cried.

"Oh! Sorry," Alex offered nonchalantly.

"Let's take him to the infirmary," Chris suggested.

"I don't think we should move him. One of us should go for help," Leena insisted.

"Move, let me see," Jacks said coming up behind Alex.

Jacks looked at E-man's leg and then his face. She easily noticed his great discomfort and asked, "Do you want to be healed?"

E-man hollered, "Yes!" He shut his eyes tightly and tried to bear the pain.

"Okay," she said, "here goes."

She placed her hand gently behind his head and the other one on his leg and closed her eyes. Her lips were moving as she said a silent prayer. Some of the others had their eyes closed too. Suddenly, while she prayed the, bleeding stopped and new skin started to form over his injured knee. Those with opened eyes were shocked to fright. Others opened their eyes at hearing the gasps and could scarcely believe what they were seeing. Their mouths fell open at the sight, but Jacks continued to pray. With just a little more time and prayer, E-man's foot too began to change; it slowly began turning and in no time he could move it again just as before! E-man rose to his feet and examined his leg as if he were Pinocchio. He kicked it back and forth.

Everyone was wide-eyed and numb. Bo stood up slowly examining Jacks with wide eyes of disbelief.

"How in the world did you do that?" Chris asked.

"I didn't…God did," she replied a matter-of-factly dusting off her pants.

"The gift of healing," Alex added.

"Exactly," she said looking at him.

"Is that magic?" Casey asked still amazed.

"No," Alex said, "it is the opposite actually. The source of magic is evil. That was God's power we just witnessed."

"I don't understand," Casey said sitting down on the bed.

Alex pulled up a chair beside her while Chris was staring at E-man as he jumped up and down with a huge smile on his face.

"Once you join God's team he gives you a gift, a piece of his spirit, which comes and lives inside of you.  That's where the source of power comes from - not the person," Alex explained.

Casey stood up and pointed to Jacks, "So she had a piece of God in her?"

"Yes, and healing is the gift He gave me," Jacks said.

Alex nodded his head in agreement.

"So everyone that joins God's team will be able to heal people? Because that would be just great! Because we could just go to the hospitals and heal everyone, and there will be no more sick and suffering," Casey said excited, as told by her flailing arms.

"Don't think it works that way Casey," Bo inserted.

"I wish it did, but it doesn't." Jacks continued. "Just like I can't go into a hospital and heal everyone there unless God tells me too."

"Well, why not?" Casey said.

"Because it has to be God's will. Everything happens for a reason even if it is bad. He might need someone to be sick so it will bring a family closer or whatever the case might be," Jacks instructed.

"But if you have any doubt, one little drop, whatever you are believing for won't come because God needs us to completely believe. When we have faith, we can do all things!" Alex said.

"You guys are right," Bo said.

"The only reason God healed E-man through me was because it was His will to do so. I asked Him, He said yes, and I had the faith that He would carry out what He said," Jacks taught the fascinated group.

"And just to clarify, God doesn't give everyone the gift of healing. Some get the gift of wisdom, speaking and interpreting the language of God, discernment - "

"What is discernment?"

"When people can tell whether someone is good or evil!" Leena said jerking her neck around and hands on her hips. "I was exercising discernment earlier with Floo-Ellen!"

"Oh," Casey said.

Alex continued, "Then there's the gift of faith, and prophecy with dreams and visions."

Casey looked over at Chris. "Visions?" Casey asked.

"Yes, when God shows you something that is about to happen or warns you. Or it could be he wants you to deliver a message to someone."

"Chris! God showed you that vision?" Everyone turned and looked over at Chris.

"Uhh," he grunted giving a half-hearted chuckle and sat down in hopes of stifling any curiosity.

Regardless, Chris had to sit and explain the whole story and reason that he and Casey were there at Camp Come Along. Everyone was glued still and their ears peeled for every detail of the occurrence that unfolded just days before he arrived at camp - from the beginning all the way to the visit to the therapist. Once again, the crew was as taken aback as they were by the healing of E-man; the testimony of God's abilities through people was almost more than they could take.

"Wow! I wonder what the reason was for showing you if you couldn't save her," inquired Bo.

Chris shrugged his shoulders.

"There's a reason for everything. God will reveal it to him in due time," Alex said.

"So Chris has the gift of prophecy, and Jacks has healing," Casey surmised.

"Leena has the gift of discernment, and I have the gift of knowledge and wisdom," Alex added.

"I'm still developing my gift," Bo added. "I have the gift of faith, but I'm still developing it. I get a little afraid sometimes because the miracles can be a bit overwhelming."

"The spirit of fear is not from God," Jacks said a little upset because he hadn't learned to take hold of his gift.

"I know, I know," Bo said feeling bad.

"That sounds like a cool gift," Casey said, "Why don't I have a gift?" she asked looking at Alex.

"You probably do. It's just not recognized or developed yet."

"Well how do I develop it?"

"You must have a relationship with God himself by talking to Him and knowing His word," Alex informed her.

E-man was sitting Indian style on the floor listening to everyone.

"Don't feel bad Casey I don't have a gift either," he said.

"Well you don't know that yet," Jacks said.

"It's rare that you find others with true gifts from God," Bo said. "So maybe it's not a coincidence that we are sharing the same cabin after all!"

*Knock, knock…* the door opened.

*Chapter Five*

## ⊗ FIRST NIGHT OUT ⊗

It was Jill and Bella.

"Having a group meeting?" Jill asked jokingly when she saw everyone huddled up looking serious.

"Something like that," Leena said.

"Oh, we're just making sure that everyone in here is assigned to this cabin."

The two ladies stepped in and Bella pulled out her clipboard and started calling roll. "Emanuel Amin, Alex Fitzsimmons, Leena Lee, Jacqueline Martinez, Casey and Chris Prentice, and Bo Richardson."

"All here," Alex said.

"And your team name?" Bella asked.

The group turned their necks one toward the other eyeing to see if anyone had any ideas, since they had not yet come up with one.

"What about God's Gifts?" Casey suggested.

"No," Bo protested.

"You guys haven't come up with a name yet?" Jill yelped.

"Just give us a minute," Alex insisted.

"What about The Seven?" Bo suggested.

"There are other teams with seven members," Leena said.

"I know, I know, but they will just be seven – we are *The* Seven."

"I don't think so," Jacks argued.

"I'm with her," Leena added.

"I was thinking 7-Alive," E-man submitted.

"I like it," said Alex as if he had just gotten a bright idea.

"Me too," Casey said. "So, we all agree on this name?"

They agreed and Bella recorded their name on her clipboard and handed it to Jill as she reached for the doorknob.

"Thanks guys. Now you *7-Alivers* need to get ready for bed. We gotta busy day tomorrow," she said following Jill out the door.

"Oh, yeah," Jill peeked back in, "Chris and Bo, you two need to be in the Mess Hall at seven-thirty in the morning if you want breakfast. I talked to Ms. Lambert and she informed me that your chores start tomorrow morning and will run through the week. Everyone else, breakfast is at eight in the morning. Good night," she said and shut the door.

Chris looked at Bo and shook his head disappointingly.

"He attacked you! Why should we be punished for that?" Bo threw up his arms in protest.

"Just do the chores and steer clear of that guy," E-man said almost like a demand. "That's what I would do."

E-man was sitting on the floor next to Casey who was examining his healed leg.

"I won't mess with him, but if he comes to me, I can't promise nothing," Chris said standing up to stretch.

"Something's not right about her," Leena said.

"Who, Jill?" Jacks asked.

"No, Bella. I can't put my finger on it. I don't feel right about her - Floo-Ellen either. Ya know, I think we should sneak out to her cabin tonight so we can find out where she's staying – you know – so we can keep an eye on her," Leena devised.

# First Night Out

"Leena, I just got one question for you," Bo said trying to keep a straight face, "How do you feel about me? Do you feel right about me?"

She sucked her teeth, "Shut up Bo! This is serious."

"I don't think it's a good idea to go out sneaking around at night. We have five weeks here. We'll find out in due time. Things done in the dark are always revealed. Plus, we have a busy day tomorrow so we should listen to Bella and get some rest," Alex insisted.

"Fine," Leena sighed.

The crew prepared for bed and all turned in promptly, but Leena would not rest. Her sleep was broken for hours. As the hour grew later and later, Leena found herself wide awake in the middle of the night. So, she got out of her bed, got dressed, and went over to Bo's bed and kneeled down.

"Bo," she whispered.

He peeked at her through one eye.

"Wake up. We need to go to Floo-Ellen's cabin and find out why Ms. Lambert is so afraid of her!" Bo sluggishly sat up.

"But Alex said we shouldn't – "

"Last I checked he wasn't your daddy," she said in a harsh whisper.

"*Shhh…*ok," Bo spat.

"Go wake Chris up, and we'll go," he said rubbing his eyes.

"Make sure you dress in something dark," Leena whispered going over to wake Chris.

Bo slid on a black tee shirt and slogged over to the window. As he peered out he saw Ms. Lambert and Floo-Ellen standing outside of the director's cabin talking.

"Hey look," Bo whispered as he arrowed with his chin.

Leena had gotten Chris up, and they both went over to the window, too.

"I wonder what they're talking about," Bo said putting on his shoes now.

In the midst of the goings on, Jacks sat up out of her sleep.

"What's going on?" she asked groggily.

"*Shhhhh!*" Leena said placing a forefinger over her lips, looking suspiciously around the room.

Suddenly, at the sound of someone shifting about in the bed, everyone froze in place in hopes they had not awakened anyone else. Once there was silence again Leena tiptoed over to Jacks.

"Get ready. We're about to go find out what's up with Floo-Ellen," she whispered in her ear.

Bo waved his hands to get their attention and motioned for them to come over.

"Look," he said pointing out the window.

They all peeped out and watched the two conversing women in the distance. Ms. Lambert held up a silver key that sparkled in the moonlight and was obviously passing along instruction concerning it, as was told by the tight grip she had on it as she directed with it as she spoke.

The crew from the cabin, turned detectives, were now about to become expert lip readers, too.

"Hey," Chris whispered, "I can see what Floo-Ellen is saying."

"Yeah, she just said, 'thank you'."

They remained glued to the window as if they were at home in the den watching television. After deciphering most of the conversation, they watched as Floo-Ellen snatched the key, turned and walked away, while Ms. Lambert's head dropped into her hands. It was obvious that she was weeping as she made her way back inside her cabin.

"Wait! Why is Ms. Lambert going into the director's cabin?" Bo asked.

"Yeah, I thought Floo-Ellen was staying there," Leena said.

"We'll follow her to see where she goes," Chris said.

"Everybody ready?" Bo whispered.

"Yeah," Chris said opening the front door.

"Wait!" Jacks said tying up her shoes, "Look in there," she pointed to a chest in the front room. "Let's take walkie-talkies just in case we get separated."

Leena quietly dug through the chest and found the two yellow walkie-talkies.

"Good thinking, Jacks," Leena said. "Let's go out the side door. We won't be seen."

Bo peeked out the window once more and ran out after the others.

"I just saw her cross over the east bridge," Bo said once they were outside.

"Why would she be crossing the east bridge? There is nothing over there except the forest." Jacks wondered out loud.

"Guess we're about find out," Chris said.

The four scrunched down low and ran single file the entire span behind the cabins that were parallel to the water leading up to the bridge. The distance was much further than the crew of four had expected; so, when they got to the last cabin before the bridge, they stopped almost breathless. Chris placed a finger over his lips to message to the crew to quiet down, if possible, as they were all practically heaving by now.

He looked around the corner at the bridge but there was no sign of Floo-Ellen. All he heard was the quiet rustling stream of water that flowed beneath the bridge and into the larger body of water. "Come on! Let's go!" Leena directed and started off towards the bridge.

"Wait!" Bo commanded, "Let one person go to make sure the coast is clear."

"So who's gonna go?" Jacks asked.

"I think Bo should since it was his idea," Leena said with a smirk.

"Alright…fine, I'll go," he said, bothered.

He began his jog over toward the bridge, but halfway there, he froze in place and looked back over his shoulder at the crew, but they just waved him on.

"Keep going!" they mouthed.

When he got to the bridge, he ducked down beside it, craning his neck in an effort to lay an eye on Floo-Ellen. Bo glanced at the water and considered taking his chances crossing it instead of the bridge.

The stillness of the night was pierced with noise from chirping crickets and crocking frogs. Bo's vision was draped by the darkness, and the deep massive forest that stood before him was an obvious no-no; so, he crossed the bridge and looked once more. Then, he threw up a hand signaling to the rest that it was safe to pass on over, then resumed his squatting position. As the rest arrived on the other side, they each knelt down beside him and waited for further huddle talk.

"Ok, change of plan," Bo said. "It's too quiet for all of us to follow her. Leena and Jacks take my walkie and go hide behind that old canoe over there."

A couple of feet toward the shore sat an old, rusty, red canoe that was flipped up-side-down on a debris littered ground.

"We need you two to be the lookouts anyway. If you see anyone cross, buzz and tell us!" Chris instructed holding up the other walkie-talkie.

"Alright," Jacks said, "come on Leena."

Once they were behind the canoe, and out of sight, they quietly ran forward in search of Floo-Ellen. The would-be spies made sure the coast was clear; they jumped from tree to tree and crouched a while; they peeped around making sure the coast was clear before moving forward avoiding the lightly treaded path that she was on.

Further down Chris spotted her, "There she is."

Bo looked up the path and saw her walking slowly but confident.

Chris whispered into the walkie-talkie, "We see her. You guys alright?"

He turned the volume down low before they had a chance to respond.

"We're alright – you two be careful," Jacks whispered.

"We will," he said running over to the tree where Bo was.

Chris beckoned for Bo to come, but instead he stood still.

"What's wrong?" Chris asked.

"The deeper we get, the scarier the trees look," he answered.

"I noticed that too, but I just try to ignore it, "Chris told him. "Look, Bo, let's just do what we came out here to do, or do you just wanna go back and let this be a waste of time?" Chris asked hoping Bo would choose the go-back option.

"Okay, let's go," he said continuing along.

But before they could get too far, a burst of static come blaring out of the walkie-talkie.

"Turn it off! Turn it off!" Chris hollered startled by the sudden outburst.

He started fumbling and struggled to get it off. Jacks' cracked voice came through, "tzzzz BLUE EYES tzzzzz." He turned it off and froze, and so did Floo-Ellen.

Chris peeked around and saw that she was looking in their direction.

"Is she looking over here?" Bo asked in a panic.

"Yeah, I think Jacks was telling us Zanku is coming. What are we gonna do?"

"I got an idea," Chris said tossing the walkie-talkie away from them.

"Follow me," he said as he began to climb the giant cedar tree they were hiding behind. Bo followed him up without question.

*I sure hope she does not see us*, Bo thought. Once they reached the top of the tree, they saw that it sunk in like a giant nest, and they crawled in and hid. Seconds later they heard a deep voice say, "Everything alright?"

"No. I heard noise coming from over there," Floo-Ellen said walking towards them.

"What kind of noise? An animal maybe?" Zanku inspected whipping out his flashlight.

"It sounded like static," she said. "I don't think we're out here alone."

They heard them get closer.

"What is that?" Zanku asked with the flashlight spotlighted on the walkie-talkie.

He picked it up.

"This must be what you heard."

She looked at it suspiciously, "Possibly."

Chris and Bo quietly peeked over the treetop and watched them. As he examined it, more static shot out.

"It looks like the batteries are going dead." he said, "When these things run out you only get static."

"Humph. Let's get going," Zanku tossed the walkie-talkie back on the ground and followed Floo-Ellen back to the trail.

"The place is perfect. The basement is even better."

"How many kids are here this summer?" he asked.

"About ninety," she said as they both burst into cynical laughter.

Chris and Bo looked at each other.

"Let's get back to the girls," Chris suggested.

Bo looked out of the tree to make sure the two were gone before they dared to begin their descent from the tree.

Chris went immediately to the spot where the walkie-talkie was and scooped it up. Then, the two boys trekked their way back to the canoe to get the awaiting girls. Once the girls saw them at close range Leena and Jacks jumped out and ran towards them.

"Are you alright?" Leena asked.

"Let's get back to the cabin and we'll talk about it there," Bo insisted.

He knew stopping to chat was not wise, and they zipped off hurriedly.

Once they reached the cabin, they slowed down and stood behind it near the water. They checked their surroundings ensuring no one was around before they told the whole sorted story to the girls. Leena gripped her chest as she was breathing really hard.

"That was close," she gasped.

"Too close," Bo agreed blowing out a hard sigh.

# First Night Out

"I wonder what place is perfect. The camp? But what does a basement have to do with anything?" Jacks inquired.

"And why did he want to know how many kids there are?" Leena continued.

"We'll look for answers tomorrow. Let's grab some sleep," Chris said opening the cabin door.

"Yeah," Bo agreed. They each tip toed into the cabin and crawled into their beds without so much as a wash-up.

## Chapter Six

## ⊗ BOAT RACES ⊗

The sun illuminated brightly through the clouds that hung high over Camp Come Along early the next morning. The campground was fairly quiet; the sound of water babbling under the bridge was a calming exception. Chris' sleep came to an end when a singing bird outside his window began its morning solo. He tossed and turned beneath the covers in search of that deep place of sleep again, but to no avail, because the bird continued to whistle out a melody that now overtook his slumber. So, out of the bed he rolled in defeat.

He crept over to the window to see if he could lay an eye on the feathered culprit, but instead was hit with the realization that he had chores that he could not be late for. Chris stretched long and hard then glanced at the wall clock.

Oh no, he thought, seeing the time. He dashed over to Bo and began shaking him wildly.

"Get up man, its seven forty-five!" Bo sat up obviously startled looking around as if he'd forgotten where he was.

"The alarm didn't go off?" He asked making his way to the

bathroom.

"Uh…forgot to set it," Chris confessed apologetically.

He slid on the same dirty jeans from the day before then dived into a tee-shirt. Bo was ready in no time, and the two boys made their way across the open field to the Mess Hall for breakfast.

"I'm starving!" Bo complained rubbing his belly.

"Me too. I haven't eaten anything since lunch yesterday," Chris added opening the Mess Hall door.

When they stepped in, the place was empty except for a heavyset, black lady preparing the breakfast buffet. She wore a blue hat and tee-shirt that bore the camp logo and tight, fitted jeans that were giving way in the seams.

"You two must be the trouble makers, "she implied turning around with her hands on her hips - her tone weighty. "Ya'll late."

"Sorry about that Ms. … is that…O'Dale?" Chris questioned struggling to read her nametag.

"Yes it is. You boys go on over there and get a plate so you can get out there and help Mr. Andrew," she instructed. "Better yet, go on over there and sit down…TRUDY!" She yelled to the back.

Chris and Bo sat down at the table beside the buffet but were not satisfied to just sit there; they wanted to know what they should expect and became fidgety, turning to and fro trying to see the activity going on in the back. Looking around, they noticed quite a lot.

"Looks like Cleofus and his crew are late too," Chris said seeing that they weren't there. "They're probably still asleep."

Trudy, a petite, brown-skinned, soft-spoken lady emerged from the back and approached Ms. Odale.

"Yes, Ms. O'Dale," she responded timidly.

"I need you to fix our trouble makers here some breakfast and quick, before they don't eat," she instructed her looking at her watch. "They gotta be outta here by eight o'clock sharp."

"Yes, Ma'am."

# Boat Races

They watched Trudy rush off to the back.

"You boys lucky to be eatin' cause if you woulda came in ten minutes later you wouldn't be."

"Mama, please be gentle – we over slept," Bo said jokingly.

"I ain't yo' mama!" she snapped.

"So… you don't love me?" he asked sweetly, teasing her. She gave him a stern look and remained serious at which time Bo dared to reach out and hug her in spite of herself. She broke into a smile and couldn't take it back.

"Boy, shut up and sit down," she said in a facetious tone and waved him off as if he were an irritating fly. "I'm going back to work. Get outta here," she said suppressing a smile and went back to preparing the buffet.

Bo sat back down and looked at Chris and started singing, "She's a MEAN one! Mrs. Grinch…."

"You can say that again."


Groups of children started pouring in for breakfast just as Ms. O'Dale finished spreading the buffet. They all rushed on the buffet, piling their plates high and scurried back to their seats to scarf their food down like the hungriest of children. It seemed as if some inhaled their food!

"This food is nasty," Chris said with a mouth full of boxed eggs.

"It's soldier food," Bo said.

"Soldier food?" Chris inquired.

"Yeah, we're not eatin' this for pleasure. We're eatin' for survival."

Chris laughed and chomped into his dry toast. A group of girls came in and sat at the table behind them and immediately started giggling. The two boys, still chewing like cows, lifted their faces from their plates to see what was so funny. Chris' eye caught something that froze him in place. He stopped chewing and could not speak; it was as if he had seen a ghost, but it was a girl.

To him, she was stunning. She had green, almond- shaped eyes with sweeping brown eyelashes. Her hair was golden and cascaded from the top of her head along her tanned arms and stopped at the tip of her elbow. Chris was smitten and speechless.

"Hey, man! Snap out of it!" Bo charged, "What's wrong with you?"

But Chris didn't take his eyes off of her, "She's beautiful."

"Who?" Bo asked irritated looking over at the table.

"The girl in the green and yellow striped shirt."

"Summer?"

"Is that her name?"

Bo shook his head and took a sip of his orange juice. "All the guys go crazy over her when they first see her, but she never gives *anyone* the time of day."

"I bet she'll give *me* some time," Chris challenged.

Bo burst into deriding laughter. "No, man. Don't do it to yourself! I don't wanna see you get your feelings hurt."

"I won't!" Chris said confidently.

Bo laughed even harder, "Ok, I wanna see this."

The girls peered over to see what Bo was laughing at. Chris caught her eye and smiled at her; she blushed and quickly turned her head.

"Summer," he soothed under his breath, nodding to himself.

The noise level in the room began to rise as the Mess Hall filled up with the late groups arriving for breakfast.

"Bo and Chris!" Jill shouted from across the room in the doorway.

As always she had her clipboard and stopwatch which she waved at them and shouted, "It's 8:05. Let's move it!"

The girls giggled again and started whispering amongst themselves as Bo and Chris got up like dancers having to follow the piper. They carried their trays to the front, discarded them, and then went out the door which Jill had propped open with her foot just for them.

Once outside, they saw several groups of people coming toward the Mess Hall.

"You see the guy with the dark blue shirt over there trimming the hedges?" Jill asked.

"Yeah."

"That's Andrew. Go let him know who you are and then he will give you your assignment for today."

Just then, Cleofus and his group walked by snickering at them.

"See what happens when you mess with me? You get chores," Cleofus huffed. His friends started laughing.

"Mr. Sline!" Jill bellowed.

"Sorry, sorry," he said raising his hands in surrender only to appease Jill.

Shining a vindictive smile at Chris he turned and disappeared into the Mess Hall with the rest of his friends like the crook who got away.

Chris turned and looked at Jill in disbelief.

"What are their chores Jill?" Chris asked calmly, "since he started the fight and all."

"I know – I know, it's not fair," she said trying to brush the matter off until she had some real answers.

"WHAT?" was the one word Bo managed to get out, "You mean to tell me that we gotta do yard work and chores for a week, and they don't?"

"Walk with me," she said leading them towards Andrew. "I know you guys are mad, I'm mad too, but you gotta understand, I'm not the one in charge here."

"What's going on?" Chris asked.

"Floo-Ellen gave the order that you two were to fulfill the punishment and everyone else was off the hook," she admitted preparing for a backlash.

"No way," Chris said shaking his head.

Bo laughed, "This is a joke…right?"

"I'm afraid not."

"How did that happen, Jill?" Chris asked.

Jill was grimaced and began shaking her head, "Good question. I just hate that I don't know the answer. But, I do know something strange is going on and Lambert isn't talking. Last night, I checked cabins with Bella, and she made me feel like she was running the show."

The boys listened intently.

"Listen, I'm going to talk to Lambert and see if I can get you off the hook for the rest of the week."

"This is…this is…maaan I don't believe this!" Bo said fuming.

"Look, I need you two to cooperate quietly while I figure this thing out," she said lowering her voice.

Chris let out a long sigh. "Alright Jill, we'll cooperate. We'll do your chores, but when you find out what's going on, we want to be the first to know." Chris demanded as politely as he could.

"Deal," she said, "just go over and help Andrew, and stay out of trouble."

Jill turned and marched back into the Mess Hall.

"Maybe Leena was right after all," said Bo.

"Yeah, especially if Jill thinks something strange is going on."

The two went over to Andrew, who was working feverishly. As the two boys approached, Andrew put down the trimmers and pulled a hand towel from his rear end pocket and wiped his sweaty brow. Andrew was grimy from head to toe; his t-shirt had a tear that stretched diagonally across his stomach, and his jeans were dingy with big, jagged holes in the knees.

"Check out dude's ring," Bo whispered to Chris.

"Ring? Where?"

"There on his thumb…right hand."

Puzzled, Chris studied the ring a while.

*Where have I seen that ring?* Chris thought.

"Hola mi amigos!" The smiling worker said startling Chris out of deep thought.

"You speak Spanish?" Bo asked.

"Yeah, I speak a bunch of different languages," Andrew responded.

"Yeah right," Bo said. "What are you like…thirty?"

Andrew had his arms folded listening and smiling at the inquisitive youngster.

"Unless you study day and night, how are you gonna know a bunch of languages?"

He nodded his head in agreement.

"Well, with this job, we know I don't study day and night!"

They all started laughing.

"Is this your first summer here?" Bo asked.

"Yeah."

"So, who hired you - Ms. Lambert or Ms. Floo-Ellen?"

"Ms. Lambert did. Why?"

"…uhhh," Chris flubbed trying to find the right words, "just curious about Floo-Ellen and what she has going on, that's all."

"She and the people she brought on seem a little…questionable," Bo said hesitantly.

"I've noticed the same thing," Andrew said. "Don't turn around now, but since you two came over here, the guy standing over by the water hasn't taken his eyes of you."

Scott was slowly pacing back and forth near the bank of the water suspiciously watching them. Andrew gave Bo the yard scissors.

"Take these and go over the hedges, and make sure that they are nice and even. Chris, take the rake and rake up the excess grass where I've cut," he said pointing over to the open field.

He snatched up the rake and glanced over at the lake and saw that Scott was still glaring over toward them.


Meanwhile, Leena, Jacks, Casey, Alex and E-man were finishing up their breakfast in the crowded, noisy Mess Hall.

"Uhmmm! The cheese that they put in these eggs are addictive," Leena exclaimed.

"Well, I don't like them. You want mine?" Jacks offered.

Her plate was all but empty with the exception of her eggs; they were left in place untouched.

"Sure," Leena said scraping them off with her fork.

"It just isn't fair!" Casey said looking over at Cleofus and tearing up the napkin in her hand.

Cleofus and his friends were in the distance laughing obnoxiously and she didn't like it one bit.

"He starts the fight but Chris and Bo get punished?"

"Calm down, Casey," Leena said looking at the shredded napkin pieces collecting on the table.

Casey was so upset, the others hoped she wouldn't bring attention to their table because they knew Cleofus would gladly be up for the added drama.

"When Ms. Lambert comes in, we'll talk to her about what happened."

"And you never know, they might have evening chores too," Alex added. "Don't worry, everything will work out."

He picked up the tournament schedule Bella just handed out to read up on the activities, and a frown washed over his face.

"What's the matter?" Jacks asked.

"They have us scheduled to compete today in the raft relay," he complained.

"We can't compete today! We don't have Bo and Chris!" Casey lamented.

"With less man power, we don't stand a chance," E-man asserted.

"Maybe we can trade with another cabin," Leena surmised.

Their minds were tinkering for a solution. As fate would have it, Bella entered the room to E-Man's utter joy.

"There's Bella!" E-man squealed. "Let's go ask her can we switch."

The crew charged in her direction. She was leaning against the wall near the door reading over the papers that hung from her clipboard when they approached.

"Excuse me Bella, I'm Alex and we are all from cabin thirty-seven."

"What's your cabin name?"

# Boat Races

"7-Alive."

"Yes, I remember you guys from last night. You're Leena, Emanuel, Casey...uh, don't tell me - Jacqueline..."

"Call me Jacks."

"Of course, Jacks."

"Wow, that's pretty impressive," Alex commented giving her a once over.

"Thanks. So, how can I help you?" she asked resting her chin on the tip of the silver clip of the clipboard.

"Two of our cabin members have chore duties for the week, and we are on the schedule to compete today. So, we were wondering if we could switch with another cabin that competes next week..."

"...Of course, if it's ok with that cabin," Leena added.

"No, no we can't do that," she said flatly.

"But we're short-handed – we'll lose!" Casey inserted.

"I'm sorry. It's just not possible," Bella insisted.

"All things are possible!" Leena yelled.

Bella gave her a weak smile, "I know that Leena, however I don't make the rules around here. I just help to enforce them."

On that note, Bella turned and walked away. The crew stood abandoned and befuddled.

"What do we do now?" E-man asked.

"We race," Alex said staring out the door at the water.

Jill came in the door and bellowed, "The races start in twenty minutes! Those who are competing need to be out here and ready to go in five. Those cabins racing today are: The Kidder Krew, Total Eliminators, and 7 Alive! See ya out here in a minute!"

The groups that were announced for the day's competition scrambled to finish their food and wrap up what they were doing to make it out in time.

Cloefus stood up and shouted over all the noise, "KIDDER KREW AND 7 ALIVE MIGHT AS WELL STAY HERE 'CAUSE IF YOU RACE,

# Summer of Seven

IT WILL BE A WASTE OF YOUR TIME. NOBODY BEATS THE TOTAL ELIMINATORS!" He said high-fiving his teammates.

"We'll see about that," Andy challenged standing to his feet.

He was short, stocky, and a very competitive member of the Kidder Krew. 7-Alive left the Mess Hall and slowly walked across the field over to the huge lake where the competition would be taking place.

"I really don't care about this competition," Leena said.

"Why not?" E-man asked.

"It's obvious they don't want us to win – Chris and Bo get chores, but Cleofus and his goons are still able to race! Then, they won't even let us trade with another cabin!"

"You got a point," Jacks agreed.

Once they reached the bank, they saw that there were three orange flags posted in the water, which was about a quarter mile away. Floo-Ellen was out front giving instructions to the helpers on how the rafts should be set up. The shore quickly began to fill with anxious onlookers curious to see who would take the first win.

"Look!" E-man said poking Leena in the side. "What is he doing?"

Cleofus held his T-stick upside down while he taped down something.

"Is that a blade?" Leena asked.

"Don't know. Everett got his arm in the way," Jacks said.

"Ok, we have The Kidder Krew in raft number one," Floo-Ellen announced through the megaphone, "The Total Eliminators in two and 7 Alive in three! Will these cabins please board your rafts?"

Leena looked around worried at the roaring crowd. People were chanting the name of the team they wanted to win. Others were placing bets on the team they thought was the strongest. Most of the bets were placed on the Kidder Krew. This team was lead by Kevin Kidder whose team was made up of all athletic types plus one girl who was undoubtedly a tomboy and actually among the strongest on the team. They held their T-sticks in the air as they loaded their raft, and the crowd cheered them on.

Charles, a camp counselor, held the raft still as they entered and took their seats.

"What is he doing?" Casey asked agitated.

Cleofus and his team were in the raft, but Cleofus seemed to be preoccupied with his T-stick lying in his lap. Leena made her way to the back of the raft.

"Excuse me, Mr. Charles, I'm not sure what's going on, but Cleofus over there is doing something with his T-stick," she said discreetly gesturing over towards Cleofus.

He looked over at the Total Eliminator's raft spying out Cleofus.

"I don't see anything strange," Charles said glancing over. "Think you better hurry and get to your raft because the race is about to start."

Leena ran over to her raft and the others quickly helped her in.

"He said nothing was strange," she reported as she climbed in.

"I'm not so sure about that," E-man argued. "I know Cleofus, and he's always up to no good."

"The task is simple. The rafts are to race to the orange flags. Once they've reached them, they are to turn around and the first raft back to shore will win the race! Cabins! Are - you – ready!" Floo-Ellen yelled through the megaphone, "On your mark! - Get set! - Go!"

And the crowd went wild.

⊗ ⊗ ⊗

The grounds and shrubs were manicured to near perfection when Chris and Bo were finished with their chores. Sweating and tired they set out to find Andrew. Gladly, they found him over changing garbage liners.

"We're done, Andrew," Bo announced.

Andrew tied up a trash bag then stood up placing his hands on his hips.

"Well, that's all the work I have for you boys today." He glanced at his watch and told them, "It's not quite lunch time yet, but look, there's Jill.

Go let her know you're done. Maybe she'll let you guys off the hook. " He had his fingers crossed and edged them on with a wink of his eye.

The two ran over to Jill who was coming out of the main office with folded sheets in her arms.

"Jill, we're done with our chores," Chris announced with anticipation.

"Ok, Chris, I want you to go in the main office and help Bella out, and Bo, you go into the Mess Hall and see if Ms. O'Dale needs any help with lunch preparations. And, don't worry, I talked to Ms. Lambert about the unfair punishment, and we're working on it."

Chris took a deep breath and kept his brooding sarcasm to himself.

"Alright Jill," he said with a sigh.

The boys went their separate ways while Jill headed on to the main cabin.

When Bo arrived at the Mess Hall, he found that the place was empty. In the distance, however, he saw a glimmer of light shining and heard music playing through a static riddled radio mounted on the kitchen wall in the back. Curious, Bo moved toward the light and the singing voices of Marvin Gaye and Tammy Terrell tuning out *Ain't No Mountain High Enough*…through the static. The closer he got to the kitchen a delicious smell of food surprised him and put pep in his steps The scent of meatloaf, potatoes, and veggies got stronger and stronger. He plowed through the metal double doors and met face-to-face with Ms. O' Dale. Surprised, she stamped her hand on her hip and quipped, "Can I help you?"

"*Don't think you can*," Bo said under his breath. "I was sent here to help you with lunch."

"Oh yeah…you one of 'dem trouble makers," she said rolling up dough into little circles.

"Didn't know I earned the title…but, yeah," Bo said with a chuckle.

"Well, this is my kitchen, and I don't need you in here messin' thangs up!"

"Oh ok! I'll just go out on the field with the other kids so I won't be in your way," he said turning to leave.

"Hold it there, Sonny!" she bellowed with a frown on her face.

"MAN!" Bo huffed to himself grimacing.

"Look," she said, "I confess, I really don't want you in my kitchen. Heck, I don't care to have anyone in my kitchen," she blared then calmed down. "See, this is like a home away from home in a strange sort of way. This is a place where I can come and be away from all the children and the madness. At first, I thought, 'What was Jill thinking sending this little trouble maker into my kitchen?' But it's okay. If I send you away there will be trouble later on."

She scanned the room, to find something for him to do, something where he wouldn't be in her way.

"There," she pointed with a nod, "take that rag over there wash it out and clean the walls – and make sure you get that wall over the stove real good."

"Ooh, yeah it is a little nasty," he said frowning at the splattered food hanging on the wall.

He took the dishtowel over to the sink and dipped it into the warm, soapy dishwater and got ready to put his elbow to the grind. "So how long have you been working here?"

"I've been with Ms. Lambert from the beginning. I've known her most of her life."

"What? How's that?"

"I use to be her nanny – use to work for her father... Mr. J. C. Lambert," she said pausing smiling in a reminiscent gaze. "Oh he was the sweetest man you could've ever known – I sure do miss him...God rest his soul. He died when Sarah was about twenty eight," she continued, opening the oven to put the rolls in.

"Who is Sarah?"

"Excuse me, you know her as Ms. Lambert," she corrected then continued. "When he passed, he left her all of this land, including the mansion. His death devastated her so bad she started the camp to keep herself busy, and I was right there to help her with anything she needed."

"Wow! I didn't know you guys had so much history together," he commented scrubbing the grimy wall a little harder.

"Yep! I love her like she 's my own daughter."

"So, you said he left her a mansion?"

"Yes sir, beautiful too!"

"Where is it?" Bo inquired.

"About a quarter mile past the east bridge," she informed him.

*So that's where Floo-Ellen was going*, Bo thought to himself.

Just then there was a loud knock at the back door...bam, bam, bam, bam! A little startled Ms. O'Dale took a wet dishtowel and quickly wiped her hands then patted them dry on her apron. "Wonder who this is," she said.

When she opened the door, there stood Herman with a large cart of mini bowls of vanilla pudding.

"What's all this?"

"Dessert...Floo-Ellen wants the children to eat this with their lunch today," he answered directly.

"Whatchu mean *'what she wants the kids to eat?'* I run this kitchen!" she commanded slamming the door in Herman's face.

Bo burst into hilarious laughter as Ms. O'Dale stood leaning on the slammed door inhaling and blowing out slowly.

"Let me calm down fo' my blood pressure rise."

"Ms. O'Dale I gotta admit, you're one tough cookie!"

"How he gone try to intrude in my kitchen? Sara told me to run this kitchen how I want to as long as the food is ready and on time – breakfast, lunch, and dinner!"

"Where is your assistant?"

"Trudy?"

"Yeah," Bo said ringing his dishtowel out in the sink. "Oh, she's at the library of course – you know she's the librarian too."

"No, didn't know that," Bo responded as he stepped back to admire his clean wall.

"Uhh…she ain't doing too well though…constantly talkin' 'bout seeing monsters inside people and stuff…told her not to come round here with that mess trying to scare folks! I told her to come back when she got her mind right."

"Monsters?"

"Uhmm huh," she muttered as she slopped the mashed potatoes into a large aluminum serving dish.

About ten minutes had passed when Ms. Lambert came rushing into the kitchen followed by Herman still pushing the cart of pudding.

"Ms. O' Dale please don't be upset…" she begged, "…but from now on Floo-Ellen wants to prepare the desserts for the lunch meals."

She turned around and motioned for Herman to push the cart in. "You can still prepare whatever meals you want, Ms. O'Dale, just add whatever dessert she brings to the menu and everyone will be happy."

Herman placed the cart near the table, and Ms. O'Dale peered at him as if she was about to growl.

"Ya know, Ms. Lambert, ya can't please everybody," she quipped and turned back to finish preparing the lunch trays.

Ms. Lambert turned a wounded eye and walked away without a word.

The bells jingled as Chris entered the door to the main office, alerting Bella from behind the counter.

"Chris, what's up?"

"Wow, you remember my name?"

Bella chuckled, "I make it my job to remember names and faces."

Smiling, Chris informed her that he and Bo were finished helping Andrew.

"Jill sent me in here to help you now," he informed her further.

"Ok then, you can take these files over there and start putting them in alphabetical order," she said plopping a large stack of files on the counter.

"Over on that table?" he asked pointing to the table in the corner.

"Yes, that'll be fine."

⊗ ⊗ ⊗

"GO!" and they were off! The three teams took off all at once. As suspected, The Kidder Krew took a two inch lead over The Total Eliminators, and 7-Alive was not too far behind them both.

"Row! Row! Row!" Kevin Kidder bellowed.

His team was in the lead and rowing fiercely. The sound of the roaring crowd fed their adrenaline. The Total Eliminators were trying to bridge the gap, but The Kidder Krew was too fast.

"You would think because we have a lighter load we would have a chance!" Alex yelled against the noise and the strain of rowing.

"Just row! And put your elbows into it!" Casey shouted.

The Kidder Krew was close to approaching the flags and The Total Eliminators were right behind them. 7-Alive was about two raft lengths back, but still giving it all they had.

Once The Kidder Krew reached the flag Kevin shouted, "Left stop – right row! Row! Row!" sinking his T-stick paddle deeper into the water.

Their raft began to turn toward the crowd as The Total Eliminators started to turn at their flag also.

"Push a little closer… I can almost reach them," Cleofus said with a grimy smirk, glaring down at the shinny blade taped to the end of his T-stick.

"Ok, now both sides row! ROW!" Kevin shouted.

"A littttle more," Cleofus said slyly raising his T-stick out of the water.

7-Alive finally reached their flag and slowly turned and navigated around it with little hope of catching up to their competitors.

"We're almost there! Stay focused!" Kevin insisted.

Marci, the only girl in the Kidder Krew, frowned hard as droplets of water from the lake spotted her face.

Cleofus was finally close enough to make his scandalous move. He pulled his T-stick up as if he were going to row further, but instead of thrusting it into the water, he sliced the side of The Kidder Krew's raft causing them to lose air and speed quickly. They were stopped dead in the water and sinking fast!

"Oh no!" E-man said pointing, "Did you see that? Cleofus popped their raft with that blade on his T-stick!"

" He cheated!" Alex exclaimed.

Frantic because of the sudden drag in their momentum, Kevin snapped his head about looking for the problem. In no time he discovered the huge tear in their raft.

"Oh, no! There's a hole in the side! What kind of shoddy nonsense is this!" he yelled furious but worried.

"Should we swim back to shore?" Andy asked frantically. "We're going to have to! Can everyone swim?"

"Well, we have our life jackets!" Marci huffed.

"We'll row until the raft is completely flat," Kevin said looking at The Total Eliminator's ride by in pursuit of their victory.

7-Alive passed the struggling Kidder Krew raft looking sorry for them.

"Yes! Yes! Yes!" Cleofus said jumping up from his seat pumping a fist in the air.

He threw his T-stick paddle down and held both fists in the air to claim his victory before he even reached the shore, and the crowd was cheering him on.

The Total Eliminators' raft was now gaining water fast; everyone's feet was getting soaked. As the water was rising, Everett looked down and noticed that the blade on Cleofus' T-stick went right through the middle of their raft.

So, that's why... Everett thought to himself. "Man, look!" Everett said jumping back from the growing geyser.
"The water is like spewing up the middle of this raft, and I can't swim!"

At the sound of the raucous and the reduction of speed, Cleofus turned and looked toward them. It was if he had seen a ghost at the sight of all the water filling in their raft. Everett's teammates were all standing preparing to swim the rest of the way without him as Everett had no intention of getting into any water.

"How could you be so stupid?" Everett shouted at Cleofus.

"I'm not stupid!" he said as he shoved Everett into the water!"

Frightened to no end, he started crying and screaming as he splashed broadside into the murky cold lake.

"Help! Help! I can't swim!" he cried.

Just before Cleofus jumped into the water too, he couldn't help but notice 7-Alive cruising by. Jacks looked back and saw that The Kidder Krew members were all swimming toward the bank. The crowd was cheering wildly waving them on the closer they got.

"And the winner is ...7-Alive!" Floo-Ellen announced through the megaphone.

Willing helpers scurried to the edge of the lake to assist 7-Alive holding on to the raft and extending a hand to aid in their climb out of the water.

"Congratulations," Floo-Ellen said to 7 Alive, "you have earned the first win."

At that she handed Alex a large copper medallion with a "W" carved into the middle. Leena took the medallion from Alex and handed it back to Floo-Ellen.

"But we didn't really win. The Kidder Krew... they –"

"It doesn't matter how you win. A win is a win," she said tightly pushing Leena's hand away from her.

Leena's head jerked back as if she were smacked by her words. Floo-Ellen smiled and started clapping with the crowd.

"Enjoy your win – celebrate your victory!" She stepped back as the Kidder Krew and The Total Eliminators made their way out of the water and made their way through the crowd dripping wet.

"I don't believe this," Leena said to the others.

E-man stepped up to her and took the medallion and looked down at its gleaming surface. "I think we should go give this to the Kidder Krew because they deserve it," he insisted.

They all agreed with him and quickly turned and marched through the dwindling crowd and across the field in hopes of finding some remaining Kidder Krew members. When they arrived in the middle of the field, they saw that kids were starting up games of their own to kill time until the lunch bell rang, but there was no sign of them.

"What is their cabin number?" Casey asked.

"They should have their cabin name posted on the door," Alex said scanning cabins from a distance.

"Did we put our name up?" Jacks asked.

Leena answered no with a shake of the head.

"We better before Floo-Ellen has something to say about it."

"There it is!" Alex said pointing to their cabin beginning to run toward it.

When the crew arrived at the door, Alex was the official knocker.

"Door's open!" they heard someone yell.

He opened the door, and they all spilled in. The place was a mess. Old tennis shoes, dirty underwear, and tee-shirts littered the floor, and the aroma of wet socks filled the air.

"Congratulations," Kevin said flatly as he and the others were changing into dry clothes.

"Actually we don't deserve this - you do," E-man said holding out the medallion.

"We can't take that," Kevin said throwing a clean shirt over his head.

"It should've been yours. If Cleofus had not popped your raft, you guys would've won."

"What!"

"Now, now. We aren't here to start a fight," Alex said trying to calm the Kidder Krew down.

"What do you mean he popped our raft?"

"I mean he had a blade tacked on the end of his T-stick – and he popped your raft with it," Casey inserted.

"We tried to tell Floo-Ellen you guys deserved the win, but she said it doesn't matter how you win. A win is a win," Leena added.

"So Floo-Ellen condones cheating?" Andy shouted angrily.

Casey shrugged her shoulders nonchalantly. "I guess so," she said.

"No, I don't think she knows about Cleofus cheating," Alex argued.

"This is crazy!" Kevin shouted kicking a pile of dirty clothes in frustration.

Casey told them about the unfair chores given to Bo and her brother while Cleofus and his crew got off scott-free.

"Wow! What does Lambert think of all this?" Kevin asked.

"Not sure, but we're going to find out," Leena answered.

"Well, did you want the win?" E-man asked still holding the medallion.

"Yeah, we'll take the win," Andy agreed.

He received the medallion from E-man and said, "We really appreciate this."

"Yeah, we really do," Kevin added. "And if there's anything we can do for you guys just let us know…we gotcha back."

"Well, it's the right thing to do," E-man said.

No sooner than they were all done, the lunch bell rang and everyone filed out for lunch.

*Chapter Seven*

## ⊗ TRUDY AT THE LIBRARY ⊗

After Bo left the cafeteria with Ms. O'Dale he ran over to the office to see if Chris was done. He pushed opened up the front door of the office and there was Chris, over by the filing cabinet, filing his last batch of folders.

"Hey man, you almost done?"

"Yep, just got a couple more."

"Where's Bella?" Bo said looking around the room before he came all the way in.

"She ran out. Herman was having some kinda problem in the kitchen."

Bo chuckled as he jumped up and sat on the counter.

"You heard about it?"

"Yeah, but I'll tell you about it later."

Chris fingered through and filed the last folder.

"We need to go to the library to see Trudy."

"Who's that?" Chris asked as he made his way over to Bo.

"The little, skinny lady who was in the cafeteria working with Ms.

O'Dale this morning," Bo answered.

He got down, and they walked to the door.

"So, why do we need to see her?"

"Because I think she might have a connection with Leena…you know, about Floo-Ellen and all." Bo understood the crazy look Chris gave him and said. "Just wait 'til you hear this!"

When they arrived at the library, it was pretty much empty except for a girl sitting over at a table by the window reading her book. Most of the light that filled the library came from the many surrounding windows. Old reading posters encouraging the young to read were stapled on the wall. The colors were faded, and the edges were beginning to curl. Trudy was in the middle of an aisle putting misplaced books back on the shelves in the order that they belong. Bo and Chris spotted her and went over to her.

"What's up, Ms. Trudy? How are you?" Bo inquired.

She looked up cautiously at the two of them shook and her head without a word.

"Uhmm… wanted to know if we could talk to you for a second?" he asked.

"How can I help you?" she asked not looking at him directly.

"Just curious about something Ms. O' Dale mentioned about you," he began.

"And what's that?" she quipped then put the book down on the cart and curiously awaited his answer.

"She said something about you seeing monsters inside peoples' faces."

Trudy's eyes shot wide open and she looked around to make absolutely sure no one heard his comment.

Chris also looked at Bo in shock and leaned over and whispered, "Monsters in people's faces?"

Bo nodded his head, yes, without taking his eyes off Trudy.

"We shouldn't be having this conversation out in the open," she said pushing the cart over to the side parking it. "Come with me."

She continued to look around paranoid as she led them to a small cramped room in the back. When they went in, the smell of old paper infused the room. Torn, ragged books littered the desk and the floor. Looking around, the boys found two wooden chairs in the middle of the floor and sat in them.

"So, how are you able to see that?" Bo asked folding his arms looking like a detective.

She slowly shook her head side to side and answered, "I've been seeing demons inside of people since I was a young girl. Sometimes I see people talking and their faces are normal but when I blink my eyes… their faces turn into terrifying monsters!"

Trudy tensed up and threw her face into the palm of her hands as the boys sat speechless.

After a moment, "Wow!" burst from Chris' mouth. "So how do the demons get in these people?"

"Sin! It's through sin that the demons are able to enter into people!"

Bo snickered, "Man that's crazy!"

"No!" Trudy said with her eyes as wide as a deer's in headlights,

"I'll tell you what's really crazy," she said as she looked around again. "I've seen some demons in the faces of people here! That's what I was trying to tell Ms. O'Dale before she started screaming at me!"

"What?"

"Here at this camp?" Bo said standing up.

Trudy said nothing as she looked to the floor and began to rock back and forth.

"Who?" Chris asked.

In a panic she shook her head no. "I cannot say. I cannot tell you that! Wait…I've said too much. You must leave! You two must go now!" she said, running to the door and pulling it open. "Hurry! Please leave!"

Bo and Chris got up agreeably and walked to the front and out of the library.

Later on that night, the kids were getting ready for bed when they heard a light knock on the door. Casey jumped up and opened it.

"Hey," Jill said quickly easing her way inside.

Chris stood up, "How are you?"

"Good. Just came by to pass the information I found out just like I promised."

"So what's going on?" Bo inquired.

"Well Floo-Ellen has a secret club called Society 36," she said sitting down at the foot of Chris' bed. "I'm not sure what kind of club it is but Cleofus and his friends joined last night. That's how they got out of chores today."

She saw the look on their faces and decided not to take that bullet and went straight to the good news.

"BUT... I spoke with Ms. Lambert and she said you two wouldn't have to finish out your chore punishment for the rest of this week."

The harsh words she was about to catch disappeared with an exhale.

"Oh yeah, as long as you two behave yourselves," she added.

"Secret club? How crazy does that sound?" Leena ranted.

"Something's not right about this lady, and when you guys finally decide to listen to me, it's gonna be too late!"

"Now she is really a nice lady; she's just strict and about business. She's doing a good job and she seems to have everything under control," Jill said standing up.

Casey looked at Leena to see her reaction.

Leena gave an 'I'm not convinced' look and muttered, "We'll see."

Jill made her way to the door, "On behalf of the camp, I apologize for the whole chore mix-up. I think it's unfair as well."

"Not your fault Jill! We still love you," Bo said.

Jill smiled, "Get some rest, and I'll see you guys in the morning," she said turning to exit the room. "I'll let myself out, guys. Thanks."

## *Chapter Eight*

## ⊗ BAD BREAKFAST ⊗

Chris was a little sluggish at breakfast the next morning because he had stayed up most of the night thinking about how his vision has changed him. Meanwhile the rest of the 7-Alive crew had already gone to the Mess Hall earlier that morning to practice for the next challenge.

"Yuck! Eggs again," Jacks complained.

Leena slid her plate over to Jacks' and scooped the eggs off her plate.

"There you go," Jacks said making sure none of the eggs touched her other food.

"Thank you, ma'am!"

"Oh yeah, we won the race yesterday, but you guys didn't tell us how," Chris said to Alex.

Alex took a deep breath and told him the details of the race and their trip to the Kidder Krew's cabin. Everyone was quiet and chewing.

"So, you gave away the win?" Bo quipped trying to soak in the full story.

Chris nudged him on the arm.

"What? I'm just asking," he sang.

"Yes, because it was the right thing to do," E-man inserted.

Bo nodded his head and pretended to understand.

E-man started laughing, "I can't believe we won though! It was pretty amazing. When we began the race we didn't put forth our best because all odds were against us!"

"What!" A loud voice blew in from the table behind them.

Cleofus stood up and the entire Mess Hall suddenly hushed.

"Win? You guys didn't win! We just lost! You guys suck! It doesn't matter if you got the medallion; you're still losers in the end!" Cleofus spat.

After a moment of silence, with Cleofus peering hatefully at 7-Alive, E-man stood up pushing his chair back with the back of his knees.

"Listen here, Cleofus!" he said pointing his finger at him, "We know you cheated! That's why you lost! Cheaters never win!"

Cleofus was riled to no end at E-man's charge toward him and jumped over his chair toward E-man, tearing up a path of other chairs to get to him.

"Boo!" he yelled in E-man's face, almost nose-to-nose.

E-man flinched, jumping from fright and fell backwards tumbling over his chair. His body slapped the floor with a splat! A roar of laughter tore through the room encouraging a smug smile on Cleofus' round fat face and making E-man feel smaller than he already was. Chris shot up on his feet in no time.

"Go sit down Cleofus before I sit you down!" Chris threatened him.

"Oh, look! It's chore boy to the rescue! So, how did you enjoy your manual labor, huh?" Chris stared at him fuming.

He wanted to dive into his chest, but Bo grabbed him and pulled him back before he had the chance to act.

"Don't even think about it," Bo said in his ear.

E-man got up off the floor and dashed out the door. Leena dropped her fork and ran after him, as did Alex. Bo finally got Chris to sit down and calm down.

"Very smart!" Cleofus said making his way back to his seat as his cabin continued laughing at the antics that had just occurred.

"Why don't you just shut up you big coward!" Casey screamed.

Cleofus turned back around and balled up his fist.

Casey jumped up bitterly excited, yelling. "What you gonna do, hit me? Come on! Do it! Oh, I dare you!"

Jacks pulled Casey's arm forcing her to sit back down, "Calm down! He's not worth getting in trouble for, and he's certainly not worth you getting hurt!"

Casey was in no mood to follow a voice of reason, but taking deep breaths did help her calm down just a little bit. Cleofus snarled at Chris.

"You might want to control that little sister of yours before she ends up getting a sample of what you got the other day," he threatened.

Chris snickered at his words and asked, "Why don't you come a little closer…so I can hear you a little better."

Cleofus looked down at Chris' restrained arm that Bo was still holding and cautiously declined Chris' invitation. Everyone's eyes were on the two of them and everyone was curious to see what Cleofus' next move was going to be.

"Just wait until we get outside. I'm gonna beat you down and watch you do the chores for it!" he laughed along with his gang.

Jacks stood up and waved her arms at Zanku who was standing in the back corner leaning against the wall with his arms folded watching everything.

"Aren't you going to do something?" she asked getting no response.

E-man ran across the field, behind the cabins, all the way to the edge of the lake. He grabbed his chest and tried to control his breathing by taking deep controlled breaths, but that didn't work so he reached into his pocket for his inhaler and took a couple puffs and sat down by the lake.

He gathered both knees up into his chest and buried his face between them and wept quietly. A flood of tears traveled down his cheeks and on to his pants. E-man cried and cried seemingly endlessly.

Leena and Alex's running came to a halt as they finally approached him. Leena sat down beside him and softly rubbed his back. Alex stood at the edge trying to contain his concern, so he picked up a rock and threw it into the water. Before looking up E-man wiped his face with his shirt sleeve.

"It's okay, E-man. Don't cry," Leena spoke sweetly.

Sniffling, he looked at her wishing he could believe everything would be okay. "People don't bully you...you wouldn't know how I feel," he said putting his head back down.

"Oh, if only that were true," she chuckled.

"Since I was born things were messed up for me, too. Are you kidding? My mother is Japanese and my father is a black man from Alabama, and they met while he was in the military. When my mom got pregnant with me, her family disowned her. So...she gave me up just like that," she said, snapping her finger. "I've only seen pictures of her."

E-man listened attentively still catching his breath from crying so hard.

"My father took me in, which should've been good for me, but he travels a lot! So, guess where I ended up next? With his family in Mobile, Alabama! My cousins treated me like crap," she paused and closed her eyes for a second,

"...because they were jealous! They constantly called me ugly and teased me about my eyes. I was so miserable, E-man... I had no one to play with, no one to identify with. So, God became my best friend. I used to talk to him and hope he was real.

"So one day, I asked him. I said, 'Hey, if you are real, please respond to me in some way that will leave me with no doubt that it is you. But, in the meantime I'm gonna keep talking until I know'. And guess what, E-man? He proved his existence and his love for me. He doesn't care what I look like."

"Yeah, guess not since he basically made you the way you are,"

# *Bad Breakfast*

E-man said softly now gaining some strength.

Leena laughed, "Yeah, he protected me while I was in that situation. So, trust me, I know how it is to be rejected, bullied, made fun of, and to feel that no one in the world loves you. God loves you, and you should be good with that."

"Wow. Is that really true?"

"Yeah, in a nutshell."

"Sorry to hear that," E- man said, "I would have never thought that. You seem so strong."

"Not all the time."

"Tell me about it," Alex said.

"Most of my life I grew up without a father because he was in and out of jail."

"What for?" E-man asked.

"Theft. And he was really good, too. At the tender age of eight, he taught me how to pop almost any kind of lock. And the last time I saw him, he showed me how to hot wire a car. Great, huh? Good daddy, I'd say. I could grow up to be a thief too. That would get me really far in life," he said sarcastically.

"What!" Leena laughed. "No way!"

"Yeah, mate... I'm serious!" Alex said picking up another rock.

"Now, looking at you I would have never thought that was the case," she said.

"Yep... I wish I were just joking."

"Cleofus has been bullying me this whole school year!" E-man said with much frustration in his voice.

"It's good you stood up to him back there," Leena said.

E-man sucked his teeth, "What good did it do... except give everyone a good laugh?"

"I'm not worried. You'll be fine. Just keep hanging around with us!" Leena said patting him on the back.

"I hope so," said E-man wearily.

# Summer of Seven

After the breakfast brawl, everyone was out on the field anxious and excited to see the competing cabins in the relay races. Floo-Ellen stood in the front sporting her camp tee-shirt and hat.

"Okay! We have the Roaring Lions in lane 1 – The Hot Stepper in lane 2 – and The Hands Down Winner in line 3!" Floo-Ellen yelled into the bullhorn.

A supportive crowd gathered behind each team and gave loud cheers. Bo stood on the sideline with his arms folded, watching intensely, checking out his pending competition. Two of the teams were doing stretches while the other was huddled up together, and the leader was distributing tasks from the game plan to win. Chris came up and stood beside Bo.

"This is too easy," Bo said. "This competition is ours."

Chris scanned the three teams as they got ready too. "You might be right," Chris told Bo.

"Might be?" Bo responded giving Chris a wry look.

"You never know, they might have a trick or two up their sleeves."

Just then, Summer walked up from behind the boys and approached Chris. When he turned and saw her, he froze for a second.

"Hi," she said fluttering a wave. "I'm Summer."

He nodded his head, "Chris."

"Nice to meet you," she said flashing a perfectly white smile.

"You too," he stammered.

Floo-Ellen blew the whistle and the runners were off! One of the girls from the Hands Down Winners immediately took the lead.

"I wanted to come over and let you know how sorry I am for what happened earlier in the Mess Hall with Cleofus."

Chris rolled his eyes, "I'm not worried about him. He better be worried about me though."

"Oh! Well, that's good. Hope he doesn't bully girls."

# Bad Breakfast

"Don't worry. I wouldn't let him touch a hair on your head."

Bashfully, she looked away and a wisp of her sun colored hair fell softly along one side of her face. Chris surprised even himself by his nervy move.

Meanwhile, Bo was no help at all because he was behind Summer flipping out - making all kinds of faces, jumping up and down in a sort of irritating dance in celebration that Chris and Summer were finally talking face-to-face! Chris tried his best not to be distracted by Bo's antics; it was all he could do not to laugh by focusing on Summer instead.

"So, is this your first time at this camp?" he asked.

"No, I came here last year."

"This is my first summer here," Chris announced.

"It's fun. So what do you think about the tournament?"

"Oh, I love it. Makes things much more challenging and exciting." Summer's emerald green eyes seem to sparkle when she laughed.

"For a $20,000 win? I would say so!"

"That's a lot of money," he said.

"OH, LOOK!" Summer said distracted by the field activities.

"Hands Down Winners were in the lead but it looks like The Roaring Lions are gaining ground in the end!" Floo-Ellen shouted in the bullhorn.

"This is a good race!" Chris said.

"He's sooo close!" Summer added.

"Caught him!" Chris hollered watching the boy from The Roaring Lions pass his competition.

The crowd cheered louder with each close call, with each win! As the boy from the Roaring Lions took the lead, the crowd erupted piercing the sky! Every supporter ran toward the winner and before he knew anything he was lifted off the ground and surfing through the air on top of collected raised hands cheering and chanting his praises. The kids were euphoric! Floo-Ellen presented The Roaring Lions with a bronze medallion inciting more cheering and smiling red faces. The losing team, on the other hand, was sullen but still congratulated their teammates for trying.

Chris and Summer had stood watching the whole electrifying outcome but seemed to have no preference for a winner. Summer's eyes widened as The Roaring Lions accepted their win, as she was genuinely happy for them, but Chris only had eyes for Summer now.

"Well, it was nice talking to you, Chris," Summer said blushing a little.

"Maybe we can hang out a little more this summer," Chris said.

"I would like that," she smiled.

*Chapter Nine*

# ⊗ HILLTOP TALK ⊗

Dusk was descending upon Camp Come Along at a time when all the 7-Alive cabin members sat atop a hill to eat watermelon and talk among each other privately. They all watched quietly, even contemplatively, as the light blue sky faded to an indigo night lit only by the dimness of the moon hidden among the cloud thickened sky. The clouds moved slowly through the sky capturing their attention as they sat and lay beneath it and enjoyed the change, especially the pinkish hue that encircled the clouds.

The night began further to take on peculiar beauty in that it was being wardrobed gradually by layers of silhouetted mountaintops set off in the distance. Alex was standing the whole time with his hand on his hip looking over the horizon while the others were sitting eating watermelon.

"I think I would enjoy summer camp so much more if everything flowed peacefully like that sky there - and Cleofus wasn't here," E-man said.

"He's such a coward," Leena added slurping her watermelon.

"He only does it because he can," Chris stated. "If E-man really stands up to him, he'll leave him alone."

"I wish I were strong and mighty," E-man said.

"With God, you are," Leena responded.

"Thanks, but I'm not special. I don't have gifts like you guys."

"You are special E-man. You are God's. Just because you haven't fully grown into your gift yet, don't write yourself off as useless and not important because that is not true. God cares for you, and he is interested in the things you do," Leena told him.

"God sometimes takes us through the wilderness or hard times so when he blesses us, or uses us, we will know for sure where we came from; so we will appreciate and cherish where he brought us," Jacks said.

"Well, I want God to use me! I want to learn how to use my gifts… whatever they are," E-man confessed.

"What you need to do is listen to His voice and obey His commands," Jacks explained.

"But He doesn't talk to me!" E-man said frustrated.

"God is always talking…you just have to learn to listen," Bo interjected.

"When did you hear from God? When did He decide to use you?" E-man asked Jacks.

"When I was nine, still living in Puerto Rico with mi familia… sorry…my family, my aunt that lived with us got very sick. For weeks she was bed ridden and no one could understand why. It turned out she had bone cancer and it had already started spreading throughout her body. At night, she would scream horribly because of the pain and I would cry myself to sleep listening to her.

"One night it was really bad, and I couldn't sleep at all so I started praying. Before, whenever I prayed, it was a general prayer - like the same kind of prayer you say before eating, or before you go to bed. But this night was different. I really talked to God…like he was my friend. I prayed for about 30 minutes then I heard a voice…a small, gentle, but powerful voice, told me to go to my aunt's bedroom. Then I knew that voice was God speaking to me. I went not knowing the purpose for going. As I walked over to her, my vision was blurred with my tears, but I could see that she was lying on the bed crying with her eyes shut tightly.

"God told me to touch her chest, and I did. I closed my eyes and prayed and while I was praying, He asked me if I believed that he had the power to heal her. In my prayer I told him I believed with every inch of me that he could do it! While I was talking to God, my aunt stopped crying. When I looked down at her face, she seemed to be glowing. She smiled at me, and when I gave her a kiss on the cheek she whispered, 'thank you' in my ear. I told her that God did it, and I went to bed thanking him and telling him how awesome a God he was to me and certainly to my aunt. I just wanted to tell God how good he was. After such a wonder, I couldn't stop praising him.

"In the morning when I woke up... oh boy, my mom, dad, aunt, brother and sister were all sitting around my bed looking at me like I was the Virgin Mary! They didn't pray to Jesus like I did; they were Catholic. The difference was that my old babysitter taught me about Jesus and told me never to forget him and I didn't. My family saw that my aunt was instantly cured of her bone cancer. Whether they wanted to or not, they believed there was power in the name Jesus and gave their lives to Christ, and they believed in Him, and they began to pray to Him."

"Wow!" Casey shouted.

"God is truly amazing! He did all that for her!" Alex exclaimed.

Bo put his well eaten watermelon rind on the ground next to him.

"Remember the first night of camp when Jacks healed E-man's leg and we were naming the different gifts God blessed us with?" Bo asked.

"Yeah what about it?" Chris asked as everyone else nodded. Bo spat a seed over the edge and watched it fall.

"Well, my gift is faith. I was a little afraid of it at first but not anymore. Let me tell you about my faith that saved my family."

"You saved your family?" Casey repeated.

"Yep... when I was about eight years old our doorbell rang one night, and my dad went to go answer it. He looked out and saw that it was the pizza delivery man and chuckled to himself because he had not ordered any pizza. He opened the door to let him know he had the wrong house when the guy pulled out a sawed off shotgun from underneath the box and forced his way in. Once he was in two other guys came in from behind the door. I was asleep but got awakened from a bunch of commotion downstairs in the foyer of our house.

"I heard my mom scream. That's when I got outta bed and peeked over the banister to see what was going on. I saw the men taser my father. My mom left the cordless phone on my dresser earlier, so I picked up the phone to call 911 only to find out that they had cut the phone line, so I ran into the closet and prayed real hard! I was so scared. While I was in the closet, I heard someone open my bedroom door pushing things over. That is when a peace came over me. I heard a voice tell me that my family would all be safe.

"God told me that my family would be fine because he sent angels to protect us. With this peace, I knew the robbers had no chance. I believed He would do this for us, and I had no doubt in my mind that he wouldn't come through. So God told me to call the police, which was strange because I know God knows all, right? So, he knows the line is cut, why would he ask me to use the phone, right? But hey, I was obedient and did it anyway, and do you know when I picked up the phone there was a dial tone on the other end! I called 911 and told them we were being robbed, I gave them our address and they said that two police cars were in the nearby area so they would be there shortly. That's when I heard the robber's car revving up outside, but it wouldn't start. They came back in and took my dad's keys to his car and left.

"The police came and untied my family, but the detective that took all of our statements was puzzled that I was able to call the police when the lines were cut. Another strange thing was after they robbed us they tried to kill my family because they didn't wear any masks and they didn't want my family to be able to identify them. They tried to shoot, but the gun was stuck and it wouldn't fire. So, they tried the other two guns, and they were both jammed! None of the guns would work! Not only that, but what were the chances of their car breaking down in our driveway!" Bo shook his head and thanked God again.

"Eventually, they found my dad's car, and they caught the bad guys because of the car they left behind!"

"Oh, my goodness! So glad God protected you guys!" Jacks said.

Just then Summer came up behind them and waved at Casey who was already staring at her.

"Hello," she said as everyone turned and looked at her.

Chris inhaled deeply to calm his nerves.

"Hi Summer, what brings us the pleasure?" Bo asked.

"I came to see if Chris would like to ride a canoe with me since we have some free time."

"Sure, I would love to," he said hopping to his feet.

Leena and Casey gave Chris a wry look and kept him in their sight as they watched him walk away with Summer toward the lake.


"Thank you for coming with me. You seem like a really nice person," she said.

"You're welcome, and I am really nice."

She chuckled, "I guess we'll see about that."

Summer sat upright in the canoe as Chris rowed them parallel to the camp. She looked out into the rich green forest and breathed in the fresh air.

"So, what's the happiest day of your life?" she asked him.

"Today," he said looking into her eyes, his face reddening.

She blushed too and quickly turned away.

"Ok, what's the saddest day of your life?" she asked.

"The day my dad left us. He said he was only leaving mom…but he left us too. So now I have to play the father role for my little sister a lot."

"Sorry to hear that. My parents split too. How old were you when he left?"

"Eight. Before that, I was a pretty good kid, but after he left, I went totally rebellious. I would sneak out my bedroom window at night, and soon my mom would come looking for me. I would skip school, talk back, not bathe…" he paused quickly looking over wishing he had left the bathing part out.

"Why did you do all that?"

"Because I thought it would bring my dad back. I thought he would say, 'my son needs me' because I had never acted that way before. I was just hoping that he'd come back because he would see that I really needed him to get me back on track. But he never did."

"Oh, Chris," she said and touched his hand.

"It's ok, I'm a big boy now," he chuckled leaving his hand in place.

"Were you sad when your dad left?" he asked her.

"My mom left us."

"Oh," Chris responded lowering his head.

"It's ok. She left when I was five. It's fun living with Dad," she explained shrugging her shoulders. "He didn't really know how to care for me, but he tried. He would feed me icecream sundaes for dinner pretty often!"

They laughed as Chris paddled to keep them moving.

"So, you're an only child?" he asked her.

"Yep!"

"It's just me and my sister," Chris revealed.

"So what career do you want to go into one day?"

"I want to be an architect so I can create and design my wife the house of her dreams," Chris explained proudly.

"Oh, that's so sweet!"

"Whatever you do, don't tell Bo I said that!"

They both laughed again as they continued to move forward. Quietly, they looked around admiring the mountain-sides and the greenery of the forest. As they paddled along, the trees became less dense where they could actually see through them.

"Look at that!" Chris pointed.

"Where?"

"There. You don't see that huge house?"

# Hilltop Talk

"What is a house doing in the middle of the forest?"

Chris turned the boat around.

"I wonder if that's where Floo-Ellen stays," Chris said.

"Not sure, but speaking of Floo-Ellen, have you heard of Society 36?"

"Yeah, but I'm not too sure what it is."

"You should come with me tonight. My roommate, Tess, joined and she has a lot of benefits!"

"I think Cleofus is a part of that club."

"Yeah, I heard he was."

"I don't know about that, Summer. It doesn't sound too good."

"We're at camp, relax. What harm could there possibly be?"

Chris laughed, "You might be right. So, keep me posted on what goes on when you join."

"Yeah, then maybe you will join too."

"Yeah, maybe," he said with a crooked brow and a smirk.


Chris paddled the canoe onto the shore. Meanwhile Cleofus and his crew were on the court playing a game of basketball.

"Hey Cleofus, isn't that the girl you like over there in that boat with that little punk Chris?" Everett instigated.

Cleofus stopped dribbling his ball and went over to the fence to lookout. Chris hopped out of the boat and took Summer's hand to help her out.

"What's she doing with him? Let's go see," Pete said.

"No... I'll deal with that later," Cleofus fumed and threw the ball hard at the basketball goal.

"I really enjoyed the ride," Chris said with a smile.

"Me too!"

Cleofus and his boys watched Chris as he escorted Summer, hand in hand, to her cabin. Disgusted, Cleofus stormed off the court mumbling under his breath.

*Chapter Ten*

# ⊗ BIKE RACES ⊗

A couple of days went by and it was camp as usual. The seven played their hearts out and took part in most of the camp activities. Including losing a medallion to the Hot Rods in a swimming relay. It was late morning when 7-Alive was informed that they were to compete in the bike trail race with Sugar and Spice, Hot Rods, and The Winners. Each team was to elect one person to represent their team in the bike race. All of the teams were standing at the beginning of the bike trail that led deep into the forest.

"I think Chris should ride for us. I've seen him on a bike and he is pretty fast and he also has strong legs," Casey said boasting on her brother.

The rest of the team members agreed.

The four people from each team picked up a bike and mounted it. Chris looked over and saw that Summer was riding for her team and waved at her. She flashed him a smile.

"Ahem!" Bo said, snatching Chris' attention, "man, focus on winning, not on her!"

"I am! - But not on her!" Chris said fumbling his words as if he was confused.

Bella stood on the sideline holding a bright orange flag up in the air.

"Riders are you ready?"

The four sat upright, ready for takeoff.

"The first one back with their flag wins the race! On your mark, get set, GO!" she swung the flag down and the racers took off!

The trail was a bit narrow for four bike riders which caused some close calls early in the race. The kid from Hot Rod braised Chris causing him to lose focus for a second. Then, that same guy veered sharply to the left forcing Chris' position next to Summer's. Summer raised up off her seat and pedaled faster; her back was now in Chris' full view. He not only saw her hair flapping in the wind, but he also saw that her back tire was going flat.

"Pssssstt!"

Chris was unsuccessful at getting her attention. Every racer was focused and pedaling super hard and fast--everyone wanted to be the winner. Chris was gaining on Summer, but his mind was more on her deflating tire than winning now.

"Pssssssttt!" he tried again.

She heard him and whipped her neck around and smiled at him, then snapped her attention back on the race. The unexpected smile sent flutters through him, and he became tongue-tied for a moment.

"No, Summer!" he called out to her and before she turned again, he flipped over a branch that was lying on the path that the others had avoided.

Chris was quickly sprawled all over the ground; he was one place and the bike another. The members from the Hot Rod and The Winners both looked back to see what the ruckus was all about. When they turned and saw Chris struggling on the ground they both started laughing, slowing down to get a better look.

Summer, on the other hand, pedaled even faster and took the lead.

# Bike Races

Humiliated but determined, Chris jumped back on his bike and pedaled hard, but he was too far behind to catch up to anyone. Summer reached her flag first and quickly turned around and headed back to the awaiting crowd and the finish line.

The boy from Hot Rod gained some ground, but it had not been enough to catch Summer. Chris pedaled with all his might. He was already embarrassed and didn't want to add finishing-last to his list of things to be remembered for. All of Summer's teammates as well as the other campers, particularly girls, had cheered her on as she crossed the finish line. There were rounds of congratulations on her victory against the boys.

Chris finally pulled up to the finish line where Bo was standing on the sidelines with his arms folded slowly shaking his head. When Chris saw the look on his face, disgust covered him like a blanket. He knew he had some explaining to do.

"And the medallion goes to Sugar and Spice!" Bella yelled.

All the girls from Sugar and Spice were screaming and jumping up and down. Bo came up to Chris. "Man, what happened?"

"I fell off the bike," he said nonchalantly and shrugged his shoulders.

"How does that happen?"

"Well, I was trying to warn Summer that her tire was going flat..."

"Oh, Summer – the girl who just won?"

"I didn't want her to fall, Bo," Chris said irritated.

"Ohhhh, like you fell?"

"Whatever," Chris said and walked away.

A couple of people patted him on the back and let him know that it was ok and he would do better next time.

Shortly after the crowd settled down, everyone was seated in the Mess Hall to take in some good eating, they'd hoped. Bo was still upset because he felt like Chris didn't put his all into the race, as told by his long face. From time-to-time, Bo would still look at Chris and shake his head without a word.

"What? I lost – I'm sorry!" Chris said to him.

Bo still shook his head.

"Would you have lost if Summer wasn't racing?" Leena quizzed.

"I don't know. I tried my hardest today and if she was not racing I would've done my best then. So, I can't tell you who would've won."

"How about laying off Chris. He tried his best, and that's all we can ask for," E-man said.

"Thanks!" Chris said.

Trudy finally delivered their food, and they dove right in. Summer came over to Chris and placed her hand on his shoulder.

"Good race today," she said hoping to boost his confidence.

"Apparently not good enough," he said looking over at Bo.

"Can I eat with you guys today?" she asked.

"Sure," Chris said.

"Sorry but there is no room," Leena quipped suddenly.

"Oh, yes there is," Bo said getting up with his tray.

"You can sit here, I'll go over to your table and keep those ladies company," and took Summer's seat at her group's table.

Summer sat down in Bo's seat next to Chris.

"So, what's going on?" Summer asked the table as she chomped into her sandwich.

"Just a little upset cause we didn't win," Casey said.

"Eh, we all win some and lose some," Summer said.

"Yep!" Chris agreed.

"Sooo, I hear you are a part of that secret society thing Floo-Ellen has," Leena said turning instigator.

"I am apart of Society 36," she said chewing her food.

"What goes on there?" she asked.

"Well, that's privileged information, and I'm not at liberty to say," she answered. "Are a lot of people in it?" E-man asked.

"Yeah, there's a few of us."

"I think Floo-Ellen is evil! Her eyes tell it all," Leena said.

# Bike Races

"Floo-Ellen?" Summer laughed, "Evil? You definitely don't know her if you think that. She might have ones that she shows favoritism to, but evil – definitely not."

"Floo-Ellen doesn't come across as evil to me either - a bit mean though…sometimes," Alex said.

"I am not saying she's evil based on how she acts and how she treats us. I can feel that she is evil!"

"Ok, Leena, you can't accuse people of something with no proof," Jacks said.

"Just forget it. You guys don't understand – but you'll see. My feelings are never wrong."

"Alright, how about a game of truth or dare at the cabin?" Casey asked eager to put an end to the testy conversation.

Everyone agreed and strolled back to the cabin.

*Chapter Eleven*

# ⊗ TRUTH OR DARE ⊗

7-Alive combined space with Sugar and Spice in their cabin for a game of Truth or Dare. The two cabins-in-one were sprawled comfortably throughout; Summer and Chris had a space on the floor next to Casey while most of Sugar and Spice took spots on the sofa. Everyone else was propped on a bed somewhere.

"Okay, we're playing Truth or Dare guys and the rules are as follows! You have to tell the truth if you pick truth, and if you pick dare, you have to do it! If you do not wish to share the truth or choose to do the dare then you must kiss everyone's feet and you will create a reputation for yourself as a big loser!" Casey said.

Everyone in the room agreed to play by her explanation.

Casey looked around the room for her first target, "Leena, truth or dare?"

"Truth."

"Okay, what is the most embarrassing thing you have ever done?"

Leena thought for a second and began to turn red. But she remained quiet.

# Summer of Seven

"Uhhhh…." Leena stalled.

"The truth!" Casey reminded her.

Letting out a sigh, Leena said, "…A couple years ago when I was in the fifth grade, I moved from my dad's house to my grandmother's. She lived in the next town over so, naturally, I had to change schools. Well, it was Wednesday and we were moving that weekend, so I went to school and told all my friends and teachers that I was moving and Friday was my last day. My close friends were crying, and people bought me gifts! And on Friday, my teachers threw me a going away party. At the end of the day on Friday. everyone was giving me hugs and kisses. I never knew I was so loved. They all told me how they would miss me and made me promise to write them.

"Well, that weekend we moved to Grandma's, and Monday morning my dad came a little late to pick me up to take me to my new school…or so I thought. I got into the truck and asked him what was the name of my new school, and he said, 'New school? You're not going to a new school. You're gonna finish the year out here, and then you are going to your new school down the street from grandma's'. I said, 'But Daddy, this is far from where grandma lives!'

"I know that's why I will be picking you up and dropping you off everyday.' I begged him, 'No Daddy, please don't take me back!' and I had explained to him what I told all of my friends and teachers. I pleaded with him all the way there, but he wouldn't listen. He took me back to my school. When we got to the school it was really late and he walked me to class. When he opened the classroom door everyone was quiet listening to the teacher. I walked in and found my seat.

"Everyone was looking at me and whispering. I was mortified! What made things worse, my dad was talking to my teacher about my misunderstanding, and his voice carries, so the whole class overheard him talking. My dad waved bye to me, and I just put my head down. People laughed and made fun of me the rest of the year! It was just horrible!" Leena finished.

Everyone in the cabin also laughed at her story.

"Okay, Bo, truth or dare?" Casey asked him.

"Truth!"

"Have you ever peed in a swimming pool?"

"Yeah," he said.

Most of the room burst out in disapproval!

"That is sooo gross!" Jacks said.

"What? It just happened!" Bo said.

"Why wouldn't you get out and go the toilet?" Alex asked.

"I can't always make it in time when I'm in the water!"

"In time? So you've done this more than once?" Summer asked in disgust.

Bo sat there and couldn't find a reasonable explanation.

"Ewweee!" some of the girls from Sugar & Spice moaned and squealed.

Most of the room got a good laugh.

"Okay, I have a confession," Chris said with his hand raised. "I have peed in a pool too!" The whole cabin was in an uproar at hearing Chris' confession and Bo high-fived Chris then fell out on the floor laughing.

"What?" Casey screamed, "I'm always with you when you're swimming! You mean to tell me I was backstroking in your pee!"
She tackled him and they were on the floor wrestling. Everyone in the room was bent over laughing. Chris was laughing so hard he couldn't fight back so Casey got some good blows in.

"Chris!" Summer said, surprised at his breaking news.

But since Chris was laid out on the floor from Casey he laid there laughing with Bo. He had no response and didn't care what anyone thought at the moment.

"I can't believe you," Jacks said.

"Look, everyone has done it! If you've been in a pool, then you've peed in one. It's just that Chris and I are man enough to admit it!" Bo said.

"That's not true! We all don't have barbaric tendencies!" Leena objected prompting others to agree with her.

"Okay, let's move on!" Casey said before Bo had a chance to respond. "We now know who the nasty ones are. Chris, truth or dare?"

"Dare!" He shouted feeling pumped up.

"Alright, I dare you to sing and act out the song 'I'm a Little Tea Pot'." Chris hesitated and took a deep breath. Everyone clapped and cheered him on as he stood up in the middle of the room with one hand on his hip and the other stretched out for his best rendition of a spout. He sung the whole song and everyone got a hearty laugh.

"Okay, Alex!"

When he heard his name, he cringed involuntarily.

"Truth or dare?"

"Truth."

"If you were stuck on a private island with one person, who would it be?" Casey asked him.

"Well, I don't know who the person would be, but their profession would be that of construction worker or builder, so we can build a boat together to get off that wretched island and back to civilization."

"Oh, Alex you're no fun!" Casey said.

"You asked me a question and I gave you my answer!" Alex said.

"Okay, next!" Bo yelled above the arguing.

"E-man truth or dare?"

"Truth."

"Okay...," Casey pondered, "how old were you when you had your first kiss?"

E-man's face flushed beet red, and he looked as though he wanted to vanish from everyone's sight. Everyone gawked as he began to stutter. "I...I uhh..."

"Oh no, man! Don't say it! Don't do it to ya self!" Bo shouted.

"He has to. It's the rules!" Leena snapped at Bo.

E-man looked more nervous than ever; he was actually afraid to speak.

"Go ahead E-man, speak your truth," Casey encouraged him.

"I...never had a kiss from a girl other than my mom and aunt," he said bashfully.

"What? You never kissed a girl?" Summer asked him.

He shook his head no and nervously looked down at the floor.

"Stop, guys! Can't you see that he's embarrassed. Let's move on Casey," Leena said.

Casey asked some of the girls in Sugar and Spice a couple of questions and dares, but, E-man sat numb and wished he never agreed to play the stupid game anyway.

"Alright, Jacks."

"Truth."

"Hardly anybody's choosing dare!" Casey complained.

"You gave me a choice."

"Okay, if someone in this room had to be your servant who would you choose and what would you have them do?"

She took a deep breath and looked around.

"Casey, I would make you my servant."

Casey was very surprised and little offended by her answer. A couple of people chuckled when they saw the look on her face.

Jacks continued, "And I would make you rub my feet and back and feed me grapes while you read to me."

"I can see that!" Chris said laughing with everyone else.

But Casey didn't find it funny. Jacks gave her a friendly wink and smiled at her.

"Okay thanks, Jacks. Let's move on," she said in the midst of the noise of their laughter.

Casey looked over and saw that Summer was still laughing so she smiled.

"Summer, truth or dare?"

"Truth."

"Is it true that you like my brother?"

With that, Chris' laugh turned into coughing, then slowed to silence as he was now uncomfortable about what the answer would be.

"Of course, I like your brother. I like everyone. In fact there are few people I don't care for," she said with a 'you didn't get me' smirk on her face.

"You know what I mean!"

"I know what you asked me, and I answered."

"Fine," Casey rolled her eyes, "Bo, truth or dare?"

"Dare!"

"Okay, I dare you to..." she said rubbing her hands together, "... take off your shirt and run around the camp screaming, 'Help somebody call the mental institution! I need to be admitted! Somebody – anybody – everybody – please!'"

"Oh, no!" Bo immediately responded.

Everyone in the room was cheering him on to do it.

"You don't have a choice," Casey said.

"You have to. It's the rules."

Bo stood up and pulled off his shirt. Some of the girls in Sugar & Spice started screaming. Leena looked over and rolled her eyes at them. Bo popped his neck and went over to the door and opened it. He ran out screaming, and everyone in the cabin rushed over to the door to watch him. He ran past cabins screaming, "Help! Help! Call the mental ward! Somebody sign me in! Please help me! Somebody! Anybody!" he shouted running past the fields.

People all around the camp were pointing and laughing. Some came out of their cabins looking to see what the ruckus was all about. They saw Bo and laughed until they were breathless. "Somebody Please!!!" he continued running about until Jill heard him from her cabin. She came out and saw there was nothing wrong and stopped him.

Jill blew the whistle that always hung low around her neck; she blew it long and hard until she hushed Bo and got his attention.

"Get over here," she mouthed.

# Truth or Dare

Bo caught his breath as he made his way over to Jill.

"Just exactly what are you doing?" she asked looking him square in the eyes.

"It was a dare," he admitted.

"Ok, why would someone dare you to do this?"

"Truth or dare...it's a game we're playing."

"Not anymore. Go back to your crew, and shut that game down. Find something else to do," she said walking away.

In an instant the game was over - no more confessions, no more embarrassment, and no more offenses to be stirred by anyone.

*Chapter Twelve*

# ⊗ ARTS AND CRAFTS ⊗

It was about mid afternoon when 7-Alive and two other cabins were called to the Assembly Hall for the arts and crafts period. When the children entered the Hall, Jill was sitting behind the desk patiently waiting for everyone to enter and take their seats.

"Okay guys, I want everyone to close your eyes and think of your happiest moment, or the last time you laughed so hard you had to cry. Now there's a piece of paper in front of you, open your eyes and try your best to capture that moment using all the colors in front of you," Jill said pointing to a long table up against the wall. "Paintbrushes are in the jars over here, and the paper is over there."

"I love to paint!" Jacks said.

"So we have three teams here today and they are," she said looking down at her clipboard.

"7-Alive, Total Eliminators and the Kidder Krew. So, to make this a little bit more interesting Floo-Ellen gave me a medallion," she said holding it up. "Whoever creates the best picture, that person wins a medallion for their team."

Naturally, everyone got excited and began putting their all into creating the best piece of art even though it was just a friendly competition. Cleofus rubbed his hands together and said to his team, "We can do this, guys!"

"When do we start?" Kevin Kidder stood up and asked.

"You can start now."

Everyone got up and grab their supplies. Several people clipped their papers to the easels that were lined along the windows and began painting their pictures while others took their paper back to their tables.

"What are you painting?" Casey asked Leena.

"I'm making a picture of a sunset. What about you?"

"Not sure yet."

Bo was very focused on his piece and could not be distracted. Chris was one of the ones standing at an easel; he was drawing a fancy house. Every camper there was so intensely working, that one could hear a pin drop. Pictures all around were coming to life - sunsets, faces of people, houses and other things of interest to the campers. Bo was drawing a picture of his baby sister, and Cleofus was painting a picture of a $20,000 bill.

Compliments were being passed around the room among the little artists as pictures were being completed. Chris was hard at work now filling in details with a tiny paint brush much to Jacks' amazement.

Jill patrolled the room like a watchman observing everyone's progress. She was stunned by a picture done by a girl from the Total Eliminators. She stared at it until the girl finished it completely; it was a close up depiction of a very detailed flower in full bloom.

What talent this girl has, Jill thought to herself.

Others began peeping around to see how paintings were turning out, but all that did was stir up some jealousy and worry about who would win the medallion.

"I didn't know you could paint that well," Alex said observing Chris' creation.

"Me either," Casey added.

Chris chuckled, "Actually, I didn't know I could paint that well either. I need a sponge," he said looking around.

Chris marched up the front where Jill was sitting and asked for one, and Jill got up to take Chris to pick out his own sponge. When they were gone, Cleofus looked over at Chris then at his picture and gave a disapproving frown. A mischievous smile crept up on his face.

"Watch this," he said dipping his paintbrush in black paint.

He took his paintbrush and went over to Chris' painting. In the meantime, Jill found a sponge in the cabinet and gave it to Chris. On the way back, he looked up in time to see Cleofus marking up his picture. Chris dashed over to his painting and Cleofus took off running back to his seat. When Chris got to his picture, he saw that Cleofus had put a big black blob right above the house.

"Why'd he do that!" Casey screamed.

The members of 7-Alive were in an uproar yelling and screaming about what Cleofus had done. Jill, alarmed at the sudden outbursts, looked up to see what was going on.

"He cheated!" Leena yelled to Jill.

"He messed up Chris' picture!" Casey yelled.

When Jill looked over and saw that Chris was not upset, but instead using his sponge to blot the black glob of paint, she signaled for them to sit down and finish their painting. Chris mixed a little white into it and made gray smoke coming out of one of the chimneys in the picture. Bo came over in quiet support to see what Chris was doing.

"Love what you did with it. Fixed it up nice. Can't even tell it wasn't a part of the picture."

"Thanks," Chris said and glared back at Cleofus.

He sat with a smug look on his face as if he'd defeated Chris in some way.

"I think it's so unfair! How does he think he can just walk around doing things with no consequence!" Bo said.

"Oh, don't worry. As soon as class is over I'm going to talk to Jill and ask why she didn't get on him, because if it was me, and I did that to him, I would be sitting in detention somewhere."

"Five more minutes!" Jill announced.

Everyone started scrambling, putting the finishing touches on their work. Leena and Casey were finished and were sitting with their arms folded, frowning, and talking about what happened with Cleofus. Casey kept trying to get Jill's attention with her eyes so she could give her a dirty look, but to no avail.

"Okay, time's up! Everyone stop working and put your work where I can see it, please."

Jill walked around the room slowly and looked at everyone's finished picture and made her decision.

"The winner for the best picture is Emma Gray from the Total Eliminators!"

Cleofus was ecstatic and his team jumped for joy and gave each other high-fives as they rushed on Emma patting her on the shoulder for a job well done for the team. 7-Alive and the Kidder Krew members wore looks of disappointment as they watched the winners celebrate.

"Yes, congratulations are in order for Emma who did a superb job in expressing her artistic ability; however, her team will not receive the medallion."

The Total Eliminators froze and fixed a confuse glare on Jill.

"The medallion will go to the second-place winner. Everything you do right or wrong, good or bad, affects your whole team, not just one member. Cleofus tried to sabotage the work of another member that was not on his team; therefore, he forfeited the win for his team. Second-place winner is Chris Prentice, so the medallion goes to 7-Alive. Congratulations team!"

A rush of sadness and pride came over Cleofus. He wanted to apologize to his team, but his pride would not let him. He snarled at Chris as if his loss was his fault. When Jill presented the medallion to Chris, the room was filled with applause, but the Total Eliminators stood with their arms crossed angry.

After the room cleared and the campers moved on to the next activity, Bo, Chris, Jacks, and Leena lagged behind to talk to Jill.

"One question, Jill," Bo began.

"Yes sir?"

"Why didn't you get on Cleofus for what he did when you first noticed him doing it?"

"Why does he always get away with things?" Leena asked.

"If I thought Chris wouldn't have come in second place, I would've said something. The reason I didn't is because I wanted to teach Cleofus, and everyone else who was watching, a lesson on ethics and good behavior.

"Yeah, ok," Leena said unsatisfied with her answer.

And they left the room and went out to play on the field.

## Chapter Thirteen

## ⊗ TUG-OF-WAR ⊗

Before lunch it was announced that Sugar & Spice would be competing with the Total Eliminator's in tug-of-war. Summer was not happy about it and complained to Bella that they only had six members on their team while Total Eliminators had seven. Not only were they mostly made up of boys, except for Emma, Sugar & Spice were all girls. There was no way the competition could be fair. But Bella turned a deaf ear to Summer's complaint.

"Your team doesn't have to compete if you choose not to, but you will forfeit your game and the medallion will automatically go to the Total Eliminators. Is that what you want?"

Summer rolled her eyes and walked away angry at her response.

Moments later, on the open field, everyone was gathered around to watch the event. The Total Eliminators were excited about their easy win. Some of their members were already celebrating a victory, 'another medallion under the belt' they chanted.

"Total Eliminators and Sugar & Spice team members please line up on your side of the rope and pick it up without pulling or tugging!"

Cleofus was in the front of his line, and Summer was in the front of hers; face to face they stood. When the teams picked up the rope, Cleofus yanked it without Bella noticing then gave Summer of sneering wink of his eye. She frowned back at him. 7-Alive was among the crowd of rowdy onlookers. Nobody expected Sugar & Spice to win.

"My teams, are you ready?" Bella yelled.

She was standing on the middle line holding the rope with one ready hand.

"Yes!" both teams answered.

"Alright - The struggle begins with a word — the word war! Tug-of-War!" With that she released the rope and the war was on.

Immediately, The Total Eliminators pulled the opposing team forward intimidating the girls terribly, but Sugar & Spice regained themselves pulling with all of their might but the rope would not budge. Cleofus laughed hard and let go of the rope and threw his big arms in the air as if to say 'we won! No contest'! He grabbed the rope again and tugged harder than ever. The Total Eliminators started to move backwards, forcing Sugar & Spice forward with great resistance. No matter how they tried to keep their ground, they were losing it fast. The Total Eliminators pulled harder, and before they knew it, Sugar & Spice found themselves tumbling over the midway line.

"The Total Eliminators win!" Bella shouted.

The Total Eliminators spun into euphoric celebration.

Cleofus looked over and saw their whole team sprawled on the ground and went over with an extended hand to help Summer up.

"I don't need your help!" she barked lifting herself from the ground and brushing herself off. She marched away focused only on helping some others up, also.

Chris and Bo were among so many others who were talking about how this game was unfair, and Bella overheard it all and had had enough. She got everyone to quiet down so she could speak.

"Listen up, everyone! I feel the need to say something – to clarify some things. The Come Along Competition won't always be fair. It is designed to test you at your highest and lowest points. We don't match up the teams that play. Whatever team comes up on the rotation, those are the teams that compete, and we don't change them for any reason at all," Bella explained.

Some groaned with disapproval because they could not see the fairness in it. Chris caught Summer's eye and tried to send comfort and assurance. She smiled at him and started to make her way over to him when she was stopped. She turned and saw that Cleofus had clasped her arm.

"What are you doing?" she said yanking her arm away.

"Just wanted to say that was a nice try," he said in a genuine tone.

"Thanks," she said and turned away.

"Wait, I have one more thing," he said coming very close to her.

"What's that?"

But he didn't say anything.

"What?"

He zoomed in and gave her a kiss on the lips.

"Ewwwwee!" she screamed and pushed him off of her.

People turned around just in time to see what was happening and they began to laugh. Cleofus got embarrassed and retaliated with a forceful shove to Summer which sent her spiraling to the ground with a painful thud! Chris, of all people, had seen the whole thing. Chris took off running after Cleofus with every intention of beating him to a pulp, but in mid stride Chris was snatched back. Bo had him by the shirt.

"Let me go!" Chris shouted his gaze locked on Cleofus.

Jill saw what was happening out of the side of her eye and ran over before Chris reached him.

"Calm down. Chris, I got this one!"

Knowing that someone might finally be on his side in the matter of Cleofus, Chris immediately calmed himself and fixed his ruffled clothes.

Jill helped Summer up off the ground and turn to Cleofus.

"Office! Now!" She said pointing for him to leave right then.

Cleofus sucked his teeth and rolled his eyes. He was mumbling something under his breath as he made his way through the crowd.

"You okay?" Jill asked Summer.

She nodded yes and wiped the dirt off her pants and rubbed her aching backside.

"Okay then, let me go deal with Mr. Cleofus," she said and went to the office.


Later on that night, Summer found Chris on the softball field. 7-Alive was playing a friendly game of softball with the Kidder Krew. Chris was sitting in the dugout when Summer approached.

"Hey, how are you?" Chris asked coming out to talk to her.

"Doing good. A little upset though."

"What's wrong?"

"Earlier today…the incident with Cleofus."

"Yeah, what about it?"

"He didn't even get in trouble!"

Just then, Leena and Casey could be heard rejoicing - jumping up and down screaming for their team because E-man hit the ball out into left field and the boy in the outfield had failed to catch it.

"How do you know?" Chris asked her.

"Tess, my teammate, told me. Plus he's out there playing soccer! So not fair!" Chris gazed out over the field to see if it was true. He shook his head. "Don't worry, he'll get what's coming to him."

*Chapter Fourteen*

# ⊗ BOOGER DINNER ⊗

Earlier that day all of the cabins had a giant shaving cream battle. Kids were equipped with their bowls and bags of shaving cream ready to cream anyone who wasn't on their team! The battle lasted about an hour and a half and it was intense! Some kids were running around looking like they were dipped in shaving cream, others were getting hit with globs of cream on the side of their heads. However, everyone had a blast and quickly cleaned up before lunch.

The Mess Hall was nearly filled to capacity with hungry kids who had still not come down from the elation of the shaving cream battle earlier.

"Look, Chris, you still have shaving cream on your ear! Jacks told him.

"That was fun!" E-man said.

"The guy who won –"

"Kevin from the Kidder Krew," Bo said.

"I can't see how he was the only one who didn't get creamed – how did he do it?"

"Not sure, but he's good," Chris admitted.

# Summer of Seven

Leena sat with her elbows on the table and her chin propped in the palms of both her hands looking a bit morose.

"What's wrong?" Alex asked her when he noticed her.

"I'm a little homesick – miss my grandma."

"Me too, this is the longest we've ever been away from home," Casey said.

"Well, I have good news, girls!" Bo exclaimed. "You just got a couple more weeks here and you'll be home!"

"Yeah, then you'll find yourself missing camp," Alex joked.

Chris had only taken a couple bites of his ravioli when Cleofus and the rest of the Total Eliminators came marching into the Mess Hall.

"Is the food extra good tonight or am I just hungry?" Chris asked.

"You know Ms. O'Dale be throwin' down in the kitchen!" Bo said taking a big bite.

"And they have banana pudding, my favorite dessert!" He added.

"No desserts man!" Bo reminded him.

Disappointment covered Chris' face.

"Leena, you got ravioli sauce on the side of your mouth," Casey pointed out just as Cleofus was passing their table.

He couldn't resist taunting them and just had to spit some unpleasantries their way.

He laughed and hollered, " 7-Alive! When I'm finished it will be 5-Alive cuz I'm gonna take you and E-man out!" He said pointing at Chris.

Chris continued forking up and enjoying it like he never heard a word Cleofus said. When Cleofus saw he couldn't get a rise out of Chris, he went over to him with his finger up his nose! He pulled out a big booger and buried it in Chris' ravioli! Chris dropped his fork, and everyone surrounding him gasped then froze with their eyes wide. They were too stunned to move.

"Eat that! It's good for your health!" Cleofus jeered and walked away.

Chris stared at his half eaten plate without a word.

"That's it! I'm going to Ms. Lambert tonight!" Leena protested.

E-man shook his head.

"That guy has some serious issues," Alex said.

Cleofus sat down at his table laughing loudly with his friends. Chris stood up and calmly picked up his tray.

"Chris, sit down. I'll go get you another tray," Casey said.

"Don't worry. He's going to get what's coming to him," Jacks said.

Chris had turned a deaf ear to everyone and focused on Cleofus only. He stood still. He was breathing deep, long, and hard - furious as he peered darkly at Cleofus, but all other eyes were on him. Slowly, Chris started walking over to Cleofus. Again, gasps could be heard throughout the Mess Hall. Some of the girls clutched each other.

When Chris arrived at his table, Cleofus looked up at Chris.

"How can I help you? Did you need more seasoning?" he asked sardonically.

His table burst into ridiculing laughter. That was all Chris needed to take his tray of food and whack it hard across Cleofus' face sending him straight to the floor! Chris hit him over and over again in the head, chest, and stomach until he drew blood! In spite of that, Chris kept going and started stomping him, too. Cleofus squirmed on the floor trying his best to block Chris' blows. Chris didn't get off of him until a camp counselor came up and grabbed him from behind.

"Get off him! That's enough Mr. Prentice!"

Two other counselors came in and carried Cleofus' limp body straight to the infirmary. Jill ran into the Mess Hall out of breath.

"What happened?" She asked the counselor.

The Mess Hall was in an uproar with frightened and excited kids.

"He beat him with a tray!" a counselor answered looking at Chris.

"Chris, what has gotten into you?" Jill asked.

Chris remained quiet and calm.

"Come with me, young man," Jill insisted and Chris did just that. When he walked passed his table, they all felt for him; they wore looks of shock and pity.

When Jill arrived to the office with Chris in tow, Ms. Lambert and Floo-Ellen were engaged in conversation, but upon seeing a huffed up Chris, with Jill obviously annoyed, they put their conversation on hold.

"What's wrong?" Ms. Lambert asked.

"Chris beat Cleofus up. He's in the infirmary… banged up pretty bad!" Jill relayed.

Ms. Lambert gasped with surprise, and Floo-Ellen just stared at him almost admirably.

"Sit down," Miss Lambert said walking over to Chris. Floo-Ellen and Jill had arrived by now also.

He took a seat on the wood bench behind him, with a frown on his face he looked only at her. Ms. Lambert knelt down in front of him.

"What is the problem, Chris? Why you acting out like this? This isn't like you."

"Well, Cleofus keeps messing with me, and I try to 'turn the other cheek' all the time," he said with his fingers gesturing quotations. "You guys simply ignore everything he does!"

"So that's why you felt the need to go after him?"

"No, he put a booger in my food while I was eating."

"You beat him bloody, Chris, and there is no telling what injuries he has," Jill said.

Chris shrugged his shoulders nonchalantly.

"So you're not even sorry?" Ms. Lambert asked.

Floo-Ellen watched him for his response. Chris shook his head no. Lambert stood up eyeing the others.

"Chores for a week!" she said.

Chris acknowledged his punishment by nodding his head.

"Chris, I'm very disappointed in you! Report here at eight a.m. tomorrow morning," she instructed.

"Off to bed," Jill said shooing him off to his cabin.

# Booger Dinner

A couple days later, Chris was still serving his detention, and Cleofus was still healing in the infirmary. He had an hour break from detention and used the time to spend in his cabin. Everyone was there when he arrived. Of course everyone wanted to know how things were working out in the office for him. Jacks expressed excitement that so far their cabin hadn't been up for any challenges since he had been gone.

"Chris, I would like to speak with you," Alex said then looked over at Bo.

"It's about what we talked about earlier so maybe you should come too," Alex said to Bo.

"Okay," Bo said getting up.

Chris looked at them both. "About what?" he asked.

"Come on outside. Let's take a walk."

Alex walked on Chris' right and Bo on his left. "What's this about?"

"It's about the incident with you and Cleofus."

"What about it? He got what he deserved! End of story!"

"Yes, but vengeance should not have come from you," Alex said.

"So what was I supposed to do?"

"Pray for him."

"What!" Chris stopped in his tracks, "Are you crazy? I should have beat him down a long time ago! He was constantly testing my patience—just asking for it!"

The boys walked toward the big rock that sat in the middle of the camp. People were out playing their free time activities as usual.

"You know, Chris, I probably would have done the same thing! I'm still struggling with self-control," Bo admitted.

"Bo!" Alex shouted.

"Oh sorry. But seriously Chris, in God's eyes, that was wrong. Very wrong. Vengeance is the Lord's. When you pray and tell God to handle Cleofus for you, he will do it! In some way or another, Cleofus won't be a problem for you any longer."

"I don't think Cleofus will be a problem for me from now on," Chris surmised.

"Yes, Chris, but that lesson was not yours to teach. Let me tell you what happens now," Alex said then took a deep breath.

"Now that you have taken your own vengeance out on Cleofus, God will not punish him for messing with you because you already punished him. Who knows what God would have done for you as it relates to Cleofus? But now God is looking at you for vengeance for Cleofus."

"What? But he started it with me!"

"And God should have finished it!"

"Well, what do I do now?" Chris asked, worried now.

"Anytime your sin causes hurt or offense to another, you must make it right with God by asking him to forgive you. Then, you must make it right with that person you offended and ask them for forgiveness. Now, whether or not they forgive you is another issue altogether. The main thing is that you are right with God and that you at least apologized to that person for the wrong you have done to them."

"What happens if that person won't forgive you?"

"I told you, that's another matter; that's between them and God when you've done all you're required to do," Alex said matter-of-factly.

"So, I gotta go apologize to Cleofus and ask him for forgiveness?"

"Yep!"

Both Chris and Bo looked like they were both swallowing a large pill.

"You gotta be kidding me!" he yelped.

Alex gave him a very serious look.

"No, Chris. I don't think he's kidding," Bo said.

"Okay, I'll do it."

"After you ask God for forgiveness, then go do it," Alex said.

"On the way to do that now," Chris said heading to the cabin.

When Chris got back to the cabin, everyone had gone, which was perfect for what Chris had to do. He knelt down in the empty cabin and talked to God.

"Dear God, first of all please forgive me for taking matters into my own hands with Cleofus. It's just that he just kept on…I know I shouldn't make excuses; you know very well what was going on. Help me, Lord, to have more self control. Give me patience in these situations. Thank you, Lord, for having mercy on me. In Jesus name, Amen."

He got up and felt better about himself.

Chris made his way to the infirmary to see Cleofus. He knocked on the door, and there was no response, so he opened it. The lights were low, and the room was cool. Ms. Humphrey, the nurse, was nowhere in sight, and the room was empty except for Cleofus asleep in the twin sized bed next to the window. The left side of his face was bruised black and blue, and his head was wrapped in gauze stained with a little blood. His left arm was cast from his wrist to his elbow because it was broken from blocking Chris' blows. A little dried blood was also caked around his nose.

Chris felt bad at seeing Cleofus for the first time since the incident. Chris walked over to the foot of his bed. Cleofus was still asleep. Chris placed his hand on Cleofus' foot as a compassionate sign but instead startled him out of his sleep.

"Hi," Chris said trying to break the ice.

Cleofus looked frantically around the room for Ms. Humphrey or anybody else who could help him.

"I…"

"What you doing here?" Cleofus asked terrified.

"I just came by to tell you that—

"Get out!" He screamed not allowing Chris to finish. "Please! Get out!" He started to cry.

"Cleofus, you don't have to be afraid of me. I'm not here to hurt you; I just came to tell you that I'm sorry and to ask for your forgiveness."

Cleofus got real quiet and looked at Chris as if he was a stranger.

"So, do you forgive me?" Chris asked.

"Heck no! Get out of here!"

# Summer of Seven

Chris took a step back, hesitated, and then without another word, walked out of the infirmary feeling satisfied because he knew he did what he was supposed to do.

$$\otimes \quad \otimes \quad \otimes$$

Chris was in the office alone completing the task sheet Ms. Lambert had given him earlier that day when Summer came walking through the door.

"Hey!"

"What's up?" Chris said surprised to see her.

"I miss you since you've been locked away. I thought I'd come by to visit," she said leaning over the counter.

"Yeah, isolation is no good for me. What's been going on out in the free world?"

"Same ole, same ole... except there hasn't been much bullying going on lately."

She looked at him and smiled. Chris bashfully looked away.

"Never seen that side of you Chris."

"I know. I'm working on controlling that side... that dark side."

"I wouldn't have believed it if I hadn't seen it with my own eyes!" she said pressing the issue.

"I saw him a couple of days ago, actually."

"He's out?"

"No, I went by the infirmary."

A look of surprise came over Summer's face. "I went to apologize to him."

"Really? What did he say?"

Chris chuckled, "He told me to get out!"

Summer slapped her hand over her mouth, shocked, "Are you serious?"

Chris nodded.

"Well, at least you did the right thing."

Chris got focused again and started wiping the counter down while Summer moved out of his way and went to the window and perched herself there.

"So how many medallions has your team racked up?"

"...uhhh..."

Chris frowned at such a response.

"Floo-Ellen, Bella, and Zanku are coming!" She jumped back from the window. "I'm going to get in trouble for being in here!"

"Quick! Behind the door!"

They both ran behind the office door and opened it so wide that the doorknob touched the bookshelf. Chris looked over at Summer in their cramped space and placed his pointer finger over his mouth. Summer nodded. Chris held on to the doorknob just in case the door might ease closed and reveal them.

The bell clanged against the door as Zanku opened it. Floo-Ellen was still talking when she and Bella came strolling in.

"No Bella, everything is perfect! I couldn't ask for a smoother plan," she said walking into the office.

"But what about the others who haven't joined yet?" Bella asked.

"Don't worry Bella. They will join. Society 36 has its perks. They'll see the other children with benefits, then there's always peer pressure; that will get them. And if that doesn't work, we still have the dessert to feed them. Speaking of, is Herman still delivering that to the kitchen?"

"Everyday," Zanku said.

"What if the ones we have recruited try to leave the society?" Bella asked.

"They can't. Do you listen to the chant we speak at the beginning of every meeting?" Floo-Ellen asked her. "That is a contract, and it is spiritually binding... Once they join, their souls belong to me," and she snatched the air.

Summer looked at Chris with terror in her eyes.

"I think we are doing well," Zanku said.

"Why is that?" she asked.

"Because we have recruited twenty-nine members already," he said.

"So we're just 7 children short of having the complete circle of power," Bella said excited.

"Come let's go into the office so Zanku can give us the rundown on everyone," Floo-Ellen said.

Zanku followed the two ladies into the office, then he grabbed the doorknob which Chris was holding on the other side and closed the door. Chris let go in enough time so there was no resistance, so they never knew that they were behind the door. Summer and Chris stood frozen plastered against the bookcase and could hear muffled talking coming out of the office behind them. Chris looked over at Summer and mouthed, 'let's go!' She nodded fast as they high-stepped quietly to the door.

Chris reached up and held the ball inside the bell before Summer opened it so they could make their exit undetected. She eased the door open and they ran out leaving the door slightly cracked. In no time she was lengths in front of Chris. Chris dashed hard to catch up with her.

"Summer…we're clear now… slow down!"

But, Summer kept running. When she got near the water she slowed down and Chris grabbed her hand and saw that she was crying.

"Did you hear… that… that evil woman!" she cried.

"Yes," Chris tried consoling her.

"They said that I couldn't get out!" she cried on Chris' chest.

"I promise you - it will be okay," he leaned her back so he could see her face.

"I was told that Society 36 was a summer club that you join to get VIP status and benefits! That's it! Not some crazy, evil people trying to steal kids' souls!"

"It'll be okay."

"I want out! I have to get out! Now! Let's go to Ms. Lambert."

Booger Dinner

"Before we do that, let's go tell the others. Then, we will make a move," Chris said leading her back to the 7-Alive cabin.

*Chapter Fifteen*

# ⊗ ASSEMBLY HALL ⊗

When Chris and Summer arrived at the cabin, everyone was there relaxing and having fun with each other. Casey and E-man were in the front playing cards; Jacks and Alex were having a debate on some unknown subject, and Leena and Bo were arm wrestling, which stirred a playful argument about who was the strongest.

"You're not stronger than me, Leena," Bo said not breaking a sweat as Leena gritted her teeth and struggled to flatten his arm to the table.

"What's up Chris?" Bo shouted not losing his stride.

"Guys, stop what you are doing! We've got something incredible to tell you. Summer and I heard Floo-Ellen saying some really disturbing stuff!"

Everyone turned front and center, all eyes on Chris, with their ear gates wide open. Chris began telling what had gone on and what was said in the office, but was stammering so much, apparently still in dismay; Summer insisted that she tell the story instead.

"Bottom line," she said, "Floo-Ellen is evil and wants the souls of all of us! And that 'special elite' group called Society 36? Oh, that's just another name for cult! I want out at any cost, but make sure no one sucks you guys into it. I'm telling you!"

She told them every sordid detail of the conversation between Floo-Ellen, Zanku and Bella right down to the mind altering dessert. The entire crew was astonished. Fear seemed to touch each one of them, one at a time...except for Leena.

"I told you guys that something wasn't right with her!" Leena said.

"She-is-a-witch. Period."

"You think that she is a witch?" Jacks asked.

"She very well could be!" Alex said.

"I think this is a whole lot worse than what we thought." Casey said.

"You think!" Chris exclaimed.

"Okay, fun and games are over," Alex said. "We need to call our parents and tell them to come get us."

"And tell Mrs. Lambert!" Summer said.

"Nobody has a cell phone?" Chris asked.

"No cell phones," Summer said.

"Camp rules," Bo added.

Just then, the community bell rang indicating a change-up.

"Oh yeah, all the campers are supposed to meet in the Assembly Hall. Let's go, we will talk about this later," Alex said as they all made their way out the door. It was movie night in the Assembly Hall - usually an exciting time where the kids could sit relax and enjoy. No rough competitions, just entertainment and maybe a little assessment about the movie. Everybody filed in and took seats next to their preferred partners or groups. 7-Alive sat dab in the middle of the Assembly Hall.

"Look, there's Ms. Lambert! Let's tell her!" Summer insisted.

Floo-Ellen stood in front of the hall while Bella loaded the movie.

"How is everyone?" she asked cheerfully.

Generic answers blew across the crowd; 'I'm just fine,' some said.

'Doing great,' said others. A few proclaimed how tired they were.

"Good, good...we are going to get some down time. I'm sure you all will enjoy the movie."

Every member from 7-Alive sat stoically with glowering looks on their faces; suddenly they did not like Floo-Ellen at all as they were very suspicious of her now. Summer was clearly upset and did not even try to hide it. The more she thought about how they betrayed her and tricked her into joining the Society 36, the sicker she got.

While Floo-Ellen spoke with everyone, Chris, Summer, and Bo went into the back to find Ms. Lambert. She was tacking the assembly events on the bulletin board when they came in and unintentionally startled her. Bo closed the door, and they walked over to her.

"Ms. Lambert, we need to talk to you," Summer said looking nervously back over her shoulder.

"What is it?" Ms. Lambert asked very concerned.

"I was in the front office with Chris--"

"Why were you guys in the office?" she asked with crumpled brows.

"I was serving detention, and Summer came to visit," Chris explained.

"But that's besides the fact!" Summer insisted, trying to get to the point.

"Floo-Ellen, Zanku, and Bella came in unannounced and we hid behind the door..."

"While we were there, hoping not to get caught, we heard them saying some very disturbing things," Chris said.

"We heard with our own ears that they have special plans to recruit people into that secret club of theirs."

Summer and Chris told her absolutely everything. Ms. Lambert took a seat and dropped her face into her hands and began to cry. The kids looked at each other not sure what they should do or say next.

"Why did you give her control over your camp, Ms. Lambert?" Bo asked.

"Because," she said lifting her wet face from her hands, "she threatened me!"    "What? What do you mean?" Chris asked.

She looked over at the door and lowered her voice to a whisper.

"She told me at the beginning of camp that I was to give her control over the camp and I was to be reduced to a camp counselor, and if I get in her way or tell anyone what she said, then I would have major trouble to pay. And when Floo-Ellen says trouble, you have no idea what that really means. I just couldn't risk it."

"Where did Floo-Ellen come from anyway? And why are you so afraid of her?"

"How bad could this trouble really be?" Chris asked.

"Alright, alright, guys. Look, she threatened to torture my family while I'd be forced to watch! She is known for torturing people to no end. Some have not survived and she doesn't care. She even threatened my life," she cried. "As for where she came from? I don't know. She came about a week before camp started looking for a job. She presented herself as someone with just the right experience for what we needed, so I hired her. She stepped right in and helped me put everything in order. And this Camp Come Along Competition? I knew nothing of it! There's no way I would approve of children competing everyday for money!"

She shook her head, "I don't know. There's something about Floo-Ellen - something unnatural. I can't explain it. This woman is no one to mess with."

"Call the police!" Summer suggested.

"And say what? I have no recourse; she hasn't done anything physically. Plus, I don't want to risk my life or my family's life."

"Well, there's gotta be something we can do! We can't just sit back and wait for something to happen," Bo said before the door swung open.

"Lambert, I need you. Oh, I didn't realize you had company," Floo-Ellen said, miffed by seeing the children in there with her.

"Its fine," Ms. Lambert said as she stood up quickly. "They were just leaving." "Okay, talk to you later," Summer said and followed the boys out of the room. Floo-Ellen watched suspiciously as they left.

After the movie ended, all the campers filed through the campgrounds back to their several cabins. In 7-Alive's cabin, everyone was alight with the drama of the day; they recapped and chattered until bedtime.

"...I agree with Alex. This has gone too far! I wanna call my grandmother to come get me!" Leena said.

"Yeah, that's a good idea."

"How about me and Chris go to the office and call our parents, then we will come back and two others go to call theirs – we'll take turns."

"Sounds like a plan!" Alex agreed.

Chris and Bo ran over to the front office to use the phone. When they got there, the lights were off and the office seemed empty. Chris opened the door and crept in.

"Come on, the phone is over here," he whispered going behind the desk.

He picked up the beige phone and put it up to his ear. There was no dial tone. Chris put the phone on the hook and tried over and over again, but still no dial tone. He picked the base up to make sure it was plugged up.

"What's wrong? Don't tell me it's not working!"

"Nope," he said placing the dead phone back on the receiver.

"What are we gonna do now?"

"First, let's just get outta here, we'll figure something out."

They left the office on their way back to the cabin when they saw smoke rising from across the way.

"Look! What's going on over there?" Bo said pointing to the rising smoke.

"I don't know. Let's go see!"

The two inquisitive boys ran over to the fire pit where they saw Floo-Ellen, Bella, Zanku, Scott, and Herman dancing in a circle, singing and chanting around the fire. The two boys watched in horror from behind a tree.

At points during chanting, Floo-Ellen and the rest would be overcome with something unseen as their bodies would jerk and flail almost violently. The fire in the middle of the circle would rage and form into what looked like a huge dancing serpent! The fire actually responded to their gyrating bodies as if they were calling something out of the fire!

Bo looked at Chris with terror in his eyes.

"She *is* a witch!" he mouthed.

"What are we gonna do?" Chris asked.

"I'm going over to say something!" Bo declared.

But before he could walk from around the tree he felt a hand grab him around his mouth! He was so afraid he thought he would faint. He tussled with all his might to see who had grabbed him from behind and finally the corner of his eyes picked up an image of Andrew behind him with his hand also around Chris' mouth also.

Bo pulled back, strangely comforted by the fact that it was Andrew, and not some other demon seed from around camp.

"What the –!"

Andrew put his finger over his mouth telling the boys to keep quiet. He lead them away from the fire pit and back over to their cabin.

"You boys shouldn't be out here!"

"We saw smoke and we thought –"

"I know what you thought but you need to get back to your cabin," he said and walked away.

"Did you see that snake of fire?" Bo shouted out to Andrew.

He nodded his head, yes, and kept on his way. They went in and told the others about the dead phone and the fire pit activities.

"What? No phones?" Leena said.

"Phone. No dial tone," Bo corrected.

"Look, let's just get some rest and we will talk to Ms. Lambert about the phone first thing tomorrow morning," Alex said.

# Assembly Hall

The next day, Alex, Bo, and Chris found Ms. Lambert in the Mess Hall and told her about the phones not working and the late night fire pit activities. Ms. Lambert became saddened by what she was hearing from the children, mainly because she knew they could not be lying. She hung her head in shame that she could've allowed things to get this far; if only she'd kept things in her hands in the first place, she thought. It took everything she had not to break down crying in front of the kids.

Instead, Ms. Lambert began to explain. "The phones have been down for a while now. The other day, we received some mail from a concerned parent checking on their child; Floo-Ellen told Bella to write the parent back in a child's handwriting explaining how much fun they were having and because the camp was in the mountains, the phones systems go down frequently so not to worry."

Taken aback by what he was hearing, Chris looked off forcing himself not to respond.

"Please think of something without getting us all killed," she whispered.

"Don't worry Ms. Lambert – we will," Alex said, and they left the table.

On their way out, Chris noticed Cleofus sitting at his normal table with his teammates. As Chris walked by, Cleofus gave Chris a look that said, 'I'm mad at you, but I'm scared too.' Chris paid it no attention and went on his way. He was not interested in anymore disturbances with Cleofus.

*Chapter Sixteen*

## ⊗ WATER DEMONS ⊗

The clock on the wall in the Assembly Hall read 9:45 p.m. when Society 36's meeting was adjourning. The dismissed members shuffled toward the exit and back to their cabins as they engaged in quiet chatter. Summer remained seated, however, in the back of the room listening half-heartedly to a chattering Tess. Her true focus was in the mouths of Floo-Ellen and Bella who were engaged in busy conversation on the other side of the room.

Summer occasionally responded to Tess with short nods and 'uh huh's' while she was trying to come up with the best way to tell Floo-Ellen she wanted out. Five minutes had passed when Floo-Ellen finally finished talking with Bella and headed towards the back door right towards Summer. Summer bolted from her seat.

"Sorry, Tess, I gotta go," she said charging after Floo-Ellen in hopes of having a word with her.

She opened the back door and there was Floo-Ellen standing outside of the building talking to Zanku.

"Oh sorry," she said immediately regretting interrupting them.

"No problem, Summer. Do you need something?" Floo-Ellen asked pleasantly

"Uh, I wanted to speak with you privately," she said nervously.

Floo-Ellen turned to Zanku and said, "I'll see you back at the black mansion when Summer and I are finished."

Nodding his head in respect and agreement he went on about his way in the direction of the east bridge.

"What's on your mind?" Floo-Ellen asked looking Summer square in the eyes. Summer swallowed hard then began to speak.

"I've been thinking about this for a while now – I don't think Society 36 is for me."

"Why is that?" Floo-Ellen asked looking off, her ears peeled.

"Not sure. I just don't want to be a member anymore, I want out."

Turning her gaze back onto Summer, she said, "Never. Once you're in you're in. You don't remember the oath you took?"

"Yes, I thought this was what I wanted, but it's not."

"Trust me darling. It's easier to stay in and get used to it - than it is to get out."

Summer was quiet as was Floo-Ellen. After a while she continued to instruct Summer on the ways of Society 36 membership.

"You will continue to come to the meetings. You will keep your mouth shut about what we do here, and you will continue to be a part of Society 36 social activities. If you do not, the punishment is worse than torture," Floo-Ellen said eerily calm and casting a stern look into Summer's eyes.

Then without a word she turned and walked away in the same direction as Zanku. Summer stood in place speechless and watched as Floo-Ellen walked away from her. When, at last, Floo-Ellen disappeared into the night, Summer relaxed her stare and let it sweep across the ground then set her sights in the direction of the 7-Alive's cabin and began walking fast.

When she arrived and stepped onto the porch, she heard voices laughing and talking; obviously, somebody was having a really good time. The sound of it slowed her stride to a crawl. She decided to stand there a while to take it all in. Closing her eyes her mind snapped a picture of the days when she was so free to laugh and carry on with friends - not having to worry about anything; no adult sized burdens; no bitterness or a heavy heart. Since she had been involved in Society 36, Summer secretly felt she'd lost so much freedom and gained too much weight of the wrong kind.

She closed her eyes and reminisced, forgetting where she was for just one wonderful moment. She missed the days of innocent, free fun.

"I just want my life back," she said sighing to herself. "How did I even allow Tess to convince me to join anyway? How could I have been so stupid?"

Rousing herself out of the moment, she finally lifted a hand and knocked on the door.

E-man opened it with a cheerful greeting. "Hi!" he said bright-eyed.

"What's up?" Summer responded blandly.

She walked further in and saw that Bo and Leena were wrestling in the front room and that Casey was their referee. Chris was doing push-ups on the floor beside his bed while Alex was lost in a book as usual. As for Jacks, she was laughing like mad at the wrestling match. In the throes of his push-ups Chris managed to catch a glimpse of Summer, so he cut his regimen short and went over to her.

"Hey lady, how are you?" he said.

"I told her," Summer responded softly.

But before he could respond, Casey yelled from the across the room.

"Told who what?" she asked.

Alex looked up from his book and lowered it to his lap. Bo and Leena even quit wrestling and waited to hear the answer from Summer. Just then Chris thought, *My sister needs a 'Nosiest Sister Ever' award right now.*

"Floo-Ellen. I told her I wanted out of Society 36."

"What did she say?" Casey continued to probe.

"She said no," Summer answered turning from Chris to Casey. "Actually she said never."

"What? She can't do that!" Leena said jumping up from the floor, "She don't own you!"

"She said if I got out then I would be tortured."

"Tortured?" Alex replied looking up from his book.

Everyone in the cabin had a look of shock and confusion on their faces.

"Whatever!" Bo said getting up off the floor. "What she gonna do? What can she do to you that won't land her butt in jail?"

"I don't know."

Chris had no honor for such a threat. It only bothered him because of the fear he saw on Summer's face.

"What exactly do they do in Society 36?" Alex asked.

"Wish I could answer that, but she also said I still had to keep everything a secret."

"Who's gonna tell? We won't," Jacks assured her.

"Well," Summer said taking a seat on the bed at which time everyone gathered around her.

"It's a little hard to explain," she said with her eyes cast down.

"Just try," Casey pressed.

"Ok," Summer said letting out a hard sigh. "In the meetings – it's weird. People vent about who they don't like and Floo-Ellen makes them come up with ways to get revenge on their enemy. Sometimes if their ideas aren't bad enough she would say, 'Think harder! Make it worse!' or 'Is that all you got?'"

The crew was shocked silent by what they were hearing.

"Oh yeah, by the way, Cleofus really hates you," she said to Chris, and he chuckled.

"At the end of every meeting, she makes us meditate on hurting and crushing the people we don't like. We are to ask for supernatural powers to make us stronger – Floo-Ellen said the more we invite powers to come inside us, the stronger we get, and in due time, we can start making things move without touching them and hurting people while we are somewhere else."

Some of the kids' mouths were wide open as they covered them with their hands.

"So, from where do you summon these so-called powers?" Alex inquired quizzing Summer.

"I don't know. I just know I hate being there. The more I go, the more I find myself being bitter for no real reason at all. I'm barely happy anymore. I'm more sad and depressed than I've ever been. I just want my normal life back, but she said there's no way out," she said and started to cry.

"If Jesus is in your heart and the Holy Spirit in your body, then it doesn't matter how tight they have you. Jesus can break you free from them. He is the only one who can save you from this," Jacks said.

"She can't make you do anything," Chris said. "When's the next meeting?"

"Tomorrow at nine p.m."

"At that time tomorrow you will be here with me," Chris said.

Summer gave a weak smile of thanks and relief and laid her head on Chris' shoulder.

⊗ ⊗ ⊗

A couple of days went by and it was business as usual. Heated competitions were still going on and in between competitions you could find kids all over Camp Come Along preparing for the next big opportunity. All was in flow and every camper accounted for with one exception. Floo-Ellen was on the hunt for Summer now because as directed by Chris, Summer had missed the last Society 36 meeting, and she didn't like it.

It was Sunday and the sun was setting brilliantly over the tree-covered mountains towering over the vast lake that flowed through the center of campgrounds. There were just a few campers and counselors left out on the playing fields. The temperature was falling and coolness was blowing over the mountains tickling the trees a bit and rippling the water gently. All was serene and happy until Summer came storming out of her cabin after having a heated argument with Tess.

*I thought she was my friend. How could she talk to me like that!* Summer fumed.

Biting her bottom lip, she fought back the tears. She marched hard and long wanting not to stop until she was home. Inhaling and exhaling deeply trying to contain herself, she was a mix of angry and hurt; her eyes were teary, her face was red and her nostrils flared like that of a racehorse! Next, an angry Tess came bursting from the cabin and ran up behind her.

"Don't be so stupid...so easily influenced, Summer!"

"I'm not easily influenced, and I'm not stupid! I just don't want anything to do with the society or you!" Summer continued walking really fast and Tess kept up with her.

"The only reason you want out is because Chris isn't in!" she spat.

"It has nothing to do with Chris! I'm miserable! Have you not heard a word I've said?"

"Whatever," Tess rolled her eyes.

At that, she stopped cold and let Summer continue on. She watched her walk away for a while then yelled, "You better think about what you're doing!"

Summer turned around to return fire yelling, "When I listened to you and joined, I wasn't thinking! I just hate that it took me this long to start!"

Then she turned and continued on her way. Summer slowed down as she approached the lake. She made her way over to the bank of the water, walking very slowly, fiddling with pebbles and sticks with her feet. Trying to quiet her mind, she began to pretend to walk a tightrope using the very edge of the lake as the rope.

# Water Demons

*Let's see if I can do this without getting my feet wet,* she thought.

Extending her arms to keep her balance, she walked toe, heel, toe, heel....along the damp edge of the water. Trying to concentrate, all she could really think of was how one stupid decision had dramatically changed her life in just weeks. She stopped and stepped gingerly off her imaginary rope and looked into the rippling water right at her own reflection and let out a sigh. She gazed as if she hadn't seen her own reflection in quite some time.

The hour was drawing later, and the water was becoming calmer. She watched long enough to see her face become more still as the ripples slowed almost too total calm.

"This is nice," she thought.

This is the kind of peace I'm talking about. This is what I want to get back to," she said to her reflection. "Oh, just give me strength. Bring me back!"

Summer squatted down and leaned in still closer to the water. Searching her reflection, she seemed to look for something that perhaps had not come to life yet.

"What causes me to make such dumb decisions? And why was I so scared to run away when I felt I needed to?" she asked her reflection out loud. "It's me, Summer. Talk to me," she whispered now still looking into the water.

"I know, I know, you're not gonna answer because I have my own answer," she said to the reflection in the water.

She picked up a pebble and plopped it square in the middle of her face in the water and smiled.

Sighing, she continued to gaze throughout the peaceful water still not quite satisfied, but happy for the long moment of peace and time alone with herself. Since it was getting late, she decided it might be smart to be getting back to her cabin.

"Well, me," she said to her reflection, "I wish I could just get a little more right now but it's getting late." Smiling a little she asked, "Are you sure you don't have an extra boost to help me make it through the week? I know I have a lot to deal with…good ole' Floo-Ellen and all…."

Just as she was about to stand up she thought she saw something in the water next to her reflection. Her brows furled as she moved in as close as she could get without falling in.

What is that? Am I seeing things? As she got closer she saw that indeed there were five pairs of red eyes staring back at her! Summer gasped as she jumped back as if someone had uppercut her! She fell back and scuffled away from the lake. Finally she got up screaming, tearing away from the lake as fast as she could. Before she knew it she was beating on 7-Alive's cabin door. Chris opened the door and Summer dashed into his arms.

"What is wrong with you?" Chris asked looking out to see if anyone or anything was behind her. Summer was so out of breath, she could hardly speak.

"Okay, calm down. Just calm down," he said bringing her inside the cabin and closing the door behind them.

Everyone in the cabin was alarmed and concerned about Summer, but all she could do was cry leaving them with no answers.

"What happened, please?" He said lifting her chin in order to see her eyes. "Look at me and just talk real slow, Summer."

"Demons! Demons in the water! I saw them floating and…"

"What? Demons? Are you sure?"

"Yes! They had red eyes… and…" she closed her eyes tightly as she recalled the scene at the lake. Taking a deep breath she continued, "…look, I'm sure."

"Maybe we should go check it out," Chris said looking around at the others. "Anybody with me?"

Casey's answer was obvious as she darted beneath her covers without a word.

"I think we can take her word for it," Bo said.

"It's Floo-Ellen, I know she's doing this because I didn't come to the meeting tonight," Summer concluded.

"Remember what she said about being tortured?"

"Do you think Floo-Ellen is a witch?" Alex asked.

"Hmm, I don't know! She could be," Summer answered looking to Chris.

"I don't feel safe in my cabin. Can I stay here with you?" she asked.

"Of course you can," he said holding her tighter.

*Chapter Seventeen*

## ⊗ FIGHTS IN THE NIGHT ⊗

"Casey, are you absolutely sure you changed the batteries in this thing?" Chris asked shaking the yellow walkie –talkie.

"Yes, I'm sure," she said tying up her sneakers.

"Where are my trainers?" Alex asked looking under his bed.

"Trainers?" Jacks asked.

"Sorry, my tennis shoes…sneakers…whatever it is that you Americans say."

"Oh, I saw them over by the bathroom," Leena informed him, pointing.

"Hurry up so we can get there and back," Chris commanded.

Alex tied up his shoes, and the others made sure they had everything in order.

"Alex, Jacks, you guys ready?"

"Ready as I'll ever be," Alex said putting on his black cap.

"You guys be careful," E-man said affectionately.

"Yeah and make sure you don't do what I would!" Bo chided playfully.

"And what could that be?" Leena said pushing his head to the side. "What's wrong with you?"

"I'm looking out for their best interest, Leena!"

"Ok, guys, it's almost two o'clock. They should be sound asleep. You should get going," Leena said on a more serious note.

Chris looked at his little sister. "Case, I really don't want you to go. I promised Mom that I would protect you and…"

"Well, shut up and protect me," she said swinging the door open and going out in front of Chris.

She looked back at Jacks and Alex.

"Let's go!" she bellowed and they promptly jumped out and headed out behind her.

The crew of four crept through the night like graveyard detectives towards the east bridge.

Chris caught up with Casey. "Make sure you stick with me," he instructed her.

"Okay," she whispered.

They ran over the east bridge and started on the dirt trail to the black mansion. The silver moon that shone from the night sky was their guiding light.

"You ok?" Jacks asked Alex.

"Yes, I'm fine," he said nudging his sliding eyeglasses back up the bridge of his nose. They kept up a steady jog with Chris and Casey in the lead.

"How much further?" Casey asked.

"If we keep up this pace, we'll be there in about five minutes," Chris answered.

Suddenly the crew heard a voice crackling through one of the walkie-talkies.

"I think you guys need to turn around and come back!" the voice cried.

Slowing their pace just a bit to cater to the message; it turns out that it was Bo's voice coming through the walkie-talkie.

"What's the matter?" Chris whispered, pressing it close to his lips.

"It's Leena...she's gone mad! She's attacking me! *Aaaahhh!*" Bo screamed into the walkie-talkie.

Chris broke into a smile then tried to hide it, as he informed the crew that Bo was just clowning around and to ignore him.

"I'm tired," Casey said slowing down.

"Me too," Alex said slowing down also.

"Tell Bo and Leena they should be looking for anything suspicious, not goofing off," Jacks warned.

"Stop goofing off, and look out!"

"It's hopeless," Jacks said taking off into a slow jog while the others followed suit.

"Ok, I'm sorry. Whew! I think she might be a bit crazy," Bo said chuckling inside the walkie-talkie.

"You guys are supposed to be letting us know what's going on out there anyway."

"Well, it sounds like there is more action going on there at the cabin," Chris said.

Bo continued to clown around being an annoying goofball throughout their entire trip to the black mansion. Indeed, he kept them company in his absence by saying all kinds of silly things in the walkie-talkie possibly to keep everyone's mind off the seriousness of their venture.

"Look!" Casey screeched pointing, "There it is!"

All four of them stopped cold, stood up, and gawked at the sight of the grey stone covered, black mansion that actually resembled a small castle.

"We're here," Chris whispered into the walkie-talkie. Leena snatched the walkie-talkie from Bo and began a long string of sentences spoken in an unfamiliar tongue. No one understood a word she said as she went on and on.

Finally, Bo snatched the walkie from her shaking his head, "You see why I say she's crazy –talking gibberish for no reason!"

Casey's mouth fell open and her eyes lit up. "Did you hear that?" she asked.

"What? Leena playing around?" Chris responded.

"That strange baby talk?" Alex asked chuckling.

"No! She wasn't playing around! You didn't understand what she said?"

"No Casey, what did you hear her say?" Jacks asked.

"She said, 'Thus says the Lord, beware as you enter in there. One of you is not fully prepared for what is up ahead.'"

"Oh my God! Leena was speaking in spiritual tongues, and God allowed you to interpret what she was saying! Interpretation! That's your gift Casey!" Alex said, as only a Brit can.

Casey stood still, taking it all in with a nervous smile on her face, proud that at last she knew her gift from God.

"Wow," she said sweetly, "I have a gift too like you, Chris."

Chris grabbed her gently by the head and pulled her in close to him.

"Yes, Casey. See, you're not left out. I'm proud of you for not being afraid to use it, too. But we better get on with this little journey now."

"So, one of us isn't prayed up or ready for this, huh?" Chris said looking at Casey.

"That's what she said…well, what He said."

"Well, then let's pray," Jacks insisted.

The four of them held hands in a small circle and asked God to protect them from any hurt, harm, or danger that they may incur while they are in the black mansion. Chris put the walkie-talkie up to his mouth.

"Bo, Leena, E-man, we're about to go in so my walkie will be off. I'll let you know what happened when we get out."

"Ok. Be safe," Leena said.

Chris turned the knob on the walkie-talkie until it clicked off.

"Come on," he said walking toward the colossal house.

# Fights in the Night

There was a flowing moat surrounding the black mansion. Chris jumped over it easily as did Alex. Then they extended their hands to help the girls across it. Thick, prickly bushes were planted on the sides of the stone steps that lead to the front door.

"Come on," Chris whispered as he went up the steps towards the door.

He slowly turned the knob, but it wouldn't budge.

"It's locked from the inside. No way to get it from here."

"Well, that's not surprising," Alex commented.

"I thought we would try and peek through some windows to see what we could see."

"Let's go around to the back," Jacks suggested.

Everyone agreed and followed along the circling water to the back of the mansion and saw that it flowed into an opening that lead into a basement entrance of the mansion.

"Look! How's it going into the house?" Casey asked.

"There must be underground pipes that recycle this water back up to the front," Alex guessed.

"Looks like we gotta get wet to get in," Chris said staring at the opening. But no one was in agreement with getting wet.

"What? A little water never hurt anyone," he quipped.

"I have an even better idea! Why don't you go through the water and once you get in come open up this window and let us in," Casey devised.

"I like that idea," Alex chimed in as Jacks nodded in agreement with them.

"Guess I'm outnumbered on this one." Chris took a deep breath and let it out hard. "Okay, wait right here."

"Oh, we will," Casey said smirking.

He walked towards the water, and no sooner than he got both feet into the water, a strong current carried him in snatching him out of their sight in no time. The remaining three winced at how fast Chris was sucked away.

The current carried him all the way to the middle of the basement where he immediately started being swung around in what was obviously a huge whirlpool. The closer he was slung toward the middle he began to feel suction pulling him under. Chris' arms flailed and his legs kicked wildly as he tried like mad to stay afloat and not get pulled under. *I will not go under*, he encouraged himself. It took all of his energy, but he fought with great determination, splashing against the might of the current to swim to the edge and climb out. Sloshed onto solid flooring at last, he laid there with his faced pressed to the cold stone floor, heaving, until he could catch his breath.

The basement was dark except for a flitter of light that shone from the hallway by the stairs. When Chris was finally able to pull himself together and realize his surroundings, a wave of fear came over him and he dragged over to the window to let the others in.

"What took so long?" Jacks asked as she came through the window into the shadowy atmosphere.

"The water has some suction action going on that is really overpowering," Chris explained, panting. "I had to fight like crazy to get outta there!"

"Wow, it's a good thing we all didn't get in after all. One of us might not have made it, huh."

He extended a hand for Casey to come in, and Alex followed right behind her.

"Are you okay, Chris?" Casey asked after seeing how wet, flushed and exhausted he was.

"I'm good. I just didn't expect such a ride."

"This looks super creepy," Casey whispered as she eyed her surroundings.

The smell of stale water and wax candles stiffened the air. Grey stones covered the walls and ceiling while stone tiles made up the floor. The crew stood huddled together roving their eyes throughout.

# Fights in the Night

"Look at this!" Alex said examining the large cage that hung from the ceiling.

"And there's another one over there on the floor," Jacks added.

"...and there," Alex noted pointing to the other side of the room.

"They're big enough to put a whole person in!"

"Crreeeppy!" Casey repeated.

Jacks walked over to a long stone table that stood in the middle of the floor. Sitting on the surface was a knife that looked like a small sword. Its narrow handle was encased in dark leather with two small tassels dangling from the end.

"What are you so engrossed with?" Alex asked Jacks.

"This knife on this cool, stone table. Never seen anything like this before. This blade looks like it could split a hair in two!"

Two thick ropes lay on the table as well - each on the two far ends of the table.

"Wonder what this is used for?" Jacks muttered.

"Yeah, it looks medieval," Chris said inspecting it more closely.

Alex had gone over to inspect the water. He had squatted down and was bent over with one hand in the water trying to determine where the suction was coming from.

"Are those torch holders on the walls?" Casey whispered loudly.

"Looks like it," Jacks said walking away from the table.

"What's this?" Chris asked pointing to the large star inside a circle etched into the stone floor.

Alex gasped, "That's a pentagram! ...it's used for demonic practices," he exclaimed.

"What? Let's get outta here then!" Casey demanded. "We found out what we needed to know."

"Casey's right," Jacks exclaimed, "and this is more serious than we thought. We don't need to stay here."

Just as the crew was thinking about running away, a revving sound rose from the depths of the mansion sending shivers through all of them. It was the sound of the rickety furnace they soon figured out.

"So, you think Floo-Ellen's a witch?" Chris asked Jacks.

"There is no thinking about it," Casey said.

"I don't know, but this place is starting to convince me of just that," she replied.

"Look," Alex said pointing to some white melted wax on the floor.

The little droplets of wax made a trail to a closed door with a crystal clear diamond shaped doorknob. Alex erected his index finger and pressed it to his lips and began walking slowly towards the door. The others stayed at a distance and watched him. He put his ear to the door to see what he could hear, but he heard nothing, so he gripped the doorknob, inhaled deeply and shut his eyes hoping to get access to the room. No sooner than he would turn the knob, he stopped, opened his eyes, and turned back to the group with a blank stare in his eyes. Lifeless, he crept back over and joined them.

"Mission abandoned, I guess," Casey said.

"Glad you chose to make the right decision and not open that door," Jacks whispered into his ear.

But Alex said nothing and, instead, looked back at her with empty eyes.

"Let's go," Casey said.

"Alright," Chris agreed walking back to the window that he let them in through.

By now, Alex had picked up a candle holder that was on the floor at the rim of the whirlpool and was standing with it lifted high above him preparing to clock Chris in the head with it! Out of the side of her eye, Jacks noticed what was going on and power-kicked him on the side of his knee causing him to go crashing to the floor. Startled, Chris turned to see what all the commotion was and saw Alex crumpled on the floor with the candle holder still in his hand.

"Man, what's wrong with you?"

Alex responded with a roaring grunt and shot up from the floor to

# Fights in the Night

lunge at Chris again, but he dodged just missing being swiped by the iron candle holder. Once again, Alex ended up in Jacks pathway, so Jacks— unafraid— jumped him and pinned him to the floor. Alex squirmed like a snake on fire.

"Chris, he is being controlled by something! He's possessed!" Jacks screamed.

Casey pressed both hands over her mouth as she was completely overcome with horror and surprise. *This couldn't be Alex*, she thought.

"Here! Hold his shoulders!" she yelled snatching away the candle holder and tossing it.

Chris straddled him and held his shoulders down as best he could. Alex growled and jerked like a rabid animal.

"Alex! Be quiet! Calm down." Chris whispered loudly.

He insisted, trying to reason with him.

Alex stilled himself long enough to lift his head, look Chris in the eye and hiss at him before falling back to the floor squirming and growling wildly. Chris glanced over at the stairs to make sure no one was coming.

"Casey, I need you to come and hold his knees. Sit on them if you have to!" Jacks instructed.

Jacks knew this madness had to end quickly. She began to talk to what was inside him. "Demon, what is your name?" she began.

A voice blared from within Alex and answered in an unfamiliar deep voice," Balachew!"

Casey shut her eyes tight and tried to show no fear. Trembling, she held her post.

"Balachew, I cast you out of him in the name of Jesus, and you are to never return. Leave NOW!" Jacks commanded.

Alex's body stiffened like a board first; then, he went into uncontrollable shaking as if he were having a seizure. Chris and Casey pinned him down with all their might. Slowly but surely, Alex stopped resisting, and his body went limp. Casey and Chris climbed off of him and rolled him over on his side as he was coughing profusely now. In fact, he coughed until he threw up.

When he was done, he suddenly passed out cold. Casey was mortified and ran into Chris' arms whimpering. Unexpectedly, a light shone from underneath the door with the diamond-shaped doorknob.

"Look!" Casey screeched.

Breaking from Chris, she bolted for the window!

"Hurry, Chris!" Jacks said running behind Casey.

Chris struggled but managed to pick Alex up and put him over his shoulder and ran, limping, as fast as he could to the window. Jacks and Casey had made it outside the window quickly and waved Chris on.

"Here, help me get him through," Chris begged putting Alex's head and shoulders through the window while Jacks and Casey pulled him through to the outside. Chris heard the door with the special doorknob unlocking but jumped through the window before anyone caught sight of him, and he ran with the rest off into the night.


Zanku crept out of his room and looked around for the commotion that had awakened him. He rolled his eyes over the room and saw that the candle holder on the floor was out of place, the vomit on the floor, and the window was wide open. Instinctively, he ran over to it and looked out, but he saw nothing. He smelled the scent of perspiring warmth left behind as the kids ran away.

"What's going on?" he heard a woman's voice behind him ask.

He turned and noticed Floo-Ellen coming down the stairs in her long white night gown.

"Not sure. I heard some noise and got up. When I came out, I saw that candle holder knocked over and I saw the vomit on the floor and this window up. I smell something, though. Somebody has definitely been here," he said.

She looked around suspiciously and folded her arms tightly.

"Where's Balachew? Does he know what might be going on?"

"I don't know, but I think—"

# Fights in the Night

"Well Zanku, you don't seem to know much of anything now do you," she snapped. "Never mind, I'll summon him myself."

Very quickly she went to work to conjure up Balachew with incantations. Throwing her head back and rolling her shoulders she muttered chants until Balachew stepped into her spirit.

"Balachew...what happened here tonight?" She asked moving her lips with only a whisper escaping. Pausing she awaited a response that only she could hear.

"Children? How many were there?" she asked louder.

While she continued conversing telepathically with Balachew, Zanku picked up the candleholder and examined at it as if it would reveal a clue of some sort.

With every answer from Balachew that only she could hear, she answered out loud.

"Four children – meddling around? Well, listen closely Balachew, I want you to go find the leader of that pack and torture him…tonight! Then we'll see if they'll be foolish enough to follow him or her back here again." She put her head up, opened her eyes and stormed off back up the stairs.


When Chris, Casey, and Jacks returned to the cabin they laid Alex in his bed and sat down beside him. He started coming around as told by his fluttering eyelids. When he was able to finally awaken completely, the first thing he asked was if he had been dreaming.

"Afraid not," Chris said.

"Was what a dream?" Leena asked alarmed at the sight of Alex having been carried in.

She came over and kneeled down beside them. The small crew told her and the others everything that happened while they were at the black mansion.

The others were flabbergasted by what they heard, especially Leena.

"You know…" Alex said pondering on the earlier event, "as soon as I grabbed the doorknob, my body felt very strange - like an invisible force took me over."

"So…there was a demon in the door knob?" Bo asked trying to understand.

"Yeah, as soon as he touched it, he went nuts!" Casey inserted.

"So, that's what God was trying to warn you about," E-man said.

"I'm just glad we made it back in one piece!" Jacks commented, "Whew, that was close - way too close!"

"I know," Chris added solemnly standing to his feet. He stretched and went into the bathroom to remove his damp clothes and take a shower.

"All I really want to do is go to bed," he said as he slogged away.

"I can't believe Floo-Ellen is a witch," Bo said. "What do we do about that?"

"Whatever is to be done about it, we need to worry about it tomorrow because we have to get some sleep," Jacks insisted.

"It's already morning," Casey said.

"You know what I mean, sweetie. Good night."


About an hour later, while it was still dark outside, the cabin was quiet with sleeping campers with the exception of Bo's light snoring. The peace of the night was suddenly interrupted when Chris was awakened by a searing pain that shot through him like lightening cutting through the sky. His eyes popped open and he wanted to scream but discovered he could not because his mouth was shut so tight it was as if it was nailed. No matter what his mind told him to do, he could not do it. In his head he heard, move…lift your leg…turn over…all to no avail. He had become pinned to his own bed not able to speak or move.

As he lay there like an entombed mummy, he was able at last to blink his eyes, and in doing so, a vision spread out before him that resembled a very large television - nothing new to Chris. The only difference was this time there appeared to be a swirling blackness with a hole in the center. No real picture. No other activity. Just total blackness encompassed everything he saw before him.

Chris continued to peer, wondering if anything would change.

*What is in this black hole?* he wondered. *Anything?* Chris continued to stare, as that was all that he could do, when finally something appeared to be emerging from the black hole. It was hideous! Chris wanted to scream for help. The image grew closer and larger and revealed its ferocious intent with a wide-open salivating mouth filled with fangs ready for tearing Chris apart, and he was coming straight for him to do just that!

This beastly image blew a gust of hot reeking stench into Chris' face that made him want to vomit. Chris felt as if he would smother. He tried all he could to breathe normally but the squalid air that filled his surrounding was choking him seemingly to death. The creature moved in closer with its nostrils flaring and dripping strings of slime all over areas of Chris' body: his stomach, his chest and arms.

He could feel each thud as glops of mucous splatted onto the thin blanket that covered him; it was sickeningly warm and flowed along his body like loose jelly. Shaking his head in disgust and dismay Chris began to feel hopeless and worried. He prayed that none of the goop would get in his face. Now, he was glad he couldn't open his mouth.

Sweat beaded up all over his face and began to trickle down his temple. Tears streamed from his eyes. A single vein of fury embossed his forehead and, again, Chris tried to make a sound to alarm his roommates, but still he could not.

Chris started getting tired; his fight was beginning to weaken. His eyes were losing its life when suddenly he could clearly see another set of eyes in front of him.

*Oh, my God*, he thought to himself.

The crimson eyes peered back at Chris, unmoved. The two eyes resembled two ladybugs set in charcoal. This beast rose up higher towering over the immobile young man displaying black wings that spread up and out as if he was going to take flight and tear through the roof of the cabin, taking Chris with him clutched in his talons. This menacing creature donned thick, black hair that framed its ugliness resembling a lion's mane. Chris began to sweat profusely and tried all he could to scream out.

The beastly demon shook his head violently growling so loud it pierced Chris' heart. This terror in the night was none other than Balachew, Floo-Ellen's assigned torturer. He was determined to follow her instructions to the tee. Balachew lifted a leg that was now like that of a gigantic eagle and pounded it into Chris' chest and clinched it digging deep into Chris' flesh. Then he repeated the pounding over and over again. He tore and scraped into Chris for minutes that seemed like bloody, endless hours.

Balachew had nails that were six inches long and curved under a bit, and with them, he proceeded like a hungry, vicious animal going in for the kill. He even performed a ceremonial ripping into the air showing off his very intimidating talons, as if he were striking matches, until with one foul strike, he tore into Chris' chest again. The cutting impact was more than Chris could bear as tears poured from his eyes and formed a puddle in his ears. Balachew let out a load roar that rattled Chris' brain.

*Oh, God, why! Is help ever going to come?* He cried to himself.

Right at the point, when Chris was tottering in hopelessness, E-man awakened needing to go to the bathroom. Groggily, he got up and plodded across the dusty floor and fumbled for the bathroom. Balachew turned his head at the faint sound that someone was stirring, but he did not let up. He pounced on Chris and lowered his face so that his eyes met Chris' and his nostrils practically touched the tip of Chris' nose.

Chris felt as if he would faint away or surly dissolve through his now soaked body; his bed was a mere pile of mush now too. Balachew opened his mouth wide displaying his fangs and the bubbling gums from which they grew. No! Chris hollered from within. If *only* God would send someone, anyone to rescue me. Balachew hissed and spit acid in Chris' face and hair scorching him severely.

Soon Chris began to feel an unusual sensation on the surface of his skin that quickly turned to burning! His skin was being eaten; it was melting and dissolving like ice in hot tea. He longed for the simple ability to get up and run, but that was still impossible. More tears wrung from his eyes when he shut them tightly in a brave effort to bear the never-ending pain.

Chris, skin-soaked with perspiration, felt like a boulder sunken in mud and could not get up no matter how hard he tried. Right at the time when Chris was on the brink of giving up, E-man opened the bathroom door and turned off the light. He was more alert now but still eager to get back to his bed.

In the darkness of the room, E-man noticed some movement around Chris' bunk and stopped in his tracks. Scratching his cheek, he was baffled as to what could be going on. The more he gazed the clearer the picture was becoming. Chris was jerking violently as he was being rumpled terribly by Balachew! E-man was alarmed and confused by the flopping silhouette against the darkness.

"What in the world is going on?" E-man whispered, walking over to Chris' bunk. "I didn't know Chris had seizures," he whispered to himself.

"Chris! Man, are you ok?" he called out grabbing Chris' shoulder.

Chris' eyes were wide and blank.

"Chris!" E-man shouted shaking him. "Snap out of it!"

Balachew turned and gazed at E-man a second then let out a deafening shrill before retreating quickly into the black hole. In an instant, the entire vision that was held up before Chris' eyes vanished and he was able to move normally again. All at once, he sat up in the bed heaving, grasping his chest.

"Are you ok...what was all that about?" E-man asked in a huff.

With trembling hands, Chris frantically began unbuttoning his pajama shirt. E-man sat down next to him trying to stay calm.

"It was a monster," Chris said stammering and examining his chest.

"Where?" E-man asked carefully.

"He did this - this right here," Chris stammered some more looking down at his chest. He turned toward the window so that the moon could cast some light on the area so E-man could see. There were four long scratches across his chest, and just below his neck, were splotchy red marks where the acid had burned him.

"Oh my God!" E-man screeched jumping back.

"What's going on?" Leena asked rousing from sleep, her eyes half closed.

"It's Chris!" E-man cried. "Something is wrong! Everybody, get up!"

"Huh? What happened?" Leena insisted climbing out of her bed and rushing to Chris' bunk.

When she saw his chest she yelped, "What happened here?"

Bo got up and darted over to the crowd that had formed around Chris.

"I had another vision," Chris began to explain panting furiously, " — but this time it was of a monster attacking me. Everything he did in the vision happened to my body," he said looking down eyeing his body again. "But, when E-man came over here it left."

"I saw him shaking like mad when I came out the bathroom," E-man inserted.

"Did you see the monster?" Leena asked him.

"No, I didn't see any monster, but from the looks of things when I saw him it looked as if something really was attacking him!"

"I wonder why this happened," Bo said.

"Maybe Floo-Ellen sent it," Leena suggested.

"Maybe, I don't know," Chris said dabbing his forehead with his sheet.

"Hey, help me from my bunk guys," Chris asked.

"Where are you going?" someone asked.

"To the bathroom. I need to clean up…sooth this burning pain with a wet towel or something."

"Towel? Looks like you need stitches!" Bo said.

"Yeah, I'm surprised you were not bleeding all over the place!" Leena said.

# Fights in the Night

"Oh, my God, but I was, I know I was. That thing literally stabbed me repeated with long claws cutting me to no end. Or at least it felt like it," he explained tiredly. "I'm just going to go to the bathroom and see what I can do."

By this time, no one had noticed that Casey was standing off in a distance listening and watching with tears rolling down her cheeks. *I want to call Mom to come get us. I hate this place,* she thought.

When Chris got into the bathroom, he ran cool water into a towel and cradled his face in it awhile. He ran more water and pressed it into his chest for much needed soothing.

Soon Leena interrupted his concentration and asked, "Chris, do you wanna go to the infirmary?"

"No, I'll be fine. I just need to get some sleep," he insisted heading back to bed only to discover that it was still pretty wet so he went over to Casey's bunk and curled up at her feet until sunrise. Concerned, grimaced and confused everyone followed suit without another word.

$\otimes$ $\otimes$ $\otimes$

"Wake up, Bella!" Floo-Ellen said excited, ripping through the black mansion switching on lights everywhere.

"Scott, Herman, get up now and go to my room!"

She went downstairs and got Zanku and brought him to her room too. Herman sat in a chair in the corner, and Scott and Bella took a seat on her bed. Sleepy and puzzled, they wondered what Floo-Ellen was up to and why they were awakened in the middle of the night.

Floo-Ellen entered the room brightly smiling and said, "Sorry to wake you up like this, but good news cannot wait."

She was so happy, she clapped her hands then rested them on her chest smiling wide. "Tonight we had some intruders…" she began almost singing.

"What!" Herman said shooting up from his seat.

Floo-Ellen patted the air and he sat back down.

"...Yes, four children meddling around," she turned and looked wryly at Zanku who was leaning nonchalantly in the doorway.

"So, this is good news?" Scott asked dryly.

"No, Scott," she responded shaking her head, smiling. "The good news is I sent Balachew after the leader of those nosey kids to make him pay for what they did. But here is the exciting problem...Balachew told me that when he was attacking him, he was interrupted by another boy who came to his aid. His name is Emanuel!"

Floo-Ellen was almost not to be contained. The others sat quietly and continued to look puzzled.

"Okaay...and," Herman inserted snidely.

Turning and eying everyone in the room Floo-Ellen continued.

"My dears, this Emanuel is the one...he is the one we have been waiting on for hundreds of years!"

For a moment, Floo-Ellen's eyes faded to black, and she closed them taking in a deep breath and blowing out slowly to calm herself. When she opened her eyes again the whites of her eyes had returned.

"The one?" Zanku repeated changing his stance from leaning to standing.

"YES!" she answered practically hissing. "The pure one – the child of innocence – he has been right here under our noses this whole time! He must be sacrificed!"

"When do you want us to pick him up?" Herman asked.

"No!" Bella spoke up, "His blood will be much sweeter if we can convince him to come over to our side."

Floo-Ellen nodded in agreement. "First we will try to lure him – and if that doesn't work, then we'll snatch em'," she said grabbing the air in front of her.

"Once we've done this, every witch and wizard, demon and devil, will know my name. This will make me the greatest of the great in the dark kingdom!"

# Fights in the Night

"His blood will bring you power beyond measure," Zanku said looking into her eyes.

"Yes, I know," she said looking off into a distance. "That's why everyone must turn all of their attention to him and his friends! Forget about every other camper and Society 36! He is much more valuable to us!"

Everyone in the room was quiet and contemplative on that note.

"Alright, everyone is dismissed. I just wanted everyone to know the good news. You are free to go back to sleep now, but while you are sleeping be sure to dream of ways that we can make his capture a success."

"Okay"

"Sure thing."

"No problem, I'm on it."

Everyone filed out of Floo-Ellen's room and headed up the stony hallway to their rooms.

*Chapter Eighteen*

## ⊗ SUMMER AND E-MAN ⊗

Late that night, an hour into bed time, Floo-Ellen unlocked Summer's cabin door with her master key and eased it open quietly. She looked into the dark cabin and saw that everyone was asleep. Floo-Ellen crept over to Summer's bed and sat down on the edge. Summer shifted in her sleep and Floo-Ellen watched her.

After awhile she whispered, "Wake up, Little Pretty."

Summer jumped, startled, and when she saw Floo-Ellen, she quickly sat up.

"Shhhhh...." she said with her pointer finger over her primped lips.

"I need a favor from you."

Summer was in no mood for favor requests from Floo-Ellen, the very woman who'd continued to hold her captive in Society 36.

"What is it?" She asked coolly.

"I'm making you responsible for making sure that Emanuel joins Society 36."

"Emanuel? Who is that?"

"Don't act like you don't know him! He's in 7-Alive! I see you playing around with them all the time…I know you know who he is."

"E-man?"

Floo-Ellen chuckled, "Yes E-man."

"What? He won't join! None of the kids from 7-Alive would! And besides I wouldn't dare want him to come join. I'm trying to leave myself!" she said whispering harshly.

Floo-Ellen smiled and gave her a dark piercing stare.

"I'm not asking you," she said with a crooked smile, "I'm telling you."

Summer stared at her in the dark, trying to figure a way around this ludicrous favor.

"What makes you think he would listen to me anyway?"

"I'm sure you can be quite persuasive my dear."

"Sorry, Floo-Ellen, I won't do it," she said flatly.

"Oh, you will," she snickered looking around the room to make sure everyone was still asleep before pulling Summer in nose-to-nose with her.

"And if you don't, you will be sorry," Floo-Ellen threatened.

"I don't care! You can give me chores for the rest of the summer I still won't do it!"

"Well fine," she said standing up, "since you aren't moved by chores, then I have to take greater measures."

"And what's that?" Summer asked snatching the covers off of her lap.

"Your friend Chris… the one who you adore, and it's so obvious that he adores you too," she said with a cynical smile painted on her powdery face.

"What about him?" she stood up in front of her showing no fear.

"I'll kill him. I'll torture him slowly before I put him out of his misery. And please – do call my bluff! I've been waiting to make an example of someone…you know… show off my power."

# Summer and E-man

"I don't believe you, Floo-Ellen. Even you couldn't be a cold-blooded murderer. People go to prison for a lifetime for murder, you know!" Floo-Ellen sat and stared at Summer completely expressionless and without a word.

Summer knew she had struck an unfamiliar cord with her. She had not known this side of Floo-Ellen. Summer batted her eyes hard fighting back tears of anger.

"Please don't...don't hurt him." Her voice was shaky as she fought back the tears.

"Oh, I don't want to. It's just imperative that Emanuel joins Society 36 as soon as possible. If not, then Chris will have to suffer. And if you tell anyone, I'll let you watch me kill him. Then, I'll kill you."

Summer burst into sobbing.

"But why would he listen to me if everyone knows I want out?" she asked sniffling and whimpering.

"Like I said, you have the power of persuasion. I'm sure you'll think of something, my dear," Floo-Ellen turned and meandered out the door like nothing ever happened.

⊗ ⊗ ⊗

The next morning, the sun hung in the midst of the blue sky sparing Camp Come Along of its hot rays allowing wind to swoop around lending some cool relief. The trees were swaying especially much this day, and the ripples in the lake were beautifully enlivening the lake. It was a beautiful morning, and after breakfast, the campers were taking full advantage of the free time they had before the competition began. Campers were canoeing and some even took their chances on swimming on the other side of the cool lake. Still others were playing basketball, tennis, and softball.

Chris, Bo, Leena, and E-man were playing in a volleyball match against a team of other players, and 7-Alive's team was losing by five points.

"It ain't over till it's over!" Bo ranted, swiping the back of his hand over his sweaty brow.

"Come on!" Chris yelled to the server on the opposing side.

Just then he caught a glimpse of Summer sitting underneath a tree reading a book.

Chris had noticed all morning that Summer had kept an unusual distance from him. She had not even given her usual greeting during breakfast…not to him or any of the others in their cabin.

"Maybe she isn't feeling too well, or maybe Society 36 is really taking a toll on her." Chris pondered.

He was really concerned.

"CHRIS!" Bo shouted. Chris snapped out of it at the sound of Bo's voice and ducked, then dived to the ground in time not to get hit, but too late to make a point. Instead, E-man hit the ball high in the air and Bo spiked it over!

"Dude, you didn't see that ball coming right for your face. You better look out! What are you thinking about?" Snapping his fingers at Chris, he quipped, "Pay attention. Focus, please!"

Bo always got serious when it came to sports, and when he would lose he would say, "Just fun and recreation…"

"You alright man?" E-man asked helping Chris up.

"Yeah, yeah…" Chris said dusting off his pants holding his side.

Instinctively, he turned and looked at Summer to see if she had seen his blunder. She was staring right at him. Embarrassed, he quickly turned and focused on the game.

Casey and Alex were sitting on Rock Mountain, the large rock that sat in the middle of the campground. Alex was reading a book, and Casey was eating an apple staring off into space more than likely reminiscing about the other night. Out of nowhere, Alex slammed the book closed and blew out a breath of frustration. Casey blinked and returned back to the moment. Raising her brow, she turned an inquisitive eye towards Alex.

"Sorry, I just get so frustrated sometimes. It's this book. I've wasted my whole morning reading it and now that I'm done with it, I can't take anything from it – in fact I could've given the author some pointers." He looked at her and giggled. "Sorry, a lot of people aren't that bright."

"Well, why don't you call that author up and give her your advice – ya know, get it off your chest," she joked.

Alex laughed as he climbed off the rock to go and return the book back to the library. "You know... I just might!"

"Casey!" someone yelled, startling her a bit.

"Come here!" E-man yelled.

She climbed down from the rock and ran over to the volleyball court.

"I gotta go to the bathroom. Need you to sub for me."

"No problem," she said happily taking his spot.

Summer put her book down when she saw E-man jogging off the court. He went into the cabin and closed the door. Summer tried her best not to be seen as she crept up to the cabin. Chris spiked the ball and scored a point for his team and they went wild cheering and high-fiving each other. Chris whipped his neck around as usual to see if Summer was there seeing everything. She was gone. He took a quick glance over the field but still no Summer. He turned towards the cabins just in time to see her slip into their cabin. Finding it a bit odd but not too strange he turned and continued to play.

*All that orange juice at breakfast'* he laughed to himself, *she probably couldn't make it to her own cabin.*

Summer heard the water running from E-man washing his hands. She closed her eyes, took a deep breath, and exhaled slowly.

*I hate that Floo-Ellen put me in this position. This is so stupid and degrading. Just when I am no longer ashamed to admit that I'm in love with Chris here comes Floo-Ellen putting my heart in jeopardy by messing up everything that Chris and I have worked on,* she thought to herself.

She walked over to the bathroom and saw him shut the water off and dry his hands. When he turned around and saw Summer standing in the doorway, he threw his hand on his chest and gasped.

"Summer, you scared me!"

"Oh...sorry," she lied.

"It's okay. So, what brings you to our humble cabin home?"

"I saw you coming in and well... I was hoping that I could talk to you about something."

"Of course! What's on your mind?"

"Why don't we sit down out here?" She walked over to a bed, sat down, and patted the space next to her for him. He sat down and gave her a curious look and waited to hear what she had to say.

"What's wrong?" E-man finally asked.

Summer choked up and fought back tears. She inhaled and exhaled as calmly as she could.

"The problem is that I really like this guy—"

He smiled and interrupted her in mid-sentence and blurted out, "I know who - Chris! But why is that making you so sad?"

She forged a smile shook her head and said, "Yes he is a good guy and I care for him a whole lot... but there's another guy that I like even more," she lied.

The smile faded from E-man's face.

"You know he really likes you. It's gonna really hurt him when he finds out you're..."

"He's not going to find out anything because we're not going to tell him anything. This secret is between me and you, E-man," she said scooting closer to him.

"No one else, you know what I mean?" she said pulling her face a little closer in looking deep into his eyes.

E-man looked mesmerized and began nodding to whatever she had to say.

Meanwhile, the others were still outside engaged in an intense game of volleyball but by now Chris called a timeout because when Casey got the opportunity to hit the ball, she popped it hard to the far left way out of bounds. Chris agreed to run and get it. The other side was laughing at her, and she was slightly embarrassed by her lack of skills out on the court, but she was determined to hang in there. Even Bo laughed at her.

"Let me go get E-man before we lose this game while I'm at it," Chris said and ran off to the cabin.

"So, you aren't telling Chris anything?"

"I can't."

"Why not?"

"Because the guy I like is his friend." E-man gasped.

"Who? What friend?"

"You, E-man!" she lied convincingly.

E-man's eyes became ghostly wide. And before E-man could say a word she pushed him down on the bed and pounced him.

"E-man, it's you that I like, and I want you to be with me in Society 36."

Before he could do a thing, she planted a kiss on him that took his breath away. He was in utter shock. He shut his eyes tight and his body froze with his arms plastered by his sides.

Just then, Chris came jogging through the door, "Hey, E- man, we –" Chris began but stopped cold at the sight of him beneath Summer, on a bed no less.

E-man pushed her off of him and sat up. They both looked at Chris with shock and shame on their faces.

"It's not what you think," Summer said.

Without a word, Chris simply walked out and closed the door behind him.

"Look what you have done!" E-man said.

She broke down and started crying, and E-man left her and ran after Chris.

By the time E-man caught up to him, Chris had already gotten back into position on the court when E-man approached him. "Listen, Chris –"

Chris pushed him hard, and he almost fell to the ground.

"Hey man!" Bo shouted at him, "What's the problem?"

"No problem - let's play," Chris insisted, focused on the net.

E-man fixed his shirt and walked off the court. Summer had come out of the cabin holding a wad of tissue and ran up to E-man.

"Look, I don't think it's a good idea for you to be around me right now," he said to her.

"E-man, I'm so sorry! Please hear me out!" she begged.

They were standing near the tree that she was reading under earlier.

"She made me do it! Floo-Ellen planned the whole thing!"

"What?"

"She wants you E-man...bad too!" she wiped her eyes with her tissue.

"What's going on, Summer?" he asked folding his arms.

Sniffling, she began to tell him everything. "Floo-Ellen came to my cabin last night and told me that if I don't get you to join Society 36, she would kill Chris!"

"What?"

"So you see that's why I did all that!" she said looking for forgiveness in his eyes.

"Was she serious though, Summer?"

"YES!"

"We need to let Chris know," he said finally believing her story.

She sniffed and blew her nose again. "Well come on, let's go tell him!"

"Oh no, now wouldn't be a good time," he said looking back at Chris who was hitting the ball harder than ever.

E-man couldn't believe how easy it was to get caught up in a horrible misunderstanding like this.

"Summer, you need to tell him what you just told me."

"But you said now wasn't a good time."

"Uh, it's not for me, but you... you should be fine," he tried to reassure her.

She looked over at Chris and began to cry again.

"I'll just talk to him later," and she ran off.

Later on that day, everyone had gathered in the Mess Hall for lunch. All the camp counselors were sitting at their table in the back of the room, and people filled up the roundtables that covered the rest of the very large room. Ms. O'Dale, Trudy, and Jill passed out trays of food to everyone. Floo-Ellen whispered something in Bella's ear; she looked over at E-man, and after a moment, nodded her head yes.

"You know, they really played a good game," Bo said popping a potato chip in his mouth.

Everyone looked tired as though the sun drained every ounce of energy they had.

"We lost. Get over it" Leena said.

"I'm not mad. We just lost by one point."

"A loss is a loss whether by one point or thirty!" Leena teased.

"You're right. We woulda won, but it seemed some people had other things on their mind," he said looking over at Chris.

"Chris, what's wrong with you?" Casey asked.

"Nothing," he said cutting his eyes at E-man.

E-man looked nervous and felt guilty for no good reason at all, but he ignored the look and kept eating.

"That's a lie. I know you, and I definitely know when something's wrong," Casey kept pressing.

"Nothing Case, drop it," he said taking a bigger bite of his burger.

Alex looked back and forth at Chris and E-man suspiciously and wondered what was really going on. Bella walked up to E-man with a gentle smile on her face. Then. she squatted down to be face-to-face with him since he was seated.

"Floo-Ellen wants you to bring your tray and have lunch with her. She would like to ask you something."

"What does she want to ask me?"

"Not sure. You would have to go and see."

The others at the table were curious to know exactly what Floo-Ellen wanted with E-man.

"Okay," E-man said a little nervous.

Because of Summer, he had a pretty good idea what she wanted. He stood up, got his tray, and walked towards Floo-Ellen. When she saw him coming, she stood up and pulled Bella's chair out for him to sit in. E-man placed his tray on the table and took the offered seat. When Cleofus saw E-man pass his table heading for the counselors corner, more specifically to Floo-Ellen's spot, he stopped chewing and dropped his fork on his plate.

"What's he doing up there?" he said with little particles of food flying from his mouth.

The other members of The Total Eliminators turned to see what he was gawking over.

"That's the little wimp! What does she want with him?" another member asked.

"Thank you for joining me," Floo-Ellen said, taking her seat after E-man. "So how are you doing today?"

"I'm fine, thank you," he answered looking toward his tray.

"That's good. That's good. I'm just going to cut to the chase here, young man. I've been watching you for a while now, and you are very well mannered. You're never in trouble, and you follow directions. You're a very special boy, Emanuel. There's no doubt about that."

"Well, thank you for noticing."

"You don't have to thank me. I would like to thank you," she said focusing only on him.

"For what?" E-man asked somewhat firmly.

"For coming to camp this summer. For allowing me to have the honor of meeting you."

"Oh," E-man grunted feeling a little awkward.

*Why would she feel honored to meet me? I'm nobody special, I'm just*

*E-man.*

He looked out in the body of children and caught Cleofus' eye peering at him through his frowned up face. It was obvious he was languishing at the fact that Floo-Ellen was having lunch with E-man and never extended the invitation to him. Not even once.

E-man shot a smile at Cleofus which sent him spinning out of control. Fuming, he stood up and marched toward the back where they were sitting. The brightest, biggest smile ever was pulled across E-man's face now.

"Ms. Floo-Ellen! Why are you in the company of an—"

Floo-Ellen swiftly threw her hand up, an indication for Cleofus to shut his mouth. She turned and looked at him as if she would smash him like the annoying gnat he'd now become like.

"I don't recall you being invited over here. Leave."

Cleofus struggled to hold his tongue as he looked at E-man with the utmost disdain and disgust. Before he could turn to leave, Floo-Ellen spoke.

"Before you leave, I think an apology is due to Emanuel for the offense you were about to speak upon him."

Cleofus was aghast at the request. He couldn't say a word.

"Come on, SAY IT!" she demanded.

He looked at her, begging with his eyes to be dismissed from the pride washing assignment. He could not bear to apologize to E-man of all people. Floo-Ellen was growing impatient and gave him a piercing look and parted her lips to speak once again.

With her voice subdued this time, she insisted, "say it."

"Sorry," he said and stormed off to the nearest exit.

"Sorry about that," Floo-Ellen said looking sweetly at E-man.

"Not a problem," E-man said with a Kool-Aid smile.

"I can reassure you that he won't be a problem for you anymore."

"That's good," he said relieved.

"But back to what I was saying before we were rudely interrupted.

I think you are special and I would like for you to come and join my elite society."

"Society 36?"

"You've heard of it...good." Her eyes became beamy.

"Yeah, I heard it mentioned a couple times."

"Well, I would like for you to come aboard as a VIP member."

"I don't think so," E-man responded quickly washing the light from Floo-Ellen's face; her smile immediately faded.

"I was talking with Leena about it and we don't think it would be in our best interest," he explained.

"Emanuel, because you would be a VIP member, that would give you plenty of benefits. One of the benefits," she began explaining as she leaned over to whisper in his ear, "would make your cabin the winner of all the competitions! You guys would automatically receive the $20,000."

She leaned back and searched E-man's face for some sort of reaction. When she saw that there was none, she exaggerated some more.

She added, "The money would be rewarded to you personally and you would decide how it's divided, Emanuel." She said that low enough so that only he could hear.

E-man looked over at his table and knew they would agree with his decision.

"It's sounds tempting - real tempting. But I'm gonna have to pass this time."

Floo-Ellen was quietly furious and taken aback.

"Well, think about it. Hopefully, you'll change your mind," she said through a forged smile.

"Ok," E-man said and got up, took his tray, and went back to his table.

Everyone, except Chris, was curious about the short meeting and why E-man was the chosen one. E-man didn't mind at all. He sat down, and told them everything.

## Chapter Nineteen

## ⊗ OUCH!! ⊗

The last week of camp was approaching and Floo-Ellen was growing increasingly impatient with E-man.

"We will give him a day or so to change his mind. If he doesn't, then we will have to do it for him," Floo-Ellen had told Zanku.

"Just let me know when," he answered.

Later on in the day, the kids were outside playing by the water near the east bridge.

"Did you see him?" Bo asked laughing.

"Don't even go there, Bo," Leena demanded even though she knew there was no stopping him once he started joking on someone.

Meanwhile, Chris stood near the edge of the lake and gazed out over the water. He was not in the mood to do much talking to anyone. Leena, Jacks, and E-man were temporarily captivated by Bo's take on Cleofus' angry reaction to E-man's privileged position during lunch. Bo talked and laughed about it seemingly for hours mimicking Cleofus and contorting his face to match Cleofus'.

Bo laughed so hard that tears were rolling down his cheeks. The others could not help but laugh too as they watched Bo's antics and listened to him make fun of Cleofus. All of them were laughing hysterically at his rendition of the apology scene in particular.

"I won't do it!" Bo had repeated imitating Cleofus.

That is when they each took turns mocking Floo-Ellen's response. They were laughing uncontrollably when Jill walked up on them.

"You guys behaving over here?"

"Absolutely not!" Leena laughed.

Chris stood up and turned around when he heard Jill.

She chuckled, "You guys look like you're up to no good!"

"Nobody's plotting to do anything crazy or nothin'. We're just having a little fun," Jacks explained catching her breath from laughing so hard.

"What's up with you?" Leena asked.

"Came to see what Floo-Ellen wanted with E-man because that little display of affection was unusual for her."

"I know. Obviously, everyone didn't agree with it," Bo said.

"So what does she want?" she asked turning toward E-man.

"She wanted me to join society 36 as a VIP member."

"Really?" She looked off. *I wonder why she wants him to join as VIP? Hmm...* Jill took some steps back as if to make thinking room.

She placed her hands on her hips and stood still a moment obviously thinking deeply.

"We've been trying to figure that one out too," Leena said.

"Well, we need to keep an eye – AWWHHH!!" Jill cried suddenly.

Everyone looked to see what could possibly be the matter when they looked down and saw a hissing snake at her feet! Leena saw it and began jumping up and down and screaming to the top of her lungs. Now, everyone nearby was alarmed by the curdling scream. Jill started moving away from the snake but only made it a few feet before fainting onto the ground with a thud, at which time the snake struck out and bit her again!

Chris ran over towards the old canoe and grabbed one of the planks of wood from it. Jacks kept her eyes on the coiled, slithering snake and started moving back slowly. Bo grabbed Leena, who was still screaming, and tried to calm her. Chris cautiously approached the snake then began striking the snake repeatedly until it no longer squirmed. People gasped at the sight of Chris beating the snake to death.

Since the snake was no longer a threat, everyone rushed over to Jill to see if she was okay. She lay there barely moving. Bo and Chris picked her up and rushed her over to the infirmary. They burst through the door and startled Ms. Floyd, the camp nurse.

"What's wrong?"

"She got bit by a snake!"

"Oh, no! Lay her here," she directed them patting a bed over in the corner.

They laid her on the bed and stepped back to give Ms. Floyd the space needed to tend to Jill. First, she felt her forehead then her cheeks.

"She feels clammy."

Jill was sweating profusely and going in and out of consciousness.

"What kind of snake was it?"

"I don't know. It was red, yellow and black."

"Oh, no! That's a poisonous snake!" Ms. Floyd threw up her hands.

"My goodness. I don't know what I could possibly do for her then.

We are not prepared for an injury this serious here. This is just a small infirmary for cuts, bruises and upset stomachs. Just maybe we can tend to a child who is having a seizure or something but this? This is beyond our staff and supplies. She will have to be transported to the nearest hospital and hopefully before it's too late!"

"Someone run a get Ms. Lambert to see if she can call 911!"

E-man ran out to see if he could find her. Jacks said a silent prayer: *Oh, God. Please help Jill. Don't let her die. I know that Jesus already bore this kind of thing so that Jill would not have to die from it, that's one reason Jesus went to the cross and suffered and died. He did it for Jill. Please Lord, save her.*

When she was done, she waited to hear anything from God. Perhaps, He might want to say something too. And He did! He told her just what to do about the grim circumstance surrounding Jill. When she finished listening to God, she began walking over to Jill where she lay limp like a helpless soul. The nurse had placed a cool cloth on her forehead.

"All we can do is keep her comfortable until someone can get the help she needs or until she…"

"Excuse me," Jacks said as she made her way through the people that started to crowd the room.

As word got out about Jill's mishap, more and more campers came and crowded in and around. When she finally made her way to Jill's bed, she found that she was trembling and very pale. Jacks carefully moved in a little closer to her bed then leaned over and whispered in her ear.

"Jill, would you like for God to heal you right now?" Jill lifted her weak eyes, sweat streaming down her temples, and nodded her head yes.

"Okay, Jill, I am going to touch you right here and pray."

With that, Jacks laid her hand on the bite and closed her eyes and prayed silently. Some onlookers snickered, some cried, some quipped,

"Who does she think she is?"

Jill remained still awhile but soon felt a wave of energy flow through her body. Jacks even noticed her skin color returning slowly but surely. Within minutes, she was no longer weak or in pain. Ms. Floyd was astonished.

"Get her some water somebody!" Ms. Floyd bellowed, nervous.

Jill asked, "I need to sit up. May I please sit up?"

When she sat up, the first thing she wanted to do was ask questions and get answers. "How did you do that - that prayer thing?"

"I didn't. God did."

"No, for real," she said looking dumbfounded.

Ms. Lambert and E-man came barreling through the door.

"Oh dear! Are you okay?" Ms. Lambert asked. "Please move, MOVE! Everyone clear out!" She said shooing everyone that was in her

# Ouch!!

way.

E-man looked at her and knew that she'd been divinely healed. Jill sat reclined and didn't move a muscle even as Ms. Lambert came racing over, feeling awful that she was late. By now, Chris was also among the crowd of well wishers. When E-man looked over at Chris, the thankful smile for Jill's recovery faded away.

He stepped over to him and Chris looked ready to shove him again.

"She was gonna kill you Chris," he said, but not too loud.

Chris looked at him as if he was unfamiliar. E-man finally had his attention without being in the line of fire, so he continued.

"That's the reason Summer kissed me! She did it to save you!"

Hurt and insult washed over Chris' face.

"What are you talking about?" he asked uninterested really.

"Floo-Ellen," he looked around and lowered his voice some more,

"she threatened Summer and told her she would kill you if she didn't do it!"

Chris stood with his arms crossed but looking confused.

"Let's go outside. I'll explain everything" E-man told all he knew to Chris.

"I'm so sorry, E-man. Why didn't you tell me sooner?"

"Because I thought you would hit me again!"

"Oh, no!" Chris cried, "Summer...I completely ignored her earlier."

"I'm sure she understands, looking at the circumstances and all."

"Did you tell the others?"

"Not yet."

"Alright," he said panning the field in hopes of seeing Summer.

"Okay, I gotta go find her. I'd never forgive myself if I let our relationship end this way."

Chris took off for her cabin and knocked on the door. Tess opened it and gave him a nasty look.

"Yes?"

# Summer of Seven

"Is Summer here?"

"No."

"Do you know where she is?"

"I don't know. She said she was going for a walk," Tess said and before Chris could get another word out, the door was slamming in his face.

He ran over the playing fields looking for Summer. He went to the Mess Hall and the Assembly Hall, and still no Summer. He ran over to the water and went up and down the shore, and still no sign of her. Finally he ran toward the West Bridge near the camps entrance, and there on Rock Mountain sat Summer quietly weeping. Chris ran over to the rock and called her name. She looked up a bit startled and stared speechless at him as he stood at the bottom of the rock.

"Can I join you?"

She shook her head yes and began scooting over to make room for him. Chris climbed the big rock and sat beside her. He looked at her and wiped the tears from her eyes.

"E-man told me what happened," he started.

She blew her nose loudly before she spoke.

"Chris, I am so sorry. You know I would never do anything to hurt you. I was so upset because I knew you didn't understand what was going on, and I was hurting because I knew you were."

Chris shook his head as he remembered the feeling he got when he saw her kiss him. It was the same feeling one might have if he got hit by a car.

"You should have told me," Chris said.

"But Floo-Ellen said…"

"I don't care what she said. You should've come to me."

She started to cry again. "Chris I didn't know what to do! This lady is dangerous, and I don't know what I would do if she caused something bad to happen to you!"

"She was just bluffing!"

# Ouch!!

"No, she wasn't! Look what she did to me, Chris!" She lifted her shirt, and big ugly sores covered her stomach. She turned around so he could that they covered her back as well. She pulled up her jeans and saw that her legs were covered too! She looked at Chris and saw the shock on his face.

"What happened?"

"Floo-Ellen! She's torturing me!" she cried harder, "I can't eat. I can't sleep, and if I do get to sleep, I have terrible...terrible nightmares. I wake up screaming. It's embarrassing because my roommates are starting to complain. I just want it all to stop. I want to go home."

Chris held her tight in his arms, and she closed her eyes.

"I feel so safe here with you. Can you make it all stop?" she asked.

"I can't make it stop, Summer. Jesus can make it stop."

"But how?"

"Summer, you must repent, ask him to take this away, and believe he will."

She shook her head, "Ok."

"Just pray and asked him. It'll get better, I promise," he said and held her again.

## Chapter Twenty
## ⊗ POWER OF PRAYER ⊗

"Ouch! You didn't have to hit me that hard, Bo!" Leena screamed.

She wanted to charge him! Bo stood before her smiling, tossing the ball from one hand to the other.

"This is dodgeball, baby! You're out!"

Leena gave him a nasty look as she walked out of the middle of the circle. She made her way to the sidelines and watched the rest of the game with her arms folded.

"Get em', Chris!" Bo yelled.

Chris threw the ball at a boy from The Hard Hitters, but the boy was too fast. Chris missed him. While Bo was looking in one direction he threw the ball in the opposite direction, striking a girl sending her out.

"Gotcha!" Bo turned and winked at Leena, but she just shook her head at him.

As the game went on, Bo and Chris struck more and more people out. In the end only E-man, Jacks, and the little boy from The Hard Hitters remained in the game.

"Okay," Bo said tossing the ball up and down. "It's time to end this."

He looked over at Chris to see if he was ready to play hardball. Huffing pretty hard, Chris gave him a confirming look and wiped his sweaty forehead with his tee shirt. Bo threw the ball fast and hard at E-man smacking him with it. E-man was almost knocked off his feet.

"Man!" he complained under his breath, and made his way over to the sidelines where Leena was standing.

Floo-Ellen and Bella were staked out on the edge of the tennis court watching them play.

"Don't worry," Leena said noticing E-man's disappointment, "he got me too – so we'll get him later!" she said putting smiles on both their faces.

"Emanuel!" Floo-Ellen called from across the field.

E-man turned toward the sound of the voice calling his name and saw a smiling Floo-Ellen waving for him to come to her. E-man started towards her when Leena grabbed his arm.

She leaned over toward him and lowered her voice, "Stay away from her, I don't trust her."

He quickly turned away from Floo-Ellen and remained beside Leena. When Floo-Ellen saw this, she gasped and clinched her chest.

"Ah! I can't believe that little hussy would over step me."

"I saw that!" Bella said.

"Did you see her deliberately detain him?"

"Yep, sure did!" she said adding fuel to the fire.

Gritting her teeth, Floo-Ellen turned and walked towards the office ranting, "No one gets in my way! That's one problem that will be eliminated today!"

Bella marched behind her listening to every word Floo-Ellen blew out. Leena turned and peeked over her shoulder just in time to watch them storming away. She smiled and was satisfied that she had done the right thing in protecting E-man.

A couple hours later, everyone was seated in the Mess Hall for lunch.

"Who got the medallion today?" Alex asked.

"The Bully Dogs," Casey answered looking around for the food.

"I'm starving!"

"Me too!" Leena added.

"I wonder when's the next time we compete," Chris asked.

"Well, according to the number of teams competing, and the times that we have competed, I would say we will be up on Friday," Alex deduced.

"Every group needs a geek...we have Alex," Bo commented rudely.

Alex ignored him initially then said, "Because I was able to figure out a probable answer, where you could not that makes me...what you say? A geek? Hmm."

Chris played peacemaker and intercepted. "Guys, come on. Let's just eat and not get into anything here. Bo was just messing around as usual, Alex. You know Bo."

"I understand," Alex said, "he's just a little miffed that his strength lies in athletics, but he's not much on thinking. It's okay."

Bo was about to dive in for an argument. Instead, Trudy came from the back with a food cart and started passing out trays of food which diverted their attention. Applause filled the room.

"Guess we weren't the only ones hungry," Casey said happy for the food and the shutdown of an argument.

Floo-Ellen made her way into the kitchen as Ms. O'Dale was loading another cart with trays full of food. Floo-Ellen made herself busy and slid two trays off her cart.

"I'll take these two," she said and carried them over to the counter.

Ms. O'Dale frowned at the unusual request and kept a close eye on her. Floo-Ellen reached into her pocket and took out a small vile of green liquid. On the vile was pasted a small image of a skull and crossbones. She unscrewed the cap and poured the green substance all over one of the trays of food.

"And just what do you think you're doing?" Ms. O'Dale questioned sneaking up behind her like a quiet cat.

"Minding my business," she said calmly.

Floo-Ellen picked up the trays and pushed the door open with her foot. However, before she exited the kitchen completely she turned and looked at O'Dale and said, "And if you know what's good for you, you'll do the same." Then, she rolled on through the double doors leaving them swinging wide behind her.

Floo-Ellen teetered across the floor of the Mess Hall quickly making her way down the middle of the aisle in between tables. O'Dale peeked out of the small window in the kitchen to see where she was going with the contaminated food. O'Dale was very intimidated by Floo-Ellen, but she knew a child could be endangered because of her. All she knew to do was to clamp her eyes shut and pray real hard.

Floo-Ellen stopped over at 7-Alive's table and put the clean tray in front of E-man and the contaminated one in front of Leena as she peered over toward the kitchen to see if Ms. O'Dale was watching. Indeed she was, but she had jumped back out of sight when she saw Floo-Ellen turn and look her way.

"Oh, Lord!" she mumbled under her breath.

Trudy delivered food to everyone else at 7-Alive's table and had continued on to the next. The crew at the table was engaged in yet another confrontational conversation, this time about dodge ball.

"Now, Bo, you're not being fair," Jacks said.

Hearing the conversation but choosing not to engage, Leena pulled her plate in closer to her and picked up her fork ready to chow down. Her food was piping hot as steam rose from her plate.

"Okay, I'll admit, the little squirt was good - but I'm the king of dodgeball and if I were in the middle, I would've won!" Bo said.

Leena laughed and couldn't resist jumping in now.

"I don't know, Bo, he was pretty fast!"

Laughter rounded the table, and Bo crumpled his face.

"I'm the king, and I'll prove it to you!" he said as they continued laughing.

Leena started stirring up her noodles, and Floo-Ellen watched every move from the small window in the kitchen. Leena was smiling at Bo and wrapping the noodles around the end of her fork.

"Get over it, Bo. You can't win everything," she said.

"So, you're really upset that you weren't able to get that little boy out?" Casey asked.

"I'm not mad," Bo said in his defense. "It just fun and recreation, I mean, since my strength is in athletics and all," he said mocking Alex now.

Just as Leena opened her mouth to slurp some of her food, she remembered she needed to pray first. She dropped her fork back in the plate and clapped her hands together to pray.

"Forgive me, Lord, for getting ahead of myself. Thank you for this meal. Let it be nourishment for my body, to do your will, Lord. In Jesus name, Amen."

She opened her eyes and eagerly grabbed her eating utensil and took in the first fork full.

"Mmm… alfredo, my favorite!" she mumbled with a mouth full.

Floo-Ellen watched in delight smiling scornfully.

"Leena, everything is your favorite," Jacks joked.

"True," she said nodding her head, "I do have a lot of favorites."

Leena slurped up more noodles and the creamy sauce dripped from her lips a little which she quickly licked clean.

"This is good," Chris agreed slurping his up by the fork piles.

Taking another bite Leena nodded some more. It was as if all that mattered was the food. The table was alight with smacking, chewing, slurping, and very little conversation now. Floo-Ellen watched Leena carry on as if everything was fine; Leena and the others talked a little and ate a lot. But, Floo-Ellen was eager for the poison to kick in and do its job. It wasn't long before Leena cleaned her plate and looked around for seconds.

Grimaced, Floo-Ellen wondered how this could possibly be.

"That little bit should be out cold already. The counselors should be writing a letter to her parents by now telling them to come pick up her dead body!" she mumbled to herself.

She reached in her pocket and pulled the little bottle out again and examined it to make sure that she had used the right stuff. What's going on? Floo-Ellen thought because when she had used the concoction before, the person couldn't get down the second bite before falling over dead on the floor.

"Is it me, or was this the best lunch yet?" Leena commented sitting back in her chair rubbing her belly.

"Uhh… it's you, Leena," Bo said.

Chris sat frozen at the table for about 30 seconds stunned by yet another open vision.

"Oh my God! Did you guys see that?" he screeched.

"All we saw was you sitting there looking like you'd seen a ghost and not talking to us. You should have seen yourself, dude," Bo said.

"That's not the point," Casey inserted." You know this happens to him. Go ahead, Chris."

"See what?" Alex asked looking around, as did the others.

"The vision that just played right here, that's what!" Chris was making gestures with his hands trying to get the group to understand.

"No, but what did you see?"

"I saw Floo-Ellen poison Leena's food and deliver it to her. When Leena prayed I saw a green substance lift off of her plate and disappear into thin air! Then I saw Floo-Ellen waiting and watching from the window in the kitchen," Chris snapping his neck toward the kitchen real quick.

"And don't turn now…" he said lowering his voice and head, "… she's still looking!"

Leena closed her eyes and thanked the Lord for saving her life in more ways than one.

"I told you guys from the beginning about her," Leena said.

"I know – you were right," Alex admitted. "

"Okay, think about it. It's time to go home. Who tries to kill a kid?" Casey said.

"Floo-Ellen obviously!" Leena said clearly upset.

"Oh nooo! I'm calling my mom tonight," Bo said, and they all got up and left the Mess Hall.

Once they were back in the cabin, everyone sat down and tried to soak in the earlier event with Floo-Ellen. Not that didn't understand what was going on, it was just hard to believe that they would find themselves in this situation. Leena stared at the wall with an angry expression on her face. Bo went over to her and started rubbing her shoulders.

"Don't worry, Leena. Camp will be over soon and you can go home where it's safe," Bo said.

"And I would only have to worry about doing the dishes instead of worrying about someone trying to take my life," she added.

"I don't want to eat anything else that this camp serves," Casey said.

"I won't be," Leena said.

"You gotta eat," Jacks said.

Leena turned and gave her a nasty look.

"Maybe we can have Ms. Lambert personally prepare and deliver our food," Alex suggested.

"Yeah, or Ms. O'Dale since I'm in her good graces," Bo said. "I'll talk with her in the morning about the situation."

"That will be good," Alex said yawning.

Leena looked a little satisfied with their efforts.

"Alex you know yawning is contagious," Bo said yawning as well.

"Well let's take the hint and hit the sack," Chris said and they all laid down.

Hours later Chris lay in his bunk unable to sleep because his mind was filled with the goings-on of things happening all around him since he and Casey arrived at Camp Come Along.

"*This couldn't be what the therapist recommended,*" he thought to himself.

Tossing and turning a bit, he decided to sit up. He sat on the edge of his bed and looked out over his sleeping roommates then got the notion to go check on Casey. He felt like a true big brother as he gazed down at her peacefully sleeping. A surge of responsibility came over him as he gently reached out and stroked her hair.

*Wow,* he thought. *I actually see my mom's face, too. Yeah, Casey looks like her. I miss Mom. Wish I could call her right now. Not sure I like this place. I'm not seeing the benefit.* Chris' thoughts were running wild and his heart was growing tenderer, especially when it came to protecting his little sister.

Chris dabbed her cheek then stood up and walked over to the window to perhaps take in the bright moonlight. Folding his arms and settling into a stare at the moon, he listened to all the sounds of the night. Crickets were chirping loudly and he could hear bullfrogs bloating. He closed his eyes awhile and let the moon shine on his face.

*It would be cool if I could feel the moon,* he thought from behind his closed eye-lids. *The sun has heat…what would the moonlight feel like?*

Chris stood and thought and listened peacefully with his face skyward enjoying his moments of peace. Suddenly, he thought he heard something that clashed with the sound of the nature he was enjoying at that moment. He lifted his eyes open and saw the door of the Mess Hall opening and soon two men emerged from behind it. It was Scott and Herman looking around suspiciously and whispering to each other. Chris quickly left the window and darted over to Bo to wake him up.

"Get up man! Get dressed!" he whispered rather loudly then looked around to see if he'd disturbed anyone else in the cabin.

He especially did not want to awaken E-man and Casey. Bo jumped up already dressed because he'd fallen asleep in his clothes.

"Go look out the window," Chris said and went over to get Leena and Jacks up too.

"Hurry up!" he whispered. "They're on the move!"

The girls jumped up and everyone scrambled quietly. Chris opened the back door.

"They're headed towards the east bridge, I'll meet you guys at the last cabin," he said as he darted out behind the two men.

Scott and Herman were strolling along as if they were enjoying a walk in the park in broad daylight. Chris tried to make out what they were saying but couldn't get close enough without being detected, so he went to the last cabin and waited for Leena, Bo, and Jacks. The two men stopped at the foot of the bridge and carried on their conversation.

Scott mouthed something as he pointed to the far right.

*Where are they?* Chris wondered growing impatient but keeping his eyes on the two men who were now beginning to walk over the bridge. They started walking over the bridge and into the woods.

"Oh, no!" he whispered out loud.

Finally, Chris turned to find Bo, Jacks and Leena running toward him.

"What took so long?" Chris asked.

"Leena couldn't find her other shoe so Jacks gave her a pair of hers," Bo said.

"Good thing we wear the same size," Leena said nervously, sorry she had held everyone up.

"Alright," said Chris, "I saw them pointing over to the right so we should go that way instead."

"So, we aren't going to hide behind the canoe and wait for you guys?" Jacks asked.

"Since we don't have the walkie-talkies there's no need to split up," Chris said.

"You gals are coming with us!" Bo said pinching Leena's cheek.

"Stop," she said and slapped his hand down.

"Stop horsing around guys!" Jacks said. "We should get moving!"

They all ran over the bridge, one after the other, with Chris leading - the two girls in the middle and Bo following in the back. They ran until they entered the forest behind Scott and Herman.

"Come on!" Chris said running faster.

Scott and Herman were still lollygagging on the trail, so the kids were gaining on them faster than even they thought they would. Chris used his hand as a stop sign for Jacks, Bo, and Leena because he didn't want Scott and Herman to hear them. It worked. They hadn't heard a thing and were still strolling and talking, seemingly enjoying the night.

"We should go in pairs – less noise," Jacks said.

"Good idea," Chris agreed.

"Leena and I will go together," Bo said giving her a tight side hug.

Leena rolled her eyes.

"Ok, but remember this is serious. Don't let your fooling around get us caught," Chris said seriously.

"Have we ever been caught?" Bo asked.

"No," Chris said through gritted teeth.

"Ok, we won't start now," Bo assured him.

"Come on, Jacks. Bo, wait a couple of minutes before you guys come, and make sure you watch us for signs of trouble," Chris said.

"Oh, please believe I will be watching out for that!" Bo said curtly. Chris and Jacks jogged slowly to catch up with Herman and Scott, and when they were in eyesight, they walked. He looked back and saw that Bo and Leena were zigzagging through trees as if they were Bo Bond and Spy-girl.

Chris chuckled and wagged his head. "It's no use getting ticked off at him. Bo will be Bo," he said.

"What?" Jacks whispered.

Chris gave a head gesture toward the two for Jacks to see what he was talking about. She turned and looked.

"What are we going to do with them?" she asked.

"I don't know," Chris said and kept walking.

After a couple minutes of walking, he noticed that the two men had slowed and turned right which meant they were delving deeper into the forest. Chris and Jacks jumped behind the closest tree.

"Jacks, run back and get them so they won't bring any noise. I'll stay here and watch these guys," Chris instructed her.

"Ok. Be back in a minute," she agreed running back with her hand up so Bo and Leena could see her.

Chris watched them closely then soon noticed a large circle of grass that appeared to be cut out perfectly among the trees a couple of feet up from where he stood. He was careful to stay out of their sight, but he was close enough to make out what they were saying. He observed the circle was outlined by eight large trees, but no trees in the middle. The grass was strange looking - brown, perhaps even scorched. Chris heard them coming up behind him, and he turned around with his index finger pressed to his lips. They all watched and listened to Scott and Herman. Hopefully they would find out something.

Scott pulled an onyx-black skeleton key from his pocket.

"Now, Herman, this is the only key left," he said, "Watch closely."

Scott stood in the center of the circle and lifted the key. Herman watched as Scott jabbed the key into the ground and turned it. In no time at all, the ground began to quake a bit. Knowing what was going to happen next, Scott ran over to where Herman was on the edge on the circle and waited.

"Oh my goodness! What's going on," Leena whispered.

"I don't know," Chris said, his heart beginning to race.

"Everyone, just be calm," Jacks whispered.

"Oh, I'll just be calm as the earth cracks open and we all fall in!" Bo whispered.

Once the shaking stopped the ground split apart and opened outward, like two huge double doors, and a dim light peered through the large hole in the ground. The kids looked at each other in disbelief.

"WOW," Herman said in a deep lazy voice.

"Come on," I'll show you more," Scott said leading him to the dim light.

They walked down the steps and disappeared.

"Oh my God, oh my God, oh my God," Leena repeated framing her face with her now shaky hands.

"What is this place?" Bo asked.

"Your guess is as good as mine," Chris said.

"Oh my God, oh my God."

"Has anyone heard of anything like this happening at a camp before?" Jacks asked.

"I haven't," Chris said.

"Me either," Bo added.

"Oh my God. Oh, my God."

"One of us go over and take a peek?" Bo said. "It would be worth whatever trouble we get in just to find out what's down there. Any volunteers?"

"Oh, my goodness. Oh, my goodness."

"Shut up!" Jacks said louder than a whisper.

Leena quieted herself and gave Jacks a look to let her know that she was offended by her apparent insensitivity.

"I'm sorry, but you're making the situation worse with all that panicking," she tried to explain.

"Uh…" Bo said clearing his throat, "…any volunteers?"

"Why don't you go, Bo, since you're so curious," Jacks snapped.

"Hey, hey, hey," he said with his hands raised, "don't be mad at me."

"I'll run over and take a look," Chris said.

"Ok. Well, hurry before they come back," Leena said.

Just then Scott and Herman were coming back up the steps and up from the ground

"Man!" Bo whispered.

"And as long as it is locked," Scott said forcing the ground back closed, "no one, and I mean no one, can get in - not even if they dig."

Once the ground was back to a simple patch of land, Scott gave Herman the key.

"Make sure you guard this key with your life," Scott warned him.

"I will," Herman said shoving the key in his shirt pocket, and they started to walk off.

"You think we can get it opened?" Bo asked.

"You heard what he said," Chris said, "but it's worth a try."

"You're right. It's worth a try," Jacks said.

They watched as Scott and Herman walked away. They watched attentively for the men to get out of sight when, all of a sudden, Herman tripped on a rock and fell to the ground. Bo's eyes got wide.

"You alright man?" Scott asked helping him up.

"Yeah," he said brushing himself off. "Just didn't see that stupid rock."

He finished dusting himself off and kept walking.

"Did you guys see that?" Bo asked.

"Yeah the big oaf fell," Leena said.

"No…I mean, yes he fell, but the key fell out of his pocket!"

"Really?" Chris asked.

"Yes! You guys didn't see it?"

"I didn't see it," Jacks admitted as matter-of-factly.

"Ok, stay here, and I'll go and get it," Bo said leaping from behind the tree and running over to the place where he fell.

He searched for a second and retrieved the key. When he had the key in hand, he dashed behind a tree and looked out to make doubly sure the two men were completely out of sight, and then he held up the key for them to see it. They all ran out on to the patch of brown grass.

"Man, you got good eyes out here in the dark. I didn't even see it fall," Chris said gawking at the key.

"And I couldn't see the key when you held it up, either, but I knew you couldn't be lying," Leena said.

"Okay, well, let's test this thing out," Bo strongly suggested eying the key.

"Wait before you do," Jacks interrupted, "let me run out to the path and make sure they are nowhere near because remember the ground shakes."

"Good thinking," Chris concurred.

Jacks jogged over to the center pathway and cautiously looked around a tree that stood before the path. She didn't see anything so she stepped out onto the path and started jogging in the direction she saw them go – still no sign of them - so she went back to the circle where everyone was waiting.

"Looks like they're gone for real!" she confirmed.

Bo stuck the key into the ground, the way he had seen Scott demonstrate, and turned it. He stood up and anticipated the thrill of the tremor. In mere seconds, the ground began to shake, and they all ran out of the circle and watched as the ground opened once again like double doors.

Once it was open, the ground settled and a dim light came through. Standing side-by-side, they looked at each other.

"Well, come on. Let's see what's down there," Bo said walking towards the light.

They all kneeled down and looked in.

"Oh, my goodness!" Jacks said.

"What is all this stuff?" Chris asked wide-eyed.

The space inside was massively deep and wide. Beyond the light was everything they could imagine. There were luxurious cars, bars of gold and silver, diamonds, gems, jewels—all the luxuries of life as far as the eye could see! There were even houses and businesses. There were several sets of steps and different levels that separated all the goods.

"Why is all this stuff down here?" Bo asked.

Just then they all heard someone walk up behind them. Chris could hear his own heart beating in his throat, and his body immediately went numb.

"What are you guys doing?" Andrew asked.

They all turned around and were so relieved to see him.

"Andrew, because of you, I know how it feels to almost have a heart attack," Bo said.

Andrew kneeled down beside them and looked down into the ground at all the treasure. Bo noticed that his shoulder blades were so large that they made an imprint in his tee-shirt so he asked him, "Andrew what's up with your shoulder blades?"

"You know I work out. But we have more important things to deal with. You guys need to come with me, and fast – Herman just realized he no longer has the key!" Andrew said closing the ground.

He took the key from Bo and tossed it over to where Herman had fallen. They all jumped up and followed Andrew back to the bridge.

Once they were over the bridge on the way back to the cabin, Chris asked, "How did you know we were out there?"

"Yeah! And how did you know about the key and the open ground?" Bo asked.

They started to look at him suspiciously.

"Listen, if there is anyone here you can trust, it's me. I'll explain as soon as we get out of range of Scott and Herman," Andrew said pointing the way.

Chris turned around to see Scott and Herman in the distance running toward the patch of land.

"Quickly, back to your cabin, I'll explain everything later," Andrew said and took off.

"How did he know about everything?" Bo asked.

"Don't know," Chris said.

"You think he's with Floo-Ellen and her crew?" Leena asked.

"He did say this was his first year here," Bo said.

Chris shook his head as he opened the door. "Yeah it is his first year here."

"Maybe he works with them and feels bad about what they do so he tries to protect people from them," Bo guessed.

"Maybe," Chris said not knowing what to believe. "I'm going to bed, I know that."

Chapter Twenty-One

## ⊗ HIDE AND SEEK ⊗

The night was still as they stepped outside the Mess Hall and onto the damp ground as it had been raining. The camp grounds seemed deserted.

Bo stretched and let out a noisy yawn, "Ohhh that meal hit the spot."

"Yeah it was good tonight," Jacks added.

E-man and Casey skipped ahead to the cabin.

"I'm really looking forward to Friday," Leena said stepping over a rock.

"Last day of camp, and you're still alive," Chris said playfully.

"I know. I hope I can hang on until then," she said.

"Things are definitely crazy around here," Bo said.

They were almost to the cabin when Casey and E-man came running back to them.

"Look what we found in the cabin door," Casey said holding a black envelope.

Alex grabbed it and tore it open. The sheet of paper that was stuffed inside was white with a gray faded out skull and crossbones that watermarked the paper.

He read it aloud: HIDE AND SEEK IN THE DARK!! TONIGHT AT 11:00PM SHARP. STAFF VS. KIDS. IT IS MANDATORY THAT KIDS ARE OUT OF CABIN ON TIME! THE LAST PERSON STANDING WILL RECEIVE A MEDALLION FOR THEIR CABIN!

"See. Creepy. Who gets an invitation to play hide-n-seek, in the dark no less…late at night!" Leena said in disgust.

"I never got an invite to play hide-n-seek," Chris said.

"Why would they make it mandatory?" Alex questioned with a confused look on his face.

"Because it's required that we have fun the last couple days," Bo said excited about the challenge.

"I love hide and seek in the dark," Casey added.

"No, no, no! These people are crazy! They tried to kill Leena! Look at what Summer is going through and all that other weird stuff they got going on! Why all of a sudden they wanna play hide-n-seek in the dark?" Jacks quizzed.

"I agree with Jacks. We can't play. Who knows what evil plan they have laid out," Chris added.

Kids from other cabins were also outside reading the invitation from Society 36 trying to figure out if this was the grand finale of the competitions for the summer.

Alex looked at his watch. "Well, it's nine o'clock now."

"What are we going to do? Stay in our cabin while the rest of the camp plays?" Bo asked.

"We might be asking for trouble if we don't play since it's mandatory," Chris said.

"How about we show our faces at the beginning and then we come back here to the cabin one by one," E-man suggested.

"I like that idea," Alex said as the others agreed.

So they went into the cabin to relax before the game.

# Hide and Seek

When Cleofus read the invitation he saw this as an opportunity for revenge. An opportunity to pay Floo-Ellen back for embarrassing him in front of everyone --for not paying him any attention when he was trying so hard to please her!

*Why would she even pay that Emanuel one ounce of attention? He's not even in our Society! How dare she!* Cleofus balled up the invitation and became skew-jawed then made his way over to the Kidder Krew's cabin.

Kevin Kidder opened the door and realized he was grinding his teeth when he saw Cleofus.

Cleofus put his hands up in submission, "I'm not here to cause you any trouble. Just want to let you know two things: Sorry for popping your boat in the first competition. That was stupid of me," Cleofus said humbly.

Kevin said nothing. He just looked at him to finish so he could get back to what he was doing.

"I'm also here to warn you."

At that, the other members of the Kidder Krew came to the door and peeked around at Kevin's face as he was looking at Cleofus. They would respond according to Kevin's reactions, if there were any.

"Warn us about what?" Kevin finally spoke.

"Well, I felt really bad about the boat races and I don't want to see this cabin get cheated again."

The door opened all the way and more faces were visible, and Cleofus now saw every camper present. Now that he had their undivided attention, he continued. "I know that you guys have collected the most medallions so far – and congratulations for that – but there's no money!"

Shock reddened their faces.

"What?" Kevin said furious.

"The $20,000 doesn't exist! Floo-Ellen lied to us!"

"How do you know?" one boy asked.

"I'm in her secret society, and I'm very close with her," Cleofus confessed.

"Oh yeah, I've seen them together a lot," another boy said.

"We are very close," Cleofus confirmed before he continued. "Last night in our meeting, I overheard her telling Bella to make sure she's packed and ready. They're planning to leave two days before the end of camp. It didn't really upset me because my team won't win the money one way or the other," he said shrugging his shoulders. "But I did want to warn you."

He looked into all of their faces and saw that he was succeeding in his plan to get them to help him carry out his revenge on Floo-Ellen. Kevin Kidder was livid, and one of his teammates placed a hand on his shoulder to calm him down.

"I don't believe this!" Kevin shouted.

"I know. That's such a low down dirty thing to do," he said supposedly sympathetically.

Kevin balled up his fist and looked over the field.

"You guys received this invite, didn't you?" Cleofus said holding up the hide and seek invitation.

"Yeah, we did," Kevin answered.

"Listen, I have an idea! I know how we can get her back," he said letting himself inside the cabin and closing the door behind him.


Around nine forty-five p.m., a member from the Kidder Krew knocked on 7-Alive's cabin door. When Jacks opened it, he quickly let himself in.

"Did you guys receive the hide-and-seek letter?"

"Yeah," Chris said.

"Well, Kevin is calling his own mandatory meeting at ten o'clock and we're in cabin five, so make sure you guys are there in fifteen minutes," he said making his way out the door.

"Wait, what's this all about?" Chris asked.

"It's important. We'll explain everything when you get there. I have to let the other cabins know," he said rushing out.

"We'll be there," Bo said watching him run to the next cabin.

He closed the door, turned around, and said, "Wonder what this is all about."

"The Kidder Krew – throwing an emergency meeting - who knows," Alex said and shrugged his shoulders.

At ten o'clock p.m., they all went over to cabin five and saw that it was packed out with people from other cabins. Using his bed as a stage, Kevin stood up on it and made an anxious speech about why everyone was asked to come. The crowd was eager. They grew angry as he explained with passionate detail how Floo-Ellen and her crew lied to them about the money from the competition, according to Cleofus of course. The crowd roared with grumblings and complaints.

"Okay, alright –" he said trying to quiet them down. One kid from the crowd said, "Let's egg them while they're counting!"

"All in favor of egging Floo-Ellen and her crew, raise your hand," Kevin said.

Almost every hand went up.

"We can also throw balloons filled with milk!" someone else yelled.

"Milk balloons and egging it is!" Kevin shouted with his fist in the air.

"Now how do we get this stuff from the kitchen?"

"I can get the keys from Ms. O'Dale," Bo said with his hand raised.

He knew that he made a special impression on her when he did chores for her that day.

"Wow," Leena mumbled under her breath.

"Listen up, everyone. This is the plan," Kevin shouted from his makeshift podium. "Bo and I are gonna go and get the eggs and milk. Everyone else, go back to your cabins, and we'll deliver them to your cabins through the side door. When eleven o'clock comes and they put on their blindfolds to start counting, everyone will throw the eggs and the balloons at them when I give the signal. Then, run for your lives! With all the chaos going on they will never know who did it."

The kids looked excited about their new plot to get back at Floo-Ellen. After the plan was laid out, everyone went back to their cabins.

# Summer of Seven

Fifteen minutes after 7-Alive got back to their cabin, they heard a knock at the side door. Jacks ran over to get it. Kevin and Bo were standing there with 12 cartons of eggs.

Kevin had a mischievous smile on his face. "How many you guys need?"

Jacks looked to see if anyone wanted any, but nobody responded. Then she turned and gave Kevin a warm smile. "We're gonna pass on the very tempting offer."

"Suit yourselves," he said. "I think you guys are making a big mistake," he said as he went off to the next cabin.

At eleven o'clock the lake brought in a cool breeze, and the kids walked out of their cabins dressed in all black, and met everyone in the middle of the field near the big rock. All ten of the staff members were standing shoulder-to-shoulder in front of the rock with their flashlights behind their backs. Zanku had an untrusting smirk on his face that made a few campers uncomfortable. The Kidder Krew and their followers had small bags on their backs, and some had pouches around their waist full of eggs and milk balloons. They were walking gingerly as not to make a wrong move in fear of breaking or busting one.

"This is gonna be good," Bo whispered in Chris' ear.

"Very," he chuckled.

"I would like to thank everyone for being on time," Floo-Ellen said taking out a hand full of blindfolds out of her pocket, taking one and passing the others down.

"These are the rules: No hiding in the water. No hiding in the cabins. We all have flashlights and if you are spotted and you get flashed then you are caught. You are to report to the base immediately, which is this rock. Any questions?" Floo-Ellen asked looking around.

Most everyone agreed with a nod, but a few from the crowd sang out in disagreement. But they were ignored.

"Alright, blindfolds on, and we are counting to 35," Floo-Ellen said tying the blindfold to her face, as did the rest of the staff.

"Remember," Kevin whispered, making facial gestures, "only Floo-Ellen and her crew!"

The active participants nodded in agreement.

"Ok...1!... 2!... 3!...4!...5!"

"NOW!" Kevin said taking the first egg and throwing it right at Floo-Ellen's mouth. The egg broke on her tooth and the yoke slowly slid down her lip and chin. Before she realized what happened, everyone was throwing eggs at her and her precious Zanku, Scott and Herman. The girls that were participating were happy to throw theirs at Bella. Bo was pointing and laughing so hard that Chris had to help him up. A milk balloon burst on the side of Zanku's head drenching the side of his face and shirt in milk. The eggs and milk were coming so fast they didn't have time to take off the blindfolds. Instinctively, they shielded their faces with their hands and arms instead of going for the blindfolds. Alex was standing on the sidelines stunned by it all. For that one moment he really wished he was an adult and away from this place.

Leena and Jacks were laughing and walking backward out of the crowd. When the last egg was thrown everyone turned laughing, screaming, and running for dear life. Floo-Ellen's mouth was still open when she snatched off her blindfold and looked around to see exactly what had just attacked them. Furious, Zanku snatched his blindfold off, and his fists were balled tight. He was breathing so hard, his nostrils flared and fluttered with every hard breath and pant. Without saying much, Floo-Ellen and her crew ran out looking for the culprits. They were livid and out of control.

"YOU FILTHY BRATS WILL PAY!" Floo-Ellen spat.

Campers were laughing and running in every direction. It was total chaos! Alex was leaning on the rock trying to steer clear of all the mayhem when Andrew came up behind him slightly out of breath.

"There is danger here and we must flee. I have E-man, Jacks, and Casey hiding over by the west bridge. Leena is grabbing Bo and Chris.

# Summer of Seven

Come quickly!"

Alex ran with Andrew to the west bridge and ducked down with everyone else once he got there. Two minutes later, Chris, Bo, and Leena came across the bridge and saw everyone crouched down.

"Shhh...quietly, follow me," Andrew instructed them taking off running low to the ground.

The kids followed Andrew across the parking lot. They all ran quietly into the night. The only sound you could hear were the crickets chirping and the stony asphalt crunching beneath their sneakers.

Chris caught up with Andrew and asked, "What's going on? Where are we going?"

"I...will explain... everything... once... we get to safety," Andrew said between huffs of breath.

"But why do you think we're in danger?"

"HEY!" they heard a loud deep voice shout from behind.

They turned to see Scott, Herman, and Zanku on the south bridge with flashlights pointed at them.

"Stop right there!" Herman spat; but everyone ran faster.

When Casey turned around and saw they were being chased she began to squeal, but Chris grabbed her hand and kept going faster.

"Don't look back! Just keep going," Andrew shouted.

About half a mile away from camp on the left of the roadway, they came up upon an old broken down church that was sitting on an abandoned piece of land. The white paint had cracked and faded. It looked like no one had been there in ages. Many of the wood planks hung out of place, and there were countless holes in the roof. The place was overgrown with brown weeds and grass. The shrubbery was thick and untamed. Andrew ran up on the wooden steps that led into the church and pulled the big heavy door open. The top hinge broke with a loud screech and the door almost fell off.

"Come on! Hurry!" he said motioning for them to come in while he held the door up with his back.

# Hide and Seek

He looked up and saw Zanku and Scott were only seconds away from them with Herman lagging behind. When the last child entered the church, he let the door go and it hung to the side with the bottom hinge holding it just above the ground. The air inside the church was fusty. The smell of rotting wood and mildew was smothering. The kids faces were so frowned up they looked like they all had mouths full of lemon juice. Leena held her shirt over her mouth and nose.

"Someone tore this place up," Chris said following behind Andrew trying not to step on the broken glass that was splattered on the floor.

The place looked like a tornado had ripped through it. Some of the pews were turned upside down, and the back was broken off of one. The colorful stained glass windows, that once upon a time displayed pretty pictures, were all broken or cracked. As they made their way through the church, they heard the floorboards creaking as if they ached. On the floor, in front of the podium, laid an old Bible. The pages were brown and curled; it looked as though it had been soaked and baked in the hot sun and rain over the years.

"Hurry this way," Andrew said leading them through the back door.

When he opened the door to the back and let everyone out, they sunk thigh high into wild grass and shrubs.

The front door started to creak loudly and Andrew could see Zanku's legs and arms appearing through the slight opening. Zanku was too close now! They swiftly went out the back and through all the overgrown grass and shrubs. Andrew quickly guided them to a small pond not far from the church.

"Now what?" Bo asked looking at the water and then back at the door.

Everyone was starting to panic.

"You must follow me into the bottom of this pond. Don't worry if you can't swim," he said looking at Leena. "You will be fine."

He dove into water and started to swim to the bottom. Chris

jumped first, then Casey and E-man, Alex and Jacks, but Leena hesitated.

"Come on Leena. I got ya," Bo said grabbing her waist and jumping in with her curled in his arm.

As soon as Leena and Bo jumped in Zanku and the others came bursting through the door. Once they were under water Leena panicked and grabbed Bo's neck almost choking him. Her eyes were closed and her cheeks were inflated like a blowfish. They swam all the way to the bottom of the pond and met up with the others who had arrived just before them. Everyone was in mid-float over the pond floor and watching Andrew who was standing flatfooted and firm on the floor like a watchful guard.

He knelt down, balled his fist tightly and slammed it against the pond floor with a tremendous splat! The ground began to shake and the water became turbulent. The floor of the pond tore open as if an earthquake was occurring. As the floor widened brilliant beams of light shot up through the crack - light so bright and awe-striking it could only be compared to morning sunlight.

Chris was mesmerized as were all the others. No one could hide their expressions, and no one could explain how they felt.

Andrew motioned for them to follow him along the beams of light further still beyond where they had already gone. Once they were all inside the light, the ground closed up after them.

*Chapter Twenty-Two*

# ⊗ THE HANGOUT ⊗

The crew swam through an underwater cave constructed of pure crystal rocks and stones and waded awhile. Iridescent beams of light crisscrossed the cave bouncing from one crystal wall to the other. The children's eyes were alight with wonder as to how such splendor could engulf an underwater cave.

Sun-rays from a heavenly canopy shot straight through the cave and seemingly nicked and bounced off the edges of the jagged crystals that made up the walls of the cave. It was breathtaking!

Jacks pointed wildly to the bottom as if to say, "Look!" Pumping her arm through the clear waters she noticed the floor beneath the water was carpeted with shimmer, twinkling noticeably through a translucent sheaf of sort.

Andrew threw his head back and laughed at the innocence of the children as they all folded their heads downward to see what all the excitement was about. Their eyes widened as they beheld the most magnificent ocean floor imaginable. The floor of the body of water they waded in was speckled with every kind of diamond and natural jewel known and unknown to man. As they peered through the moving waters, lights twinkled in their eyes; hues of periwinkle blue, sea foam green, star bright gold, pleasant pink, royal purple and bronzes lit up their unsuspecting faces. Andrew turned and smiled as he watched them take in their surroundings.

"Breathe!" he shouted muffled by bubbles and the water.

Chris sloshed his head about trying to find Casey. He needed to know how she was making it under water this long without panicking.

When he made eye contact with her, he mouthed to her, "Just breathe normally, Case," then used himself as an example.

When he turned to find E-man, he found him with his lips puckered and his cheeks blown up to capacity. He looked really funny, and Chris used the last of his breath to laugh at him. Afraid, he frantically looked to Andrew who quickly reassured him the same as he had just told Casey.

"Just breathe normally," Andrew said mouthing and motioning.

Chris followed his lead and soon found that breathing under these obviously special waters were just the same as breathing air on land. Andrew went to each of the seven children, one by one, to sure up breathing lessons because their journey had just begun, and he didn't want anyone passing out on him before he was able to get them to the destination. Once they each realized the ease of breathing in the special water they learned to smile and even laugh a little without losing all their breath. They were overjoyed.

Bo felt at ease at last and began doing a swim dance, mouthing, "I'm a fish, y'all! I'm a fish!" causing a round of watery laughter.

Andrew gave them the sign that it was time get serious now, and they followed him further. They followed Andrew out of the cave and into the clear lake. Andrew seemed to swim like a creature who lived under the waters. He zoomed away beyond them and swam up to the top and broke through the surface.

"Whew, just as I was getting used to breathing under here, we're about to get hit with new air," Bo mouthed bracing himself for the surface.

# The Hangout

Bo floated, balancing on extended arms, with a curious look on his face as he was heading for the surface. Chris turned to him as if to answer his wordless question and shrugged his shoulders.

Leena came up behind Bo and motioned for them both to catch up with Andrew because he was already at the surface. So they swam faster and soon broke the surface as well. Once Chris reached the surface he gasped taking in gulps of air and breathing out hard fighting to get his rhythm of breathing back.

"You don't have to fight for it, Chris," Andrew told him.

"Just breathe." He wiped the water off of his face and out of his eyes and looked around as he floated on the surface of the water.

One after the other, each one emerged from the water and lost no time turning their small hands into squeegees to clear their eyes and faces. When Leena popped up, she smoothed her soaked hair back from her forehead and was surprised by something floating next to her practically touching her shoulders. In fact, as she looked out, there were hundreds of them spotting the surface as far as she could see; oversized golden lily pads were everywhere.

Casey floated backward on the surface giggling and singing. She floated between lily pads running her finger along each surface. "They can't catch us now!"

"Look at this place!" Jacks said as water trickled down her face and dripped from her long lashes.

"What is this place?" Alex asked scrunching his eyes in the absence of his eyeglasses and patting around for them.

"You won't be needing those here," Andrew said with a smile.

"Welcome to the Angels' Hangout," Andrew announced coolly, extending a guiding arm. The children were speechless and awestruck. As they slowly eyed the place, no detail escaped them.

Tremendous white chain mountains spread out against a rich, blue sky along the horizon. They gawked at the strangely beautiful flowers which smelled unfamiliar and mostly looked that way too.

"My grandmother has more flowers in her yard than I've seen anywhere, and I've been to a million garden exhibits with her and my mom, and I've still never seen or smelled any flowers like these before," Alex explained.

Even the grass was greener and fuller than the usual as it flowed like an endless field before their eyes.

"Angels'… Hangout?" Alex repeated a bit confused.

"Yes. Follow me and I'll explain," he said before he shot off like a rocket to dry wondrous land.

Andrew got out of the water and stood barefoot in the perfectly manicured grass with no shirt on, and his arms were folded waiting for the rest of them to get out of the water.

"Look at the mountains!" Casey said practically screaming.

"Andrew, what's going on? What is this Angels' Hangout? Where are we?" Jacks asked ringing her ponytail out.

"The Angels' Hangout is where we angels come to chill out."

"We?" Bo repeated.

"Angels?" Chris said.

"Yes… we angels," he emphasized flexing his chest and rolling his shoulders as if he was loosening something.

The kids looked at him waiting for further explanation when suddenly Andrew erected his back and squared his shoulders releasing gigantic, white feathered wings that spread out from behind him and out to his sides. They spanned so wide all of the children could have shelter in them.

Frozen, the children looked on in disbelief not knowing if they should be afraid or happy as Andrew was now glowing before them like a light in a golden hue. Each child was mesmerized by some detail of Andrew's reveal.

"Look!" Alex cried pointing to Andrew's head.

Just as each one lifted their heads to see what could be so alarming, they saw what could only be described as a halo circling the top of his head like a weightless crown.

"You're an angel?" Chris asked in disbelief, his forehead lumpy from confusion.

"Yep," he said slowly nodding, "that *seems* to be the verdict."

"So, that's how you knew about the key and the fire," Bo blurted out as the light bulb came on in his head.

Andrew nodded.

E-man stood speechless, his eyebrows raised practically to his hairline. "*No, no,*" E-man kept repeating softly to his self.

Leena dropped her face into her hands shaking her head. "I must be dreaming, I mean... this can't be *real!*"

"It is my dear," Andrew assured her.

"So—this Angels' Hangout—where is it located exactly?" Alex asked nosing around.

"Next door to Heaven. Actually, we are connected. So, look at this place as an extension of Heaven," he explained.

"So we're in Heaven?" Casey asked.

"Noooo. Heaven is a much, much more established place than this. This is only the hangout, sort of like the playground for us angels."

His halo glowed brighter suddenly and Andrew averted his attention from the children to speak into the halo.

"We'll be there in about ten minutes," he said.

When he was done talking to it, he turned back to the children as the halo hovered normally again.

"What was that all about?" Chris asked.

"I'll explain later. We gotta go. I have some special friends I think you guys would find interesting. So grab a lily pad," he said walking over to the water.

"What are the lily pads for?" Alex asked reaching for one.

"Transportation!"

Andrew picked up his lily pad and at his touch, it adjusted in size to fit him perfectly.

"You want to keep your lily pad because this is how you're gonna get around here," he said.

"Let me show you how it works," he added snapping it in the wind like a towel fresh out of the dryer and laying it on the grass.

"When you put them on the ground they expand. See?"

The lily pad expanded to the size of a large cushion, then he sat down on top of it Indian style.

"Depending on how big or small you are will determine how the lily pad will adjust to you."

Everyone grabbed a lily pad and crouched down to sit on them. Crossing their legs and gripping the edges, they were ready and set to do whatever Andrew said.

"We're ready!" Casey called out excited—for what, she was not sure.

"Once you sit down," he continued, grabbing the stem of the lily pad. "This is what controls the lily, when you pull it up, you fly!" He said taking off into the sky. ZOOM!

They all looked up at him in trembling amazement.

"When you push it down, you're going down," he said landing slowly but not touching the ground.

He gave them one last bit of instruction.

"It's real simple. When you want to go forward, push it out. When you want to go back, then pull it back - just like a joy stick. And this right here," he said pointing to the tip of the stem, "When you firmly press your thumb against the stem, you will go in whatever direction faster!"

"Flying through the sky on golden lily pads! How cool is that!" Bo exclaimed.

The crew of seven fearlessly tested their lily pads out. The girls and E-man took off slowly, making sure they would not mess up or fall back down to the ground. Chris and Bo zipped all over the place with Andrew, like they were professionals at it. Alex carefully shifted his lily stem back and he ended up floating over the lake carefully to keep his balance.

# The Hangout

For about five minutes the kids were testing out their new rides trying to get the hang of it. Casey had her thumb firmly pressed on the accelerator, and screaming as she shot straight into the air.

"Be careful!" Chris shouted to her, keeping an eye on her.

He'd hoped like crazy she would not have a mishap. Andrew got a kick out of seeing Chris in his protective big brother roll, as told by his raucous laughter.

"Oh, yeah, don't worry about falling, because if you do the ground will catch you."

"Catch you? I know this is the coolest place ever, but I doubt the ground can catch anyone, really," Chris argued.

"Well, young mister Chris, the ground actually does cushion falls that could be otherwise dangerous, because the soil is feather soft, and very giving. So your body is safe and cannot break or be hurt in any way, even if you don't have your new bodies yet."

"New bodies?"

"Here at the hangout you won't have your new bodies, but the problems that you currently have now won't exist either. That's why I told Alex he wouldn't need his glasses here."

Turning to E-man, he said, "You don't have to worry about having an asthma attack here, so you won't be needing that inhaler."

The rest of the seven glided in closer to listen to what Andrew was saying to the others.

"So what are our bodies, and when will we get them?" Casey eagerly asked.

"You get your new body when this body dies. The new body will be immortal, it will never be destroyed, and it will never die. That's why it is so very important that when you die for real, you go to Heaven because, if you go to hell – this new body won't die there either, it will live forever and ever and ever, even in the fire."

Everyone sat dumb for a while after hearing such an explanation.

"Well, kids, we will continue this most interesting conversation later," he said noising the silence.

"We mustn't keep our friends waiting."

"What friends?" Jacks asked.

"I'm about to show you," he said with a happy smirk. "Follow me!"

With his wings spread wide, Andrew lifted off and turned towards the clouds high into the sky. The kids all followed behind him on their golden lily pads with wide smiles on their faces, and hair waving in the wind.

As everyone reached equal heights in the sky, Andrew yelled,

"THIS IS ONE OF MY FAVORITE SPOTS! YOU GUYS WILL LOVE IT!"

With his eyes squinted Alex took deep breaths inhaling the crisp clean air; and Leena lifted her face to the sun throwing her damp hair back. In no time, the warmth had dried back to normal; Bo was enjoying the ride as if he was at an amusement park, weaving in and out between everyone teasing them, telling them how slow they were.

Chris caught up to him, "Who are you calling slow?"

This set off a race through the sky! The two of them started to race flying through the sky at top speed. They zipped so fast they found themselves on Andrew's heels pretty quickly.

Once they were up in the clouds, Andrew turned around, wings slowly flapping, as a sign for the kids to slow down.

"This is it! The Clouds!" he said landing on one and reclining with his hand behind his head.

The kids floated and watched as he demonstrated the ease and freedom of resting on a cloud.

"Now the clouds on earth — "Alex began.

"Don't even think about it!" Andrew interrupted. "You will fall straight through them; even though they look pretty thick at times - don't be fooled. These clouds are different, you won't fall through. This is where I come to get away…when I just want to relax or talk to someone."

He stretched out his arms and closed his eyes.

# The Hangout

"Can we try?" Casey asked.

He sat up, "Of course. That's why I brought you up here."

The seven landed their lily pads on the enormous cloud right next to the small one Andrew was reclined on. The kids were fascinated. Leena slid off of her lily pad and stepped onto the cloud and immediately started bouncing up and down.

"It's so fluffy…" she commented like a happy two year-old.

Silky, too!" Jacks added.

"I still think I'm dreaming," Leena said bouncing higher and freer.

Bo was doing back flips while Jacks knelt down and brushed her fingers across the surface of the cloud as if she were trying to scrape some into the cup of her hand. She pressed her thumb and forefingers together hoping to get a feel of the cloudy substance, but nothing. Only air. No texture at all! "It doesn't seem real!"

Alex steered his pad onto a separate cloud and cautiously stepped off.

"This is completely amazing!" he said with a seemingly thicker British accent than usual. Casey and E-man went over to the edge of the cloud and hung themselves over looking down below.

"This place is beyond beautiful!" Casey said.

Chris happened to turn and notice Casey's stance and yelled,

"Casey come away from the edge before you fall!"

"I'm not gonna fall – stop treating me like a baby," Casey shot back.

"Don't worry Chris she can't get hurt here, everything will be fine," Andrew encouraged him.

Right then his halo began glowing again, and he pulled it down and held it in front of his face.

"We're all here… you're on the way?" Andrew stood up and looked off into the sky and the kids' curiosity was stirred.

"Our friends are on the way," he told them.

"Just who are these friends that we've never met?" Chris inquired.

"These are friends I know you would love meet."

"But who are they? Where are they coming from?"

"If I told you their names you still wouldn't know who they are, he said looking off into the distance expecting them any second now.

"Look!" Alex said pointing upward. In the distance there were six figures descending towards them.

"Look, they're coming," E-man said pointing, too.

As the figures got closer they could see that they were five angels in an arched formation around another much larger angel which soared underneath the five. They were coming down fast.

"Yes, there they are," Andrew agreed, smiling brightly.

"Leena," Bo whispered, "Close your mouth."

The angels settled down gracefully on the cloud and peered into the children's faces; the angels faces illumed with peace and joy that the children's hearts were immediately impressed by. As the small angel host stood before the seven, the radiance that beamed brightly from them lit up the faces of the seven as they gawked with mouths wide open.

The angels wore brown leather sandals and long loose garments of white laced in gold roping. They also wore gold ropes as belts around their slender waists and each one of them had different colored jewels that hung from the tips of their belts.

"These are the angels I wanted you to meet," Andrew said. "These are your guardian angels. The ones that watch over you on earth."

"Oh my! Are you serious?" Leena asked.

"No way!" Jacks said shaking her head in disbelief.

"Way," Andrew responded. "Alex this is Fiorra and she is your angel."

Fiorra stepped forward; she had long brunette hair, and big bright blue eyes.

"Boy do I have some questions for you," Alex said standing with his arms folded.

"How did I know that?" she smiled tenderly and walked toward him.

"Casey, Zeth is your guardian angel."

"Uh…hi," she said nervously wringing her hands.

"Hello, Casey," he gave her a warm smile, and took her by the hand.

"This is Bruno," Andrew said looking up at him. "He is E-man's angel."

Bruno was 10 feet tall and built like a linebacker and his wingspan was at least three feet wider than the others.

"I'm not trying to be nosey, but why is E-man's angel so…huge?" Leena asked.

Bruno spoke in a baritone voice and answered her saying, "Because God has a great calling on E-man's life, and thousands of souls are attached to him. You won't believe how many times evil forces have tried to kill him. So that's why I, and others are assigned to him. When you're fighting off that many demons," he said flexing his muscles, "size helps."

"A calling…on *my* life?" E-man asked, not so sure if he believed what the angel had just said.

"Yes," Andrew emphasized.

"There must be some mistake."

The other kids looked back at his small fragile body and secretly agreed with him.

"God does not make mistakes E-man. Many are called, but few are chosen and you're one of the chosen," Andrew corrected him.

"Come, E-man, it is imperative that I tell you some things," Bruno said scooping E-man up and carrying him away to a separate cloud.

Andrew continued introducing the rest to their angels.

"Bo, this is Marianna, and she has been your guardian angel since you were…how old was he?" He asked turning to Marianna.

"Since you were four. Your angel before me was reassigned and I've been with you ever since. It is really good to be able to shake your hand after knowing you for so long," she said embracing his hand and shaking it ever so gently.

"Good to meet you too, looks like you've known me a lot longer than I've known you," Bo responded tickling the angel into some laughter.

"Bo you keep me laughing, I like being assigned to you, come, let's sit down together," she said and they sat down.

"Alright, Jacks, Alakin is your guardian angel," Andrew introduced them and they walked away smiling.

"I'm very impressed at your ability to recognize and use your precious gift of healing," her angel told her.

Jacks blushed and thanked him. Alakin's face radiated through a flawless complexion on a perfectly chiseled face. He took her hand and led her over to the edge of the cloud where they sat down to talk, swinging their feet over the edge like two kids in a big chair.

"And, last but not least, we have Carleea here. Leena this is your guardian angel."

Leena was thrilled speechless for a minute with a smile fixed on her face. "You're beautiful," Leena said smiling at the angel.

Carleea's long golden baby doll curls delicately graced her shoulders, and her rose lips curled into a soft smile. "Give glory to God, for he created me," she said sitting down beside her. We have a lot to talk about Ms. Leena. Come let's step over here."

Very gently Carleea put her arm around Leena's shoulder and walked off.

Chris was finally getting excited until he realized that all the angels were assigned to someone with the exception of him. He looked around wondering where his was or if he had one at all. Chris stood up and respectfully confronted Andrew.

"Where is my guardian angel?" Andrew's shoulders shook and bounced as he tried not to let out a belly laugh.

"I am your guardian angel, Chris."

"What? All this time?"

"Yes sir. Sorry to keep it from you, some things are better off unknown until the proper time. Come on with me," he said walking back to his small cloud.

Chris followed. He heard is sister saying to her angel, "I don't wanna go back, I want to stay here with you!" Her angel had responded to her softly, "If you live your life right on earth you will be here with God and myself ...forever."

"So, Fiorra, tell me this, how many people do you estimate will get into Heaven?" Alex asked.

"I don't know that answer Alex. It is not revealed to me," she said.

"Well, I think about 20,000 will get in."

"How did you come up with that number?"

"Well, God, who is an unchanging God, lead 600,000 of his people through the wilderness and only two were delivered and made it to the promise land. Now, if we use that formula currently, then if there is roughly 6 billion people in the world today, then about 20,000 people should get in Heaven based on the law of math," Alex deduced.

"God is greater than math, Alex, some things aren't meant to be known."

Leena was lying back on her elbows, and her legs were relaxed, extended and crossed at the ankles.

"So how big is this place?"

"The Angels' Hangout is about the size of Texas."

"Wow! What about Heaven?"

"The New Jerusalem...or Heaven has four sides like a square. Each side is 14,000 miles long. So, to put it in context of how big...it would stretch around half the globe," Carleea said.

"Wow!" Leena said.

"Got a question for you Andrew," Chris said with his face balled up.

"I'm all ears."

"When I first got to camp and Cleofus came up behind me, why didn't you help me?"

"Chris I'm your guardian angel, not your bodyguard. Besides our protection is mostly spiritual."

"What does that mean?"

"That means we protect you from things you can't see like demons and evil plans against you…that type of stuff."

The kids spent over three hours talking with their guardian angels sitting, standing and reclining on plush, white clouds. They asked every question imaginable about themselves, their families, the world and Heaven. Andrew moved into their social time to round everyone up.

"We need to all get moving now."

"Andrew, if you don't mind I would like to stay here and talk with my angel a little longer," Alex said.

"If it's fine with Fiorra it's fine with me." Fiorra looked at Andrew and gently nodded her head yes.

The others gave hugs and thanks to their angel, and went over to Andrew with their lily pads ready to go.

"Follow me," he said taking off from the cloud and zooming off toward the Heavens.

The children flew behind him on their lily pads better drivers than they were before. They flew passed the chain mountains and over a concentrated group of unrecognizable fruit trees. They flew for miles passing raging waterfalls and breathtaking greenery, then Andrew yelled,

"Look! There it is," he said pointing.

In midair, just above the water below was a waterfall rainbow that was in the shape of a roller coaster! The water was constantly flowing on the rainbow roller coaster and recycling back into the huge rainbow lake that fed the river.

Andrew landed on a piece of land beside the lake and the kids all landed beside him.

"Wow look at this!" Casey said with glorious smile lighting up her face, but soon her eyes were squinted as droplets of water began to mist her face.

"Yes," Andrew said looking up at the massive body of moving water in mid-air. "It is the water rainbow roller coaster!"

"It doesn't have a track," Bo said puzzled by the sight.

"It's just a loopy rainbow and water."

"You're right it doesn't have a track – it's not man made," Andrew explained.

"This rainbow is solid. Once you put your lily pad on the edge of the coaster, hang on because it takes off with the speed of the rushing water."

"How does it work?" Jacks asked.

"Simply fly to the beginning, right there," he said pointing to the tip of the rainbow. "And when your lily pad grips the rainbow – then hang on!"

"Uhm…is that thing safe?" E-man asked trying to appear unafraid.

"Of course! Everything in the Hangout is safe. If any one of you should happen to fall off of a cloud or the rollercoaster or anything else, remember the soil turns feather soft because it is getting ready to catch you without a scratch or bruise. So, if you fall, get up, take your pad and take another go at it."

"Ok," he said pulling his lily out of the pocket of his damp jeans.

He took off to the coaster, and the kids were fast behind him. The closer they got they could begin to feel a fine mist of water hitting and covering their hair and face.

"Now when you put your pad on the rainbow don't worry about trying to steer and control it, the coaster will guide you!" He yelled over the rushing waters.

Andrew sat on his lily and landed it right on the tip. The lily pad folded its sides around both edges of the rainbow and took off!

"Wow!" E-man shouted.

The children looked in amazement at Andrew as he sped through the loops and dips of the roller coaster.

"So who's going to go first?" Leena asked putting out a challenge.

"Me!" E-man volunteered.

No sooner than the words left his mouth he pushed the stem of the lily pad forward and took off like a flash straight to the tip of the watery rainbow!

"Woo Hoo!" Was all you heard before the coaster shot him off!

The rest took off behind him zipping like rockets through the air headed for the rollercoaster. Casey landed after E-man and then Bo who was actually very nervous.

"Oh, where is my mom!" Bo cried.

Chris laughed at Bo until it was his turn to land, a rush of nervousness came over him. When Chris landed on the coaster it gripped and took off going about 60 miles per hour! It shot straight then fell into a deep dip, and let up into a double loop. Then it circled back around and took a small dip and looped to the right, and then took another dip, but the dip started looping around and round and round and round, like it was a small tornado letting him out straight down into the lake right below with his lily pad floating on the water.

"Oh…my…goodness! That was the most fun I've ever had!" Casey exclaimed.

"Can we do it again?" Jacks asked.

"Be my guest."

The seven rode the roller coaster over and over again, and each time they went it was as if it was their very first.

"This has got to be the coolest thing I have ever done!" Chris said as he headed back to the tip.

"Well, you ain't seen nothing yet!" Andrew said flying out of the water. "You guys ready to see more?"

"Yeah!" Bo said soaring up in the air on his lily pad while the others were floating on the water.

Casey and E-man looked at each other, and without a word, decided that they wanted to stay.

"Can me and Casey stay here and ride the rainbow?" E-man asked.

"Of course!"

Chris looked a little disturbed.

"Case maybe you two should come along and we'll come back to this," Chris said motioning for her to come.

"But I want to stay!" she cried.

"Chris, it's fine – she is safe," Andrew assured him. "We'll meet back up with them later."

"Alright," Chris said shrugging his shoulders.

Jacks punched him lightly on the arm. "Loosen up, she'll be fine, what place is safer than the Angels' Hangout?"

"Come, follow me, there is much more to see," Andrew said flying off.

Chris, Leena, and Jacks lifted up out of the water and started after Andrew. Bo laid on his lily pad, stomach down, and propped himself up on his forearms.

"Hey Chris, lay on your pad like this and fly – it's so much cooler!"

"Alright," he said taking Bo's suggestion.

High in the sky they flew parallel to the white mountains and the clear river that flowed beneath them. Mighty oaks and cedars were rich with vegetation and colorful fruit. Andrew began to slow down and descend a bit. The children did the same and followed Andrew's every move and ended up landing in a wooded area with Andrew.

"What is this place?" Bo asked.

"It's just a fruit garden. There are so many places like this in Heaven, as well as in the Angels' Hangout," Andrew answered.

The garden was a magnificent display of colorful, sweet fruits growing on the trees that had sprouted up from the precious sweet soil. Chris picked up his golden lily and it shrunk to the size of a quarter, then he dropped it in his pocket for safekeeping.

"Is this the garden of Eden?" Leena asked.

"No. Eden is still on earth, but is hidden and guarded by cherub angels. However, these gardens are equally as ravishing, and rich with good things to eat, as the Garden in Eden is," Andrew explained admiring the immense fruit hanging from the trees.

"I tell you what, take the best piece of fruit, the juiciest and the sweetest you have ever had in your life, and compared it to a piece of fruit here. The best piece you ever had would taste bitter by comparison!" Andrew bragged. "Go ahead, pick one and taste it. You'll find that you have never tasted anything so delightful in your life."

The children's faces were alight with wonder as there were so many trees to choose from. Finally, Chris picked a huge red-orange peach that was so red he initially wondered if it was an apple. But when he touched it he knew from the cottony fuzz that it was not.

"Wow! That's a big peach, Chris," Bo exclaimed.

"Think you can eat it all?"

"I'm going to try, that's for sure," he said opening wide and clamping down on the peach.

Juice burst into his mouth and painted his lips then poured down his chin. Chris chewed and chewed. Taking another big bite, juice splattered in Bo's face as he stood, almost spellbound, too close to Chris' face watching him enjoy his peach.

Bo jumped back wiping his face and yelped, "Okay, man, so how is the heavenly peach?"

"How is it?" Chris closed his eyes and rolled the meat of the peach and its juices around in his mouth tickling his taste buds thoroughly then said, "There are no words to describe it and even if I chose the word delicious, it would not come close."

Leena happily picked a rich purplish-red plum, and Jacks picked a fat green fig. Bo walked along the garden looking for a piece of fruit, cautiously walking past the apple tree.

"Here, Bo, try this," Andrew suggested picking a mango.

"These are my favorite." Bo took the mango from Andrew and took a bite.

The skin was as soft and chewable as the skin on a peach or an apple! As Bo took the first bite his eyes lit up.

"Ummm! This is too good!" he exclaimed looking down at the fruit as if it was some strange thing.

In the thick of the excitement Andrew's halo began to glow brightly. He looked up into the halo and listened attentively, "Yes, they're fine. Ok…I am on the way."

"I know…we have to go, right?" Leena asked.

"No, actually I have to go."

"Who are you talking to when your halo glows, anyway?" Leena asked.

"This," Andrew said pointing to his halo, "is how we angels communicate."

"That is really cool!" Chris said.

"And it works everywhere! All of Heaven and earth!"

"Wish we had one," Jacks said.

"But I must go, I'll come find you guys later," he said spreading his wings for takeoff.

"Oh yeah, make sure you eat the core of your fruit, it's the best part!" He said soaring away.

"Man I can't believe that this is all happening," Leena confessed.

"I can't believe this fruit is so good," Bo said.

"Oh, bananas!" Jacks said running over to the tree.

"I hope none of this fruit is forbidden," Bo said glancing back at the apple tree.

"Of course not. Andrew would've warned us," Chris argued.

"Well, one little juicy apple brought on the fall of all of mankind," Bo inserted.

"No. Disobedience brought about the fall of mankind," Jacks corrected him.

"And if you read it, the Bible doesn't say anything about Adam and Eve eating an apple," Leena added.

"Help me Chris! They're ganging up on me."

Jacks laughed, "Bo you're so silly. Nobody's ganging up on you."

"Why are you guys ganging up on Bo?" Chris asked playfully.

"We're not. We're just trying to educate him – that's all," Leena quipped walking over to the apple tree.

As she reached for an apple to tease Bo with, she saw something move in the corner of her eye. She looked at the tree beside her and saw nothing. *Humph, maybe I just thought I saw something,* she thought to herself.

"Do you eat apples on earth?" Jacks asked Bo, her back turned to him.

"Yeah, who doesn't?"

Leena let go of the apple and cautiously walked over behind the other tree.

"What is it Leena?" Chris asked.

"Don't know…thought I saw something," she said without taking her eyes off of the tree.

She walked up and looked on the side of the tree, then jumped back and screamed.

"What is it?" Chris asked.

He looked beside the tree and there stood a small white furry lamb with white leathery wings, like those of a bat. He had big blinking eyes all over his body.

"Hello, I'm sorry, I did not mean to frighten the female," it spoke out.

Chris' eyes were wild as he stared at the unusual creature hoping it was an illusion.

"Did that thing just talk?" Bo whispered.

Chris nodded his head like a wind-up toy. Leena slapped her hand over her mouth to keep from letting out another scream. Slowly she began walking backwards.

"Andrew said nothing here will hurt us," Jacks whispered.

"Oh, no, I would never hurt anyone or anything."

"How are you able to speak?" Chris asked.

"All animals speak, the question is can you understand the language they speak," it answered promptly. "By the way," his wings fluttered as he spoke. "My name is Shazook and I am the child of one of God's living creatures."

"Hi, Shazook, I'm Chris, this is Bo, Leena and Jacks," Chris said pointing to each of them.

"Nice to meet you all," he said bowing courteously.

They all bowed in return and shared the same respect. "So how did you get into the Angels' Hangout?"

"Andrew brought us."

"I see."

"He was showing us around before he had to leave," Leena said.

"If you'd like I could show you around until he comes back," Shazook offered.

"That would be nice, "Jacks responded.

⊗ ⊗ ⊗

While on the clouds still talking with Alex, Fiorra's halo started to glow bright. She pulled it down and held it in front of her face like a hand mirror.

"Yes…. Okay… I am on my way," she said and placed her halo back over the crown of her head.

"I do apologize Alex, but I must go now," she said getting up from the cloud.

"That's perfectly fine Fiorra. Thank you for letting me take so much of your time."

"We'll meet again," she said and flew away. Alex stood up with his hands on his hips and watched her fly away.

When she was completely out of sight he reached into his pocket and took out his golden lily pad and shook it so it could expand.

"Ok, now what?" he spoke audibly to himself.

He laid it down on the cloud and sat on it.

"I can do this," he said grabbing the stem, and he took off through the clouds into the direction he saw the others go into. He passed the mountain and flew over many fields. Alex was thoroughly enjoying his flight throughout the Angels' Hangout and hoped he'd run into his friends soon, however, scenes like mountains and vast fields was quite fulfilling until then.

He enjoyed the clean crisp air blowing on his face and through his hair. As he flew over the land he noticed a large field covered with flowers, so he decided to land near the riverbank, and trekked over to the curiously beautiful field.

"Wow!" he said looking over the miles and miles of flowers, but not just any flowers, these flowers were unique - unlike any flower he had ever seen on earth. There were many vibrant colors and textures and oddly formed, too. Some were shaped like tulips but their petals swirled upward. Other flowers were shaped like daisies, but turned and twisted in a downward spiral as if it were housing something.

Alex's curiosity grew and he stopped and examined a bright orange flower with long slender petals that had a velvety feel like the inside of a rose petal.

"Splendid," Alex muttered.

He started to walk through the field and noticed that butterflies were hovering over the closed pedal flowers like honeybees. He kept walking through the field looking toward the horizon, breathing in the delightful aroma the flowers were giving.

Alex bent down to smell a dark purple flower when he heard a tiny little voice say, "Hey watch where you're stepping, buddy!"

Startled, Alex looked up but he didn't see anyone.

"Uh...hello?"

"You hard of hearing?" the small attitudinal voice asked.

"Who's...who's that talking?" Alex demanded.

He looked behind and around him and still didn't see anyone.

"Down here! I'm the one you were about to crush!"

He looked down at the ground and there stood a shiny blue beetle that was quite agitated.

"Is that you talking?" he asked the beetle.

"Of course!"

Alex stood looking at the beetle in total disbelief, silent. He noticed that the beetle's antennas stood straight up, but had tiny orange jewels at the tips of them, making them droop a bit. Alex was fascinated now.

Alex disturbed the awkward silence and said, "Well uh - it's nice to meet you?"

"The name's Carter," the beetle responded.

"I'm Alex."

"So what are you doing out here in the Jewel Meadows?"

"Just exploring," Alex said getting down on his knees.

"Exploring? Is this your first time here at the Angels' Hangout?"

"Yeah! It's wonderful, and I've never seen flowers like these."

"That's because these flowers only grow here in this meadow. These flowers are special," Carter explained with pride.

"Why are they special?"

"Because the flowers in this meadow produce all of the jewels in Heaven."

"What? How is that possible?"

Carter snickered and said, "Well you do know that with God, all things are possible?"

"Yes, yes of course," Alex answered.

"We're not just your everyday average beetles," Carter explained. "God made us for the sole purpose of helping produce every kind of jewel, gem, and precious stone known and unknown to man.

"Who's we?" Alex asked puzzled.

"My family. It's thousands of us out here. So it's rare to find someone just taking a stroll through the meadows."

"Oh, sorry," Alex said.

He flinched and began looking around hoping he was not about to squash any of Carter's family members.

"It's ok."

"Now Carter would you explain to me your purpose? How in the world do you produce jewels?" Alex asked.

"Well if you look out into the meadows you will find that some flowers are open and some are closed," the beetle began.

"Yes, I see that," Alex said nodding his head.

"We beetles crystallize the soil, and the special flowers grow from the soil with their pedals closed. Then a butterfly comes, and deposits one drop of a special glaze, on the top of the flower. When the butterfly leaves, a little glowing bulb floats out of the flower and then the pedals open."

"Whoa! So where does the glowing bulb go?"

"It goes up into the sky. Each bulb gathers with the same color. That's how rainbows are made!"

"Wow! So what happens when the glaze goes into the flower?" Alex asked very interested.

"It mixes with the liquid in the flower and it creates a jewel, and when the jewel is formed it drops down through the stem of the flower and comes out to the ground. When the pedal opens, the jewel is removed by one of us beetles, and the flower withers away. Then a beetle will come along and crystallize that piece of soil and another flower, usually a different color will grow in its place."

"Fascinating! How long does this whole process take?"

"It depends on the color of the stone. Lighter jewels take about a week. Jewels that are deep and rich in color take about a month."

"So when the jewel comes out on the ground what happens to it?"

"Beetles carry them down to the Crystal Cave underwater," Carter explained.

"That's the cave we came through to get here! All those jewels that were on the floor!"

"Yes, the floor is where we store them. It's also where the jewel gets its ability to glow!"

"Why is that?"

"Because this water flows from the river of life in Heaven!"

"So why do the beetles store them underwater?"

"Because the angels in Heaven that are building houses and other constructions like lampposts, buildings and furniture – anything needing jewels – are able to pull from the storage which is the bottom of the cave.

"That is awesome! So the angels come to the Angels' Hangout to get to the Crystal Cave?" Alex asked.

"No. The Crystal Cave has two entrances, one that leads to the Angels' Hangout and the other leads to Heaven, the angels use the Heaven entrance. The cave is several miles long."

"This is all so cool – so organized. Seems like everything has its purpose," Alex said.

"Yep, sure does!" the beetle said proudly.

⊗ ⊗ ⊗

E-man and Casey spent hours riding the rainbow roller coaster until they were just too worn out it ride it any more. Casey slid down for the last time still laughing as hard as the first time. She was belly down on her lily pad and she propped herself up with her elbows, and E-man was lying on his back.

"What do you wanna do now?" E-man asked.

"Let's explore this place, we might find something even cooler than this!" she said pointing at the mass of rushing water behind her.

"Ok, we could ride the river and see where it takes us," he said.

The river started about a quarter mile down the way, and many great cedar trees stood tall on both side of the river.

"Well come on!" Casey said shooting up in the air.

"I'll race ya there!" she took off and E-man was right behind her.

"This is too cool!" E-man yelled as he flew passed her.

Casey tried her hardest to catch him, but he reached the mouth of the river first. E-man smiled as Casey arrived.

"The only reason I didn't win is because –"

"I beat you!" E-man answered finishing her sentence.

"Whatever," she quipped flicking her hand at him. "You ready?"

"Yes, ma'am!"

The two zoomed off and landed on the boisterous waters and were thrust downstream at top speed. They sailed along slicing the crystal water and admiring splendor new to their young eyes.

"Look at these beautiful trees! Have you ever seen water so clear?" Casey asked excited.

"It doesn't seem real," E-man said.

"If I'm dreaming I don't ever want to wake up!" she said with one hand in the water.

They rode down the river for a while, when something deep in the woods caught Casey's eye.

"Did you see that?" she said raising her lily off the water.

E-man stopped and looked in the direction she was referring to.

"Nothing but trees."

"No," Casey said spanning going over the area again, "I saw something."

She landed her lily on the bank of the river next to a large tree. She got off of her lily pad, shrunk it down to coin size, and slid it in her pocket. E-man did the same and followed her into the forest.

"Come on, it's this way." She trekked deeper into the forest and found exactly what it was that caught her eye.

It was an enormous horse about twelve feet tall, and his coat was scarlet red. She and E-man darted behind a tree and peeped.

"Let's get closer," she said moving towards it.

E-man snatched her arm.

"What?"

"Are you completely insane? Let's go back!" E-man insisted.

"Andrew said nothing will hurt us here."

"Well I'm not willing to find out."

"Ok, then, wait right here," she whispered.

Casey ran up to the next tree, and the red horse stood still looking right into her direction. The horse let out a loud grunt and spoke in a very deep voice.

"Who's there behind that tree?" The red horse asked.

Casey slowly came from behind the tree, her eyes glued to the horse. Slowly, carefully she moved in closer getting a better look to her amazement. The closer she got the further back her head tilted as she lifted her widening eyes and peered

She moved in a little closer as her head slowly tilted back and her eyes lifted higher peering at the unusually tall horse.

"Uhh....hi," she said lowly. E-man stood at a distance watching and trembling.

"You can talk?"

"Of course I can talk," he said with a loud gruff.

The power of his voice shook Casey's little body causing her to jump back.

"Andrew said nothing will hurt us here," Casey asserted almost crying.

"Hurt you? No. You need not be afraid until my rider comes …then destruction is on its way."

Three other horses came walking slowly toward them. A black one, a white one and a pale one, these three were just as vast as the first.

Casey chuckled nervously, "Uh – these must be your uh… friends."

The black stood up on his hind legs and steam came from his nose as he exhaled heavily, and looked at her through his mid-night eyes. Casey took another step back.

"Who is this?" the black horse asked.

"Andrew's friend," the red one answered.

"There is another," the pale horse said with a heavy gruff.

With wobbly legs E-man came from behind the tree and stood behind Casey.

"This is my friend E-man."

Upon introduction he stuck his head out and waved from behind Casey.

The black horse neighed loudly releasing air from his large nostrils which blew out like steam.

"What did you mean by destruction when your rider comes? Because I was gonna ask if I could ride you," Casey said, hands on her hips.

"We patiently wait for our riders," the white horse spoke.

"When my rider comes we will bring war and incurable *disease* to one third of the world!" the red horse announced neighing loud and hard.

Then the white horse spoke of *conquering* one third of the earth! The black horse whipped his tail about, flapping it like a flag on a windy afternoon.

"My rider and I will bring *famine* to one third of the world. One loaf of bread will cost you one day's wages! When that day comes."

The pale horse took a couple of steps toward them and pierced them with the stare from his dark yellow eyes. "We will bring *death* to one third of the world."

"Oh, ok," E-man conceded, nodding his head. You don't have to tell me twice."

"Look I know we just met, but I think you horses need to take some anger management classes. Why are you guys out here in the woods plotting - angry at the world?" Casey asked.

"This is what we're made for," the red horse told them.

"God Almighty created us for this reason alone," the white one interjected.

"Oh, that's real nice…uh I think we should be on our way," E-man insisted reaching for Casey's hand.

"Where are you headed?" the red one asked.

# The Hangout

"Don't know, we are just exploring," Casey answered.

"Well, why don't you go to Heaven? It's much better than this place," the white one suggested.

"Really? How do we get to Heaven?" E-man asked.

"Just ride the river of life down until you see the gates. This river will take you all the way to the Throne Room where God the Father sits."

"Well, it was nice to meet you all," E-man said and grabbed Casey's elbow and ran back to the river.

Casey gave her waves and good-byes and she was being pulled away by E-man.

"See you later, maybe next time we meet you'll change your mind about you taking me for a ride!"

Riled, the red horse reared back and stood high on his hind legs, kicking his fore legs into the air. Neigh!!

Casey and E-man ran back to the River of Life, and rode their lily pads down to the end. When Casey and E-man reached the gate they hopped off their lily pads and looked around inquisitively. The gate was made of thousands of rubies and it was attached to a solid gold wall that extended as far as the eye could see.

The wall stood five miles high and there were two archangels blocking access beyond the entrance of the gate. Casey and E-man spotted Alex meandering along the river in their direction.

"Hey, Alex, where are the others?" Casey asked.

"I don't know. You guys left them, remember? Meet my friend Carter, anyway."

"Where?" E-man said glancing behind him.

"He's here on my shoulder," Alex pointed.

"Hello," Carter said. E-man jumped when the beetle spoke.

"Oh my," E-man said.

"Well it's nice to meet you too!" Carter said.

"Snappy little thing aren't you?" Casey proposed.

"And you are?" Carter asked turning towards her.

"Casey."

"I like you Casey, there's nothing like a girl that speaks her mind.

She smiled erecting her chin.

"Not everyone would agree with that."

"I'm assuming these are the gates to Heaven," E-man said looking at the gleaming red gate and massive golden wall.

"Yes, actually this is the back door to Heaven. The pearly gates in the front are the ones people usually come through when they get to Heaven," Carter explained from Alex's shoulder.

"I never thought Heaven would have a back gate," Casey said.

"Yep, and a couple of side gates too! The place is huge!" Carter said with a little jump stretching out his hair-sized legs and arms.

E-man spotted Chris and Bo coming up fast with Shazook in the front of Bo's lily, leading the way. Leena and Jacks were flying close behind them. They spotted them and landed beside them. At last Andrew appeared seemingly out of thin air behind them.

"Perfect timing!" he said.

"That was so fun!" Shazook yelled. "Never rode on one of the golden lily's before."

"Me either," Bo said putting his, now shrunken lily, back into his pocket.

"You guys want to see Heaven?" Andrew asked.

"Of course!" Chris agreed.

Everyone was excited at the thought of actually seeing Heaven! Leena and Casey were jumping with joy in celebration. E-man looked at the entrance with awe in his eyes! The thought of actually entering into Heaven was overwhelming. He noticed that one of the archangels that stood in front of the gate held a large white book.

"Andrew, what book is that angel holding?" E-man asked.

"That's the Lamb's Book of Life. No one can enter into Heaven unless their name is written in that book."

"Why is it called Lamb's Book of Life?" Casey asked.

# The Hangout

Everyone gathered in close and listened.

"To make a long story short, back in the day before Jesus came to earth, God's people used to kill or sacrifice different animals whenever they sinned."

"Wait why would they kill animals just because they sinned?" Leena asked.

"Because God has zero tolerance for sin, the price is death. You sin, something has got to die to pay for it."

"So the animals were being killed for the sins of the people! Just imagine how many rams, lambs, and goats that were being slaughtered daily," Bo said shaking his head. "Guess it's a good thing the Animal Rights people didn't have their organization back then – or it would've been protestors at every alter!"

"Bo, are you capable of being serious for one minute?" Leena chastised.

"Why aren't God's people killing animals now?" Casey asked.

"People don't have to kill animals anymore because Jesus was the lamb that was slain for the world and all their sins. So now when you sin, instead of running out and getting a goat, you simply pray and ask God for forgiveness and turn from that wicked way. So the Lamb's Book of Life is filled with the names of the people that are saved through Jesus. Only they will get in. But you must remember the only way to God is through Jesus. He is the way, the truth and the life. So when you pray it must go through him."

"I never knew about the animals, Andrew," Jacks said.

"So that's why at church they always said Jesus died for me and you," Bo said.

"Yep! You guys ready to see Heaven?"

"Yes" they jumped and shouted!

Andrew walked up to the ruby gate and approached the two angels that were standing guard. "Hello fellas, these are some friends of mine and they want to visit."

"That's fine, Andrew, but you know the rules," one of the angels said in a serious tone.

"Not a problem," he said stepping aside.

He motioned for the seven children to come up. They said their good-byes to Carter and Shazook and ran over to the gates.

"You must give them your names."

Chris stepped up, "Christopher Prentice."

The angel opened the book and found his name.

"You may enter," one of the angels said and opened the gate for him. "Emanuel Amin."

"You may enter."

Leena, Jacks and Casey went through also, once the angel found their names in the Lamb's book of Life.

"Bo Richardson."

"You may enter."

"Alexander Fitzsimmons."

The angel flipped a couple pages and looked, then flipped the other way.

"I'm sorry but your name is not in the Lamb's Book of Life. Please step back," one of the angels instructed sending Alex into a panic.

Suddenly, Alex lost his balance and fell backward. Grasping his chest he struggled to breathe.

"What do you mean? This couldn't be!" Alex cried.

Andrew went over to the angel and spoke with him quietly, and then went over to help Alex off the ground. Andrew took him away from the gate and knelt down to his level to talk face-to-face.

"You must repent, Alex. Apparently, God took your name out of the Lamb's Book of Life because you have gotten too cocky with the gift of knowledge and wisdom. You judge others and think they are beneath you because you have this gift. You got ahead of yourself, Alex, you thought you could handle everything, and you didn't need God. So repent and turn from those ways."

# The Hangout

Alex bowed his head in silence. He knew what Andrew was saying was true.

"Lord, I am so sorry. Please forgive me because I have done great wrong. Purify me Lord and fill me with your love."
Alex's eyes welled up with tears and they began to trickle down his cheeks. "Lord the wisdom and knowledge you gave me…I took for my own…I am truly sorry."

Andrew went and stood over by the two angels at the gate entrance. He looked inside the book, and as Alex stood up his name glowed as it reappeared back in the Lamb's Book of Life!

"Come on!" Andrew said holding his hand out for Alex to take. Humbly, Alex took his hand and they walked through Heaven's gates together.

# Chapter Twenty-Three
## ⊗ HEAVEN ⊗

Andrew and Alex entered through the gates of Heaven and were instantly enraptured by magnificent melodious music! The melody was one with the air and it breezed through every part of them. Their clothes and hair fluttered as the music whirled about them like wind. Overwhelmed by the sight that filled their gaze and the resounding music, Leena's grip on Bo's hand tightened. Everyone was speechless. Rolling green hills and gardens of succulent vegetation stretched for miles before them.

"So what do you think?" Andrew dared ask.

They furled their brow and crooked a look at him, but words failed them. Andrew snuffed a grin and beckoned the children to come in closer and get some new directions. He led them over to a beautifully decorated marble table close to the gate. There were two angels standing behind the table like soldiers on assignment, the only difference was they were warm and welcoming.

"Hello Andrew," one of the angels said.

"Dantel," Andrew responded with a nod. "These are my friends from camp."

"Welcome to eternal paradise," the angel said with a smile.

"Oh, no, no. They aren't here permanently – just visiting," Andrew explained quickly.

"How much time do they have?" Andrew reached in his pocket and pulled out a small round ruby red timepiece and looked at it. "Not too long."

"Well, make sure you take them downtown!"

"Oh, that's right!" Andrew realized.

"Take these," Dantel said, handing them each a detailed map of Heaven.

On the table was a scroll with the title Angelic Servant Assignment scripted on it.

"What's that?" Alex asked pointing, tilting his head trying to read it upside down.

"When you get to Heaven you are assigned an angel or angels that will serve you forever," Andrew explained.

"Cool!" E-man exclaimed.

"Here is where you come to see what angel is assigned to you and their information," Dantel added. "Then you take the information downtown and they lead the new souls from there."

Chris was almost enchanted by seeing vibrantly colored flowers that grew so plenteous; it was like plush carpet covering the ground, and trees that swayed in time with the never-ending music.

"Are the flowers and trees dancing?" Chris asked.

"Everything that is alive here praises God, dance is a form of praise."

Once Alex received his map he opened it right away and examined it. "Looks like downtown Heaven is close to the center."

Jacks looked on his map to see what he was talking about.

"Look," she said, poking the map, "the mansions surround the city and they are huge!"

"Yes, they are. One of our bigger mansions is the size of a small city!" Dantel added.

Andrew laughed and looked over at Casey and saw that she had her eyes closed with her arms out dancing to the music like no one was watching.

"Look there are different paths," Alex said following along on the map with his finger. "Looks like the golden path takes you straight into the city."

"Yep!" Andrew said.

"The pearl path makes a huge circle around the main city. Is that the residential part?" Jacks asked.

"Yes ma'am. One of them, this map only covers the north side of Heaven," Andrew said.

"What's the jumping stone path?" Leena asked peering over Alex's shoulder. "Oh, that's a pretty cool path. I gotta take you there, you guys will love it!"

"Can we go now? We can talk on the way," Bo asked, eager to see more of Heaven.

"Follow me!" Andrew said heading to the path of gold, "and can somebody grab Casey, please."

Casey was still dancing around as if she was a ballerina, lost in her own little world. As they headed for The Throne, Heaven's capital, they trekked up and through hills covered with flowers such as they'd never seen on earth. The strange thing about the flowers was that they were shaped unlike flowers they'd seen before and the colors were stunning to their eyes...and they appeared to be dancing, too! The flowers twirled and swayed to the sound of the music. They rode the music notes with ease.

The children made their way through the flowers and past many trees with their mouths open in amazement.

"Look at the designs the bark makes on the trees!" E-man said pointing to a cluster of trees.

Each tree had a different design, some bark made circles; some swirled the length of the tree like a candy cane and the branches were alive with big green leaves and heavenly fruits. The children observed the strange trees a while then noticed a long streak of golden illumination up ahead.

"Look there it is! The golden path," Jacks said as they each took off running.

The children arrived at the path and immediately set out to walk on it to get to downtown. The street was paved with pure gold and a seven-inch layer of clear crystal lay on top of the gold and even with the grass.

"Wait! Are you sure we can walk on this?" Leena asked. "It looks like yellow ice or something."

"Of course this is just one of our streets," Andrew said.

"And that yellow ice is gold, by the way."

"Gold that you can almost see clean through?" Jacks asked.

"Yeah, this path or street, or whatever it is, looks so shiny and smooth, it's like we should not dare walk on it," Bo added. I mean, we don't wanna scratch it or crack it up.

Andrew laughed at the children's sweet innocence and pointed toward the golden path.

"Now, Bo, take a look. What do you see?"

Bo looked along the path and saw various, shapes, colors and sizes moving about along the path.

"Step closer, Bo. Do you hear anything?" Andrew asked challenging him now.

He looked out onto the horizon.

"Well, Bo," Andrew prompted him.

Bo stood and looked and listened. After awhile Bo said, "I hear voices coming from the moving objects." He moved in a little closer, "Hey! Those are people!" Bo shouted.

Andrew let out a hardy laugh. "Come on, all of you so we can get to downtown."

This unusually beautiful pathway was filled with people traveling along toward downtown Heaven. The closer the children got to what Bo thought was just colorful objects from afar, the clearer it was to see joyful people of every color and nationality decked in every kind of dress, engaging in conversation among themselves, as they walked.

"Heaven is so much more beautiful than I ever imagined," Leena said looking all around her.

As the crowd moved along, they passed a nearby park that had a giant sized cedar tree growing up the middle of it and underneath it sat a small boy in a bright yellow robe with a an open book in his hand. But, the strange thing was all kinds of animals were gathered around him; monkeys, rabbits, turtles, and a couple of squirrels appeared to be attentively listening as he read because, as it turns out, he was reading a book to the animals! The seven watched as the little boy in yellow would read, and then turn the book to show the animals the pictures.

"Wow! The animals understand our language?" Alex asked.

"Yep, we live in complete harmony with all living creatures," Andrew explained.

Once again the crew was astonished and walked further down the path and into the city.

"Man, would you look at the buildings," Bo said pointing.

The buildings were grand and spacious. Some of them were made of pure gold, some were made of marble. Across the top of each building was an astounding crown that held many different colored jewels on the spikes of its many tips. Each building had a grand yard with plush green grass covering it entirely, and the gold path that the children walked ran right through it and lead them to the front doors.

As they made their way toward the city they continued to see many people of all nationalities dressed in their native wear only this time angels were everywhere, too. The rainbow of people had their eyes focused and scurried along as if there were an eagerness to complete an undone task.

"Jeeze, what is the hurry?" Casey asked throwing her gaze at the moving people as they whizzed by.

Andrew just looked at her and shook his head with a smile. The crew approached the building and noted the sign out front which read 'New

Souls Division'.

"Andrew, what happens in that building?" Casey asked.

"That's where people go when they first come here to Heaven. Inside there is where they get instructions on how things work here...and they take their servant assignment information here, and they will present the angel or angels to them."

"What would they need a guardian angel here for?" Chris asked.

"Not a guardian angel, an angel servant," Andrew explained.

"A servant?" Bo questioned.

"Yes! Just as the size of your mansion depends on your good deeds down on earth, it also determines how many angel servants you receive."

"Really?" So that explains all those smiling angels flying around all those people. It's like they are advertising!"

"Yep!"

Next the crew came up on a building with a sign that read: The Backsliders Bureau of Defense. They stopped and gawked awhile.

"What goes on in that building?" Casey asked again.

Andrew inhaled deeply then breathed out an answer. "When a Christian begins to turn from the required righteous way of the Lord and turn back to their old way of sin - that's what it means to backslide. When a person gets saved and they are headed for Heaven we begin preparing their mansion and servants and rounding up their jewels, and gathering everything that person likes, to make sure they are comfortable when they get here. But when a person backslides their labor goes on hold. That's when the Bureau angels begin pleading with that person to change their ways," Andrew explained.

"But I thought that when a person gives their life to Christ then they will automatically get into Heaven," Jacks said.

"Ohhh Noooo! Unfortunately that is a lie that is preached in many churches today!" Andrew said shaking his head.

The kids were all ears.

"Because Jesus died for you he gave you the opportunity to be saved. Once you give your life to Christ initially you are given salvation, but it is up to you to keep it! Think about it, if 'once saved always saved' were true, then why would Jesus spend so much time teaching people how to live right? If that was the case then people could lie, steal, cheat, kill, and all of Heaven would be waiting for them with gates wide open! No. I don't think so."

"Basically, a person can do everything the Bible tells us not to do, with no consequences if 'once saved always saved were true," Alex added.

"That sounds crazy," Bo said.

"It is," Andrew agreed, "Heaven is not guaranteed, you have to work hard for it."

"That makes sense," Jacks added. "And that would explain what the Bible says when it talks about the path to Hell is broad and the path to Heaven is narrow and only few will find it."

"That's right Jacks!" Andrew said.

"Now as far as the backsliders go, we don't want them to lose their spot in Heaven so we try to pull them back.

"Wow! I'd like to see inside there!" Alex said.

"Yeah, me too," another cried.

Soon Andrew was outnumbered by seven children insisting on seeing inside the Backsliders Bureau of Defense.

"Alright, alright. The best I can do is to allow you to see inside the windows and if you listen closely perhaps you will be able to hear something. I don't know."

"No, problem!" Casey said, excited.

Chris actually led the bunch to the side of the wide gold and silver stone building in order that they may get in some good peeping. The windows were open and the kids could hear clearly everything that was going on. They each took a window and peered inside and once again were astonished by what they saw and heard. The room was large and open, the only furniture that was there was a small leather bench that set against the window in the back of the room. Like busy operators on duty in a large room on telephones, the kids could hear angels speaking into the air, some were knelt down, others stood and some sat as they continued speaking to someone other than each other, and they were not using anything like telephones.

"Okay, Andrew," Chris whispered, "who are they talking to?"

Alex added, "Because, clearly they are not conversing with each other and there are no other persons in the rooms with them."

There was a huge navy wall that had hundreds of small black picture frames, some were empty and others had images of different people's souls. The souls looked lost, some were weeping, and others looked depressed. There was an image of a woman in one of the frames, who looked to be in her mid thirties and she was crying.

She shouted at one of the angels, "You've got to help me! My body is going to send me straight to hell!"

"Okay, calm down," the angel said.

"You don't understand, I'm going to commit major sin tomorrow and I know it's wrong and I don't want to do it, but my body takes over and it does what it wants to do! The Holy Spirit is speaking to my conscience, angels are sending me messages, but my body won't listen! And when my body dies and turns to dust, I'm going to have eternal hell fire to deal with! Not the body!" she screamed.

"One word for you – FAST – you've got to kill that flesh!" the angel said.

Casey looked back at Andrew, "What is that all about?"

"Shhhh…" he had his index finger over his mouth.

"Come on I'll explain," he whispered.

As Andrew walked the children away from the building he explained. "Listen, guys, these are angels that speak to the souls of people who do wrong or are thinking about doing it. People who were once living right, then stopped, need someone to encourage them and lead them back on the right path. That is what these angels are for. They are speaking directly to their souls before they start to do wrong in hopes that they make the right decision before it's too late. The souls are very concerned because they will be rewarded for the body's good deeds and punished for the bad when it's all said and done."

"So what did that angel mean when he said kill the flesh?" E-man asked.

"He didn't literally mean kill the body… like dead. He meant killing it by fasting, because when you don't eat food your body gets weak and a lot of times the body doesn't have the desire to sin. So when the body is weak the soul is stronger so the soul leads the person in the right direction. That why it's so important for Christians to fast to keep their flesh under control."

"So the person doesn't realize their soul is speaking with angels?" Chris asked.

"Usually the souls speak with angels while your body is sleep," Andrew explained.

The kids stood silent for awhile.

"Humph," Chris grunted shaking his head.

"Ha! That explains a lot," Jacks blurted out.

"I know good and well I hear someone speaking to me all the time, especially when I want to punch someone out for messing with me when I know I need to forgive and move on!" Chris said.

"What about the Bureau of Blessings?" Jacks asked pointing to the huge solid gold building sitting to the left of them.

"That's where angels round up the blessing due to God's children, and in due time divvy them out."

"Wow," Alex said.

"Remember when you guys saw Scott and Herman open up the ground back at camp?"

"Yeah," Bo said, while the others nodded their head.

"All that stuff in the ground – those were people's blessings!"

"What? How is that?" Chris asked.

"When a Christian is right with God He gives them the desires of their heart," Andrew explained, "So when they pray and ask God for what they want, whether it's a house, car, jewels, whatever it is, then this department releases that blessing from the sky in spirit form, and as it is traveling down, if that person sins then the blessing is open game and the devil and his demons are able to take it, and they do. Then they store it in the ground like what you saw at the camp."

Everyone stood speechless trying to process what Andrew was saying.

"There are millions of ground storages all over the world!"

"Well how do you get your blessings back?" Jacks asked.

"Be obedient to God and you can take back what was stolen!"

"This is all so much!" Leena said.

"Look at that building," Chris said pointing to a very tall turquoise building topped with emeralds at the top.

"What happens in the Department of Laughs and Tears?" Jacks asked looking into the distance.

Andrew pulled out his little timepiece and glanced at the time. "Well, we have a little time. You guys wanna go in and see? This place is really neat."

"Indeed!" Alex jumped up, followed by the rest who were quite excited about seeing into another one of the buildings.

"Come on," Andrew said leading them to the door.

However, as they were drawing closer to the door an angel wearing a white business suit, carrying a turquoise blue briefcase, swiftly flew in the direction of the door and landed. Once his feet touched the ground his wings disappeared and his flying turned to a brisk walk as he reached the door.

"Wow!" Bo hollered.

E-man walked up to Andrew, reached for his elbow and gripped it inside.

"So what happens here?" he whispered looking suspiciously at the angel.

"Come on, I'll show you," he said opening the huge door for them to enter.

When they stepped inside music was playing but not like the other music they'd grown used to hearing; this time the melody was more relaxing, the tempo was not as fast. The sound of water pouring off of a wall in the rear of the building was exhilarating and mixing with the music very naturally, but when the kids saw that it flowed out into the river of life, which ran underneath the wall they almost could not believe it.

Scores of exquisite chandeliers like none they had ever seen before hung low above their heads. Multi-color lights flickered from them and caught the children's eyes setting a sparkle in each one. Instead of bulbs, uniquely cut gems of every color fit into each socket, of each light, of every single chandelier. The room was alight with yellows, blues, greens, purples, reds and even white all moving like clouds intermixing on a perfect spring day...only they were inside.

"This way," Andrew said walking toward the crystal clear elevator that sat alone in the midst of the floor.

When they approached the doors, they opened as if by request then closed with a quiet click before their staring faces. The children looked around still checking out the magnificent building from inside the glass elevator. On the right side of the elevator were several, small, pink buttons and above them was a sign to match that read 'Floors of Laughs' engraved in it. The left side was the same except the buttons were blue and the label read 'Floors of Tears'.

There were about ninety floors all together and a massive lobby separated the floors of laughs from the floors of tears. Andrew pressed one of the blue buttons and the elevator glided over to the left side of the building. Everyone stepped off the elevator into silence. No more music. The floor was wooden, but white and many bright lamps floated above them.

"This way," Andrew said leading them down the long corridor. They went into a large room where the entire back wall of it was clear like a window and Heaven's skyline could easily be seen in the distance for an breath-taking view. For the most part, the room resembled a library as it was filled with shelves loaded with items of many types; this room was not by far limited to books. Clear glass bottles with names carved on them lined the shelves also.

"Are the names on the bottles all the people in Heaven?" Casey asked.

"No these are names of people on earth."

Just then a man with a purple robe came in carrying a small golden bowl. He walked steadily over to the shelf and picked up the bottle that read 'Lucy Jones'. He took off the cap and poured the contents of the small golden bowl in it. Then he capped it, put it back and walked back out the room.

"Watch this," Andrew said grabbing Lucy Jones's bottle. "This way."

They followed him down another hall into an even bigger room.

There were beautiful books neatly placed on the bookshelves that overwhelmed the room. Andrew pulled one of the books off the shelf that read 'Jones, Lucy' on the spine of it, and laid it down on a bulky wooden table that sat in the middle of the floor. The cover of the book had tear-shaped emeralds on it.

The children gathered around and watched him open the book, and noticed the pages were all blank. Andrew carefully opened the bottle and dropped a single drop onto the page and words began to appear.

"Awesome!"

He dropped another drop on the opposite page and it began to fill up with words as well.

"These words tell the story of this woman's sorrows," Andrew said.

"Wait, so our tears are here in Heaven?" Alex asked.

Andrew gave an affirming nod of the head.

"How do they get here?" Leena asked.

"Your guardian angel collects them while you're crying, and places them in a bowl and brings them here to the Department of Tears."

"So the guy we saw earlier in the purple was carrying tears!" Bo asserted.

"Yes indeed, taking them to that person's jar," Andrew answered.

"So Heaven knows our sorrows and pains." Leena said aloud.

"Who puts all the tears in these books? Jacks asked.

"The angels on duty," he answered, screwing the top back on the bottle.

"Then they take the completed books to God's library. That's one place He visits everyday He reads all the books because He likes to know what's going on with His people."

"This is all so cool," E-man said.

"The angel on duty also records how many tear drops are there and takes that number to the floor of laughs, and for every tear that's cried, there's a laugh in store. To keep it kinda balanced so to speak."

"God really loves us," Bo said.

"Man," Andrew said shaking his head, "you have no idea!" He glanced at the little ruby timepiece again. "We should get going."

They were headed to the front door when they passed a room where a lady in a blue robe stood reading someone's book of sorrows. The kids noticed how carefully she turned the pages. Chris recognized her and backed up. He stretched his neck for a closer look.

"Mrs. Harris?" he almost squealed.

She looked up at him and tilted her head. Her usual stringy hair was now a full body of curls. Her pale skin was now rich in color.

"It's me, Chris. I was your next door neighbor," he said looking down the hall.

The others didn't know he'd stopped so they kept going.

"Oh my," she said coming toward him. "When did you get here?"

"Today, I'm just visiting, though."

"Oh...so you're not dead?"

"Oh no! But it's nice to know what's in store."

She smiled at him but it faded when she looked down at the book she was holding.

"This book holds the tears of my son. He misses me so much and he is so upset that he couldn't protect me," she said turning the page. Looking up at him she asked, "Will you talk to my son and my husband for me? Will you put their minds at ease? Better yet," she said, her eyes lighting up,

"Will you deliver a letter?"

"Of course," he said looking back down the corridor.

At that point no one he knew was in sight. He went into the room and stood beside Mrs. Harris as she wrote her letter. He watched her as she wrote thinking about everything that happened on that tragic day.

"I tried to stop you. I saw that accident before it happened and I tried to stop you, but … I wasn't fast enough," he said holding his head down.

She stopped writing and looked up at him. "I hope you aren't blaming yourself for what happened to me."

Chris said nothing. She stood up and put her hand on his shoulder.

"It was my time, Chris. Neither you nor the doctors in the hospital that night could've saved me, and it's no one's fault."

"I just thought maybe if I was faster, then you would still…"

"Even if you did stop me I would've died a different way, that same day – same minute," she said looking into his eyes. "Please don't blame yourself, sweetie – I couldn't be happier!"

She folded the letter up and handed it to him. "Please give this to my husband," she said and cupping his hand tightly.

"I will."

"It was really nice seeing you Chris."

Chris told her the same, waved good-bye, and jogged off to catch up with everyone.

She stood at the table and waved back and said, "Make sure you live your life right so that I may see you again."

Looking back he smiled, "I will," and ran disappearing into the distance.

Everyone was outside waiting for him.

"Did you get lost?" Casey asked when he came busting through the front doors. "No just ran into someone I know."

"Ok, well let's get moving, I'm taking you guys to the Throne!"

"We're about to see God?" Alex asked.

Andrew chuckled, "You're about to see the Throne."

"Where is it?" Leena asked.

"It's elevated right above the middle of the city."

They passed a couple more buildings then a darting lady in pink robes appeared out of nowhere, carrying three large books in her hands. She was moving very fast as if she was on a life or death assignment. She zipped passed the kids and headed toward a cluster of five platinum buildings that were set back off the main road. The kids followed her every move with their eyes. The Prayer District, is what the sign out front read.

"Let me guess what happens in these buildings," Alex volunteered.

"They collect and sort out the prayers of course," Casey erupted instead.

"Exactly! When you pray, your prayer comes here. Angels record the prayers of the people, and then everyday at the same time, the angels on duty take the prayers up to the Throne and gives them directly to God. So now He knows what the needs and desires of his people are," Andrew explained.

"Wow! This is all too wonderful," E-man said.

"After God hears the prayers of his people, the prayer books are taken to the Magistrate Storehouses," he said pointing to the three enormous building across from the Prayer District.

"Also in the District is the Room of Records, and there every good thing a person does is recorded, but the bad is not left out. Believe me. Not only is the deed they've done recorded, but the country, state, city, county, street and time are recorded also. That is what the Room of Records building is used for," Andrew explained further.

As they traveled closer to the throne, the crowd of angels, people and even animals thickened because everything and everyone was coming from all over Heaven to worship the Lord.

"Is that the Throne?" Bo said pointing to a colossal mass of clouds in the distance that sat fifty feet above the tallest building.

"Yes," Andrew said.

The children slowed their steps and widened their gaze. They beheld what appeared to be an emerald rainbow, throwing off magnificent rays of light encircling the thrown while another one arched high above it forming a double ring that looked as if the throne was being encircled by two great Os. Penetrating music emanated everywhere. The children could feel it down on the inside of themselves and could not be sure if they were trembling because of God's presence or the strength of the melodious music.

Beams of light blazed from around the throne and were visible from many miles off. Colorful billows of smoke, smelling sweeter than perfume, extracted from every angle of the throne. Andrew led them through the crowds of worshipers. Countless voices were praising God.

"Look!" he said pointing over to little groups of clouds that hovered slightly off the ground.

"Those are cloud elevators that take you up to the throne. Just stand in the center and it will take you up there," he emphasized.

Andrew helped Casey onto one, and immediately the cloud took her up to the throne. The others stepped onto elevator-clouds and off they went. Andrew took up wings and flew alongside them.

The Throne of God was an awe-striking sight! The sky above the throne had a deep blue hue accented with dashes of purple that emphasized bright gold stars that hung low twinkling against the night time appearance. The children arrived and stepped off cautiously and onto another surface with the feel of a cloud, too.

Leena smiled at the sight then slowly shut her eyes. She inhaled deeply and savored the sweet smell. Around the throne were hundreds of ribbon dancers, colorfully dressed, leaping and praising God.

They waved and swung their batons with rippling ribbons on the ends, caressing the air, twirling, leaping and giving God their all. The children were amazed because it looked like a huge party going on. Bo was thoroughly taken by it all then he noticed among the excitement that there were some men dressed in white surrounding the Throne praying and bowing down before the Lord. They were not dancing or celebrating with the rest.

"Andrew, what are they doing bowed over like that? They don't seem happy like the rest. What's wrong with them?" Bo asked.

"Hold it, let me answer one question at a time," he whispered. First of all, those are elders - there are twenty-four of them. It is their duty and pleasure to bow always and pray to the Almighty.

On the east and the west of the throne stood two massive angels, with their wings spread wide. These angels' wings were different than the other angels. They had pointed tipped wings that displayed many colors patterned like that of a kaleidoscope. They were robed in blue with gold trimmed and glistening beads. Their heads were bowed, and their hands were raised with a bend in their elbow, which tapped the tops of the exquisite swords that hung on their sides. Five enormous white horses stood at attention as if they were knights postured on a chess board. Even they were dressed well; their backs were draped in plush red fabric edged out in gold and silver. Gold reins were clinched in their mouths.

Casey and Jacks loved the atmosphere so much they could no longer help themselves as they were overcome with all the celebrating and music. They let themselves go and were swept away by the music. They too began dancing, celebrating and praising God with the masses of other praisers. Casey was enthralled with it all. She glanced about until she made eye contact with some of the others. She even saw God's presence in the midst of a euphoric swirl, around the Throne at times. But, before long Casey slowed her dancing to a halt when something even stranger caught her attention.

Up near the front of the throne stood four very large living creatures covered with eyes; all of them were speckled with actual seeing eyes in the fronts and backs of them. One had the face of a lion; another had the face of a calf, still another was very tall and had the face of a man, but the body of a beast. The last one was like a flying eagle. The four creatures all had six wings, flapping as they sang, *'Holy, holy, holy is the Lord God Almighty, who was - and is - and is to come!'*

"Oh my goodness! What are they?" Casey asked as her jubilance seemed to drain from her.

"Don't know," Chris said.

"They might be God's pets," Bo suggested.

"No, no, no," Alex argued. "I think these are the four living creatures that the Bible talks about in the Book of Revelations…in fact I'm pretty sure they are," he said examining them.

Before the children could figure it out, a thick cloud descended around the center of the throne and a thunderous noise drowned out the music. Casey flew into Chris' arms and E-man clinched his fists and lowered his head. The rest of them moved in closer to Andrew and hoped that his promise that they'd never have to fear anything or get hurt was still in effect. God himself began to speak and immediately all within range of his voice fell to their knees in reverence to the Lord, even the animals. The five horses knelt down on one leg and bowed their heads in reverence to the Lord. His voice sounded like roaring, thunderous waters, yet he was easy to hear because he expressed himself so lovingly. God spoke as a father who wanted all to be saved and not lost.

"The blood of my son Jesus was shed for man – so all people will have the chance to be saved, and have eternal life. Come…sing praises unto His name!"

The cloud that hovered over the throne faded away and everyone started leaping, dancing and praising as the music was raised once again.

"What do you guys think?" Andrew asked walking up to them

with a Cheshire Cat grin on his face.

"I don't know the words to describe this experience," Alex said, and the others agreed.

"I know I don't wanna leave," E-man said.

"Me either!" Casey said, still twirling around.

"Well, we better get moving because there's not much time left," Andrew said.

Somewhat sad, they all returned to the cloud elevators, stepped on and began to descend slowly. On the way down they took in the city once again. Gradually it dissipated from their sight. All of the majestic buildings standing hundreds of feet tall, and the busy angels flitting about, diligently working on their tasks was all fading to a memory in their sight, now. The city became a shimmering picture in the distance as the various colored jewels and stones reflected off of the light that lit the city up. Once they were back on the golden path Andrew lead them to a path that took them away from the city.

"Where are we going now, Andrew?" Jacks asked.

Alex took out his map and tried to pinpoint where they were. Andrew looked over at his map and pointed to the jumping stone path.

"This path will take us to the pearl path where the residential area is. Before we leave I want you guys to take a peek at these awesome mansions."

Alex put the map away and said, "Andrew thank you for protecting us back at the camp."

"Don't thank me, thank God. I'm just doing my job."

"Well, we appreciate you for being obedient to your duties," Jacks added.

Just then a group of children came skipping making their way to a large white stone building with great white columns erected in the front. The sign outside read: THE HIGHER MUSEUM OF ART. The children skipped up the narrow pathway leading to the museum. Beautiful bushy trees dotted the walkway. E-man stared in amazement as the children made their way to the entrance of the museum.

"You guys have museums in Heaven?" E-man asked turning his attention to Andrew then.

"Every good thing on earth is here in Heaven and so much more! You guys want to take a look inside?" Andrew asked them.

"Of course!" Casey said before the others could answer.

"You will like this place, come on," Andrew said leading the way.

As soon as they stepped onto the pathway leading to the entrance, seemingly with each step they took, a tree changed its colors. The trees went from green to bright reds, purple, blues and yellows! The pathway became a multi-colored walking experience! The array of colors was spectacular.

"So what happens here?" Leena asked, her eyes darting about with the blinking trees.

"So many different things," he said holding the doors open for them.

"Come on in I'll show you."

When they all crept beyond the two huge red doors, they were immediately taken away in wonderment. The decor alone was of udder surprise. As they moved inside and eyed the room they notice every detail; the windows that made up the back and side walls were draped in lovely purple and green textiles, from the ceiling to the floor, which in itself was made up of silver marble. A winding stone staircase cast in the middle of the room led to the second level. Many rooms were at their disposal.

"Come on let's go in here," Andrew said as he entered into the first room.

The room was huge and empty except for large gold framed pictures that hung side by side on the walls. They were all pictures of landscape crowned by a splendid sky. Each picture had nailed to it a small medal plaque underneath it with the name of a different country etched into it. Andrew looked at the curiosity on the faces of the seven then answered their questions before they could ask.

"There are seven rooms just like this one, each room has a different continent and that room holds all of the countries of that continent. We call these rooms 'A little walk around the world' because you can literally step inside the painting and explore all of the countries you never had the chance to travel to on earth."

Leena glanced over at the names of a couple of countries and said,

"So this is the Europe room, huh?"

"Yep!"

"Can we jump inside one?" E-man asked.

Andrew gave him a regretful, no, shaking his head. "It will take much too long. We don't have enough time today, but next time, yes!"

⊗ ⊗ ⊗

Nighttime blue began to paint the sky with ease now as the children's visit to Heaven progressed on.

"Would you guys like to see an angel concert or take this time to rest?" Andrew asked.

"Why would we wanna rest?" Casey asked with her hand on her hip.

"Well, because it's getting dark. Heaven stays dark for a little over an hour according to your sense of time, and this is the time most of us gets to rest."

"You guys only sleep for an hour?" Casey asked.

"We don't sleep - nor desire to. And when you get your new bodies sleep won't be an issue for you either," he said.

"Wow! I can't wait!"

"Well, I'm still running on adrenaline so I want to go to the concert!" Bo said, as everyone else agreed with him.

Andrew took them to a field where a mass of people and angels were eagerly awaiting the start of the concert. Citizens of Heaven had camped out on blankets and many had picnic baskets filled with delicacies.

# Summer of Seven

The stage was tremendous, striped with grand white columns that resembled that of a Greek edifice. Oversized stars filled the sky above. Numerous fireflies hovered too like a canopy of light twinkling, waiting for the music to start. As they entered the gate leading to the grounds, they were given blankets to spread out and sit down on, so Andrew did just that. They all sat down and took in their surroundings.

Leena and Bo noticed two pretty girls sitting near them whispering to each other. One had smooth caramel skin and the other was fair skinned, but perfectly tanned. They each had incredibly thick hair that flowed down their backs, and they were dressed in purple and red linens.

"Wow! They are beautiful," Bo exclaimed. "I don't think I've ever seen girls so pretty!"

"Close your mouth Bo before one of these fireflies fly in," Leena said rolling her eyes.

Andrew chuckled. "Here in Heaven beauty flows from the inside out. Plus with the new bodies there are no toxins present to slow you down and age you."

Suddenly the sitting crowd stood to their feet blocking the view of younger, shorter ones, which made the kids stand up, too. Leena looked back again to find that the girls were still whispering, but now they were pointing at her, too.

Leena quickly snapped her head back around before they caught her looking back. But, now knowing that they were talking about her, she began to feel intimidated.

*Even in Heaven the girls disapprove of me*, she thought.

She fought back a tear and turned her attention to the angels that were performing on the stage.

"Give glory to God! Hosanna in the Highest!" The angels shouted from the stage inciting the crowd; the crowd went wild jumping and shouting.

They sent praises to God, and thanked him for loving them so much! The angels stood on the stage unaccompanied; there were no speakers, no microphones, no instruments or a disc jockey. When the two angels parted their lips and released their voices, they sounded like a choir of many, many voices singing out melodies in praise to God in an amphitheater! Musical instruments and harmony came from within them. It was like nothing the kids had ever heard in their lives.

Alex asked Andrew, "Are their vocal cords instruments or something? This sound is incredible, and from two, just two angels!"

"Yeah, I'm trying to figure out how this sound is literally filling this whole place, yet it's not hurting my ears," Chris inserted.

"I can talk to you and not have to try and yell over the music!"

"This is truly what the word 'awesome' means," said E-man noticing that the presence of God the Father was right in the middle of it all enjoying Himself and receiving all the praise from everyone.

The crowd was an unstoppable crowd; the more they praised and sang out with the angels, the stronger the intensity got! In time members of the crowd rode upon the wave of intense, worship and were airborne as they danced, shouted and sang to the Lord! After a while, a choir of angels joined the angelic duo on stage making the worship concert even more complete. With every symbol and every musical note that burst out into the crowd, the souls of those in the crowd became intertwined with them. It was as if the music and the praise could not stop. They could've gone on forever, and for many hours they did!

When the concert of worship and praise to God finally slowed to an end, the people and the animals slowly descended and lay upon the ground again. Some people tried to stand, but could not because they were happily intoxicated with the glory of God! The praisers felt so drunk in the spirit they had to sit or lay down until they could finally stop praising God. Everyone else applauded the angels on stage and they leaned forward in gracious bows. When one of the angels spoke, his voice reverberated across the entire field.

"Give glory to God! Applaud him for giving us these gifts to entertain and praise him!"

Once again the crowd erupted in praise and honor to Him. The kids were amazed at what they had just experienced together.

"That was *soooo* cool!" Casey said.

"I can't believe we were actually floating!" E-man exclaimed.

"Sometimes God's power sweeps you off your feet," Andrew said matter-of-factly. "Let's get ready to go."

Andrew started folding up the blanket, as the others prepared to go.

The two girls that were whispering walked up behind Leena and tapped her on the shoulder. Leena turned around and was immediately shrunken back by their striking beauty.

"Hello my name is Lydia, and this is my friend Mylinda," she informed her smiling big.

"Hi...Leena," she said and fluttered a wave.

"Mylinda saw you earlier and we were taken aback by your beauty."

"Me...my beauty? Oh, I just figured the opposite. I was convinced you were picking at me like so many others do," Leena explained.

"No, you are absolutely gorgeous on the inside!" Mylinda said.

"And your outer beauty is equally as stunning!" Lydia said then glanced at her watch, "Oh! look at the time!"

"Oh no! We're almost late!"

"Late for what?" Leena asked.

"Late for class. Nice meeting you but we must run!" she said and they darted off through the crowd.

Alex turned and asked Andrew, "What class are they talking about?"

"Not sure. There are many different courses you can take at Mt. Zion University."

"There's a university here?" Chris asked.

"Of course!"

"Can we visit?" Alex asked with excitement.

"Sure I don't see why not."

# *Chapter Twenty-Four*

## ⊗ SCHOOL OF THAI ⊗

Down the length of the golden path, several miles past the Throne, sat Mount Zion University. It spanned 22 acres and was casted very prestigiously; the architecture was impressive indeed with four turrets per building. The buildings were made of grey stones and mortar of gold. The school also had a jeweled crown atop every building. Gates of Emerald enclosed the school and wore an emblem, MZU, in the middle of it. The acres of grass were the exact color of the gates and the walkways were grey stone, and very smooth, with strokes of gold going throughout it like artwork on a canvas.

An unarmed angel stood in front of the gate. Andrew and the kids walked up to him in hopes of gaining access or at least information.

"Welcome to Mount Zion," he said to them. "And hello, Andrew."

"What's up, Carloso?"

"The usual wonders, and I'm doing well, very well!"

"Good. I'm here with some friends and they want to see Heaven's university."

Without a question, the angel opened the gates. "Enjoy!"

They entered in and were overjoyed to visit the university

"Okay, what classes did you guys want to visit?"

"What choices do we have?" Alex asked as they walked up the long pathway to the school.

"Let's see... the courses that are going on now are: How To Appear

Anywhere In Heaven, Holy Living, Heaven 101,..."

"What do you learn in Heaven 101?" Leena asked.

"This is a beginner's class for people who just got to Heaven. This class is important because everything is so different here; it can cause culture shock in the worse way, but that is actually a good thing.

"What else?" Chris asked.

"We have Animals 101, with animals that teach the class. Since we will be living amongst them in harmony, they explain their habits so we can understand them better."

"Uhhooo! I would love to see that!" E-man exclaimed.

"Me too!" Casey added.

"I think we all would like to see that," Alex said trying to contain the excitement in his voice.

"We also have the course called History of Heaven."

"What's History of Heaven exactly?" Bo asked.

Willingly, Andrew explained: "The teacher discusses a topic of history in Heaven and the students get to travel back in time to watch it play out."

"I think we would all love to see that as well," Alex concluded and that became the overwhelming choice and happily they went on to the class. As soon as they entered the classroom they were overcome by the size of it.

"Wow," the kids all sang.

"You need at least ten teachers to cover all this," Jacks whispered.

The classroom was more like a college auditorium since there was a large stage in the front of the classroom. A lovely mix of people different colors and hair textures, all ages and nationalities were sitting three to a desk with paper and pencil taking notes on what the animals were teaching.

When they walked in Andrew motioned for them to sit at a couple of vacant tables on the side of the room near the door. They sat down and listened to the lion that was pacing back and forth on the stage.

"I know it might be hard to believe, but yes we do belong to the cat family. But us lions are much different from the little kitty cats, we are more like wolves and wild dogs than the others in our cat species."

"Why is that?" A guy blurted out with his hand raised.

"Well because we travel in packs... actually they are called prides; that usually consists of two males, six females and several baby cubs. We male lions have a short life span. In the wild we might live for 12 years if we're lucky."

His pacing slowed down as he yawned.

"Whew! I guess that leads me to give you another fact about us; we sleep a lot, too!" The lion chuckled.

"We sleep a whole lot... about twenty-one hours a day. In fact I'm getting sleepy now," he said with his tail in the air.

He stretched his front legs out along the floor in front of him and knelt his face toward the floor, yawning again, then sat down. This took the students by surprise and a hum of chattering settled on the room. Only the lions recurring voice was able to snuff out the chatter and allow the teaching lion to continue.

"Now, the females...they have it good. When they get old and lose their teeth the pride will share the food with her as long as she can keep up. Nice huh? But us males don't have it so good; when we get old we get beat up and forced out by younger males, which is detrimental for us."

"Why would they get rid of the older lions who have taken care of everyone for so long like that?" Someone from the audience asked.

"Oh, it doesn't matter what we've done, or how well we did it. Youth and strength prevails. The pride has to keep going at any cost. And the cost is our lives!" the lion said with a roar! "Don't mean to frighten anyone but it is important to us that you know that when or if we get ousted we soon die because we are in no condition to hunt anymore, so that's pretty much it for us," he said with a sad look in his eyes.

"That's so unfair!" Casey stood up and shouted.

Everyone turned and look at her.

"That's life, a lion's life on earth anyway. But it's much better for us here in Heaven - waaay better."

He stood back up on all fours slowly and stuck his chest out. Even though we are the second biggest to the tiger... the lion is still KING!" he said and let out a loud roar of authority!

Everyone in the classroom stood to their feet cheering and applauding; a thunder of encouragement filled the room and the lion's heart.

While the crowd was caught up focused toward the stage Andrew, knew it would be a good time to take the kids and move on. He motioned to the children to follow him out and on to another classroom.

Andrew turned and said, "Those lion's are a trip! But they're really cool."

"I can't believe they sleep so long!" Bo said.

"Yep! You learn a lot about animals in that class. A new animal teaches the class each day," Andrew informed them.

He led them to a door with a blue sign that read: 'HEAVEN'S HISTORY'. When they went into the classroom it was empty except for the professor who was sitting behind the desk with his hands folded. He looked at them quite curiously.

"How can I help you?" he asked.

Andrew explained to him who everyone was and why they were there. The professor shook his head as he looked at the seven. Behind the professor's desk was a long linear time line with sapphire circles plastered along the line. The caption above the first circle read: THE CREATION OF HEAVEN AND EARTH. A couple circles down read: WAR IN HEAVEN - LUCIFIER & 1/3 CAST OUT! The circle next to that read: THE CREATION OF MAN. Several circles down further read: GOD INTO MAN – JESUS PREPARES TO MAKE HIS JOURNEY TO EARTH, and there were several other captions along the timeline.

"Feel free to jump in any circle you choose and witness Heaven's

History as it played out," the professor said.

"What circle do you guys want to go into?" Andrew asked.

"I wanna go into the creation of Heaven and earth!" Casey said jumping.

"Me too!" E-man said.

"I've read Genesis so many times, I would love to see it played out," Jacks said.

"I was thinking God into man," Alex said.

"I was thinking the same thing!" Bo said.

"Listen guys you can separate," Andrew suggested.

"Well, I'm going with Bo and Alex," Chris said.

"Guess I'll go with the guys," Leena said.

"Go over to the circle of your choice and lean into it. You will be gently sucked into the portal that will drop you off at the scene. Once you're inside, the scene will begin to play just as it did before. Once it is over it will bring you back here," the professor explained. Both groups of kids ran over to their circle of choice and waited for Andrew to tell them to go.

Chris was the first of those who chose to go together. He stuck his hand into the hollow circle and felt the suction of a vacuum. He leaned in sticking in his head and Zap! His whole body was sucked in! Casey's eyes got real big as she grasped her chest; she wasn't sure if she was excited or alarmed as she watched Leena, Bo, and Alex get zapped away right behind him. She and the others could hear Chris scream as he shot down the portal and into the scene. Before he had a chance to stand up Leena, Bo and Alex were on the floor next to him.

They landed hard without pain. As they sat flat on their bottoms on top of what felt like grass, they could hear rustling. When they looked to the right of them they discovered that they were right on the bank of the smooth flowing River of Life. The high dome-like ceiling was made of pure pearl and a thick solid gold boarder ran all the way around it. There were beautiful designs made of different color jewels etched in the pearl. Up against the wall was a huge wooden mantle and the top was made of a rare purple diamond that was five inches thick and it covered the entire top of the mantel. Angels were carved into the sides of the wood and canary diamonds were placed throughout the designs. On top of the mantel nine planets that looked like holograms floated and turned above the mantel. Over to their left was a table where Jesus was sitting at listening to God speak.

"Son, I am getting really fed up with my people! I just want to destroy everything! Everybody! Wipe out all the sin and start all over again!"

The four of them heard everything God said to Jesus, as he was clearly frustrated.

"But Father, you can't destroy everyone again!"

God sighed. "I know. I made a promise to Abraham that I would make him a great nation and that I would bless all families through him."

The great Heavenly Father got up and began to slowly pace up and down the river. He shook his head, "Oh, my people…I just don't know why their actions are so vile, so wicked and selfish! I bring them up out of Egypt and provide all of their needs and they still bow down and worship false gods! And Israel's evil kings – leading my people astray!"

"We've had some good ones – look at David and Solomon. Well Solomon…before the foreign women," Jesus said.

"What about Jeroboam, Nadab, Baasha!"

"Father you must not forget about Hezekiah and Josiah," Jesus reminded him.

A soft smile came across the Father God's face.

"I have not forgotten about my trusted servants. But look at all the other bad ones, Jesus, my son. The numbers are overwhelming."

And with that came the end of Jesus' argument; his eyebrows were furled in dismay because he could not deny that God his father was right; most of Israel's kings were corrupt.

God the Father returned to his pearl Throne and sat down.

"I've thought of a way to save my people…to save all people."

"And how's that?" Jesus asked curiously.

God looked at him and smiled lovingly. "I love you so much."

"I love you too, Father," Jesus responded.

Leena held Bo's arm tight and whispered, "That's so sweet!"

"I'm giving you the opportunity to save my people – to save all people."

"How can I do that Father?"

"You must die for the sins of the world, and by doing that you will be opening the doors for all people, not only the people of Israel."

"So how will I die if I am immortal?" Jesus asked.

"You will become mortal temporarily. You will become a man, even though you will be Me, God in the flesh. And you will be born of a virgin woman so there will be no mistaking the divinity of the situation."

Jesus looked down at his hands and thumbs.

"So once I become a man what shall I do?"

"You will spread the good news. You will inform them that the only way they can be saved is through you, Jesus. You are the Messiah and people will believe, and their belief in you is the only way they can be saved. You know I cannot stand sin and all of mankind is in sin! Even a child in his mother's womb is formed in sin. So, through you is the only way I will deal with man."

"But, what if they won't accept me?"

"Then I won't accept them."

"Your will be done, Father. I will do it."

"I must warn you, some will not believe you, but thousands will. You will do great wonders for our kingdom, son. Please understand though, they will destroy your body and you will die and be placed in a tomb like any other person who dies, but the difference for you is, you will rise three days later, and soon after you'll be back on the throne next to me," God explained to Jesus.

"I will do it. When will you send me?"

"I'll have my angel contact your mother on earth – her name is Mary. As soon as she gets message you will go."

"I will be honored Father."

With no control of their own, the kids were suddenly sucked out through the portal and placed back into the classroom.

"Ah!" Chris shrieked!

"So you liked it?" the professor inquired.

"Liked it? That was mind blowing! "Alex hollered.

"Insightful to say the least!"

"Can we go in others?" Bo asked Andrew.

He looked at his timepiece, "Not today, we don't have time."

As soon as he said that Casey, E-man, and Jacks came flying out of their portals like ejecting cannon balls.

"That was so neat!" Casey screamed and panting. The others agreed excitedly.

"What happened? What did you see?" Leena asked.

"Oh my goodness! It was God, Jesus and the Holy Spirit and the Holy Spirit is really a spirit he looks like a white mist! But they were all standing together in total darkness with God in the middle…and and…"

"God began to speak," Jacks said helping excited Casey out. "He said let there be light! And the Holy Spirit started to swirl around them really fast! Then spread far out into the darkness and at the end of that day there was light!"

The girls explained as best as they could about the six days it took God to create Heaven and earth and how everything came into formation.

The children followed along still reeling from their day thus far. Andrew lead them out of the school and back onto the golden path. Chris, Bo, Alex, and Leena had become professional tellers as they recalled their experience to the others.

"…and he was really disappointed in the kings of Israel," Leena finished.

"If I were king I would've served the Lord! I would've let God rule through me," E-man said as if it was a no-brainer.

"Wow, E-man! You could've been a great ruler in Israel!"

"Me? I'm just a kid, Andrew!"

"So what! The youngest king of Israel was Josiah and he was just 8. Then there's Joash, he was king of Judea at the tender age of seven!"

They all wore a look of shock and surprise at the thought of real kid kings!

"Just letting you know you are never too young to be great," Andrew said.

They followed the river for about a half-mile before it ended at the tree of life. The enormous tree stood alone on a small island with branches that spanned its length; the tips of the branches reached the island's edges. The splendor of the tree left the children mesmerized, and for Andrew, seeing it again lit up his face as it had done the first time he ever saw it.

The trunk of the tree was as wide as the lengths of twenty people encircling it with-out stretched clasped hands. It bore 12 different kinds of fruit, each kind a different color. The bark was highly textured and thick, but alive! It moved constantly reshaping and creating a design for each day or mood.

The children were awestruck as they watched the tree's trunk change right before their eyes. And when they looked up, they noticed eye catching balls that looked like gigantic fruit.

"Gosh! Looks likes I could go bowling with those," E-man said surprised by the size of the fruit.

"Can we eat a piece of that fruit?" Casey asked.

"No, only God can give permission to eat from this tree. You see those four angels guarding the tree?" Andrew pointed out.

Four expressionless archangels, heavily armed with large shields and swords, stood on the four sides of the island.

"But you can eat of the fruit from the surrounding trees out here in this field," Andrew said pointing to the ground.

Chris went over and grabbed a piece of fruit from a nearby tree.

The fruit looked like a plump cluster of raisins.

"Those are Trendits they are really good," he said showing him how to eat it. Andrew broke it open and popped two in his mouth.

"Try it you'll like it." Chris ate one and nodded with approval, then popped another.

"Let me try," Jacks said running over.

She took a couple of his off of the top and popped them in her mouth.

"You're right these are good and sweet too," she said.

Bo made his way over to another tree to grab what looked like oversized peaches. He could hardly fit his hand around it to pull it off the tree. "I love peaches!"

"That's not a peach, that's a Yocumberry."

Bo held the Yocumberry with both hands and took a big giant bite. No sooner than he finished raking his teeth into the meat, juice filled his mouth and started seeping beyond his lips. It was overflowing goodness! All he could do was close his eyes and chew slowly.

"Jesus!" Was all he could get out upon swallowing.

Suddenly Jesus Christ appeared and stood right beside Bo! He was tall and fit, and his skin was a dark olive color. His hair was long and thick like wool and His eyes were deeply intense like flames in a fire! Bo froze he couldn't believe his eyes as Jesus stood still smiling down on him. When Leena realized that was Jesus standing near she dashed over to him and gave him a big hug. He gave her a tight hug back and a warm soothing smile.

"Now that I've seen you my trip is complete!" she said leaving Jesus blushing.

Leena got the other's attention. "Look!" she called pointing toward Jesus. The others came running and they gathered around Him and gave Him hugs and kisses, with the exception of Bo, who was still practically frozen at His sight, somewhat limp as he held the Yocumberry.

"Jesus you don't look anything at all like your pictures on Earth, but we still knew it was you," Casey said.

"Is that good or bad?" Jesus asked.

"Uhhhh… I just thought…"

He laughed and so did Casey. Andrew walked over and knelt down before the Lord. His nose nearly touched the ground and his wings were erect with the tips pointing straight up into the air.

"Master for what do we owe this honor?" Andrew asked.

"My child Bo called my name."

"Oh, I just… the fruit was so good… I… I," Bo stammered embarrassed.

"I know - I hear your heart." Jesus looked at them all. "So you guys like the fruit?"

"Oh, we love it!" Jacks answered.

Everyone told him how much better it was versus the fruit on earth.

"Have you guys tasted the food here yet?"

"No, just the fruit from the trees," Alex answered for everyone.

"Actually, I'm a little hungry. Would you guys like to join me for lunch?" Jesus asked.

"Of course!" They said jumping up and down.

Everyone's face lit up and they were overjoyed.

"Good because I know a little Thai spot near the Bureau of Blessings that is marvelous!"

Andrew smiled, "Master are you talking about the little spot off Cush and 42nd?"

Jesus nodded.

"You know it, Andy!"

Andrew chuckled, "If you take them there I'm going to have a hard time getting them to leave!"

"Well, that's fine because I don't want to leave now! You may have to drag me out kicking and screaming!" Casey said with eyes of anticipation that incitied a round of laughter from everyone, especially Jesus.

# Summer of Seven

They followed Jesus to a small restaurant not too far from the Throne of God. The aroma met them as they approached from the outside and welcomed them warmly. Just the smell alone assured that it was the place to be. The sweet inviting smell of Thai food filled the entire place, the air was a pleasure to breathe.

"This is one of my favorite restaurants!" Jesus said excited.

"I've never had Thai food before," E-man responded.

"Oh, you don't know what you've been missing then," Jesus smiled down at him extending his hand to open the door for everyone.

There were a couple of tables inside, but most of the seating was on a large deck outside. The guy at the register beamed when he saw Jesus...again!

"Wow! Two days in a row, now," he said in a foreign accent. "How blessed am I to serve you again, my Lord?"

Jesus smiled and whispered to Bo. "Told you this was one of my favorites."

He looked up at the guy and said, "Hello, Robert, these are some of my friends that are visiting and I couldn't let them leave without eating here."

He smiled and nodded, hello, to the kids. They politely nodded back.

Jesus brushed a gaze over the menu on and said, "No need to look. I know what I want," he turned to the kids. "Take a look at the menu and get what you like."

"I want what you're getting!" Casey said.

"So do I," Alex agreed.

It turned out that they all wanted what Jesus liked which tickled him. With a broad smile Jesus ordered.

"Okay, we will all take the salmon on a bed of rice, with the Massaman Curry and the steam veggies on the side. Oh, yeah, Robert extra peanut sauce please," Jesus said.

# School of Thai

Alex took out his billfold and handed Jesus a twenty dollar bill for the meals. Jesus gently pushed his hand back.

"We are not on the world's system here. You don't have to pay for food. If you are hungry you go to whatever restaurant you like and eat."

"What! You don't have to pay for food in Heaven?" Chris asked.

"No. You don't have to pay for anything here. Almost like a free cruise without the hidden fees, it's all-inclusive," Jesus said.

"This gets better by the minute!" E-man said.

They sat down at a large round table in the middle of the deck outside. Everyone started eating their food as soon as it arrived from the kitchen. The food was indescribably delicious.

"I've never had food so good!" Chris said.

"I thought no food could be better than my grandma's – boy, I was wrong!" Leena said scooping up another fork full.

Everyone got quiet for a while and enjoyed. Casey broke the silence with a request for Jesus.

"Jesus, would you describe each of us in a couple of words, please? I would love to know what you think."

Jesus wiped his mouth and patted his goatee with his linen napkin.

"Let's see," he said looking at Casey, "I would describe you as… very spunky - Leena, beautiful, inside and out - Bo, very funny."

Everyone nodded in agreement.

He continued, "Chris, full of courage, Alex, smart as a whip." He looked at Jacks, "sharp as a needle…then we have Emanuel or should I say E-man." They all giggled at Jesus and looked over at a smiling E-man.

"You are brave," Jesus said to him.

"Brave? How is that?" E-man asked.

"You don't see it now, but I can, and you are very brave."

E-man sat quietly and waited for a deeper explanation or definition.

*Maybe what I think is brave and what Jesus thinks is brave are two different things,* E-man thought to himself.

"No our definitions are not different - you are brave E-man," Jesus said after reading his thoughts.

E-man sat for a moment afraid to think anything contrary to what Jesus said, so he started eating again.

"Okay, my turn. You guys give a word that describes me," Jesus said.

"I would say strong, because you died for us," Casey said.

"Loving," Leena simply said.

Jesus looked up and nodded his head because he agreed with her.

"All powerful!" Alex said.

"Patient because you give us chance after chance after chance," Chris said.

"Determined," Bo said.

"Why would you describe me as determined?" Jesus asked curiously.

"Well because anybody who can be in the wilderness and not eat or drink anything for 40 days and 40 nights has to be pretty doggone determined in my opinion."

Jesus and the others laughed and Bo shrugged his shoulders.

"What? It's true! No food! Not one bite? Oh, that's determination!"

"Bo you don't realize how much you keep me laughing when I listen to you."

Bo blushed and took another bite of his salmon.

"Jesus I would describe you as close," Jacks said, "because when I'm lonely I can feel you close to me and my loneliness fades away."

Jesus smiled. "I'm always with you - all of you," He said looking around the table at each child.

"But how can you be with all of us at the same time? How can you be in more than one place at one time?" Casey inquired.

"Because I am omnipresent, Casey," Jesus said.

"What does that mean?"

"It means that my Father God, Me, and the Holy Spirit, are able to be everywhere all the time."

"Just one of the perks of being God," Alex added and took a sip of his lemonade.

Jesus confirmed it with a nod.

"Wow!" Casey blurted out.

"Don't think about it too hard. God has abilities far beyond what our minds can conceive," Alex said.

"Jesus, brave is what I would describe you as, because you went to hell and defeated the devil!" E-man said.

"Really? Were you scared?" Casey asked.

"No. Fear is not of me or my father. Fear is a spirit, and it comes from Satan. So no, I was not afraid," He said.

"Jesus, I love you so much," Casey said.

"I love you too…all of you – more than you could ever know."

"Jesus."

"Yes Casey."

"What's the difference between Catholics and Christians?"

"Well, there are many differences, but the crucial difference, the difference that depends on that person's salvation is…" He paused and closed his eyes for a second.

They all looked at him thinking he was in deep thought.

"I just called someone who I think would like to give you that answer Casey."

Just then a beautiful woman appeared at Jesus' side. She wore a purple gown with scarlet stitching. Her long hair was dark brown, and her eyes were big and brown.

"I would like to introduce you guys to my mother, Mary," Jesus said.

The children's eyes were wide as were their mouths!

"Casey asked me what the difference is between a Catholic and a Christian," Jesus informed His mother.

"Ohhh," she said and shook her head. "My dear there are so many differences. But the main difference is that when Christians pray, they pray to my son Jesus Christ," she said and placed a loving hand on his shoulder.

"When Catholics pray they pray to me or to the Saints. But, children, that is a grave mistake that many make. People should not pray or worship me! They must worship God the Father of all mankind, Creator of Heaven and earth! And because Jesus is the only way to him then they must pray to Jesus. People must be wise and read and study the Holy Bible. If you do, you will never find where it instructs people to pray to me," Mary said.

"So what is happening to the millions of prayers that are being prayed to you and the Saints?" Alex asked Mary.

"They go nowhere, because I'm not a deliverer of messages and neither are the Saints.

"I thought all prayers went to the Prayer District," E-man said.

"All prayers prayed to Jesus go there," Mary corrected him.

The children stood in awe but very interested. They looked over at Jesus as they now began to see Him in a more understanding way. Jesus smiled and lightly nodded His head. "Yep! Mom has a way with explanations, that's why I knew that it would be better for her to answer."

"Thank you Jesus. I understand now," Casey said.

"Well, I must go now. There's a lady that just got here and I must show to her to her new home," Jesus said.

"Jesus we are headed to the residential area and then back to earth," Andrew said.

"Good. Then I might see you there," he said and disappeared into thin air.

Mary looked at everyone's nearly empty plates and decided she would also have a plate of Thai herself. So she said her goodbyes to the children and made her way inside the restaurant.

Everyone finished the rest of their food, as told by the sound of scraping plates. Everyone wanted more.

"Oh, Andrew that was too good and sharing with you and Jesus made it the ultimate meal. Thanks from all of us!" Alex said.

When they were all finished they quickly headed back to the path.

They walked and walked taking in the sights of Heaven. Just a couple of yards ahead they finally saw it; the jumping stone path! The path was like a snake winding through the white forest. The trees were fairly short and grew white circular leaves, perfect in circumference. At a distance the trees looked like big cotton ball lollipops. Little white stones, no bigger than apple seeds, constantly popped up and down like popcorn kernels on a hot surface. White grass grew everywhere and was trimmed to perfection.

"Oh this is an eye-popper," Leena said looking all around her.

"And white stuff is falling from above too! What!"

"Like a winter wonderland," Jacks added with her arms stretched out.

"Except it isn't cold!" Alex said.

"Andrew is this snow falling?" Casey asked trying to catch one of them as they fell softly, slowly.

"No they're Blush Petals. It's like snow, but it isn't cold. It only falls in this area, and this is what keeps the white forest white."

As they walked along the popping gravel path Alex asked Andrew, "How long does it take to see all of Heaven?"

"You mean every city and neighborhood? Or everything Heaven has to offer?"

"Both."

"Well, to fly over all the land it'll take…a couple days. But to see and experience everything Heaven has to offer… put it this way, I'm still learning new things and I was born here."

"Andrew, do we have to go back?" Casey asked.

"Unfortunately you do."

"How much more time do we have?" Bo asked.

Andrew pulled out the small ruby timepiece and glanced at it.

"Wow," he said picking up the pace. "We only have about twenty minutes before we have to be out."

The seven jogged behind him until they came to the pearl path. The all white street was solid pearl with great mansions on both sides, and it stretched as far as the eye could see. A house of immense grandeur stood before them. It stood about ten stories high and twenty stories wide! The roof's covering was that of artistically carved matted gold and had eight gigantic diamonds set into the roof, also. There were many large windows of pure clear crystal. A thick layer of gold framed each window, and the double doors that made up the entrance to the house were solid gold with the face of a lion engraved in them.

"This is somebody's house?" Chris asked.

"Yep!"

The front yard alone was at least five acres of perfectly manicured grass; every blade of the deep green grass was perfectly even with the next. The pearl driveway cut through the grass and went up the steps the led to the front door.

"This is actually one of the smaller houses," Andrew told them.

"No way!" Leena said.

"I'm serious. Some houses are the size of small cities!"

With that statement, their eyebrows practically rose to their hairlines.

"Why do they have big diamonds on the roof?" Bo asked.

"Let's see," Andrew said counting the boulder-sized diamonds.

"This person saved eight souls on earth. For each soul you save Jesus places a huge diamond on the roof of your house, and the people you saved will be your neighbor here in Heaven."

"Wow," Alex said shaking his head. "This really gives us a lot to look forward to!" Chris said.

"Yeah, and something to work towards," Bo added.

The music in the residential area played softly and sounded like an orchestra playing nearby. The tempo was slow and steady, more tranquil. Even the trees swayed slowly to its rhythm.

Tall street lights with posts made of pearl dotted the path. The illumination from them was more splendid than any light the kids had ever seen. Alex was mesmerized and tried to figure out why there was such a difference.

"What's wrong, Alex," Andrew asked noticing his studious face as he seemed to have an immovable gaze into the lamp posts.

"Well simply, Andrew, there is something awesome about the lights these lamp posts are giving off. I'm trying to see into the light bulb without blinding myself, or hurting my eyes anyway," Alex explained.

He grimaced and turned and got directly under one of the lamp posts.

"Hey, you guys you don't see this? Andrew, what kind of light bulbs give off rays of light in so many directions with hue to them?"

"You're the smartest among us, you tell us," Jacks said laughing.

Glancing at his timepiece again, Andrew said, "Just take a wild guess and make it quick guys."

As Alex turned and twisted his gaze, he thought he spotted the bulb, but to no real avail. Putting his head back down, he said, "Ok, before I blow my eyes out I'll just guess that these bulbs are not normal. Ah! They're crystal aren't they! That's it!"

"I tell ya, Heaven is the best, the greatest," E-man said smiling.

"Crystal light bulbs for goodness sake!"

The rest of the kids looked at Andrew. Some smiled, others commented on Alex's discovery.

"Cool, real cool," Bo said to Andrew.

"Well, that was an interesting little discovery as we end our trip," Leena said. "Huh, Andrew?"

Chris looked at Andrew again and noticed the smirk on his face. "Well, is he right?"

Alex turned and asked, "Yeah, am I right?"

"Actually, guys these bulbs are faceted clear diamonds cut to perfection to send off the most direct light possible. Being that it is faceted, meaning cut in many deliberate directions, light goes on many directions throughout, east, west, north and south all at once, and wherever color is, it gets picked up, and beamed throughout the neighborhood and the air surrounding it."

"I'm outdone. I'm just outdone," Alex said."

"On that note, guess we better move on," said Chris.

As they walked a little further, they saw Jesus with a lady standing next to him. The two of them were standing in front of a brand new mansion, obviously hers. The woman was bowled over, overcome with joy as tears splashed from her eyes uncontrollably. She was at Jesus' feet crying and thanking him with all her heart. It was hard for the kids to watch because of her intense emotion. But Andrew assured them that it was a good thing and not a thing to be sad about. Jesus received her thanks but let her know she needed to get up and begin to enjoy her new life in her new mansion, so he gently helped her up.

"Oh Jesus! Thank you, thank you!" the lady cried.

The seven watched as He escorted her to the front door. Upon opening it, a beautiful, friendly Collie jumped out of the door surprising her!

"Jonesy? Oh, my goodness! Jonesy!" she shouted happily, and hugged the dog tight around his neck.

The Collie was happy to see her as told by the licking kisses he put all over her face.

"Oh, Jesus, Jonesy is my childhood pet. He and I were best friends. He got hit by a car and died when I was a teenager and I thought I'd never get over him. I actually cried myself to sleep many nights." She then turned and said to the dog. "Oh, and here you were waiting for me all this time!"

Tears and smiles filled the girls' faces and Bo teased them.

"You're not crying because of a dog that made it to Heaven...for real girls."

"Whatever," Jacks said as they all turned toward Andrew knowing it was time for them to go.

"Guys we really have got to go now! There's no more time left," Andrew said and led them back to the gate of Heaven where angels were still standing watch.

They quickly exited as they said their good-byes and entered back into the Angels' Hangout. Andrew hurried them through so they could board their lily pads and take off for the exit.

Once they reached the lake that lead to the Crystal Cave they landed on the bank.

"Quickly," Andrew motioned for them to gather around. "Ok listen I am going to lead you guys out of here through the Crystal Cave ceiling, the same way you came in. But I must remind you that Heaven's time and earth's time are very different. You guys have been here about ten hours which is about seven seconds on earth," he said.

"So we've only been gone seven seconds?" Bo asked.

"In earth time, yes."

"So, when we get back Zanku, Scott and Herman will be closer than they were before," Chris surmised.

Andrew nodded his head, yes. "But we guardians are always here to protect you."

"You aren't coming with us?" Casey asked.

"No, not now, but I will be back at the camp later."

"But, you have to come! You can't leave us now!" Leena cried.

"I can't. I have a small task that I must attend to, but I will be back later. Now hurry you must go," he said jumping into the water.

They left their lilies on the water's surface and dove in too.

"Remember, breathe!" He said going under and jetting through the water leading them back into the Crystal Cave and up to the point where the ceiling opened.

They waved goodbye to Andrew; he saluted them and turned and swam away as the kids swam back up through the crystal cave's ceiling, only to emerge again through the surface of the dirty pond in the back of the broken down church.

## Chapter Twenty-Five

## ⊗ LOST AND FOUND ⊗

No sooner than each of the seven children pierced the illuminated ceiling of the Crystal Cave, it snapped closed rapidly behind them, putting them back in the murky pond behind the church. Their swimming sped up when they were, once again, engulfed in waters that had no allowance for them to breathe in.

As soon as they broke the surface the back door to the church swung open and there stood Zanku, Herman, and Scott. Leena let out a loud scream.

"Quick! Get out!" Chris said.

They all swam like harried guppies to the edge; splashing water everywhere in a panic. They desperately reached for the edge and began pulling themselves from the water. Chris jumped out of the pond first and Bo was right behind him. Breathing hard, both perspiration and water trickled down their faces, into their eyes, but nothing would stop them from snatching each other to safety.

"Come on, Casey! Hurry!" he said holding his hand out for her to grab.

When she finally hit dry land and stood up, she looked up and saw that Zanku and his crew were gaining ground and froze. Slowly she started moving backward away from Chris' hand. Bo held one hand out for Leena and the other for Alex. They grabbed and Bo and he pulled hard and finally everyone was out and they took off running, but not before Chris picked up his sister, threw her over his back and took off, too! Through the thick forest they ran at lightning speed with Zanku and his goons on their heels. Alex and Jacks were out front and the rest were keeping up with no problem.

"Okay, Casey," Chris said huffing and puffing.

"I'm gonna put you down, but I'm gonna keep running..... When I do... my hand will be sticking out... you grab it... and just keep up...I'm probably gonna have to pull you along...Okay? Got it?" he said between breaths.

"Uh huh!" Casey grunted, nodding wildly.

Casey braced herself and hoped not to lose her footing and fall when she landed because she knew that would slow them down and throw them right into Zanku's hands, then they may never get home.

"Come on!" Bo yelled.

Leena heard him loud and clear and encouraged herself to press and not faint. She turned her head just a bit and saw Zanku right on her and E-man's tail. E-man was running very hard refusing to look back. Leena caught up to Chris and Casey and was almost stepping on the back of Alex's knees. She soon passed them both. The kids ran and ran as their hearts began to feel as if they would burst through their chests, but they didn't look back.

"Herman, throw me your bat!" Zanku demanded.

He tossed it forward into Zanku's awaiting hands. When he caught it he raised it up high as if he was a batter on the run and as soon as he got up on E-man's heels, he swung it hard at his head. E-man turned just in time to see Zanku swing and his limp body fell to the ground; he was out like a light. Herman reached down and picked him up and threw him over his shoulders as if E-man was now just a bag of laundry. The rest of the kids never saw or heard a thing as they kept focused on what was ahead.

"Come on, we got what we came for," Zanku said looking at the other children running for their lives.

The evil thugs turned and marched in the opposite direction toward the black mansion.

Moments later Casey started to lose speed. She slapped her hand over her chest, "I...I can't breathe!"

Chris looked over his shoulder and saw that their pursuers were no longer in sight.

"They're gone!" he said coming to a halt.

The others slowed down but were breathing so hard they couldn't stop fully. Heaving, gasping and wheezing was the sound of the moment until everyone could gather themselves then make sure Casey was alright.

"Where are they?" Alex said peering into the surrounding woods.

Bo stopped, bowled over and gripped his knees. It was all he could do to catch his breath.

"Don't know, did we lose them?" Chris asked, puffing.

"Where's E-man?" Leena screamed.

"Oh no! They got him!" Casey hollered, gulping.

"Let's get back to the cabin!" Bo said taking off with a new burst of energy.

The others agreed and they sprinted all the way to the camp. When they crossed over the West gate they noticed that the camp grounds seemed unusually quiet; it was eerie because there was no one was in sight.

When they got to their cabin they burst through the door and began pacing around. Some went to the bathroom to relieve themselves and washed their faces, too, but chatter about what to do about E-man never ceased.

"They got E-man and let's go get him back," Chris said gripping the door knob tightly.

"They probably have him at the black mansion," Bo said.

"Well, why are we here then? Let's go get em'!" Leena insisted.

"No, we all don't need to go," Alex said.

"I'll go with Chris and Bo you girls stay here, just in case he comes back."

"Okay," Jacks' said, "Just hurry before something happens to him!"

It was obvious that Leena did not like the idea, but she knew not to argue, this matter was too important.

"Wait, take this," Casey said grabbing a little pouch out of the chest.

It contained a screwdriver, pocket knife, and a fingernail clipper. She handed it to Alex.

"Don't ask me why, something told me to give that to you."

The boys left out of the door as the girls stood, riddled with worry, and watched as the guys ran off over the east bridge, and into the forest. The sky seemed blacker than ever that night if not for the silver moon and stars that lit the way for them. The boys ran as fast as humanly possible down the dark narrow path that led to the black mansion.

"I don't remember it being this far down," Bo said.

"It's just a little further," Alex said. "Hold on."

After running a little while longer the mansion came into view and was glowing bewitchingly against the darkness. The boys could hear the rushing water running around the mansion amid the sounds of mid-night nature that was wide awake beneath the dark eyed night.

"Come on!" Chris said leaping over the moat.

Alex and Bo leaped like deer behind him. Chris tiptoed up to the door and leaned his ear in to see if he could hear anything. The sound of music was faint, but sure. He grabbed the doorknob and turned it, and to his surprise the door was unlocked, so very cautiously, he crept inside looking suspiciously for the slightest movement. The house was blindingly dark, only music could be heard. The boys crept on until relief was in sight in the way of a small beam of light shining from underneath the basement door. Bo tapped Chris on the shoulder and gestured for them to go downstairs. Chris nodded then took a deep breath.

# Lost and Found

"Okay," he mouthed as the two of them made their way over to the door with Alex right behind him.

Again, Chris took it upon himself to turn the doorknob and open the door, at which time, the music seemed to come alive; the sound of congas, drums and stomping throbbed in their heads. Regardless, they were determined to keep moving with only one focus, and that was to rescue E-man. The boys walked down the winding stone steps; lit by fired torches mounted on the descending stone wall. The further they went the louder the music got. As they approached the basement the light faded to dark again, but he could still see slightly. Chris wound his neck around the corner to see what he could discover and what he found were tribal dancers carrying on in the midst of a crowd.

Chris, Alex and Bo looked at each other, lost as to what to do, but when Chris turned back around he lifted his eyes at a distance beyond the dancing and the crowd and spotted the cage hanging over by the far window. The boys followed his eyes to see what he could possibly be so taken by. As he peered closer he realized that a human was in the cage. It was E-man.

"Look! There he is," Chris said pointing.

Now, alarmed, Chris knew he had to be careful at any cost as he looked around to map out a trail and a plan for them to get to E-man. Alex and Bo were in full stride right along with him. As the boys put their thoughts together spying out their surroundings soon their eyes came across flickering white candles on the floor in a circle, and to their dismay there were Floo-Ellen and three other women dressed in white, sitting in the middle of it! They too sat in a circle inside the circle of candles. As the boys continued to look they noticed that they had yet another thing they were sitting around. It was some strange looking slab of marble or stone with etchings in it. The ladies sat there around this stone with their heads bowed, eyes closed speaking silently.

"Are they praying?" Chris whispered over his shoulder to the guys.

"Yeah, they might be praying, but trust me...it's not to our God,"

Alex answered.

Zanku stood in the corner like a pompous aider, smiling as Herman did a shuffle and waggled a dance for their collective victory. People were drinking and lifting their glasses for toasts: "To the blood of Emanuel Amin!" they sang out, elated. They anticipated his sacrifice with great joy. The boys shuddered when they heard this.

"Okay, how do we get him out and escape without getting caught?" Chris asked.

Alex reached in his pocket and pulled out the pouch Casey gave him, and pulled out the screwdriver. "This is why she gave it to me...this is how we get him out. I can pop the lock with this."

"This is the plan," Bo took a deep breath. "Me and Chris will start dancing and celebrating with these boneheads. Alex you dance your way over to E-man's cage - get him out – and you two go out that window. Then me and Chris will ease our way back upstairs and meet you guys outside."

"And what if someone spots you two?" Alex looked around making sure they still went unnoticed.

"Well, then we will have to fight! But let's hope that doesn't happen."

"Sounds good enough for me," Chris approved and started dancing.

Alex nodded in agreement, and wiped the sweat from behind his neck. Chris and Bo stepped down onto the floor and started jerking their body in the same manner everyone else was. They fit right in and nobody noticed any difference.

⊗ ⊗ ⊗

Meanwhile the girls at the cabin grew restless.

"We should have given them a walkie," Leena said worried.

She had taken out nail polish and a file planning to do her nails while they all waited. Instead she sat and bit her nails nervously.

"Oh, yeah, at least we would know if they are okay or not," Casey agreed.

"What if someone gets hurt and Jacks is not there to help them? What if they don't know something that we do? What if they don't get there in time to save--"

"Enough of that Casey! That kind of talk is not helping anyone!" Leena interrupted.

"I'm just saying…I think they need us," she stood up and started pacing around the room.

"I agree. I think they could use our help," Jacks said.

"You know they can't function without us! What were we thinking when we agreed to stay here?" Leena asked looking over at Jacks' eying her for a response.

"That was a mistake!" Jacks said, jumping up. "Let's go help them!"

Jacks turned the light off and headed for the door with Leena, Casey followed them both out closing the door behind her.

⊗ ⊗ ⊗

Alex took a step onto the floor and started dancing along with the crowd of celebrants. With every leap and jerk he got closer to the window. E-man was sitting in the cage with his head buried in between his knees. Blood covered the side of his face from the blow to his head, and his clothes were filthy and glued to his body from perspiration. Alex was real close now and still unseen. Floo-Ellen and the other women were still chanting with her eyes closed. The music was growing louder and the people were dancing wildly but laughing now, too. The intensity increased and was now sweeping through the place like a brewing storm.

Bo noticed a table that had knives, perhaps swords lined up on it. In the dim light he could not quite make it out. But, he would dance over and see because he would need at least one of them. Upon approaching the table he grabbed one of the sharp knives and slid it underneath his shirt into his pants pocket. Chris saw him and flashed him a thumbs-up. They both looked over at Alex and saw that he was almost at the cage. At that Bo picked up another knife, danced over to Chris and gave it to him; Chris put it in his back pocket.

Bo leaned over and whispered in his ear, "Just a little insurance."

Alex finally reached the cage and started picking the lock. A groggy E-man felt something different and lifted his head to see what was going on. When he saw that it was Alex he gave him a weak smile with warm eyes.

"Shhh….be very still and quite," Alex whispered.

E-man nodded his head feebly.

"When I open up the cage, jump out as quickly as you can and we're going through this window."

E-man glanced over at the window that was slightly opened already and nodded. The lock popped and Alex opened the door.

⊗ ⊗ ⊗

Within minutes the girls reached the black mansion.

"Should we go around the back?" Jacks asked.

"No, look," Leena said pointing to the front door.

"It's cracked!" she ran and jumped over the rushing water and Jacks did the same. They turned and saw Casey was just standing there looking at the water.

"Come on girl, you can do it!" Leena said.

"I don't know," Casey said looking unsure.

"Take a couple of steps back run and jump. You'll be fine," Jacks insisted.

Casey backed up slowly and took off into a run. When she jumped up and over her right leg reached the other side, but her left leg slipped back into the rushing water pulling her entire body into the water. Casey let out a blood curdling scream as the rushing water carried her away.

"Oh no!" Jacks said.

# Lost and Found

"We gotta get her!" Leena hollered and jumped into the water with Jacks right behind her.

Chris looked over and saw that Alex had gotten the cage opened. He nudged Bo on the arm and gave him the signal to leave. Alex made eye contact with Chris and they both looked over at Floo-Ellen. She was still consumed in chanting, and the people all around never noticed either, as they were taken away in dance. Alex took E-man's hand and helped him out of the cage and they both crept over to the window. Chris and Bo made it to the staircase and, with ease, they started to climb until they were out of sight.

All of a sudden frightening screams filled the room and Chris froze.

"Oh, my god! Who...that sounds like my sister but I know it couldn't be," Chris said shaking his head no.

"Oh, no!" Bo mouthed with his eyes wide.

Alex and E-man were halfway out the window when they heard the surprising screams, too. They stopped in their tracks to see what was stirring such a commotion. Casey, Leena, and Jacks were now floating in the water, in the middle of the basement like helpless little puppies in front of everyone. The music stopped and everyone in the room became still. Floo-Ellen looked at them as she slowly got up from her knees. Her eyes gleamed with rage as she walked toward them.

"Now, what do we have here?" she asked folding her arms.

"Look! They're trying to escape!" Someone shouted pointing to Alex and E-man.

Floo-Ellen raised her hand towards Alex and E-man and the window that his leg was out of halfway began to shut. Alex quickly moved his leg back inside before it got crushed.

"Get them!" Floo-Ellen ordered.

Two men came towards E-man and Alex, but before they got close the two boys ran over to the stairs and stood beside Chris and Bo.

"So, your friends planned to come and save your life, but didn't realize they would be losing theirs for interfering!" Floo-Ellen screamed.

Her eyes turned completely black as she balled her fists tightly. The candles that burned on the floor in the circle suddenly spit fire high into the ceiling at the fierce sound of Floo-Ellen's voice.

The boys were huddled together over by the stairs and the girls were struggling in the water against the strong current in order to stay afloat and not drown. Floo-Ellen turned away from the boys and walked over to them and stood there staring menacingly at them awhile. When an evil smile appeared on her face Chris knew he'd better make a move. He ran over to the corner and grabbed a long rusty chain and threw one end into the water.

"Grab it!"

A couple of men ran towards him to try and stop him but Alex, Bo and E-man blocked them and they began to fight.

"Hurry!" Chris said.

The girls struggled to reach the chain but the current was too strong. Floo-Ellen looked down at the water and calmly said, "Come."

The current in the water suddenly calmed. Casey let out a loud agonizing scream and started crying. Chris dropped his end of the chain and ran over to the water. When he got there he saw the water surrounding his sister turning red.

"What happened?" Chris asked.

But Casey only cried. He heard struggling and grunting behind him and turned to see Zanku holding Bo in a headlock and E-man and Alex securely confined in the biceps of Floo-Ellen's bodyguards. Jacks and Lena swam over to Casey and helped her over to the edge where Chris was kneeling.

"My legs...my legs!" she cried.

Chris held his hand out for her, but she just moaned in pain. Leena and Jacks swam over to the edge and pulled themselves out of the water. The water turned dark as boisterous waves began to develop.

"Yes, introduce yourself to our uninvited guests," Floo-Ellen said.

# Lost and Found

Chris was unsuccessful in pulling her out because of the pain she was in. Jacks came over to help him and they both managed to pull her out of the water, and that is when they saw that her legs were covered in blood. Gashes and deep wounds covered the length of her legs and were oozing blood uncontrollably. Chris felt nauseated at the sight of it and the anger that boiled in his gut.

"It's going to be okay," he said and picked her up, blood immediately beginning to cover Chris' arms and body, and down his legs, too.

Chris carried her towards the stairs but Herman and Scott were blocking them. Floo-Ellen turned to Zanku and her followers and said,

"Let the little rats go. They will be the entertainment before the sacrifice."

Jacks and Leena ran over to where the guys were standing. So all seven stood there in a little huddle, and all eyes were on Floo-Ellen. Bo pulled out the knife and pointed at Herman.

"Get out of the way!" Bo threatened showing off the knife.

Bo's hand started to shake because the knife became searing hot in his hands! He dropped it and looked back at Floo-Ellen.

"I really hope you didn't think it would be that easy." Herman laughed.

"It don't look like you're going anywhere!"

"Meet Balachew!" Floo-Ellen bellowed.

An enormous monster emerged from the water, letting out piercing thunderous growling. Beads of sweat started to cover Chris' face as this felt all too familiar. Balachew spread his large black wings, and stepped out of the water. The kids huddled closer together frightened beyond words. Leena grabbed Bo from behind and shut her eyes tight. Balachew shook the water off of him as if he was a wet gigantic dog, then glared at the children through his intimidating scarlet eyes.

"Destroy them all… except for the little one…Emanuel."

Balachew let out a loud roar and everyone in the room jumped.

E-man broke free from the huddle and slowly made his way

299

to the front of the group, the beast watched him and took another step forward and let out another loud scream, right into E-man's face! His knees started to wobble, so he shut his eyes tight in an effort to hide any signs of weakness. The demon took another step closer toward them.

Then E-man took a step towards the beast and said," Jesus!"

The beast took a step back, confused. E-man took another step forward and spoke louder. "Jesus!"

The beast fell backwards, screaming as if it was in pain! But, in no time he got back up, opened its mouth and shot a stream of acid toward E-man and the others, but they darted out of its stream, and he missed. E-man chuckled.

"No weapon formed against me shall prosper!" he said fearlessly.

The beast let out a loud squeal, and began to jerk its head.

E-man stretched out his hand towards the beast and yelled,

"Demon I cast you back to the pit of hell from where you came…in the name of Jesus Christ the son of God!"

A harsh wail barreled up from the creature so loud everyone, including Floo-Ellen flinched a bit. She looked around the room and again at the monster in wonderment. But, what was really going on? She knew Balachew would win as always, so she waited.

However, just then Balachew burst into ten million small flies that immediately swarmed into a funnel spinning about the room. Everyone was mortified. The flies suddenly changed direction and rolled high into the air like a bullet then all shot directly into Floo-Ellen's naval. She began blowing up like a stuffed teddy bear, jerking and pulsating as if she was about to throw up. Her stuffed body fell onto the floor where it shook and flopped about like a fish out of water. Herman and the others stood in shock with their mouths covered in hopes the same would not happen to them.

Floo-Ellen's skin began to discolor as she became still. She went from pale to whitish and her black eyes stared lifeless into the distance, dead to the world.

# Lost and Found

E-man turned to the others and said, "Let's get out of here!"

They made their way over to the stairs where Scott and Herman were still standing paralyzed with fear, clasping their mouths.

"If you would please excuse us," E-man said waiting for them to move.

Confused and unsure of what to do, they slid out of the way. The ceiling was starting to crumble, as E-man led the crew upstairs.

"Hurry this place is falling apart!" E-man yelled and they ran faster. They heard screaming in the basement from all the people trying to escape the black mansion. Huge boulders from the house were crushing people and they were trampling over each other as the house was caving in. 7-Alive had just made it up the stairs when Leena shoved Jacks hard saving her from the huge boulder rock that almost crushed her.

"Thanks!" she said jumping to her feet.

The house was crumbling and falling so bad that it now started to lose form. The people in the basement were being crushed by the falling debris unable to escape with all the confusion. Bella, however, was able to make it out the back window before it caved in.

7-Alive finally made it out of the house with E-man leading the way. Casey was crying in Chris' arms because of the excruciating pain she was in. Leena's face was red and tears were flowing freely, and she held Jacks hand tightly. They ran off the porch and all carefully jumped over the rushing water. They all got across and Bo was last following Alex. He screamed when someone yanked him by the ankle making him fall head first onto the ground. He turned to find Zanku on the ground behind him still holding his ankle tight.

"Where you think you going?" he said frowning with sweat pouring down his face.

"Not with you!" Bo said taking his other foot kicking him hard in the face, sending him flying back into the rushing moat!

The current carried Zanku back into the falling house, and they all watched, as the house fell to the ground with everyone in it. The earth beneath the house started to give way too, and the rubble of the mansion fell hard into it. A mushroom of dust and smoke rose into the air as the entire edifice caved in. The children were stunned and stared at the unfolding of an end to what seemed like a summer filled with nightmares that had been borne out of that house. They were speechless and relieved all at the same time.

"Come on, let's get back to the cabin," E-man said, and they ran off through the woods into the night.

# Chapter Twenty-Six

## ⊗ HOME SWEET HOME ⊗

When the kids got back to the cabin, Chris laid Casey down on the bed.

"Jacks please!" Chris cried as Jacks rushed over and examined the bloody gashes all over Casey.

"Under the water! That demon under the water did this to me!" she cried.

"Shhh! It's gonna be fine," Jacks assured her and immediately started praying.

In no time at all Casey began to feel relief; the pain vanished, the wounds were closed; her legs were healed and she could use them again! She sat up and put her feet to the floor and stood up. Casey was elated as she then started jumping and screaming, "Thank you, God! Yes, Lord Jesus, thank you!"

"E-man you are the man!" Bo said.

E-man curled his head and smiled bashfully.

"I must admit I was not afraid," he said.

"You weren't scared?" Chris asked.

"Are you kidding me? Of course not! Not after what we saw in Heaven! I'm not afraid of anything anymore. Plus when we were on the clouds Bruno told me exactly what to expect, so I was a little prepared."

"Yeah I understand that!" Leena said pulling her suitcase from under her bed.

"Despite all of the Floo-Ellen stuff camp was actually fun!" Jacks admitted.

"I'm so glad we got a chance to go to Heaven and hangout with Jesus!" Chris said.

"Do you think we will ever get the chance to go back?" Casey asked.

Everyone in the room shouted, 'yes' and 'of course'!

"No, I mean while we are still living," she clarified.

"Oh…well, Andrew is Chris' guardian angel, maybe he can check into it for us."

"That would be awesome!" E-man said.

"I'll check into it."

"I'm gonna miss everyone so much!" Leena said taking a note pad and pen out of her bag. "I want numbers and addresses!" she said passing it around.

Everyone exchanged information and vowed to stay in touch.

"Guys we can finish packing later. We are missing the good-bye camp party.

They all ran over to the Assembly Hall for the party and upon arriving they saw absolutely everyone either embracing, dancing, chatting, or exchanging information. Even Ms. Lambert seemed to be in high spirits as she drank punch and danced about to the music. She was thrilled that Camp Come Along was back in her charge after almost losing it completely.

Cleofus, on the other hand, was circling the room like a shark. He was clearly in search of Floo-Ellen or any one of her goons. Trudy sat in the corner looking at Cleofus slowly shaking her head in disapproval. Bo saw her and went over to her.

"Trudy, how are you?" he asked.

"Fine, fine, I'm good thank you."

"Great," he said dryly.

"You know I don't see any monsters in the faces of the people here," she said both excited and relieved.

"Well, that's a good thing!"

She chuckled, "Tell me about it!"

He hugged her, "You take care of yourself Trudy because I'm not sure if I'll be back next summer," Bo said.

"I will miss you," she said hugging him back.

Leena was behind Bo and waved to Trudy.

"Hey whatcha doing?" Leena asked.

"Just saying goodbye to Trudy. What are you up to?"

"I wanted to go tell Summer she's safe now."

"Well, let's go," Bo said leading the way.

"How are you?" they asked approaching Summer.

"Good, thank you."

"We just wanted to let you know that you are free from the bondage Floo-Ellen had over you. Once she was destroyed all spiritual ties that she had to you were broken," Leena explained.

"Well, actually about an hour ago I literally felt a heavy burden lift off my shoulders and peace, instead, rested on me and through me! When that happened I went and spoke with other people who had been in Society 36 and they claim that they had the same experience!"

Leena and Bo were dancing and praising God just like at the concert in Heaven. When Summer saw how happy they were she started dancing too!

Chris saw all the commotion and went over to them.

"Hey!" she said swinging her arms out wrapping them around him tightly. "You just missed it."

"Missed what?" Chris asked.

"Lambert just informed everyone that Floo-Ellen was no longer in charge and no one would be seeing her again."

Chris and Bo looked at each other.

"She also apologized to the Kidder Krew because there was no money to give.

"But how did Lambert know about Floo-Ellen?" Bo asked.

"What happened to Floo-Ellen?" Summer asked.

"I'll explain everything later," Chris answered then turned to Bo.

"Bo, let's go speak with Ms. Lambert and see how it is that she knows what's going on."

They marched over to the joyous dancing woman. Looking hesitant, Chris tapped her on the shoulder.

"Oh, hey sweetie!" she said as she spun around to see who tapped her. "How are you boys doing?"

"Good, doing good. Now, how did you know about Floo-Ellen?" Chris asked cutting to the chase.

She bent down and got close to his ear still shimmying and all.

"She's dead," she whispered.

"How do you know?"

"God told me. He said that Floo-Ellen was destroyed and I was not to have any fear anymore and if there was something I was to worry about, bring it to Him!"

Bo slapped Chris a high five. "Our God is the best!"

Jill walked over to Jacks with a drink in her hand. She stood there for a moment, took a sip of her drink, then finally spoke.

"I've been racking my brain trying to figure out how you were able to heal me when I was so close to dying," Jill said.

"One...I didn't heal you. God did. And, two...you can do all things through him even if it seems impossible." Jacks answered.

"Ok. I believe. I believe in your God," Jill said.

"Our God? The God of Abraham, Isaac, and Jacob?" Bo quizzed.

"Yes I believe in Him – how could I not?"

"Well you can't get to Him without going through His son – no man can," Bo said.

"Who is that? I mean who could possibly be his son?"

"Jesus of course!" Chris shouted.

"Okay, I'm ready to do this thing – help me."

"Do what thing?" Bo asked her.

"Well, what is it called when you accept Jesus?"

"Oh, you accept Him as your savior...it's salvation. We call it being saved."

"Ok, well, help me through this salvation process. I'm ready to be saved. Let's go in here," she said leading the kids to a private room.

The children gathered around her with extended hands toward each other. As they all held hands Jacks prayed and had Jill repeat after her.

"Jesus, I believe you are the son of God. I believe you died for me, rose from the dead for me, and coming back again for me. Forgive me for all my sins. I confess with my mouth, and I believe in my heart...that I am saved."

Jill said the sinner's prayer and gave her life to Jesus so that she might be saved. As she repeated the prayer, she started to cry as she felt really sorry for not being all God made her to be. Meanwhile, a host of angels in Heaven were looking down on the small circle of clasped hands holding The Lamb's Book of Life in their hands and rejoicing over Jill's heartfelt repentance; they were happy that she had chosen to be saved so they could now write her name in the Book of Life, too. The Book began to glow brightly now that Jill's name was now in it on its very own line!

Jill opened her eyes and wiped her cheeks.

"Is that it?" she said faintly, but happy.

"Yep!" Bo said.

"Now you have to build a relationship with God by reading His word."

"The Bible?"

"Yes, and through prayer you'll get to know him for yourself."

"But don't think prayer always has to be formal. Prayer is just communicating to God and Him speaking back to you. Hey, you can be walking, or in your car, in your bed, you don't always have to be on your knees," Bo added.

"Okay. Thank you guys," she said giving them hug. Jill still had a tear in her eyes. "I'm going to miss you guys."

"Can't tell you how we'll miss you too!" Jacks spoke up.

"Thanks again for introducing me to your God, we will get to know each other very well."

"You will get to know Him Jill. He has known all about you before you were born!" Bo said.

"Wow! Well, I have some catching up to do!" she chuckled.

Just then the door opened and Andrew peeked his head in.

"I was looking for my friends…know where I can find them?"

"ANDREW!" Casey shouted and they all ran and pounced him almost knocking him down.

Jill stood and looked puzzled trying to figure out what the big deal was about the camp's landscaper.

"Oh, we missed you," Leena said holding him tightly.

"I wanna go back," E-man said.

"One day you will," Andrew responded.

"We are going to miss you," Jacks said.

"Chris won't," Bo said inciting laughter among the crew.

"We will meet again, here on earth, I promise!" Andrew said.

Jill looked even more confused as she continued to listen.

"But when Andrew?" Casey asked.

"Soon."

"When is soon?" Leena chimed in.

Just then Ms. Lambert's voice came through the intercom telling the kids to meet their parents in the parking lot. They fought back tears as they hugged each other tightly and promised they would always keep in touch. Leena embraced Bo tightly.

"You be good Bo, I'm gonna miss you!"

# Home Sweet Home

"Me too! Don't do anything I wouldn't do," he said squeezing her tightly.

Jacks gave Alex a hug, "Make sure you write me," she playfully demanded.

"I give you my word," he said.

Chris hugged them all and made his way out of the room to look for Summer. He spotted her over by the door laughing with her friends. She saw him coming in her direction and broke free from the girls and met him half way.

"Chris," she said shaking her head, "Please don't say that this is the end of the road for us and you're going to wish me a happy life."

"Of course not! I am just saying good-bye for now," he said hugging her affectionately.

She had her eyes shut tight, "I'm going to really miss you Chris."

"I already miss you," he held her even tighter.

Just then Casey and E-man came up behind them.

"Come on Chris we gotta go," Casey said hitting him on the back.

"You have my information. Make sure you call me and I'll be sure to write," Summer told him.

"Definitely, see ya later," he said and followed Casey and E-man out the door.

⊗ ⊗ ⊗

Parents started pulling into the parking lot in droves. Ms. Prentice was among them and could not wait to see her children and E-man. She rose up from the car and craned her neck to see if she could spot them among the crowd of cars, parents and kids all looking for each other in the packed parking lot.

"Mom!" Ms. Prentice heard through the sea of voices that filled the area. Somehow she knew that that *Mom!* belonged to her.

"Ms. Prentice!" she heard then coming from a stronger than ever E-man.

# Summer of Seven

A smile came across her face as she jumped up and down waving for them to see her. Casey rammed her mom and stayed a while taking in her smell and the softness of her clothes and her body. Chris came and wrapped his arms around them both.

"My goodness, I thought I was the only one missing somebody around here. You guys missed me that much?"

"God...yes," Casey said her face still pressed into her mother's chest.

"Mr. E-man I don't see you over here. You'd better come join this love fest over here," Ms. Prentice said to him.

E-man smiled big and walked over. Chris opened his arm to let him in. They laughed and hugged and rocked seemingly for minutes.

When they all piled into the car they threw their heads back, leaning on the cushioned head rest and appreciated the air conditioning, the music on the radio, the sound of their mother's voice and the mere fact that they could sit and be carried. There was silence but for the sound of breathing for quite a while, then the flood gates opened. All at once they tried to tell their mother everything that went on every single day. They told her all about camp and all they had been through.

"You guys have very vivid imaginations!" Ms. Prentice laughed.

Casey tried and tried to convince her that they were telling the truth but she wouldn't believe it and chucked it up to vivid imaginations.

"Mom it's true and we can prove it," Casey said turning to Chris in the back seat, "Show her your scars from that monster!"

Chris lifted his shirt and there were two light pink scratches and red splotches where Balachew spit acid in the middle of his chest.

"Oh, Chris what happened? Looks like you had a rash or Poison Ivy and scratched it up!" Ms. Prentice said still oblivious to the facts.

"Mom! Why is it so hard to believe?" Chris asked her.

"Oh, honey why would someone like Dr. Host recommend such a place if there were monsters there to attack you? It's okay, son, I understand. Kids have wild imaginations!"

# Home Sweet Home

Chris and Casey looked at each other and shook their heads.

E-man shrugged his shoulders.

This summer camp experience was far beyond Ms. Prentice's understanding so she just pretended to understand and asked no more questions.

An hour into the trip everyone had gone off to sleep and remained so for the rest of the ride. When they pulled into the neighborhood the children began to rouse as if on cue. Ms. Prentice dropped E-man off and went home.

The next day Ms. Prentice couldn't help but notice a difference in Chris. During breakfast their conversation was light and Chris seemed to have a restored youthfulness as he should at his age instead the heaviness of a grown-up that he had before camp; it was obvious that he was no longer depressed about the tragic loss of their neighbor. The more Ms. Prentice looked at her seemingly new son, the more grateful to Ms. Host she was for recommending Camp Come Along.

"Chris this afternoon I want us to visit Ms. Host so we can give her an update on how well you are doing. Grab my purse so I can book us an appointment."

Chris went into the living room where Casey was watching TV and got his mother's purse.

"Here," he said putting the purse on the table in front of her. "While you're on the phone I'll be outside – I'll be right back."

"Ok," she said shaking her head and digging in her purse.

Chris ran over to the Harris' house next door and rang the doorbell. Sean answered the door after peeking through the window.

"Hi Chris! I haven't seen you all summer."

"I've been away at camp."

"Man I wish I could've gone to camp!"

"How have you been?"

"I've had better days. But each day that passes, it gets better."

"I understand. Is your dad home?"

"Yeah he's inside watching the game."

"Will you tell him I need to speak with him for a moment."

Sean disappeared into the house and a moment later reappeared with his father.

"Hello Mr. Harris."

"Hi Chris, how are you?" he asked curious to know why he was there.

"Uhmm…I don't know how to say this, but I saw your wife."

Mr. Harris suddenly looked like someone had punched him in his gut.

"What kind of sick joke do you call yourself playing?" he asked enraged.

Sean was frowning behind him.

"I did. And I talked to her, too."

"Look here!" Mr. Harris screamed. His face was now beet red.

Chris pulled out the letter from his back pocket and handed it to him. Mr. Harris wanted to snatch it, but he took it and unfolded it.

"I watched her write it, and she asked me to deliver it to you."

As soon as he recognized her handwriting the anger vanished from his face, and he eagerly read the letter.

Sean was behind him peeking over his shoulder. As he read the letter tears began to pour from his eyes and flooded his face. By the time he got to the end of the letter he was on his knees crying and holding the letter tightly against his chest.

"She's in Heaven and she is so happy. The only thing that brings her grief is the fact that she knows you and your son are hurting," Chris explained.

Mr. Harris gave Chris an understanding, but tearful nod. Chris extended a hand to help Mr. Harris up, instead he found the strength to stand up by himself, and whispered thanks and closed the door. Chris went home feeling somewhat accomplished seeing the thankful smile on

# Home Sweet Home

Mrs. Harris' face in his mind's eye – knowing she was happy in Heaven.

Later that day Ms. Prentice took both Chris and Casey to see Dr. Host. When they arrived she hugged and kissed them like they were her own.

"Welcome back guys!" she said beaming at them.

"Please, take your seats. Let's talk."

"So, Chris how are you?" Dr. Host began.

"Better than I have ever been!"

"Oh, good! So glad to hear that."

He and Casey gave Ms. Host the run down on the whole summer, and she laughed and believed every word. Ms. Prentice on the other hand was getting a bit annoyed with her kids and their farfetched stories.

"Well, make sure you guys keep in touch with all the new friends you've made on earth and in Heaven," she said folding her hands on the desk.

Chris and Casey immediately noticed the gold ring, with the blue stone, that she wore on her right thumb. They knew it to be the undercover angel ring! They both looked at each other in amazement and before they could say a word she had her finger over her lips and signaled them not to say a word.

"So, Ms. Host, how do we get back to that place?" Casey asked.

"Someone who wears a ring would have to take you."

"What exactly are we talking about?" Ms. Prentice asked annoyed.

"Nothing," her kids said in unison.

"Chris I'm glad you found the purpose for your visions."

"Me too!" he said with a big smile.

"If you ever need anything please don't hesitate to call me – I do mean anything."

"I really appreciate that."

"So, Ms. Prentice, thanks for coming in today and letting them share their experience at Camp Come Along."

"No problem. I will be sure to bring them back if we have any other issues."

"Keep in touch! Feel free to come by anytime even if you just want to say hello."

"We will!" Ms. Host stood up and gave everyone a hug goodbye and they left.

On the way home Casey was in the front seat chatting with her mother. Chris was in the back with his head on the window looking up at the sky. He was just about to go to sleep when he saw the clouds open up like curtains, being opened, to reveal a bright Saturday morning. He raised his head off the window and his eyes opened wide! He couldn't believe what he was seeing! Behind the clouds Heaven was revealed! Waterfalls rushed down mountains as flowers and trees swayed back and forth to a heavenly breeze. Green plush hills stretched for miles; the sight was too awesome to keep to himself.

"Casey look!" he said pointing up to the sky.

A big smile covered her face as she looked up into the heavens trying not to blink. Ms. Prentice looked out of her window but couldn't see anything.

"What? What is it? I don't see anything!" she said looking up while trying to keep her eyes on the road.

"It's nothing mom, besides you wouldn't believe us if we told you anyway," Chris said.

Just then the clouds suddenly came back together and blocked the incredible sight, bringing the day back to just another sunny Saturday.

"Chris, we gotta get back there!" Casey said.

"Don't worry, we will!"

"I am the way, the truth, and the life. No one comes to the Father except through me.

-Jesus

# ⊗ SPECIAL THANKS TO... ⊗

**JESUS CHRIST** my Lord and my Savior! I am so grateful to have You in my life. Thank you for giving me the idea to write this wonderful story, that will give You all the glory. I Love you.

**MY FAMILY** - my mom **NANCY** without you, there would be no me (literally) :-). You have been the backbone of my support system, and I don't know where to begin to thank you! My sister **SARA**, thank you for your input it was greatly appreciated (except for the clown idea)! My brother **BO** thanks for being your awesome self, because without your personality I wouldn't have been able to create your character! My brother **SHAKIL** and niece **JACQULINE** thank you guys for listening and giving me your feedback, when I was forcing you to listen to different scenes, over and over again. **JESSICA** – my brilliant cousin – thanks for everything. Knowing I had you in my corner gave me comfort. My cousin **STASIA** – thanks so much for all your help. I will never forget it!

**MELVIN "ACTION" JOHNSON** – the best attorney in whole wide world! I have gained so much from you. Learning life's lessons with the best teacher; your friendship is truly priceless! Thanks for being my WWH!

**NATALIE CRAWFORD** – A great editor able to help bring my vision to life. Thank you, really appreciate you! **KEVIN TAYLOR** – A very talented graphic designer! Without your help this journey would've taken much longer.

**AMBER & MASON AND THE CHESTNUT TREEHOUSE AFTERSCHOOLERS** – Thank you guys for your excitement and support. It was your enthusiasm that encouraged me to keep on writing!

And to countless family members and friends that have supported this dream, Aunt Terry, Kayce, and Teriya. I am forever grateful. Thank you, and I love you!